Ellis William Ashton

Richard Wagners Prose Works

Volume VII. In Paris and Dresden

Ellis William Ashton

Richard Wagners Prose Works
Volume VII. In Paris and Dresden

ISBN/EAN: 9783337394592

Printed in Europe, USA, Canada, Australia, Japan

Cover: Foto ©Andreas Hilbeck / pixelio.de

More available books at **www.hansebooks.com**

RICHARD WAGNER'S PROSE WORKS.

CONTENTS.

TRANSLATOR'S PREFACE.

SOMETIMES I have regretted my not having commenced this series of translations with the works selected by Richard Wagner for the first two volumes of his *Gesammelte Schriften*, as the gradual evolution of his artistic and æsthetic principles would thus have been more manifest, and the life-record consequently more complete. But at the time when the London Wagner Society first invited me to undertake my task, it was only contemplated to issue one volume in every two years, and therefore was deemed advisable to begin at once with the prose that succeeds the Dresden period, the works that mark the great climacteric in Richard Wagner's life, instead of delaying their appearance in English for what then would have amounted to two whole years. Since the completion of my first volume (end of 1892) the rate of publication has been doubled, but there would have been no manner of sense in returning to the earlier works before the later ones had all come out. From another point of view there is an advantage in the course imposed on me, for the reader who has followed the Bayreuth master's train of thought from 1849 to the year of his death, is in a better position to judge the trend of many a hint in these earlier writings ; which correspond, with trifling exceptions, to those contained in vols. i. and ii. of the *Ges. Schr.*

Before the present " Author's Introduction," the original opens with a Preface to the whole of the standard German edition of 1871-73 ; this will be found on pages xv to xviii of Vol I. of the English series. Immediately after it, again, there occurs the author's " Autobiographic Sketch," also rendered into English in my volume I. Written soon after the success of *Rienzi* at Dresden (produced Oct. 20, 1842), it appeared in Heinrich Laube's *Zeitung für die elegante Welt* on the 1st and 8th of February 1843, i.e. just a month after the production of the *Holländer* at Dresden, and its first instalment on the very day of the author's definite entry

upon office as one of the two chief Conductors at the Dresden
Court-theatre.   The "Sketch" was accompanied in that journal
by a lithographic portrait of "Richard Wagner, Componist der
opern : Rienzi und der fliegende Holländer," and prefaced with
the following note by Laube :—

"For the last ten years I have known this young musician, who
in two months has become famous through the Dresden theatre.
His inexhaustibly productive nature, impelled and unceasingly
prompted by a lively fancy, had always interested me ; and I had
always hoped that most excellent modern music would issue from
a personality so filled with our culture of to-day.   The fortunes of
fate, which cast him so far afield as Russia [Riga], removed him
from my sight for awhile, and I was no little astonished to see
him suddenly enter my room in Paris in the winter of 1838
[should be " 1839 "].   But that is just the waywardness of artists !
To have come with a wife, an opera and a half, a slender purse
and a terribly large and terribly ravenous Newfoundland dog,
through sea and storm, straight from the Duna to the Seine, to
make his name in Paris !   In Paris, where half Europe competes
for the jingle of fame, where all must pay toll, even the most
meritorious, if it would come on the market and thus to recognition.   Heine, at other times so impassive, folded his hands in
pious wonder at this assurance of a German's.   Well, it did not
succeed, but neither did it fail ; and outwardly poorer, inwardly
richer, after a couple of years the strolling musician was back in
Saxony, which has given a glorious welcome to her son.—To
enable me to shew the great public the features and adventures
of my friend, I asked him to send me the portrait once hopefully
drawn by his faithful comrade Kietz in Paris at a time of dire
straits, with a sketch of his life-history for me to work up.   But
the Paris stress had speedily turned the musician into a writer
too : I should only spoil the life-sketch, were I to attempt to alter
it ; so let it follow in the author's words, to his own surprise."

That " Paris stress " represented a time of terrible anxiety and
privation to Richard Wagner.   With no financial resources beyond
the occasional and scanty help of his relatives, he had descended
on a city where nothing but intrigue and the patronage of influential friends could smooth the way for an artist.   Intrigue was
absolutely foreign to a nature so impetuous, and in worldly
matters almost childlike, as his own, whilst his friends were for

the most part struggling artists like himself: Friedrich Pecht, a painter and pupil of Delaroche, Ernst Kietz, portrait-painter and likewise Delaroche's pupil, "Anders" a librarian, and Siegfried Lehrs, the classical philologist and editor of Oppianus and Nicander etc. The first and fourth of these are suggested in the "End in Paris," the "philologist and painter" who followed the body of the poor German musician to the graveyard. Heinrich Laube, who had introduced Wagner to H. Heine and Pecht, left Paris early in 1840; Heine himself was scarcely of the temperament to worry about the welfare of others; with Halévy and Habeneck the young composer's acquaintance must have been of the slightest; whilst Berlioz was in no position, even had he desired it, to exercise influence in Wagner's behalf beyond the power of the pen—on the only occasion when he could have been of service in the last regard, namely after the performance of Wagner's *Columbus*-overture at Schlesinger's concert of Feb. 4, 1841, he made no mention of that work in his report to the *Journal des Débats*.

There remains one great power, incomparably more influential than them all, that of Meyerbeer. So much has been made of Wagner's so-called "ingratitude" to Meyerbeer, that it will be as well to inquire what the latter really did for him.—It is obvious that Meyerbeer at once recognised in the young composer a personage beyond the ordinary; his large and varied experience of the world would have sufficed to tell him that. It is highly probable that he also saw in him a future rival, even if he did not dimly foresee a demolisher; but the intense magnetism of Wagner's enthusiastic nature would certainly have moved the operatic Cagliostro to stir at least a finger in his aid, though the sober dictates of prudence would prompt the "patron" to put forth both his hands against him when the personal fascination was removed. And what did Meyerbeer do for him? He gave Wagner an introduction to the manager of a theatre whose reputation for going into bankruptcy was a by-word; he introduced him to a friend, the proprietor of the *Gazette musicale*, whose ambition it was to have a good list of correspondents in his journal, with the arrière pensée that the young musician would feel it his duty to speak in flattering terms of his introducer—as indeed he did in the article on "German Music"; he further introduced him to the Director of the Opéra, who coolly threw him over within a twelvemonth—to anyone acquainted with Meyerbeer's tactics, it is impossible to avoid a perception of cause and effect in this procedure; after Wagner had despatched his *Rienzi* to Dresden, at his petition Meyerbeer sent a letter to the Dresden management advocating its acceptance—the surest way of removing a dangerous rival from Paris—the only centre whence an opera could hope at that time to attain a world-wide circulation; finally he got the *Flying Dutchman* accepted for Berlin, where he was supreme operatic controller—but it was not produced there until two years later, and after the *fourth* performance (Feb. 25, 1844) it was withdrawn until December 1868, when Meyerbeer was dead! Small cause for gratitude, when weighed against the Jewish composer's perpetual and well-known schemings.

To return to Paris, it may be of interest to know what operatic works were performed during Wagner's stay there. In 1840 we find records in the *Gazette musicale* of the following operas etc. at the Académie royale de musique (Grand Opéra) :—*Le Drapier* by Scribe and Halévy, *La Vendetta* by de Ruoltz, Meyerbeer's *Les Huguenots* (107th repres. Feb. 16), *Les Martyrs* by Donizetti, Meyerbeer's *Robert le Diable* (198th repr. May 13,—205th, Nov. 9), Flotow's *Stradella*, *Le Diable amoureux* by Benoist and Reber (ballet in three acts), and the first representation of Donizetti's *La Favorite* on December 2; in 1841, Halévy's *La Juive*, *Carmagnola* by Ambroise Thomas, Mozart's *Don Juan*, Weber's *Le Freischutz*, *Giselle ou les Willis* by Ad. Adam (ballet in two acts), Rossini's *Guillaume Tell*, and the first representation of Halévy's *Reine de Chypre* on December 22. In those two years we find mentioned as having been played at the Théâtre Royal Italien, *Norma*, *Tancredi*, *Nozze di Figaro*, *Puritani*, *Lucia di Lammermoor*, *l'Elisir d'Amore*, *Lucrezia Borgia* (first repr. Oct. 30, 1840), *Pirata*, *Barbiere di Seviglia*, *la Gazza ladra*, *Mosè in Egitto*, Bellini's *Beatrice di Tenda* (first repr. in France Feb. 18, '41), *il Matrimonio segreto*, *Semiramide*, *Cenerentola*, *Sonnambula*, and *il Turco in Italia* (Rossini). At the Opéra Comique during the same period, *La Fille du Régiment* (first repr. Feb. 11, 1840), *Carline* by A. Thomas (première), *L'Eleve de Presbourg* (one act) by M. Luce, *Le Pré aux Clercs*, *Zanetta* (prem. May 18, '40), *Le Cent-suisse* (prem.) by the Prince de la Moskowa, *L'Opéra à la Cour*, a strange "pasticcio" of arias etc. from Weber, Rossini,

Boieldieu, Mozart etc., ending with "God save the King" (French musicians do not appear to have realised that for three years past it had been "the Queen"), Auber's *La Neige*, Nicolo's *Joconde*, *L'Automate de Vaucanson* (prem., one act) by Bordèse, *Jeanne de Naples* (prem.) by Monpou and Bordèse (Leuven writing the libretto for each of these two works), Auber's *Lestocq*, *La Rose de Péronne* by Adam (prem.), Halévy's *Guitarrero* (prem. Jan. 21, 1841), *Les Diamants de la Couronne* (prem. March 6, '41), *Le Pendu* by Clapisson (prem.), Boieldieu's *Dame Blanche*, Grétry's *Richard Cœur-de-lion*, *L'Ingénue* by Hipp. Colet (prem.), *La Maschera* by Geo. Kastner (prem.), *Les Deux Voleurs* (one act, prem.) by Girard, *Frère et Mari* by Clapisson (one act, prem.), *Camille*, by Dalayrac, *L'Aïeule* by Boieldieu fils (one act, prem.), Auber's *L'Ambassadrice*, *La Main de fer* by Adam (prem. Oct. 26, '41), *La Jeunesse de Charles-Quint* by Montfort (two acts, prem.), *Mademoiselle de Mérange* by Henri Poitier (one act, prem.).

Though this list may be fairly complete as regards the Italiens and the Opéra Comique—which latter institution would appear to have been in a bad way, in view of its countless trials of new works—of course it does not fully represent the repertory of the Grand Opéra, for none but "premières" and "reprises" would call for special mention in the *Gazette*. In any case, apart from the Italian composers, it is evident that Halévy, Adam and Auber were the triumvirate of the day, and above them ruled the only Meyerbeer. With the probable exception of Halévy, their influence on Wagner's music was absolutely nil, for he wrote—his *Flying Dutchman*. True, that merely the first two acts of *Rienzi* were quite completed when its author reached Paris; but the idea of the music for the remainder must already have been in his head, and whatever plans he may once have cherished of getting the work produced in Paris, it was for Germany that it was finished, and to Germany was it despatched at once.

To keep body and soul together, the young artist had more degrading work to do : the number and extent of those "arrangements for every instrument under heaven" it is impossible to compute, but on the last page of the *Gazette* for July 25 and Sep. 26, 1841, we find Schlesinger advertising the overture and three "suites" of the *Favorite*, the overture and two suites of *Guitarrero*, arranged by Wagner for a quartet of two violins, viola and 'cello, or flute, violin, viola and 'cello, with a separate arrangement of each of these for two violins. Whether he really had previously had to write "quadrilles and galops," I am unable to ascertain; but this kind of galley-work was drudgery enough, for a man who had already composed his *Faust*-overture and planned his *Flying Dutchman*. A more congenial employment was his setting of the few detached songs that date from this period; of these "*Les deux Grenadiers*, mélodie de Richard Wagner" alone is advertised in the *Gazette*, namely in the number immediately preceding his first appearance as contributor to that journal. But his songs met with neither sale nor success.

Another project was the writing of an exhaustive biography of Beethoven: Herr C. F. Glasenapp tells us that "Anders" had for many years been collecting the most abundant material for such a Life, and now asked Wagner to put it into literary form. We can imagine the boon such a work would have proved to the world when we consider the intensity and depth of the young man's adoration for the departed master, and reflect that his literary style was at this time at its brightest and most lucid. The firms of Brockhaus, Cotta, and Arnold, were offered it in turn, with the undertaking on Wagner's part that the manuscript should be ready in course of a year; but all three declined it. For a whole quarter, from March to May 1841, was Wagner busied with this plan, and it is highly significant that his article "The Artist and Publicity" was written at the commencement of this period of gestation, his "Freischütz" article (the French one) towards its close, and the *Flying Dutchman* commenced as soon as the project was regretfully abandoned. For over half a year he had done nothing in the way of composition, and it is a matter for speculation whether such a prolonged engrossment with a historical work might not have ended in his devoting to Literature too much of the time he owed to Music and the Drama. However that may be, the episode throws additional light on the joy with which he found that "he *still* was a musician" when he had once more procured a piano and tried on it some portions of the *Holländer*.

That he was naturally gifted with a sparkling literary style, no one acquainted with the first two volumes of the *Gesammelte Schriften* can possibly deny, however much it may have become obscured as years rolled on. Of all the contributors to the *Gazette musicale*, not excepting Berlioz, the articles of Richard Wagner are by far the most original and readable, especially when he was allowed a free hand—a point to which I shall have to return. Not only Laube, but Heine and Berlioz themselves admired his writings; and it was no small matter, to shine among a galaxy of talents such as the proprietor of the *Gazette* had assembled for his paper. To give an idea of the sort of literary colleagues with whom Richard Wagner was associated in this Paris period of 1840 to 1842, I need merely quote the list of "redacteurs" given on the title-page of the *Gazette* :—G. E. Anders, G. Benedit, F. Benoist, Berton, Berlioz, Henri Blanchard, Maurice Bourges, Castil-Blaze, Philarète Chasles, F. Danjou, Elwart, Fétis père, Fétis fils, Ad. Guéroult, J. Guillou, Stéphen Heller, Edme Saint-Hugué, Jules Janin, Kastner, Adrien de Lafage, Jules Lecomte, F. Liszt, J. Martin, Marx, Charles Merruau, Édouard Monnais, Auguste Morel, D'Ortigue, Panofka, H. Prévost, L. Rellstab, Georges Sand, Robert Schumann, J. G. Seyfried, P. Smith, Spazier, A. Specht, Richard Wagner. Some of the best-known of these were constant contributors to the journal, yet the articles of the practically unknown Richard Wagner were almost invariably allotted the place of honour.

The order given to these articles in the *Ges. Schr.* for artistic reasons, and preserved in the present volume, materially differs from that of their original appearance. It will therefore be as well to recall the latter and thus 'reconstitute' a chapter in Wagner's history.

The first to appear was that on "German Music," July 12 and 26, 1840. Certain fragments of a diary kept by Wagner in the summer of 1840 have been published by the body-snatchers; from these we learn that on the 29th of June he was in the very direst straits, not knowing where to turn for help, but now had "prospects of earning something by writing for the *Gazette musicale*." This first article bears a somewhat different complexion from those that followed it in point of time; for one thing, it may be considered as virtually the author's earliest studied effort in journalism, and naturally it shews a certain shyness and timidity, as if at facing a vast and unknown public for the first time, thereby confirming its own words : "But set these glorious musicians before a full-dress audience in a crowded salon—they are no longer the same men; their bashfulness will not allow them raise their eyes." Consequently it is mainly historical in drift, and only toward its close does the writer begin to half-venture a forecast of the future.

Whether Wagner managed to procure sufficient money to enable him to devote himself for awhile to the scoring of *Rienzi*, after the publication of that first Parisian article, or whether his time was so fully occupied by those hateful "arrangements" that he could spare none for literature, I cannot discover. At anyrate nothing more appears from his pen until October 11, when the review of Lvoff's adaptation of "Pergolesi's Stabat Mater" was published in the *Gazette*. Although this was obviously written to order, and for that reason has not been included in the *Ges. Schr.*, it is notable in two particulars: that it contains one of the very few references, and the longest of them, he ever made to Handel; and that his power of independent criticism is here first brought into public play—with the result that he was given no more "reviewing" to do. The faults he found were few, and mildly rated, but it is quite evident that M. Monnais, the editor-in-chief, was an advocate of that "party" system to which the author refers in his second article on the *Freischütz*.

The next week brought "The Virtuoso and the Artist," the second original article from Wagner's pen, separated by an interval of three months from the first. If the version published in the *Ges. Schr.* is from the original manuscript, a marvellous change of style must have developed in that brief space of time. But the question is open to dispute, as will be seen from the difference between that version (as translated on pages 108 to 122 *infra*) and the French translation which appeared in the *Gazette* (reproduced on pages 123 to 133 *infra*). That Wagner did not do his own translating into French, is certain; but no mere paid translator could have allowed himself such liberties with his text, and we therefore are reduced to three alternative hypotheses:—either the German of the *Ges. Schr.* is of a much later period, namely 1870-71, when the author was preparing his Collected Edition for the press; or E. Monnais insisted on a change being made in the latter half of the article, to spare the feelings of Rubini and the other Italian singers, the demigods of Paris; or again, the German was re-written at some time in 1841 with the intention, never fulfilled, of publishing it in the Dresden

Abendzeitung similarly to the reproduction of the "Pilgrimage" and "End in Paris" in this journal of that year. The first hypothesis is negatived, not only by the characteristics of style, but by the allusion to particular pieces played by Liszt at his current Paris concerts,* though it is probable that the passage on page 114 *inf.* about conductors was interpolated in the later period, namely soon after the writing of the essay on "Conducting," 1869-70. There remain the second and third hypotheses, and in favour of the former we have the record in Vol. V. (pp. 37-38) of at least one passage-at-arms between the Paris editor and his mettlesome hack, whilst the latter is supported by the general resemblance in tone to the *Abendzeitung* Correspondence of 1841. Without an expert's opinion on the manuscripts of these Paris articles, most of which are preserved in the Wahnfried archives, I could not venture to decide between the two assumptions last advanced.

In any case the author gives his wit a more impersonal tone in his delightful "Pilgrimage to Beethoven," which followed the "Virtuoso" after an interval of only a month, appearing in the *Gazette* for November 19, 22, 29, and Dec. 3, 1840. The outlines of this story are purely imaginary, as Beethoven died when Wagner was a boy of barely fourteen years; but the gist of the fictitious conversation with the older master is so remarkably prophetic of the later and more particularly the Schopenhauerian Wagner (e.g. page 41), that I could scarcely believe we had before us the exact thoughts of the composer of *Rienzi* until a stranger-friend in Paris kindly procured me those old volumes of the *Gazette*, and I then discovered that, with exception of an immaterial reference to German Court-theatres, the French was in complete agreement with the German reprint of 1871, whilst a further comparison with the *Abendzeitung* of 1841 shewed an absolute identity. Verily that "Paris stress" was thrusting the young artist forward with seven-league strides.

After Beethoven the *Favorite* of Donizetti! Does it not seem.

* On page 113 I have mentioned the pieces played by Liszt on April 20, 1840; I now have to record the very similar programmes of his two concerts in the spring of 1841 :—on March 27 he played the overture to *Guillaume Tell*, an andante from *Lucia*, Schubert's *Serenade* and *Ave Maria*, a "grande étude" entitled *Mazeppa*, a fantasia on *Robert le Diable* and his *Galop Chromatique*; on April 13 *Marche Hongroise*, Scherzo, Storm and Finale from Beethoven's Pastoral Symphony etc.—W. A. E.

b

to re-echo from the last words of the *Pilgrimage*, where the
"Englishman" is about to cap his visit to the hermit of Vienna
by another to the "very famous Mr Rossini"? In effect, the
advent of the première of the *Favorite* would seem to have
prompted those closing lines ; for its first performance took place
on Dec. 2, the day before that passage appeared in type, and
Wagner himself had been engaged to make "arrangements" from
it, as already noted. These arrangements from the *Favorite* must
have interrupted his literary work again, for it is not till Jan. 10,
1841—nearly two months from the date of the first instalment of
the "Pilgrimage"—that the article on the "Overture" appeared,
with continuation and conclusion on the 14th and 17th of that
month. Here again the French and German versions vary somewhat, as noted on pages 153-4, 156, 163 and 164, and I should
fancy that the German variants were of the Tribschen period ;
possibly in this case the German of the *Ges. Schr.* is wholly a re-
translation from the French—a hypothesis which I have no
present means of verifying. The differences, however, are of no
signal importance, and the reader may rest assured that wherever
I have added no footnotes the German and French texts are in
full accord, i.e. that the views are those of 1840-41.

We next come to the "End in Paris," originally styled "Un
musicien étranger à Paris" and printed in the *Gazette* of Jan. 31
and Feb. 7 and 11, 1841. Wagner most plainly meant this
touching tale as a sequel to the "Pilgrimage to Beethoven," for
whilst the latter puts into Beethoven's mouth the author's own
ideas upon dramatic music, the present story gives an almost
literal account of Wagner's own struggles and experiences in
Paris. The connection between the two is further proved by the
existence of a first draft of the "End in Paris" dating, as
Glasenapp informs us, from the late autumn of 1840, immediately
after the completion of *Rienzi*, i.e. the time when the "Pilgrimage"
was actually passing through the press. That preliminary draft
runs as follows :—

"*How a poor musician died in Paris.* I have helped to bury
him. He was a good soul. General estimate of his character.
How I met him. What drove him hither, as he told me. What
did he mean to do here? His explanations, hopes of the public
etc. My rejoinders. We wrangle. He withdraws his friendship
from me. For long we lose sight of each other. At last I meet

him in the Champs Elysées; he is deliberating whether to offer an opera to a Punch-and-Judy show. Most unfortunate. Fresh quarrels; affectation of frivolity attacked by me; he speaks of quadrilles, with tears in his eyes. I am moved to sympathy. He waves me off, and runs away. For long I cannot find him again. At last I receive his invitation, with the news that he is dying. How I find him. His confessions; traces of madness; the Devil sought for—the Englishman found. What passed between them. Suicide resolved on; its execution deemed unnecessary; he had discovered that an aneurism of the heart would put an end to his life of itself. Determined to die happy in God and pure Art. Last thoughts about high Art. He commits to me his *diary—Fancies of a poor Musician*;—wishes to be decently buried—and dies. Leaves many debts behind him, to be covered by the fee for the publication of the *Fancies from his Diary*. With the next number they shall begin."—This is followed by a fragment of dialogue:—"*I*: You cannot alter things.—*He*: Then I shall be granted to die of them!—He died on the Mount of Martyrs, the martyr to a faith which no one certainly disputed him, save Hunger."

In the *Gazette* the "Musicien étranger" concludes with a promise to publish portions of that imaginary "Diary" in the "next numbers of this journal"; but again we have an interval of three months before anything further from Wagner's pen appears there. That interval would have been fairly occupied by renewed "arrangements," this time of Halévy's *Guitarrero*, which had been produced at the Opéra Comique on January 21; on the other hand the author had found a fresh vent for his rejected irony in the shape of "Correspondence from Paris" supplied to the Dresden *Abendzeitung*, commencing with the 23rd of February 1841.—This "Correspondence," together with two articles for Lewald's *Europa* of the same period, has been omitted from the *Ges. Schr.*, and I therefore reserve both it and them for Vol. VIII.

With regard to the article that appeared on April 1, after the said interval of three months, there can be no shadow of doubt that "Le Musicien et la Publicité" (see page 135 *inf.*) was mutilated by the Paris editor; that allusion to a sentence of Berlioz' which had appeared in the *Gazette* just two months earlier proves the thing up to the hilt, even were the unusual brevity of the contribution not sufficient evidence that something had gone awry. What reason the editor can have had for this particular act of vandalism, it is difficult to conceive. Nothing could be more impersonal than the matter of the article, nothing finer than its style. One is reduced to the supposition that the work was quite 'above his head.' Moreover it is significant that its *Gazette* version appears above the signature "Werner"; upon completion of the journal for 1841 the "Table des Auteurs" gives this article as "par erreur signé Werner," but I cannot help thinking that Wagner was so infuriated at having his best literary creation sent back to him for amendment that he deliberately chose as pseudonym the surname of a well-known German author then many years deceased. One thing is certain : with exception of the French "Freischütz" article, he writes no more for the *Gazette musicale* till nearly seven months have elapsed, and the series of "Caprices esthétiques extraits du journal d'un musicien défunt" comes to an abrupt termination. What we have lost by this contretemps, it is impossible to estimate; what we have gained, is easy to appraise—the *Flying Dutchman.*

Despoiled of his earlier sketch of the *Dutchman,* Wagner retires to the environs of Paris—to Meudon, to be precise—with his 500 francs of blood-money, and very soon writes and composes the first of his great series of immortal dramas. Before he can settle down to this, however, the voice of his beloved Weber calls to him from the grave to protest against the grand-operatising of his most German of works, *Der Freischütz*; on May 23, accordingly, Wagner's first article on that opera appears in the *Gazette,* with its conclusion on the 30th. The first performance at the Grand Opéra took place on June the seventh : the young man's "anger at seeing himself unable to find in any shade of journal in this great metropolis of uncommonly free France acceptance for any sort of exposure of the failings in the *Paris* Freischutz" (p. 201 *inf.*) prompts him to despatch a scathing criticism to the Dresden *Abendzeitung* on June the 20th, forming the second of the two "Freischütz" articles published in this volume.

The musical sketch of his *Holländer* completed in September, on the eve of returning to Paris itself he is once more compelled to take up his literary pen to help him out of his financial straits, in order to gain breathing-space for the new opera's instrumentation : result, the "Soirée heureuse" in the *Gazette* of October 24 and November 7, 1841. This is the last of Wagner's contributions to that journal included in the *Ges. Schr.*, though it was followed in 1842 by still one other, under the title " Halévy et la Reine de Chypre," appearing on Feb. 27, Mar. 13, Apr. 24 and May 1. The article last-named differs entirely from its fellow in the *Abendzeitung* referred to below, but, its German manuscript having passed out of the author's possession—probably never returned to him by the Paris translator—, it has been omitted from the *Ges. Schr.* After a considerable amount of trouble I have succeeded in obtaining a copy of the French article, perhaps the most important of Richard Wagner's Paris writings ; its lateness and its length, however, compel me to reserve it for Volume VIII. together with the other un-republished matter.

We thus have disposed of all the articles by Richard Wagner that appeared in the *Gazette musicale*. But, following the contents of the first volume of the *Ges. Schr.*, the present book contains two further writings from this Paris period. They do not call for more than a word or two of comment, as their wit and wisdom will speak for themselves, whilst their date of composition takes us to an epoch in their author's life marked by the far greater event of the completion of the *Flying Dutchman*. These two articles are that on " Rossini's Stabat Mater " dated " Paris, 15th December 1841," which appeared in Schumann's *Neue Zeitschrift für Musik* of the 28th, and that on " Halévy's Reine de Chypre" dated " Paris the 31st December, 1841," appearing in the *Abendzeitung* of Jan. 26-29, 1842.

On the 7th April, 1842, after many a delay in the announcement of his *Rienzi* by the Dresden management, Wagner finally left Paris, to hurry up its rehearsals. Alas ! he had to take away with him the *Huguenots, Robert le Diable, La Reine de Chypre* and *Zanetta,* as he was under contract to make still more "arrangements " from them, and in fact had been advanced part of the fee to enable him to defray his travelling expenses ; see *Letters to Uhlig* page 227, where we find him saying, "as this work became impossible to me in Germany, I afterwards paid back the cash advanced." But he took something else with him to Dresden : firstly the sketches for two new dramas,.namely the *Sarazenin* (to appear in Vol. VIII.) and *Tannhäuser,* with the germinal idea of *Lohengrin* ; secondly an experience such as years of professional toil in Germany could never have given him. Though Paris had helped him to nothing but disappointments, and perhaps a speedier recognition in Germany through the glamour it cast on even the stranger within its gates, it had offered the young artist a spectacle which nowhere else could he have witnessed in such intensity; glitter, pomp of show, keen combat of wits, ardent rivalries and shrewd intrigue—all the elements in which the Germany of those days was lacking, and elements whose very contrast with his nature forced his character to a development by far more rapid than it had ever pursued before. Moreover, Paris had given him that wider horizon which marks him from every other German musician since Gluck, and from all the German poets saving Goethe—both of whom had had their range of vision extended by sojourns abroad.

Seven years in Dresden now lay before the ripening master, years in which he was far more hindered than helped by his surroundings. I have no space to dwell on that period here, but possibly may have something to say about it in my preface to volume eight; meanwhile I can only follow the author's example (p. 225 *inf.*) and refer the reader to pages 316 *et seq.* of Vol. I. To this period belong the prose-works now translated from vol. ii. of the *Ges. Schr.*, namely the Speech at Weber's re-interment, the Programme for the Choral Symphony, the Wibelungen, the Nibelungen-myth, the Toast at the Tercentenary, and the plan of re-organisation for the Dresden Court-theatre. As to the work last named, the author expresses his fear that it will be found somewhat wearisome; but, quite apart from its evidence of a constructive power that might have qualified Richard Wagner for a leading rôle in politics, had he chosen to devote his energies to constitution-making, this "plan" contains most interesting details of the artistic milieu into which he was thrown and the duties he then had to fulfil. Far more important, from a literary point of view, is the essay on the "Wibelungen," which condenses into forty pages a most remarkable philosophic history of the world of Man itself, couched in a style that may be regarded as a perfect model for the German writer; that this fascinating lucidity of expression was not preserved throughout the author's later prose-works is of course regrettable, but may easily be explained by the fact that he was afterwards too arduously occupied to find time or inclination to adopt the course pursued with this essay, namely, to lay it aside for a few months and then proceed to its revision.

It only remains to give the names of the dramatic works included in those vols. i. and ii. of the *Ges. Schr.* Between the account of the *Liebesverbot* and the "German Musician in Paris" comes *Rienzi*, and after "Halévy's Reine de Chypre" the text of the *Flying Dutchman*, completing vol. i.; vol. ii. opens with *Tannhäuser*, between the "Programme" and the "Wibelungen" comes *Lohengrin*, and between the "Nibelungen-myth" and the "Toast" comes *Siegfried's Tod*. The last-named work is the original form of *Götterdämmerung*, from which it differs in many material respects, as may be guessed from the end of the "Nibelungen-myth." It would have over-weighted the present volume to add to it an English rendering of this poem; but I propose to open Vol. VIII. therewith.

As may have already been gathered, the whole of the prose from the *Gesammelte Schriften* has now appeared in this English series; but the posthumous and un-reprinted publications, together with that "Siegfried's Death," will furnish matter for a final book of fairly uniform size to be issued during 1899.

WM. ASHTON ELLIS.

November, 1898.

AUTHOR'S INTRODUCTION.

Y greatest difficulty, as editor of my Collected Writings, has been the selection for this first volume. At the time I wrote the works now reproduced, nothing was farther from my mind than to blossom into an essayist or poet; by inclination I had become a musician, by profession a Musikdirektor. When at last in 1842 I hit the mark with an opera composed by myself to a text of my making, Heinrich Laube—who took a very friendly interest in me then—invited me to send him an outline of my life, that he might fill it up for the "Zeitung für die elegante Welt," of which he was editor. "But," so my friend remarked as introduction to the rough draft I accordingly sent him, "the Paris stress has speedily doubled the musician with the writer: were I to alter the life-sketch, I should only spoil it."

It is this "Paris stress" with which I wished the contents of the present volume to acquaint my friends, for from that period of my life, in truth, dates my first necessity to engage in literature.

As it was so courteously acknowledged by a professional writer in those bygone days, that I knew how to write, I perhaps have no especial need to apologise on that score. One writes about one's art as best one can : nowadays in fact this is more generally allowed, than advantageous to the style of our literary era. But my having to give myself the look of posing as a *poet* also, if I am to abide by the aim of this collection, will certainly expose me to great annoyances. As an act of prudence, I ought in particular to have excluded the text of my opera "Rienzi." Had I yielded to the least ambition to air the graces of a poet in

A

the manufacture of this opera-book, presumably my grade
of culture would have enabled me to shew some little correctness in verse and diction, since it was the comparative
finish of an earlier text, "Das Liebesverbot," that already
had won the recognition of my quondam friend above-
named. On the other hand, to myself it is not uninstructive
to explore the reasons which seemed to permit so striking
a carelessness of verse and diction in the execution of my
text for "Rienzi." They sprang from certain curious ob-
servations which I made about that time in regard of the
operas of our current repertory. I had discovered that,
if the subject made a telling stage-piece in itself, quite
atrociously translated French and Italian operas had an
effect that bore one over all their misery of word and
rhyme ; whereas the best efforts of professional poets to
furnish the composer with seemly rhymes and verses could
never help the choicest, nay, the noblest music to the first
element of a stage-success, if the piece itself was feeble.
In this respect "Jessonda" and "Euryanthe," for example,
had led me to most hazardous thoughts, which soon begat
a mood of desperate levity. As I was longing for a big
success at the theatre, whenever the question of an opera-
text presented itself I was seized with dread at the so-
called "well-turned verse and charming rhymes" submitted
to me here and there. On the contrary, I pounced on
every narrative or novel with the one idea of turning it
into a rousing stage-piece for a music that on its side, too,
should have nothing to do with rhetorical flourishes.

So I believe it will be quite in order, for me to start with
this step in my artistic evolution, to shew my friends its
systematic course. The "Rienzi" may thus be regarded
as the *Musical Stage-piece** from which my further development into a musical dramatist pursued its path without
any contact with the métier of the poet proper. What

* In reproducing this libretto in its *entirety* I also see a means of rectifying
the judgment of those who only know the opera in the mutilation beloved
of our present theatres, and therefore are horrified by the clumsy piling of
grotesque effects.—R. Wagner.

soon diverted that path from the light-minded tendence aforesaid, and gave it a consciously more serious direction, the kindly reader will plainly decipher from the series of tales and articles which I have ranged in this opening volume between the text-book of " Rienzi " and the poem for the " Flying Dutchman." So far as my knowledge extends, in no artist's life can I point to so startling a change, accomplished in so brief a time, as here comes to light in the author of those two operas ; for the first was scarcely ended ere the second lay almost ready.* Nevertheless the bond of kinship between the two works will scarcely escape the attentive critic. The effective " stage-piece " most certainly lies at bottom of the "Flying Dutchman," no less than of the " Last of the Tribunes." Only, everyone must feel that something of importance had happened to the author ; perhaps a deep shock, in any case a violent revulsion, to which desire and disgust contributed alike. I may hope that the " German Musician in Paris " will afford sufficient answer.

* The first definite idea of *Rienzi* was conceived after reading a translation of Bulwer's novel during a brief stay at Dresden in the summer of 1837 ; the text-book was written in the summer of 1838 at Riga, where the composition of the first act was commenced on July 26th ; the music was continued at intervals in Paris from 1839 to 1840, the instrumentation being completed on Nov. 19th of the latter year. Meanwhile the *Faust*-overture had been written, at the end of 1839 (?). Wagner's first idea of the *Flying Dutchman* dates from the beginning of 1838 ; the first sketch of the piece—ceded to the Director of the Paris Opéra—was drafted in May 1840 ; the poem was written between May 18 and 28, 1841 ; the musical 'sketch' was begun and completed in seven weeks, ending September 13, and the orchestration finished by the close of that year. So that not only were the two operas completed within a year of one another, but they actually overlapped, as was the case with all the master's subsequent dramatic works.—Tr.

"Das Liebesverbot."

Bericht über eine erste Opernaufführung.

*The following " Account of a first Operatic Performance "
is evidently an extract from Richard Wagner's as yet unpub-
lished " Memoirs," as may be gathered from its second paragraph.   Its publication in the first volume of the* Gesammelte
Schriften *was also its first, and hitherto its only, appearance.
Though I propose retaining the German title of the opera, it
may be rendered in English by " Love's Penalty " or " Love
Forbidden."*

TRANSLATOR'S NOTE.

F my second completed opera, *das Liebesverbot*,
I will merely give an outline of the so-called
text, with an account of the attempt at its
performance and the circumstances connected
therewith. Though I omit a similar report
on my earliest opera, " die Feen," since it in no way came
before the public,* I have felt it impermissible to quite
pass by this second work of youth, as it really made a
public appearance, already remarked on.†

I planned the poem of this opera in the summer of 1834,
during a holiday at Teplitz, about which I have made the
following notes in my life-recollections.

On a few fine mornings I stole away from my surroundings, to take my breakfast in solitude upon the " Schlacken-
burg," and seize the opportunity of jotting down the sketch
of a new opera-poem in my notebook. I had annexed
the subject of Shakespeare's *Measure for Measure*, and, in
accordance with my then-prevailing mood, I adapted it
very freely for a libretto to which I gave the title : "*das
Liebesverbot.*" The ideas of " *Young Europe* " at that time
in the air, as also a reading of " Ardinghello," united with
the peculiar frame into which I had fallen in respect of
German opera-music to supply the keynote of my conception, which struck at puritanical hypocrisy in particular,
and therefore tended to a frank extolling of the "liberated senses." To this sense alone I wrested Shakespeare's
earnest story; nothing would I see in it but the gloomy,
rigorous moralist of a Stateholder aflame with passion for

---

* Not until June 29, 1888, when it was given at the Munich Court-theatre
by way of indemnity for the right of performance of *Parsifal*, as claimed by
King Ludwig's successors.—The work was written in 1833, when Wagner
was just twenty years of age.—Tr.

† In the " Autobiographic Sketch " ; see Vol. I. of this series.—Tr.

the beautiful novice who pleads his mercy for her brother, condemned to death for a love-offence, and kindles the most pernicious fire in the breast of the stony Puritan by the warmth of her human feeling. That Shakespeare simply develops these powerful motives the more conclusively to load the scale of justice in the end, was not my business to regard ; my only object was to expose the sin of hypocrisy and the unnaturalness of a ruthless code of morals. So I left the " measure for measure " completely out of sight, and let avenging love alone arraign the hypocrite. From fabulous Vienna I transposed the scene to the capital of glowing Sicily, where a German Stateholder, aghast at the incomprehensible laxness of its populace, attempts to carry out a puritanical reform, and lamentably falls. Presumably the *Muette de Portici* [Masaniello] had something to do with it ; reminiscences of the " Sicilian Vespers " may have had their share * : when I reflect that even the gentle Sicilian *Bellini* must be numbered among the factors of this composition, I can but smile at the singular quid-pro-quo into which the oddest misunderstandings here had shaped themselves.

It was not till the winter of 1835-36, that I was able to finish the score of my opera. This occurred amid the most bewildering duties at the little town-theatre of Magdeburg, whose opera-performances I conducted for two winter-seasons as Musikdirektor. A strange confusion had been wrought in my taste by immediate contact with the German operatic stage, and so strongly did it stamp the cut and execution of my work, that the youthful enthusiast for Beethoven and Weber would surely have been traced by no one in this score.

* This allusion to the historical "Sicilian Vespers" (13th century) has misled one or two writers into the assertion that Wagner's earliest works were influenced by Verdi. Nothing could be more ridiculous. Not till the year 1839 was Verdi's first opera, *Oberto*, produced in Milan ; nor did he make any particular name until March 1842, with his *Nabucco*, some months after the score of *Rienzi* had been despatched to Dresden, and that of the *Flying Dutchman* to Berlin. Verdi's *Vêpres siciliennes*, composed for Paris, appeared in 1855.—Tr.

Its fortune was as follows.

Despite a royal subsidy and the intervention of the theatre-committee in the management, our worthy Director was in a perennial state of bankruptcy, and a continuance of his undertaking in any shape or form was not to be thought of. So the performance of my opera, by the really excellent troop of singers at my disposal, was to constitute a turning-point in my career. I had the right to claim a 'benefit' in repayment of certain travelling-expenses from the previous summer: naturally I decided on a representation of my work, and did my best to make this managerial favour as little costly as possible. As the management had nevertheless to bear some outlay for the new opera, I agreed to surrender the receipts of the first performance and content myself with those of the second. Nor did the postponement of the rehearsals to the very end of the season appear to me an unmixed evil, since I might assume that the last performances of a company that had often been received with uncommon warmth would have a special interest for the public. Unfortunately, however, we never reached the season's stipulated close, fixed for the end of April, as in March the most popular members of our Opera announced their departure on account of unpunctuality in the payment of their salaries, and the offer of better engagements elsewhere; against which the impecunious management had no means of redress. That was bad news for me: the attainment of a performance of my *Liebesverbot* seemed more than doubtful. It was only through my being a favourite with the whole opera-company, that I induced the singers not merely to stay until the end of March, but also to undertake the study of my opera, most exhausting in view of the briefness of time. So scanty was it, that if two performances were to be given, we had no more than ten days for all the various rehearsals. As it was by no means a simple Singspiel, but, for all the slipshod character of its music, a grand opera with many lengthy ensemble numbers, the under-taking might rank as the height of folly. Nevertheless I built my hopes on the great exertions which the singers had willingly borne for my sake with their constant practice night and morning ; and, notwithstanding that it had been clean impossible to drive them to a little conscious settledness of memory, I finally reckoned on a miracle to be wrought by my own acquired dexterity as conductor.   The peculiar knack I had of giving the singers an illusive air of fluency, however uncertain they might really be, was shewn in our two or three full re-hearsals, when I kept the whole afloat by incessant prompt-ing, singing the notes aloud and shouting out the needful action, so that one might positively believe the thing would cut a decent figure after all.   Unfortunately we had forgotten that on the night of performance [March 29, 1836], in presence of the public, all these drastic means of oiling the dramatic-musical machinery would have to shrink to the beat of my bâton and the dumb motion of my face.   Indeed the singers, especially the male ones, were so extraordinarily shaky that their rôles were lamed of all effect from beginning to end.   The first tenor, blest with the very weakest memory, tried to bolster up the mercurial character of the madcap *Luzio* by the routine of *Fra Diavolo* and *Zampa*, and in particular by an immoderately large and tossing plume of gaudy feathers. Moreover as the management could not afford to print any textbooks, it was scarcely the public's fault that it remained entirely in the dark as to the story's drift, for the piece was sung throughout.   Whereas I had intended a brisk and energetic play of speech and action,—with exception of a few of the female parts, which were greeted with applause, the whole thing remained a musical shadow-play on the stage which the orchestra did its best to drown in inexplicable torrents.   As characterising the treatment of my tone-colours, I may mention that the conductor of a Prussian military band, who was quite delighted with the work, felt it his duty to give me a well-meant hint on handling the Turkish drum in future operas.   But, before proceeding with the history of this wonderful juvenile work, I must dwell awhile upon its character, especially as regards the poem.

The piece, which Shakespeare had kept to a very earnest basis, in my version had turned out as under :—

"An un-named King of Sicily leaves his country on a journey to Naples, as I suppose, and deputes to his appointed Stateholder—called simply *Friedrich*, to mark him for a German—the full authority to use all royal powers in an attempt to radically reform the manners of his capital, which had become an abomination to the strait-laced minister. At the commencement of the piece we see public officers hard at work on the houses of amusement in a suburb of Palermo, closing some, demolishing others, and taking their hosts and servants into custody. The populace interferes ; great riot : after a roll of the drums the chief constable *Brighella* (basso buffo), standing at bay, reads out the edict of the Stateholder according to which these measures have been adopted to secure a better state of morals. General derision, with a mocking chorus ; *Lusio*, a young nobleman and jovial rake (tenor), appears to wish to make himself the people's leader; he promptly finds occasion for espousing the cause of the oppressed when he sees his friend *Claudio* (likewise tenor) conducted on the road to prison, and learns from him that, in pursuance of an ancient law unearthed by *Friedrich*, he is about to be condemned to death for an amorous indiscretion. His affianced, whom the hostility of her parents has prevented his marrying, has become a mother by him ; the hatred of the relatives allies itself with *Friedrich's* puritanic zeal : he fears the worst, and has one only hope of rescue, that the pleading of his sister *Isabella* may succeed in softening the tyrant's heart. *Lusio* promises to go at once to *Isabella* in the cloister of the Elisabethans, where she has lately entered her novitiate.

"Within the quiet cloister walls we make the acquaintance of this sister, in confidential converse with her friend *Marianne*, who also has entered as novice. *Marianne* discloses to her friend, from whom she has long been parted, the sad fate that has brought her hither. By a man of high position she had been persuaded to a secret union, under the pledge of eternal fidelity ; in her hour of utmost need she had found herself abandoned, and even persecuted, for the betrayer proved to be the most powerful personage in all the state, no less a man than the King's present Stateholder. *Isabella's* horror finds vent in a tempest of wrath, only to be allayed by the resolve to leave a world where such monstrosities can go unpunished.—When *Lusio* brings her tidings of the fate of her own brother, her abhorrence of his misdemeanour passes swiftly to revolt against the baseness of the hypocritical Stateholder who dares so cruelly to tax her brother's infinitely lesser fault, at least attainted with no treachery. Her violence unwittingly exhibits her to *Lusio* in the most seductive light ; fired by sudden love, he implores her to leave the nunnery for ever and take his hand. She quickly brings him to his senses, yet decides, without a moment's wavering, to accept his escort to the Stateholder in the House of Justice.

"Here the trial is about to take place, and I introduce it with a burlesque examination of various moral delinquents by the chief constable *Brighella*. This gives more prominence to the seriousness of the situation when the gloomy figure of *Friedrich* appears, commanding silence to the uproarious rabble that has forced the doors ; he then begins the hearing of *Claudio* in strictest form. The relentless judge is upon the point of passing sentence, when *Isabella* arrives and demands a private audience of the Stateholder. She comports herself with noble moderation in this private colloquy with a man she fears and yet despises, commencing with nothing but an appeal to his clemency and mercy. His objections make her more impassioned : she sets her brother's misdemeanour in a touching light, and pleads forgiveness for a fault so human and in nowise past all pardon. As she observes the impression of her warmth, with ever greater fire she goes on to address the hidden feeling of the judge's heart, which cannot possibly have been quite barred against the sentiments that made her brother stray, and to whose own experience she now appeals for help in her despairing plea for mercy. The ice of that heart is broken: *Friedrich*, stirred to his depths by *Isabella's* beauty, no longer feels himself his master; he promises to *Isabella* whatever she may ask, at price of her own body. Hardly has she become conscious of this unexpected effect, than, in utmost fury at such incredible villainy, she rushes to door and window and calls the people in, to unmask the hypocrite to all the world. Already the whole crowd is pouring in to the judgment-hall, when *Friedrich's* desperate self-command succeeds in convincing *Isabella*, by a few well-chosen phrases, of the impossibility of her attempt: he would simply deny her accusation, represent his offer as a means of detection, and certainly find credence if it came to any question of repudiating a charge of wanton insult. *Isabella*, ashamed and bewildered, recognises the madness of her thought, and succumbs to mute despair. But while *Friedrich* is displaying his utmost rigour afresh to the people, and delivering sentence on the prisoner, *Isabella* suddenly remembers the mournful fate of *Marianne*; like a lightning-flash, she conceives the idea of gaining by stratagem what seems impossible through open force. At once she bounds from deepest sorrow to the height of mirth: to her lamenting brother, his downcast friend, the helpless throng, she turns with promise of the gayest escapade she will prepare for all of them, for the very Carnival which the Stateholder had so strenuously forbidden shall be celebrated this time with unwonted spirit, as that dread rigorist had merely donned the garb of harshness the more agreeably to surprise the town by his hearty share in all the sport he had proscribed. Everyone deems her crazy, and *Friedrich* chides her most severely for such inexplicable folly: a few words from her suffice to set his own brain reeling; for beneath her breath she promises fulfilment of his fondest wishes, engaging to despatch a messenger with welcome tidings for the following night.

"Thus ends the first act, in wildest commotion. What

the heroine's hasty plan may be, we learn at the beginning
of the second, where she gains admittance to her brother's
gaol to prove if he is worth the saving.   She reveals to him
Friedrich's shameful proposals, and asks him if he craves
his forfeit life at this price of his sister's dishonour?
Claudio's wrath and readiness to sacrifice himself are
followed by a softer mood, when he begins to bid his sister
farewell for this life, and commit to her the tenderest
greetings for his grieving lover; at last his sorrow causes
him to quite break down.   *Isabella*, about to tell him of his
rescue, now pauses in dismay; for she sees her brother
falling from the height of nobleness to weak avowal of
unshaken love of life, to the shamefaced question whether
the price of his deliverance be quite beyond her.   Aghast,
she rises to her feet, thrusts the craven from her, and
informs him that he now must add to the shame of death
the full weight of her contempt.   As soon as she has
returned him to the gaoler, her bearing once more passes
to ebullient glee: she resolves indeed to chastise the weak-
kneed by prolonging his uncertainty about his fate, but
still abides by her decision to rid the world of the most
disgraceful hypocrite that ever sought to frame its laws.
She has arranged for *Marianne* to take her place in the
rendezvous desired by *Friedrich* for the night, and now
sends him the invitation, which, to involve him in the
greater ruin, appoints a masked encounter at one of the
places of amusement which he himself has closed.   The
madcap *Lusio*, whom she also means to punish for his
impudent proposal to a novice, she tells of *Friedrich's*
passion, and remarks on her feigned decision to yield to
the inevitable in such a flippant fashion that she plunges
him, at other times so feather-brained, into an agony of
despair : he swears that even should the noble maid intend
to bear this untold shame, he will ward it off with all his
might, though all Palermo leap ablaze.

   "In effect he induces every friend and acquaintance to
assemble at the entrance to the Corso that evening, as if
for leading off the prohibited grand Carnival procession. At

nightfall, when the fun is already waxing wild there, *Luzio* arrives, and stirs the crowd to open bloodshed by a daring carnival-song with the refrain: 'Who'll not carouse at our behest, your steel shall smite him in the breast.' *Brighella* approaching with a company of the watch, to disperse the motley gathering, the revellers are about to put their murderous projects into execution; but *Luzio* bids them scatter for the present, and ambush in the neighbourhood, as he here must first await the actual leader of their movement: for this is the place that *Isabella* had tauntingly divulged to him as her rendezvous with the Stateholder. For the latter *Luzio* lies in wait: he soon detects him in a stealthy masker, whose path he bars, and as *Friedrich* tears himself away he is about to follow him with shouts and drawn rapier, when by direction of *Isabella*, concealed among the bushes, he himself is stopped and led astray. *Isabella* comes forth, rejoicing in the thought of having restored *Marianne* to her faithless mate at this very moment, and in the possession of what she believes to be the stipulated patent of her brother's pardon; she is on the point of renouncing all further revenge when, breaking open the seal by the light of a torch, she is horrified at discovering an aggravation of the order of execution, which chance and bribery of the gaoler had delivered into her hands through her wish to defer her brother's knowledge of his ransom. After a hard battle with the devouring flames of love, and recognising his powerlessness against this enemy of his peace, *Friedrich* has resolved that, however criminal his fall, it yet shall be as a man of honour. One hour on *Isabella's* bosom, and then his death—by the self-same law to whose severity the life of *Claudio* still shall stand irrevocably forfeit. *Isabella*, who perceives in this action but an additional villainy of the hypocrite, once more bursts out in frenzy of despairing grief. At her call to instant revolt against the odious tyrant the whole populace assembles, in wildest turmoil: *Luzio*, arriving on the scene at this juncture, sardonically adjures the throng to pay no heed to the ravings of a woman who, as she has deceived himself, assuredly will dupe them all ; for he still believes in her shameless dishonour. Fresh confusion, climax of *Isabella's* despair : suddenly from the back is heard *Brighella's* burlesque cry for help ; himself entangled in the coils of jealousy, he has seized the disguised Stateholder by mistake, and thus leads to the latter's discovery. *Friedrich* is unmasked ; *Marianne*, clinging to his side, is recognised. Amazement, indignation, joy : the necessary explanations are soon got through ; *Friedrich* moodily asks to be led before the judgment-seat of the King on his return, to receive the capital sentence ; *Claudio*, set free from prison by the jubilant mob, instructs him that death is not always the penalty for a love-offence. Fresh messengers announce the unexpected arrival of the King in the harbour ; everyone decides to go in full carnival-attire to greet the beloved prince, who surely will be pleased to see how ill the sour puritanism of the Germans becomes the heat of Sicily. The word goes round : 'Gay festivals delight him more than all your gloomy edicts.' *Friedrich*, with his newly-married wife *Marianne*, has to head the procession ; the Novice, lost to the cloister for ever, makes the second pair with *Lucio*.—"

I had worked out these bustling and, in many respects, ambitious scenes, with some regard to verse and diction. The police took offence at the title, which, if I had not altered it, would have dashed my whole plans of performance. We were in the week before Easter, a time when merry, to say nothing of frivolous, pieces were forbidden at the theatre. Fortunately the magistrate whom I had to consult in the matter had not gone any farther into the poem, and when I assured him that it was founded on a very serious play of Shakespeare's he contented himself with a change in the highly alarming title, for which we substituted the " Novice of Palermo " ; that appearing to have nothing against it, no further scruples were raised on the score of propriety.—I found things otherwise at Leipzig shortly after, where I tried to insinuate my new work in place of the abandoned "Feen." There I meant to win over the Director of the theatre by offering his daughter, a débutante in Opera, the part of "Marianne"; but he had grasped the tendence of the story, and made it a not un-colourable pretext for rejection. He informed me that even were the Leipzig Magistrates to permit the represen-tation, which his respect for those authorities caused him very much to doubt, as a conscientious father he could not possibly allow his daughter to appear in it.—

In the Magdeburg performance, remarkably enough, I had nothing at all to suffer from this dubious character of my opera-text; the story remained entirely unknown to the audience, as said above, on account of its utterly vague reproduction. This circumstance, with the consequent absence of any opposition to the *tendence*, enabled me to announce a second performance; against which no one raised his voice, since no one vexed his head. Perfectly aware that my opera had made no impression and left the audience in a complete haze as to what the whole thing was about, I counted nevertheless on the attraction of the very last appearance of our opera-troop to bring me in quite good, nay, large returns; so that I was not to be hindered from demanding the so-called "full" prices for admission. Whether a few seats would have been filled by the commencement of the overture, I can scarcely judge: about a quarter of an hour previously the only people I could see in the stalls were my landlady with her husband, and, strange to relate, a Polish Jew in full costume. I was hoping for an increase notwithstanding, when suddenly the most unheard-of scenes took place behind the wings. The husband of my prima donna (the actress of "Isabella") had fallen upon the second tenor, a very pretty young man who sang my "Claudio," and against whom the offended husband long had nursed a secret grudge. It seems that, having convinced himself of the nature of the audience when he accompanied me to the curtain, the lady's husband deemed the longed-for hour arrived for taking vengeance on his wife's pretender without

B

damage to the theatrical enterprise. *Claudio* was so badly
cuffed and beaten by him, that the unlucky wretch had to
escape to the cloak-room with a bleeding face. *Isabella*
was told of it, rushed in despair at her raging husband,
and received such blows from him that she fell into con-
vulsions.   The uproar in the company soon knew no
bounds : sides were taken, for and against, and little
lacked of a general free-fight, as it appeared that this unhappy evening was held by all a fit occasion for paying
off old scores.   So much was certain,—the pair who had
suffered from *Isabella's* husband's love-forbiddal were
rendered quite incapable of coming on that night.   The
regisseur was sent before the curtain, to inform the singularly select company in the auditorium that " on account of
unforeseen obstacles " the performance of the opera could
not take place.—

To a further attempt to rehabilitate my work of youth it
never came.

A GERMAN MUSICIAN IN PARIS.

TALES AND ARTICLES, 1840 AND 1841.

Ein deutscher Musiker in Paris.

Novellen und Aufsätze.

(1840 und 1841.)

＊

＊　　　　＊

Shortly after the modest funeral of my friend R . . ., lately deceased in Paris, I had set to work and written the brief history of his sufferings in this glittering metropolis, in accordance with the dead man's wish, when among his papers—from which I propose to select a few complete articles in the sequel—there came into my hands the fond narration of his journey to Vienna and visit to Beethoven. There I found a wonderful agreement with what I already had jotted down. This decided me to print that fragment of his journal in front of my own account of his mournful end, since it deals with an earlier period of his life, and also is likely to wake a little prior interest in my departed friend.

I

A PILGRIMAGE TO BEETHOVEN.*

WANT-AND-CARE, thou patron-goddess of the German musician, unless he happens to be Kapellmeister to a Court-theatre or the like,†—Want-and-care, thine be the name first lauded even in this reminiscence from my life! Ay, let me sing of thee, thou staunch companion of my life-time! Faithful hast thou been to me, and never left me; the smiles of Inconstance thou hast ever warded off, and shielded me from Fortune's scorching rays! In deepest shadow hast thou ever cloaked from me the empty baubles of this earth: have thanks for thy unwearying attachment! Yet, might it so be, prithee some day seek another favourite; for, purely out of curiosity, I fain would learn for once how life might fare *without* thee. At least, I beg thee, plague especially our political dreamers, the madmen who are breathless to

* This imaginary story originally appeared in the *Revue et Gazette Musicale de Paris* for Nov. 19, 22 and 29, and Dec. 3, 1840, with the title "Une visite à Beethoven: épisode de la vie d'un musicien allemand." Its German original, "Eine Pilgerfahrt zu Beethoven," first appeared in Nos. 181-86 of the Dresden *Abend-Zeitung*, July 30 to August 5, 1841, under the heading, "Zwei Epochen aus dem Leben eines deutschen Musikers" ("Two epochs from the life of a German musician," applying to the present article and its immediate successor) and with the additional sub-title "Aus den Papieren eines wirklich verstorbenen Musikers" ("From the papers of an actually deceased musician"). With that German version of 1841 the text in the *Gesammelte Schriften* agrees entirely, saving for two or three minute emendations of style and the omission of a tiny clause (p. 32 *inf.*) describing Beethoven as sitting "with his hands crossed over his stick" ("die Hände über seinen Stock gelehnt"). The prefatory note, on the opposite page, also appeared in the *Abend-Zeitung* (but not in the *Gazette*), with exception of the few words between the dashes.—Tr.

† From "unless" to "like" does not appear in the French.—Tr.

unite our Germany beneath *one* sceptre :—think on't, there then would be but one Court-theatre, one solitary Kapell-meister's post! What would become of my prospects, my only hopes; which, even as it is, but hover dim and shadowy before me—e'en now when German royal theatres exist in plenty ?*—But I perceive I am turning blas-phemous. Forgive, my patron-goddess, the dastard wish just uttered! Thou know'st my heart, and how entirely I am thine, and shall remain thine, were there a thousand royal theatres in Germany.† Amen!

Without this daily prayer of mine I begin nothing, and therefore not the story of my pilgrimage to Beethoven!

In case this weighty document should get published after my death, however, I further deem needful to say who I am; without which information much therein might not be understood. Know then, world and testament-executor!

A middle-sized town of middle Germany is my birth-place. I'm not quite certain what I really was intended for; I only remember that one night I for the first time heard a symphony of Beethoven's performed, that it set me in a fever, I fell ill, and on my recovery had become a musician. This circumstance may haply account for the fact that, though in time I also made acquaintance with other beautiful music, I yet have loved, have honoured, worshipped Beethoven before all else. Henceforth I knew no other pleasure, than to plunge so deep into his genius that at last I fancied myself become a portion thereof; and as this tiniest portion, I began to respect myself, to come by higher thoughts and views—in brief, to develop into what sober people call an idiot. My madness, however, was of very good-humoured sort, and did no harm to any man; the bread

---

* These two sentences are absent from the French.—Tr.

† "Were there a thousand royal theatres in Germany" is also absent from the French, and presumably was an addition made in 1841. On the other hand, instead of the two next short paragraphs there appeared, "L'adoption de cette prière quotidienne doit vous dire assez que je suis musicien et que L'Allemagne est ma patrie."—Tr.

I ate, in this condition, was very dry, and the liquid that I drank most watery; for lesson-giving yields but poor returns, with us, O honoured world and testament-executor ! *

Thus I lived for some time in my garret, till it occurred to me one day that the man whose creations I reverenced above all else was still *alive*. It passed my understanding, how I had never thought of that before. It had never struck me that Beethoven could exist, could be eating bread and breathing air, like one of us ; but this Beethoven was living in Vienna for all that, and he too was a poor German musician !

My peace of mind was gone. My every thought became one wish : *to see Beethoven* ! No Mussulman more devoutly longed to journey to the grave of his Prophet, than I to the lodging where Beethoven dwelt.

But how to set about the execution of my project ? To Vienna was a long, long journey, and needed money ; whilst I, poor devil, scarce earned enough to stave off hunger ! So I must think of some exceptional means of finding the needful travelling-money. A few pianoforte-sonatas, which I had composed on the master's model, I carried to the publisher ; in a word or two the man made clear to me that I was a fool with my sonatas. He gave me the advice, however, that if I wanted to some day earn a dollar or so by my compositions, I should begin by making myself a little renommée by galops and pot-pourris. —I shuddered ; but my yearning to see Beethoven gained the victory ; I composed galops and pot-pourris, but for very shame I could never bring myself to cast one glance on Beethoven in all that time, for fear it should defile him.

To my misfortune, however, these earliest sacrifices of my innocence did not even bring me pay, for my publisher explained that I first must earn myself a little name. I shuddered again, and fell into despair. That despair brought forth some capital galops. I actually touched money for them, and at last believed I had amassed enough to be able to execute my plan. But two years

* From " O honoured " to " executor," of course, is also absent from the French.—Tr.

had elapsed, and all the time I feared that Beethoven
might die before I had made my name by galops and
pot-pourris. Thank God! he had survived the glitter of
my name!—Saint Beethoven, forgive me that renommée;
'twas earned that I might see thee!

Joy! my goal was in sight. Who happier than I?
I might strap my bundle and set out for Beethoven at
once. A holy awe possessed me when I passed outside
the gate and turned my footsteps southwards. Gladly
would I have taken a seat in the diligence, not because
I feared footsoreness—(what hardships would I not have
cheerfully endured for such a goal!)—but since I should
thus have reached Beethoven sooner. I had done too
little for my fame as galop-composer, however, to be able
to pay carriage-fare. So I bore all toils, and thought
myself lucky to have got so far that they could take
me to my goal. O what I pictured, what I dreamed!
No lover, after years of separation, could be more happy
at returning to his youthful love.

And so I came to fair Bohemia, the land of harpists and
wayside singers. In a little town I found a troop of strolling-
ing musicians; they formed a tiny orchestra, composed of
a 'cello, two violins, two horns, a clarinet and a flute;
moreover there was a woman who played the harp, and
two with lovely voices. They played dances and sang
songs; folk gave them money and they journeyed on.
In a beautiful shady place beside the highway I found
them again; they had camped on the grass, and were
taking their meal. I introduced myself by saying that I
too was a travelling musician, and we soon became friends.
As they played dance-music, I bashfully asked if they knew
my galops also? God bless them! they had never heard
of my galops. O what good news for me!

I inquired whether they played any other music than
dances.

"To be sure," they answered, "but only for ourselves;
not for gentlefolk."

They unpacked their sheets, and I caught sight of the

grand Septuor of Beethoven; astonished, I asked if they played that too?

"Why not?"—replied the eldest,—"Joseph has hurt his hand, and can't play the second violin to-day, or we'd be delighted to give it at once."

Beside myself, I snatched up Joseph's violin, promised to do my best to replace him, and we began the Septuor.

O rapture! Here on the slope of a Bohemian highway, in open air, Beethoven's Septuor played by dance-musicians with a purity, a precision, and a depth of feeling too seldom found among the highest virtuosi!—Great Beethoven, we brought thee a worthy offering.

We had just got to the Finale, when—the road bending up at this spot toward the hills—an elegant travelling-carriage drew slowly and noiselessly near, and stopped at last close by us. A marvellously tall and marvellously blond young man lay stretched full-length in the carriage; he listened to our music with tolerable attention, drew out a pocket-book, and made a few notes. Then he let drop a gold coin from the carriage, and drove away with a few words of English to his lackey; whence it dawned on me that he must be an Englishman.

This incident quite put us out; luckily we had finished our performance of the Septuor. I embraced my friends, and wanted to accompany them; but they told me they must leave the high road here and strike across the fields, to get home to their native village for a while. Had it not been Beethoven himself who was awaiting me, I certainly would have kept them company. As it was, we bade each other a tender good-bye, and parted. Later it occurred to me that no one had picked up the Englishman's coin.—

Upon entering the nearest inn, to fortify my body, I found the Englishman seated at an ample meal. He eyed me up and down, and at last addressed me in passable German.

"Where are your colleagues?" he asked.

"Gone home," I replied.

"Just take out your violin, and play me something more," he continued, "here's money."

That annoyed me; I told him I neither played for money, nor had I any violin, and briefly explained how I had fallen in with those musicians.

"They were good musicians," put in the Englishman, "and the Symphony of Beethoven was very good, too."

Struck by this remark, I asked him if he practised music?

"*Yes*," he answered, "twice a week I play the flute, on Thursdays the French horn, and of a Sunday I compose."

That was a good deal, enough to astound me. In all my life I had never heard tell of travelling English musicians; I concluded that they must do very well, if they could afford to make their tours in such splendid equipages. I asked if he was a musician by profession?

For long I got no answer; finally he drawled out, that he had plenty of money.

My mistake was obvious to me now, for my question had plainly offended him. At a loss what to say, I devoured my simple meal in silence.

After another long inspection of me, the Englishman commenced afresh.

"Do you know Beethoven?"

I replied that I had never yet been in Vienna, but was on my way there to fulfil my dearest wish, to see the worshipped master.

"Where do you come from?" he asked.

"From L . . . ."

"That's not so far! I've come from England, and also with the intention of seeing Beethoven. We both will make his acquaintance; he's a very famous composer."

What a wonderful coincidence!—I thought to myself. Mighty master, what divers kinds thou drawest to thee! On foot and on wheels they make their journey.—My Englishman interested me; but I avow I little envied him his equipage. To me it seemed as though my weary pilgrimage afoot were holier and more devout, and that its goal must bless me more than this proud gentleman who drove there in full state.

Then the postilion blew his horn; the Englishman drove

off, shouting back to me that he would see Beethoven before I did.

I scarce had trudged a few miles in his wake, when unexpectedly I encountered him again. It was on the high road. A wheel of his carriage had broken down; but in majestic ease he sat inside, with his valet mounted up behind him, notwithstanding that the vehicle was all aslant. I learnt that they were waiting for the return of the postilion, who had run off to a somewhat distant village to fetch a blacksmith. As they had already been waiting a good long time, and as the valet spoke nothing but English, I decided to set off for the village myself, to hurry up smith and postilion. In fact I found the latter in a tavern, where spirits were relieving him of any particular care about the Englishman; however, I soon brought him back with the smith to the injured carriage. The damage was mended; the Englishman promised to announce me to Beethoven, and—drove away.

Judge my surprise, when I overtook him again on the high road next day! This time, however, no wheels were broken; drawn up in the middle of the road, he was tranquilly reading a book, and seemed quite pleased to see me coming.

"I've been waiting a good many hours for you," he said, "as it occurred to me on this very spot that I did wrong in not inviting you to drive with me to Beethoven. Riding is much better than walking. Come into the carriage."

I was astonished again. For a moment I really hesitated whether I ought not to accept his invitation; but I soon remembered the vow I had made the previous day when I saw the Englishman rolling off; I had sworn, in any circumstances to pursue my pilgrimage on foot. I told him this openly. It was now the Englishman's turn to be astonished; he could not comprehend me. He repeated his offer, saying that he had already waited many hours expressly for me, notwithstanding his having been very much delayed at his sleeping-quarters through the time consumed in thoroughly repairing the broken wheel. I remained firm, and he drove off, wondering.

Candidly, I had a secret dislike of him; for I was falling prey to a vague foreboding that this Englishman would cause me serious trouble. Moreover his reverence for Beethoven, and his proposal to make his acquaintance, to me seemed more the idle whim of a wealthy coxcomb than the deep inner need of an enthusiastic soul. Therefore I preferred to avoid him, lest his company might desecrate my pious wish.

But, as if my destiny meant to school me for the dangerous association with this gentleman into which I was yet to fall, I met him again on the evening of that same day, halting before an inn, and, as it seemed, still waiting for me. For he sat with his back to the horses, looking down the road by which I came.

"Sir," he began, "I again have waited very many hours for you. Will you drive with me to Beethoven?"

This time my astonishment was mingled with a secret terror. I could only explain this striking obstinacy in the attempt to serve me, on the supposition that the Englishman, having noticed my growing antipathy for him, was bent on thrusting himself upon me for my destruction. With undisguised annoyance, I once more declined his offer. Then he insolently cried:

"Goddam, you little value Beethoven. *I* shall soon see him." Post haste he flew away.—

And that was really the last time I was to meet this islander on my still lengthy road to Vienna. At last I trod Vienna's streets; the end of my pilgrimage was reached. With what feelings I entered this Mecca of my faith! All the toil and hardships of my weary journey were forgotten; I was at the goal, within the walls that circled Beethoven.

I was too deeply moved, to be able to think of carrying out my aim at once. True, the first thing I did was to inquire for Beethoven's dwelling, but merely in order to lodge myself close by. Almost opposite the house in which the master lived there happened to be a not too stylish hostelry; I engaged a little room on its fifth floor, and there began preparing myself for the greatest event of my life, a visit to Beethoven.

After having rested two days, fasting and praying, but never casting another look on the city, I plucked up heart to leave my inn and march straight across to the house of marvels. I was told Herr Beethoven was not at home. That suited me quite well; for it gave me time to collect myself afresh. But when four times more throughout the day the same reply was given me, and with a certain increasing emphasis, I held that day for an unlucky one, and abandoned my visit in gloom.

As I was strolling back to the inn, my Englishman waved his hand to me from a first-floor window, with a fair amount of affability.

"Have you seen Beethoven?" he shouted.

"Not yet; he wasn't in," I answered, wondering at our fresh encounter. The Englishman met me on the stairs, and with remarkable friendliness insisted upon my entering his apartment.

"*Mein Herr*," he said, "I have seen you go to Beethoven's house five times to-day. I have been here a good many days, and have taken up my quarters in this villainous hotel so as to be near Beethoven. Believe me, it is most difficult to get a word with him; the gentleman is full of crotchets. At first I went six times a-day to his house, and each time was turned away. Now I get up very early, and sit at my window till late in the evening, to see when Beethoven goes out. But the gentleman seems *never* to go out."

"So you think Beethoven was at home to-day, as well, and had me sent away?" I cried aghast.

"Exactly; you and I have each been dismissed. And to me it is very annoying, for I didn't come here to make Vienna's acquaintance, but Beethoven's."

That was very sad news for me. Nevertheless I tried my luck again on the following day; but once more in vain,—the gates of heaven were closed against me.

My Englishman, who kept constant watch on my fruitless attempts from his window, had now gained positive

information that Beethoven's apartments did not face the
street. He was very irritating, but unboundedly persever-
ing. My patience, on the contrary, was wellnigh exhausted,
for I had more reason than he; a week had gradually
slipped by, without my reaching my goal, and the returns
from my galops allowed a by no means lengthy stay in
Vienna. Little by little I began to despair.

I poured my griefs into my landlord's ear. He smiled,
and promised to tell me the cause of my bad fortune if
I would undertake not to betray it to the Englishman.
Suspecting my unlucky star, I took the stipulated vow.

"You see," said the worthy host, "quite a number of
Englishmen come here, to lie in wait for Herr von
Beethoven. This annoys Herr von Beethoven very much,
and he is so enraged by the push of these gentry that he
has made it clean impossible for any stranger to gain
admittance to him. He's a singular gentleman, and one
must forgive him. But it's very good business for my inn,
which is generally packed with English, whom the difficulty
of getting a word with Herr Beethoven compels to be my
guests for longer than they otherwise would. However,
as you promise not to scare away my customers, I hope to
find a means of smuggling you to Herr Beethoven."

This was very edifying; I could not reach my goal
because, poor devil, I was taken for an Englishman. So
ho! my fears were verified; the Englishman was my perdition! At first I thought of quitting the inn, since it was
certain that everyone who lodged there was considered an
Englishman at Beethoven's house, and for that reason I also
was under the ban. However, the landlord's promise, to find
me an opportunity of seeing and speaking with Beethoven,
held me back. Meanwhile the Englishman, whom I now
detested from the bottom of my heart, had been practising
all kinds of intrigues and bribery, yet all without result.

Thus several fruitless days slipped by again, while the
revenue from my galops was visibly dwindling, when at
last the landlord confided to me that I could not possibly
miss Beethoven if I would go to a certain beer-garden,

which the composer was in the habit of visiting almost every day at the same hour. At like time my mentor gave me such unmistakable directions as to the master's personal appearance, that I could not fail to recognise him. My spirits revived, and I resolved not to defer my fortune to the morrow. It was impossible for me to meet Beethoven on his going out, as he always left his house by a back-door ; so there remained nothing but the beer-garden.

Alas ! I sought the master there in vain on that and the two succeeding days. Finally, on the fourth, as I was turning my steps towards the fateful garden at the stated hour, to my despair I noticed that the Englishman was cautiously and carefully following me at a distance. The wretch, posted at his eternal window, had not let it escape him that I went out every day at a certain time in the same direction ; struck by this, and guessing that I had found some means of tracking Beethoven, he had decided to reap his profit from my supposed discovery. He told me all this with the calmest impudence, declaring at the same time that he meant to follow wherever I went. In vain were all my efforts to deceive him and make him believe that I was only going to refresh myself in a common beer-garden, far too unfashionable to be frequented by gentlemen of his quality : he remained unshaken, and I could only curse my fate. At last I tried impoliteness, and sought to get rid of him by abuse ; but, far from letting it provoke him, he contented himself with a placid smile. His fixed idea was to see Beethoven ; nothing else troubled him.

And in truth I was this day, at last, to look on the face of great Beethoven for the first time. Nothing can depict my emotion, and my fury too, as, sitting by side of my gentleman, I saw a man approach whose looks and bearing completely answered the description my host had given me of the master's exterior. The long blue overcoat, the tumbled shock of grey hair ; and then the features, the expression of the face,—exactly what a good portrait had long left hovering before my mental eye. There could be no mistake : at the first glance I had recognised him ! With short, quick steps, he passed us; awe and veneration held me chained.

Not one of my movements was lost on the Englishman; with avid eyes he watched the newcomer, who withdrew into the farthest corner of the as yet deserted garden, gave his order for wine, and remained for a while in an attitude of meditation. My throbbing heart cried out: 'Tis he! For some moments I clean forgot my neighbour, and watched with eager eye and speechless transport the man whose genius was autocrat of all my thoughts and feelings since ever I had learnt to think and feel. Involuntarily I began muttering to myself, and fell into a sort of monologue, which closed with the but too meaning words: *" Beethoven, it is thou, then, whom I see?"*

Nothing escaped my dreadful neighbour, who, leaning over to me, had listened with bated breath to my aside. From the depths of my ecstasy I was startled by the words:

" *Yes!* this gentleman is Beethoven. Come, let us present ourselves to him at once!"

In utter alarm and irritation, I held the cursed Englishman back by the elbow.

" What are you doing?" I cried, " Do you want to compromise us—in this place—so entirely without regard for manners?"

"Oh!" he answered, " it's a capital opportunity; we shall not easily find a better."

With that he drew a kind of notebook from his pocket, and tried to make direct for the man in the blue overcoat. Beside myself, I clutched the idiot's coat-tails, and thundered at him, " Are you possessed with a devil?"

This scene had attracted the stranger's attention. He appeared to have formed a painful guess that he was the subject of our agitation, and, hastily emptying his glass, he rose to go. No sooner had the Englishman remarked this, than he tore himself from my grasp with such violence that he left one of his coat-tails in my hand, and threw himself across Beethoven's path. The master sought to avoid him; but the good-for-nothing stepped in front, made a superfine bow in the latest English fashion, and addressed him as follows :

"I have the honour to present myself to the much renowned composer and very estimable gentleman, Herr Beethoven."

He had no need to add more, for at his very first words, Beethoven, after casting a glance at myself, had sprung on one side and vanished from the garden as quick as lightning. Nevertheless the irrepressible Briton was on the point of running after the fugitive, when I seized his remaining coat-tail in a storm of indignation. Somewhat surprised, he stopped, and bellowed at me :

"Goddam ! this gentleman is worthy to be an Englishman ! He's a great man, and no mistake, and I shall lose no time in making his acquaintance."

I was petrified ; this ghastly adventure had crushed my last hope of seeing my heart's fondest wish e'er fulfilled.

It was manifest, in fact, that henceforth every attempt to approach Beethoven in an ordinary way had been made completely futile for me. In the utterly threadbare state of my finances I now had only to decide whether I should set out at once for home, with my labour lost, or take one final desperate step to reach my goal. The first alternative sent a shudder to the very bottom of my soul. Who, so near the doors of the highest shrine, could see them shut for ever without falling into annihilation ?

Ere thus abandoning my soul's salvation, I still would venture on one forlorn hope. But *what* step, what road should I take ? For long I could think of nothing coherent. Alas ! my brain was paralysed ; nothing presented itself to my overwrought imagination, save the memory of what I had to suffer when I held the coat-tail of that terrible Englishman in my hand. Beethoven's side-glance at my unhappy self, in this fearful catastrophe, had not escaped me ; I felt what that glance had meant ; he had taken me for an Englishman !

What was to be done, to lay the master's suspicion ? Everything depended on letting him know that I was a

simple German soul, brimful of earthly poverty but over-
earthly enthusiasm.

So at last I decided to pour out my heart upon paper.
And this I did.   I wrote ; briefly narrating the history of
my life, how I had become a musician, how I worshipped
him, how I once had come by the wish to know him in
person, how I had spent two years in making a name as
galop-composer, how I had begun and ended my pilgrimage, what sufferings the Englishman had brought upon me,
and what a terrible plight my present was.   As my heart
grew sensibly lighter with this recital of my woes, the comfortable feeling led me to a certain tone of familiarity ; I
wove into my letter quite frank and fairly strong reproaches
of the master's unjust treatment of my wretched self.
Finally I closed the letter in genuine inspiration ; sparks
flew before my eyes when I wrote the address : "*An Herrn
Ludwig van Beethoven.*"   I only stayed to breathe a silent
prayer, and delivered the letter with my own hand at
Beethoven's house.

Returning to my hotel in the highest spirits—great
heavens ! what brought the dreaded Englishman again
before my eyes ?   From his window he had spied my latest
move, as well ; in my face he had read the joy of hope, and
that sufficed to place me in his power once more.   In
effect he stopped me on the steps with the question :
"Good news ?   When do we see Beethoven ? "

" Never, never " !—I cried in despair—" *You* will never
see Beethoven again, in all your life.   Leave me, wretch,
we have nothing in common ! "

" We have much in common," he coolly rejoined, " where
is my coat-tail, sir ?   Who authorised you to forcibly de-
prive me of it ?   Don't you know that you are to blame
for Beethoven's behaviour to me ?   How could he think it
convenable to have anything to do with a gentleman wear-
ing only one coat-tail ? "

Furious at seeing the blame thrown back upon myself, I
shouted : " Sir, your coat-tail shall be restored to you ;
may you keep it as a shameful memento of how you in-

sulted the great Beethoven, and hurled a poor musician to his doom! Farewell; may we never meet again!"

He tried to detain and pacify me, assuring me that he had plenty more coats in the best condition; would I only tell him when Beethoven meant to receive us?—But I rushed upstairs to my fifth-floor attic; there I locked myself in, and waited for Beethoven's answer.

How can I ever describe what took place inside, *around* me, when the next hour actually brought me a scrap of music-paper, on which stood hurriedly written: "Excuse me, Herr R. . ., if I beg you not to call on me until to-morrow morning, as I am busy preparing a packet of music for the post to-day. To-morrow I shall expect you.—Beethoven."

My first action was to fall on my knees and thank Heaven for this exceptional mercy; my eyes grew dim with scalding tears. At last, however, my feelings found vent in the wildest joy; I sprang up, and round my tiny room I danced like a lunatic. I'm not quite sure what it was I danced; I only remember that to my utter shame I suddenly became aware that I was whistling one of my galops to it.* This mortifying discovery restored me to my senses. I left my garret, the inn, and, drunk with joy, I rushed into the streets of Vienna.

My God, my woes had made me clean forget that I was in Vienna! How delighted I was with the merry ways of the dwellers in this empire-city. I was in a state of exalta-tion, and saw everything through coloured spectacles. The somewhat shallow sensuousness of the Viennese seemed the freshness of warm life to me; their volatile and none too discriminating love of pleasure I took for frank and natural sensibility to all things beautiful. I ran my eye down the

---

* In the French the last part of this sentence ran: "Je m'interrompis subitement en entendant quelqu'un qui semblait m'accompagner en sifflant l'air d'un de mes galops." This reference to supernatural presences is signifi-cant, as Richard Wagner's favourite author, in early life, was the fantastic E. A. Hoffmann. The invisible whistler of 1840 is represented in 1841 by the "*around* me" of a previous sentence, which does not appear in the *Gazette.*—Tr.

five stage-posters for the day. Heavens! On one of
them I saw: *Fidelio*, an opera by Beethoven.

To the theatre I must go, however shrunk the profits
from my galops. As I entered the pit, the overture began.
It was the revised edition of the opera, which, to the honour
of the penetrating public of Vienna, had failed under its
earlier title, *Leonora.** I had never yet heard the opera in
this its second form; judge, then, my delight at making
here my first acquaintance with the glorious new! A very
young maiden played the rôle of Leonora; but youthful as
she was, this singer seemed already wedded to Beethoven's
genius. With what a glow, what poetry, what depth of
effect, did she portray this extraordinary woman! She
was called *Wilhelmine Schröder*.† Hers is the high distinction of having set open this work of Beethoven to the
German public; for that evening I saw the superficial
Viennese themselves aroused to the strongest enthusiasm.
For my own part, the heavens were opened to me; I was
transported, and adored the genius who had led me—like
Florestan—from night and fetters into light and freedom.‡

I could not sleep that night. What I had just experienced, and what was in store for me next day, were too
great and overpowering for me to calmly weave into a
dream. I lay awake, building castles in the air and preparing myself for Beethoven's presence.—At last the new
day dawned; impatiently I waited till the seemly hour for
a morning visit;—it struck, and I set forth. The weightiest

---

* Between this and the succeeding sentence there appeared in the French :
"On ne peut nier, à la vérité, que l'ouvrage n'ait beaucoup gagné à son re-
maniement ; mais cela vient surtout de ce que l'auteur du second libretto offrit
au musicien plus d'occasions de développer son brillant génie ; *Fidelio* possède
d'ailleurs en propre ses admirables finales et plusieurs autres morceaux d'élite.
Je ne connaissais du reste que l'opéra primitif."—Tr.

† In the French this was followed by: "Qui ne connaît aujourd'hui la
réputation européenne de la cantatrice qui porte maintenant le double nom de
Schroeder-Devrient ?"—In 1871 Frau Schröder-Devrient had been dead eleven
years ; her praises are constantly sung in the master's prose-works, especially
at the close of *Actors and Singers* (Vol. V.).—Tr.

‡ This sentence is simply represented in the French by "Pour ma part,
j'étais ravi au troisième ciel."—Tr.

event of my life stood before me: I trembled at the thought.

However, I had yet one fearful trial to pass through.

Leaning against the wall of Beethoven's house, as cool as a cucumber, my evil spirit waited for me—the Englishman!—The monster, after suborning all the world, had ended by bribing our landlord; the latter had read the open note from Beethoven before myself, and betrayed its contents to the Briton.

A cold sweat came over me at the sight; all poesy, all heavenly exaltation vanished: once more I was in *his* power.

"Come," began the caitiff, "let us introduce ourselves to Beethoven."

At first I thought of helping myself with a lie, and pretending that I was not on the road to Beethoven at all. But he cut the ground from under my feet by telling me with the greatest candour how he had got to the back of my secret, and declaring that he had no intention of leaving me till we both returned from Beethoven. I tried soft words, to move him from his purpose—in vain! I flew into a rage—in vain! At last I hoped to outwit him by swiftness of foot; like an arrow I darted up the steps, and tore at the bell like a maniac. But ere the door was opened the gentleman was by my side, tugging at the tail of my coat and saying: "You can't escape me. I've a right to your coat-tail, and shall hold on to it till we are standing before Beethoven."

Infuriated, I turned about and tried to loose myself; ay, I felt tempted to defend myself against this insolent son of Britain by deeds of violence:—then the door was opened. The old serving-maid appeared, shewed a wry face at our queer position, and made to promptly shut the door again. In my agony I shouted out my name, and protested that I had been invited by Herr Beethoven himself.

The old lady was still hesitating, for the look of the Englishman seemed to fill her with a proper apprehension, when Beethoven himself, as luck would have it, appeared

at the door of his study.   Seizing the moment, I stepped
quickly in, and moved towards the master to tender my
apologies.   At like time, however, I dragged the Englishman behind me, as he still was holding me tight.   He
carried out his threat, and never released me till we both
were standing before Beethoven.   I made my bow, and
stammered out my name; although, of course, he did not
hear it, the master seemed to guess that it was I who had
written him.   He bade me enter his room; without troubling himself at Beethoven's astonished glance, my companion slipped in after me.

Here was I—in the sanctuary; and yet the hideous perplexity into which the awful Briton had plunged me,
robbed me of all that sense of well-being so requisite for
due enjoyment of my fortune.   Nor was Beethoven's outward appearance itself at all calculated to fill one with a
sense of ease.   He was clad in somewhat untidy house-
clothes, with a red woollen scarf wrapped round his waist;
long, bushy grey hair hung in disorder from his head, and
his gloomy, forbidding expression by no means tended to
reassure me.   We took our seats at a table strewn with
pens and paper.

An uncomfortable feeling held us tongue-tied.   It was
only too evident that Beethoven was displeased at receiving two instead of one.

At last he began, in grating tones: "You come from
L . . .?"   I was about to reply, when he stopped me;
passing me a sheet of paper and a pencil, he added:
"Please write; I cannot hear."

I knew of Beethoven's deafness, and had prepared myself
for it.   Nevertheless it was like a stab through my heart
when I heard his hoarse and broken words, "I cannot
hear."   To stand joyless and poor in the world; to know
no uplifting but in the might of Tone, and yet to be forced
to say, "I cannot hear!"   That moment gave me the key
to Beethoven's exterior, the deep furrows on his cheeks, the
sombre dejection of his look, the set defiance of his lips—
he heard not!

Distraught, and scarcely knowing what, I wrote down an apology, with a brief account of the circumstances that had made me appear in the Englishman's company. Meanwhile the latter sat silently and calmly contemplating Beethoven, who, as soon as he had read my lines, turned rather sharply to him and asked what he might want.

"I have the honour—" commenced the Briton.

"I don't understand you!" cried Beethoven, hastily interrupting him; "I cannot hear, nor can I speak much. Please write down what you want of me."

The Englishman placidly reflected for a moment, then drew an elaborate music-case from his pocket, and said to me: "Very good. You write: 'I beg Herr Beethoven to look through my composition; if any passage does not please him, will he have the kindness to set a cross against it.'"

I wrote down his request, word for word, in the hope of getting rid of him at last. And so it happened. After Beethoven had read, he laid the Englishman's composition on the table with a peculiar smile, nodded his head, and said, "I will send it."

With this my gentleman was mighty pleased; he rose, made an extra-superfine bow, and took his leave. I drew a deep breath :—he was gone.

Now for the first time did I feel myself within the sanctuary. Even Beethoven's features visibly brightened; he looked at me quietly for an instant, then began:

"The Briton has caused you much annoyance? Take comfort from mine; these travelling Englishmen have plagued me wellnigh out of my life. To-day they come to stare at a poor musician, to-morrow at a rare wild beast. I am truly grieved at having confounded you with them.—You wrote me that you liked my compositions. I'm glad of that, for nowadays I count but little on folk being pleased with my things."

This confidential tone soon removed my last embarrassment; a thrill of joy ran through me at these simple words. I wrote that I certainly was not the only one

imbued with such glowing enthusiasm for every creation
of his ; that I wished nothing more ardently than to be
able to secure for my father-town, for instance, the happiness of seeing him in its midst for once; that he then
would convince himself what an effect his works produced
on the entire public there.

"I can quite believe," answered Beethoven, "that my
compositions find more favour in Northern Germany.
The Viennese annoy me often ; they hear too much bad
stuff each day, ever to be disposed to take an earnest
thing in earnest."

I ventured to dispute this, instancing the performance of
"Fidelio" I had attended on the previous evening, which
the Viennese public had greeted with the most demon-
strative enthusiasm.

"H'm, h'm !" muttered the master. "Fidelio! But I
know the little mites are clapping their hands to-day out
of pure conceit, for they fancy that in revising this opera I
merely followed their own advice. So they want to pay
me for my trouble, and cry bravo ! 'Tis a good-natured
folk, and not too learned ; I had rather be with them, than
with sober people.—Do you like Fidelio now ? "

I described the impression made on me by last night's
performance, and remarked that the whole had splendidly
gained by the added pieces.

"Irksome work !" rejoined Beethoven. "I am no opera-
composer ; at least, I know no theatre in the world for
which I should care to write another opera ! Were I to
make an opera after my own heart, everyone would run
away from it ; for it would have none of your arias, duets,
trios, and all the stuff they patch up operas with to-day ;
and what I should set in their place no singer would sing,
and no audience listen to. They all know nothing but
gaudy lies, glittering nonsense, and sugared tedium. Whoever wrote a true musical drama, would be taken for a
fool ; and so indeed he would be, if he didn't keep such
a thing to himself, but wanted to set it before these
people."

"And how must one go to work," I hotly urged, "to bring such a musical drama about?"

"As Shakespeare did, when he wrote his plays," was the almost passionate answer. Then he went on: "He who has to stitch all kinds of pretty things for ladies with passable voices to get *bravi* and hand-claps, had better become a Parisian lady's-tailor, not a dramatic composer.—For my part, I never was made for such fal-lals. Oh, I know quite well that the clever ones say I am good enough at instrumental music, but should never be at home in vocal. They are perfectly right, since vocal music for them means nothing but operatic music; and from being at home in that nonsense, preserve me heaven!"

I here ventured to ask whether he really believed that anyone, after hearing his "Adelaide," would dare to deny him the most brilliant calling as a vocal composer too?

"Eh!" he replied after a little pause,—"Adelaide and the like are but trifles after all, and come seasonably enough to professional virtuosi as a fresh opportunity for letting off their fireworks. But why should not vocal music, as much as instrumental, form a grand and serious genre, and its execution meet with as much respect from the feather-brained warblers as I demand from an orchestra for one of my symphonies?* The human voice is not to be gainsaid. Nay, it is a far more beautiful and nobler organ of tone, than any instrument in the orchestra. Could not one employ it with just the same freedom as these? What entirely new results one would gain from such a procedure! For the very character that naturally distinguishes the voice of man from the mechanical instrument would have to be given especial prominence, and that would lead to the most manifold combinations. The instruments represent the rudimentary organs of Creation and Nature; what they express can never be clearly defined or put into words, for they reproduce the primitive feelings themselves, those feelings which issued from the chaos of the first Creation,

---

* From "and its execution," to the end of the sentence, did not appear in the French.—Tr.

when maybe there was not as yet one human being to take them up into his heart. 'Tis quite otherwise with the genius of the human voice; that represents the heart of man and its sharp-cut individual emotion. Its character is consequently restricted, but definite and clear. Now, let us bring these two elements together, and unite them! Let us set the wild, unfettered elemental feelings, represented by the instruments, in contact with the clear and definite emotion of the human heart, as represented by the voice of man. The advent of this second element will calm and smooth the conflict of those primal feelings, will give their waves a definite, united course; whilst the human heart itself, taking up into it those primordial feelings, will be immeasurably reinforced and widened, equipped to feel with perfect clearness its earlier indefinite presage of the Highest, transformed thereby to godlike consciousness." *

Here Beethoven paused for a few moments, as if exhausted. Then he continued with a gentle sigh: "To be sure, in the attempt to solve this problem one lights on many an obstacle; to let men sing, one must give them words. Yet who could frame in words *that* poesy which needs must form the basis of such a union of all elements? The poem must necessarily limp behind, for words are organs all too weak for such a task.—You soon will make acquaintance with a new composition of mine, which will remind you of what I just have touched on. It is a symphony with choruses. I will ask you to observe how hard I found it, to get over the incompetence of Poetry to render thorough aid. At last I decided upon using our Schiller's beautiful hymn 'To Joy'; in any case it is a noble and inspiring poem, but far from speaking *that* which, certainly in this connection, no verses in the world could say."

To this day I scarce can grasp my happiness at thus being helped by Beethoven himself to a full understanding

* In the French the last clause of this sentence presents a slight shade of difference, perhaps due to the translator, "Alors le cœur humain s'ouvrant à ces émotions complexes, agrandi et dilaté par ces pressentiments infinis et délicieux, accueillera avec ivresse, avec conviction, cette espèce de révélation intime d'un monde surnaturel."—Tr.

of his titanic Last Symphony, which then at most was finished, but known as yet to no man. I conveyed to him my fervent thanks for this rare condescension. At the same time I expressed the delightful surprise it had been to me, to hear that we might look forward to the appearance of a new great work of his composition. Tears had welled into my eyes,—I could have gone down on my knees to him.

Beethoven seemed to remark my agitation. Half mournfully, half roguishly, he looked into my face and said: "You might take my part, when my new work is discussed. Remember me: for the clever ones will think I am out of my senses; at least, that is what they will cry. But perhaps you see, Herr R., that I am not quite a madman yet, though unhappy enough to make me one.— People want me to write according to *their* ideas of what is good and beautiful; they never reflect that I, a poor deaf man, must have my very own ideas,—that it would be impossible for me to write otherwise than I feel. And that I cannot think and feel their beautiful affairs," he added in irony, "is just what makes out my misfortune!"

With that he rose, and paced the room with short, quick steps. Stirred to my inmost heart as I was, I stood up too;—I could feel myself trembling. It would have been impossible for me to pursue the conversation either by pantomimic signs or writing. I was conscious also that the point had been reached when my visit might become a burden to the master. To *write* a farewell word of heartfelt thanks, seemed too matter-of-fact; so I contented myself with seizing my hat, approaching Beethoven, and letting him read in my eyes what was passing within me.

He seemed to understand. "You are going?" he asked. "Shall you remain in Vienna awhile?"

I wrote that my journey had no other object than to gain his personal acquaintance; since he had honoured me with so unusual a reception, I was overjoyed to view my goal as reached, and should start for home again next day.

Smiling, he replied: "You wrote me, in what manner

you had procured the money for this journey.—You ought to stop in Vienna and write galops,—that sort of ware is much valued here."

I declared that I had done with all that, as I now knew nothing worth a similar sacrifice.

"Well, well," he said, " one never knows! Old fool that I am, I should have done better, myself, to write galops ; the way I have gone, I shall always famish.   A pleasant journey,"—he added—"think of me, and let that console you in all your troubles."

My eyes full of tears, I was about to withdraw, when he called to me : "Stay, we must polish off the musical Englishman!   Let's see where to put the crosses!"

He snatched up the Briton's music-case, and smilingly skimmed its contents ; then he carefully put it in order again, wrapped it in a sheet of paper, took a thick scoring-pen, and drew a huge cross from one end of the cover to the other.   Whereupon he handed it to me with the words : "Kindly give the happy man his masterwork!   He's an ass, and yet I envy him his long ears!—Farewell, dear friend, and hold me dear!"

And so he dismissed me.   With staggering steps I left his chamber and the house.

* * *

At the hotel I found the Englishman's servant packing away his master's trunks in the travelling-carriage.   So his goal, also, was reached ; I could but admit that *he*, too, had proved his endurance.   I ran up to my room, and likewise made ready to commence my homeward march on the morrow.   A fit of laughter seized me when I looked at the cross on the cover of the Englishman's composition. That cross, however, was a souvenir of Beethoven, and I grudged it to the evil genius of my pilgrimage.   My decision was quickly taken.   I removed the cover, hunted out my galops, and clapped them in this damning shroud. To the Englishman I sent his composition wrapperless, accompanying it with a little note in which I told him that Beethoven envied him and had declared he didn't know where to set a cross.

As I was leaving the inn, I saw my wretched comrade mount into his carriage.

"Good-bye," he cried. "You have done me a great service. I am glad to have made Beethoven's acquaintance.—Will you come with me to Italy?"

"What would you there?"—I asked in reply.

"I wish to know Mr Rossini, as he is a very famous composer."

"Good luck!"—called I: "I know Beethoven, and that's enough for my lifetime!"

We parted. I cast one longing glance at Beethoven's house, and turned to the north, uplifted in heart and ennobled.

2

AN END IN PARIS.*

E have just laid him in the earth. It was cold and dreary weather, and few there were of us. The Englishman, too, was there : he wants to erect a memorial to him ; 'twere better he paid our friend's debts.

It was a mournful ceremony. The first keen wind of winter cut the breath ; no one could speak, and the funeral oration was omitted. Nevertheless I would have you to know that he whom we buried was a good man and a brave German musician. He had a tender heart, and wept whenever men hurt the poor horses in the streets of Paris. He was mild of temper, and never put out when the street-urchins jostled him off the narrow pavement. Unfortunately he had a sensitive artistic conscience, was ambitious, with no talent for intrigue, and once in his youth had seen Beethoven, which so turned his head that he could never set it straight in Paris.

It is more than a year since I one day saw a magnificent Newfoundland dog taking a bath in the fountain of the Palais Royal. Lover of dogs that I am, I watched the splendid animal; it left the basin at last, and answered the call of a man who at first attracted my attention merely

* Under the title "Un musicien étranger à Paris," this story appeared in the *Gazette Musicale* of Jan. 31 and Feb. 7 and 11, 1841. Its German original was first printed in Nos. 187-91 of the *Abend-Zeitung* (Aug. 6 to 11, 1841) as a sequel to the "Pilgrimage", and with the special title "Das Ende zu Paris. (Aus der Feder eines in Wahrheit noch lebenden Notenstechers.)"—i.e "The end at Paris : from the pen of an in reality still living note-engraver." The title in the *Ges. Schr.* becomes "Ein Ende in Paris," but otherwise the two German texts are identical, saving for one or two quite trifling stylistic alterations and the appearance in the *A.Z.* of "—denn ich bin mehr Banquier als Notenstecher—", i.e. "— for I am more of a banker than a note-engraver—", following the words "as my own access to those sanctuaries was but rare " on page 55 *infra.*—Tr.

as the owner of this dog. The man was by no means so
fair to look on, as his dog ; he was clean, but dressed in
God knows what provincial fashion. Yet his features
arrested me ; soon I distinctly remembered having seen
them before ; my interest in the dog relaxed ; I fell into
the arms of my old friend R . . . .

We were delighted at meeting again ; he was quite overcome with emotion. I took him to the *Café de la Rotonde* ;
I drank tea with rum,—he, coffee with tears.

" But what on earth," I began at last, " can have brought
you to Paris—you, the musical hermit of the fifth floor of
a provincial back-street ? "

" My friend," he replied, " call it the over-earthly passion
for experiencing what life is like on a Parisian sixth, or the
worldly longing to see if I might not be able in time to
descend to the second, or even the first,—I myself am not
quite certain which. At anyrate I couldn't resist the
temptation of tearing myself from the squalor of the
German provinces, and, without tasting the far sublimer
pinches of a German capital, throwing myself straight
upon the centre of the world, where the arts of every
nation stream together to one focus ; where the artists of
each race find recognition ; and where I hope for satisfaction of the tiny morsel of ambition that Heaven—
apparently in inadvertence—has set in my own breast."

" A very natural desire," I interposed ; " I forgive it you,
though in yourself it astonishes me. But first let us see
what means you have of pursuing your ambitious purpose.
How much money a-year can you draw ?—Oh, don't be
alarmed ! I know that you were a poor devil, and it is
self-evident that there can be no question of a settled
income. Yet I am bound to suppose either that you have
won money in a lottery, or enjoy the protection of some
rich patron or relative to such a degree that you are provided for ten years, at least, with a passable allowance."

" That is how you foolish people look at things ! " replied
my friend, with a good-humoured smile, after recovering
from his first alarm. " Such are the prosaic details that

rise at once before your eyes as chief concern. Nothing of
the kind, my dear friend! I am poor; in a few weeks, in
fact, without a sou. But what of that? I have been told
that I have talent;—was I to choose *Tunis* as the place for
pushing it? No; I have come to *Paris!* Here I shall
soon find out·if folk deceived me when they credited me
with talent, or if I really own any. In the first case I
shall be quickly disenchanted, and, clear about myself,
shall journey back contented to my garret-home; in the
second case I shall get my talent more speedily and better
paid in Paris, than anywhere else in the world.—Nay,
don't smile, but try to raise some serious objection!"

"Best of friends," I resumed, "I smile no longer; for I
now am possessed by a mournful compassion for yourself
and your splendid dog. I know that, however frugal
yourself, your magnificent beast will eat a good deal.
You intend to feed both him and yourself by your talent?
That's grand; for self-preservation is the first duty, and
human feeling for the beasts a second and the noblest.
But tell me: how are you going to bring your talent to
market? What plans have you made? Let me hear them."

"It is well that you ask for my plans," was the answer.
"You shall have a long list of them; for, look you, I am
rich in plans. In the first place, I think of an opera: I am
provided with finished works, with half-finished, and with
any number of sketches for all kinds—both grand and
comic opera.—Don't interrupt!—I'm well aware that these
are things that will not march too quickly, and merely consider them as the basis of my efforts. Though I dare not
hope to see one of my operas produced at once, at least I
may be permitted to assume that I shall soon be satisfied
as to whether the Directors will accept my compositions or
not.—For shame, friend—you're smiling again! Don't
speak! I know what you were going to say, and will
answer it at once.—I am convinced that I shall have to
contend with difficulties of all sorts here also; but in what
will they consist? Certainly in nothing but competition.
The most eminent talents converge here, and offer their

works for acceptance ; managers are therefore compelled to
exercise a searching scrutiny : a line must be drawn against
bunglers, and none but works of exceptional merit can
attain the honour of selection. Good ! I have prepared
myself for this examination, and ask for no distinction
without deserving it. But what else have I to fear, beyond
that competition ? Am I to believe that here, too, one
needs the wonted tactics of servility ? * Here in Paris, the
capital of free France, where a Press exists that unmasks
and makes impossible all humbug and abuse ; where merit
alone can win the plaudits of a great incorruptible public ? "

" The public ? " I interrupted ; " there you are right. I
also am of opinion that, with your talent, you well might
succeed, had you only the public to deal with. But as to
the easiness of reaching that public you hugely err, poor
friend ! It is not the contest of talents, in which you will
have to engage, but the contest of reputations and personal
interests. If you are sure of firm and influential patronage,
by all means venture on the fight ; but without this, and
without money,—give up, for you're sure to go under,
without so much as being noticed. It will be no question
of commending your work or talent (a favour unparalleled !),
but what will be considered is the name you bear. Seeing
that no renommée attaches to that name as yet, and it is
to be found on no list of the moneyed, you and your talent
remain in obscurity." †

* In the French this sentence ran, " Me faudrait-il craindre par hasard de
me trouver, ici comme en Allemagne, dans l'obligation d'avoir recours à des
voies tortueuses pour me procurer l'entrée des théâtres royaux ? "—and was
immediately followed by " Dois-je croire que, pendant des années entières, il
me faudra mendier la protection de tel ou tel laquais de cour pour finir par
arriver, grâce à un mot de recommandation qu'aura daigné m'accorder quelque
femme de chambre, à obtenir pour mes œuvres l'honneur de la réprésentation ?
Non sans doute, et à quoi bon d'ailleurs des démarches si serviles, ici, à Paris "
etc.—Some specific case appears to be referred to here, for, although the
passage drops out of this connection in the *Abendzeitung* and *Ges. Schr.*, we
meet with an identical allusion in the essay on " Conducting," see Vol. IV.,
pp. 294 and 297.—Tr.

† Between this paragraph and the next there appeared in the *Gazette Musicale*
" (Je n'ai nul besoin, je pense, de faire remarquer au lecteur que, dans les
objections dont je me sers et dont j'aurai encore à me servir vis-à-vis de mon

My objection failed to produce the intended effect on my enthusiastic friend. He turned peevish, but refused to believe me. I went on to ask what he thought of doing as a preliminary, to earn some little renommée in another direction, which perchance might be of more assistance to the later execution of his soaring plan.

This seemed to dispel his ill-humour.

"Hear, then!" he answered: "You know that I have always had a great preference for instrumental music. Here, in Paris, where a regular cult of our great Beethoven appears to have been instituted, I have reason to hope that his fellow-countryman and most ardent worshipper will easily find entrance when he undertakes to give the public a hearing of his own attempts, however feeble, to follow in the footsteps of that unattainable example."

"Excuse me for cutting you short," I interposed. "Beethoven is getting deified,—in that you are right; but mind you, it is his name, his renown that is deified. That name, prefixed to a work not unworthy of the great master, will suffice to secure its beauties instant recognition. By any other name, however, the selfsame work will never gain the attention of the directorate of a concert-establishment for even its most brilliant passages." *

"You lie!"—my friend rather hastily exclaimed. "Your purpose is becoming clear, to systematically discourage me, and scare me from the path of fame. You shall not succeed, however!"

"I know you," I replied, "and forgive you. Nevertheless I must add that in your last proposal you will stumble on the very same difficulties, which rear themselves against every artist without renown, however great his talent, in a place where people have far too little time to bother them-

ami, il ne s'agit nullement de voir l'expression complète de ma conviction personelle, mais seulement une série d'arguments que je regardais comme urgent d'employer pour amener mon enthousiaste à abandonner ses plans chimériques, sans diminuer pourtant en rien sa confiance en son talent.) "—Tr.

* In the *Gazette* here appeared "(Le lecteur voudra bien ne pas oublier de faire ici une nouvelle application de la remarque que je lui ai recommandée ci-dessus.) "—Tr.

selves about hidden treasures. Both plans are modes of
fortifying an already established position, and gaining
profit from it, but by no manner of means of creating one.
People will either pay no heed at all to your application
for a performance of your instrumental compositions, or—
if your works are composed in that daring individual spirit
which you so much admire in Beethoven, they will find
them turgid and indigestible, and send you home with a
flea in your ears." *

"But," my friend put in, "what if I have already circum-
vented such a reproach? What if I have written works
expressly to aid me with a more superficial public, and
adorned them with those favourite modern effects which I
abhor from the bottom of my heart, but are not despised
by even considerable artists as preliminary bids for favour?"

"They will give you to understand," I replied, "that your
work is too light, too shallow, to be brought to the public
ear between the creations of a Beethoven and a Musard."

"Dear man!" my friend exclaimed, "That's good
indeed! At last I see that you are making fun of me.
You always were a wag!"

My friend stamped his foot in his laughter, and trod so
forcibly upon the lordly paw of his splendid dog that the
latter yelped aloud, then licked his master's hand, and
seemed to humbly beg him to take no more of my objections as jokes.

"You see," I said, "it is not always well to take earnestness as jest. Passing that by, come tell me what other plans
could have moved you to exchange your modest home for
this monster of a Paris. In what other way, if you will
please me by provisionally abandoning the two you have
spoken of, do you propose to get the requisite renown?"

"So be it," was the reply I received. "In spite of your
singular love of contradiction, I will proceed with the
narration of my plans. Nothing, as I know, is more
popular in Paris drawing-rooms than those charming sen-

---

* Here, as also at the end of the next paragraph but one, the *Gazette* had
" (Le lecteur voudra bien ne pas oublier, etc.) "—Tr.

timental ballads and romances, which are just to the taste of the French people, and some of which have even emigrated from our fatherland.   Think of Franz Schubert's songs, and the vogue they enjoy here ! This is a genre that admirably suits my inclination ; I feel capable of turning out something worth noticing there.   I will get my songs sung, and perchance I may share the good luck which has fallen to so many—namely of attracting by these unpretentious works the attention of some Director of the Opéra who may happen to be present, so that he honours me with the commission for an opera."

The dog again uttered a violent howl.   This time it was I who, in an agony of laughter, had trodden on the paw of the excellent beast.

"What !" I cried, "is it possible that you seriously entertain such an idiotic idea ? What on earth could entitle you——"

"My God !" the enthusiast broke in ; "have not similar cases happened often enough?   Must I bring you the newspapers in which I have repeatedly read how such-and-such a Director was so carried away by the hearing of a Romance, how such-and-such a famous poet was suddenly so impressed by the talent of a totally unknown composer, that both of them at once united in the resolve, the one to supply him with a libretto, the other to produce the opera to-be-written to order ? "

"Ah ! is that it ? " I sighed, filled with sudden sadness ; "Press notices have led astray your simple childlike head ? Dear friend, of all you come across in that way take note of but a third, and even of that don't trust four quarters ! Our Directors have something else to do, than to hear Romances sung and fall into raptures over them.*   And, admitting that to be a feasible mode of gaining a reputation,—by whom would you get your Romances sung ? "

"By whom else," was the rejoinder, "than the same world-famed singers who so often, and with the greatest

* Here again, and after the first sentence of the next paragraph but one, the *G. M.* had " (Le lecteur voudra bien ne pas oublier, etc.) "—Tr.

amiability, have made it their duty to introduce the productions of unknown or downtrod talent to the public?
Or am I here again deceived by lying paragraphs?"

"My friend," I replied, "God knows how far I am from
wishing to deny that noble hearts of this kind beat below
the throats of our foremost singers, male and female. But
to attain the honour of such patronage, one needs at least
some other essentials. You can easily imagine what competition goes on here also, and that it requires an infinitely
influential recommendation, to make it dawn upon those
noble hearts that one in truth is an unknown genius.—
Poor friend, have you no other plans?"

Here my companion took leave of his senses. In a
violent passion—though with some regard for his dog—
he turned away from me. "And had I as many more
plans as the sands of the sea," he shouted, "you should
not hear a single one of them. Go! You are my enemy!—
Yet know, inexorable man, you shall not triumph over me!
Tell me—the last question I will put to you—tell me,
wretch, how then have the myriads commenced, who first
became known, and finally famous, in Paris?"

"Ask one of them," I replied, in somewhat ruffled com-
posure, "and perhaps you may discover. For my part, I
don't know."

"Here, here!" called the infatuate to his wonderful
dog. "You are my friend no longer,"—he volleyed at
me,—"Your cold derision shall not see me blench. *In
one year from now*—remember this—*in one year from now
every gamin shall be able to tell you where I live, or you shall
hear from me whither to come—to see me die.* Farewell!"

He whistled shrilly to his dog,—a discord. He and his
superb companion had vanished like a lightning-flash.
Nowhere could I overtake them.

* * *

It was only after a few days, when all my efforts to
ascertain the dwelling of my friend had proved futile, that
I began to realise the wrong I had done in not shewing
more consideration for the peculiarities of so profoundly

enthusiastic a nature, than unfortunately had been the case with my tart, perhaps exaggerated, objections to his very innocent plans. In the good intention of frightening him from his projects as much as possible, because I did not deem him fitted either by his outward or his inward condition to successfully pursue so intricate a path of fame— in this good intention, I repeat, I had not reckoned with the fact that I had by no means to do with one of those tractable and easily-persuaded minds, but with a man whose deep belief in the divine and irrefutable truth of his art had reached such a pitch of fanaticism, that it had turned one of the gentlest of tempers to a dogged obstinacy.

For sure—I could but think—he now is wandering through the streets of Paris with the firm conviction that he has only to decide which of his plans he shall realise first, in order to figure at once on one of those advertisements that, so to say, make out the vista of his scheme. For sure, he is giving an old beggar a sou to-day, with the determination to make it a napoleon a few months hence.

The more the time slipped by since our last parting, and the more fruitless became my endeavours to unearth my friend, so much the more—I admit my weakness—was .I infected by the confidence he then displayed ; so that I allowed myself at last to search the advertisements of musical performances, now and again, with eyes astrain to spy out in some corner of them the name of my assured enthusiast. Yes, the smaller my success in these attempts at discovery, the more — remarkable to say ! — was my friendly interest allied with an ever-increasing belief that my friend might not impossibly succeed ; that perchance even now, while I was seeking anxiously for him, his peculiar talent might already have been discovered and acknowledged by some important person or other ; that perhaps he had received one of those commissions whose happy execution brings fortune, honour, and God knows what beside. And why not ? Is there no star that rules the fate of each inspired soul ? May not his be a star of luck ?

Cannot miracles take place, to expose a hidden treasure?
—The very fact of my nowhere seeing the announcement
of a single Romance, an Overture or the like, under the
name of my friend, made me believe that he had gone
straight for his grandest plan, and, despising those lesser
adits to publicity, was already up to his eyes in work on an
opera of at least five acts. True, I had never come across
him in the haunts of artists, or met a creature who knew
anything about him ; still, as my own access to those sanctuaries was but rare, 'twas conceivable that it was *I* who was
the unfortunate that could not penetrate where his fame
maybe already shone with dazzling rays.—

You may easily guess that it needed a considerable time,
for my first sad interest in my friend to change into a con-
fident belief in his good star. It was only through all the
phases of fear, of doubt, of hope, that I could arrive at this
point. Such things are somewhat slow with me, and so it
happened that almost a year had already elapsed since the
day when I met a splendid dog and an enthusiastic friend
in the Palais Royal. Meanwhile some wonderfully lucky
speculations had brought me to so unprecedented a pitch of
prosperity that, like Polycrates of old, I began to fear an
imminent reverse. I fancied I could plainly see it coming ;
thus it was in a gloomy frame of mind; that I one day took
my customary walk in the Champs Élysées.

'Twas autumn ; the leaves fell withered from the trees,
and the sky hung grey with age above the Elysian pomp
below. But, nothing daunted, Punch renewed his old mad
onslaught ; in blind rage that scoundrel constantly defied
the justice of this world, until at last the dæmonic principle, so forcibly depicted by the chained-up cat, with superhuman claws laid low the saucy bounce of the presumptuous
mortal.

Close by my side, a few paces from the humble scene
of Polichinel's misdeeds I heard the following remarkable
soliloquy in German :—

" Excellent! excellent! Where, in the name of all the
world, have I allowed myself to seek, when I could have

found so near?   What!   Am I to despise this stage, on which the most thrilling political and poetic truths are set in realistic dress, so directly and intelligibly, before the most receptive and least assuming public?   Is this braggart not Don Juan? Is that terribly fair white cat not the Commander on horseback, in very person?—How the artistic import of this drama will be heightened and transfigured when my music adds its quota!—What sonorous organs in these actors!—And the cat—ah, that cat! What hidden charms lie buried in her glorious throat!—Now she gives no sound—now she is still mere demon :—but how she will fascinate when she sings the roulades I'll write expressly for her! What a magnificent *portamento* she'll put into the execution of that supernatural chromatic scale!—— How treacherous will be her smile, when she sings that famous passage of the future : " *O Polichinel, thou art lost* !"—— What a plan!—And then, what a splendid pretext for incessant use of the big drum, will Punch's constant truncheon-beats afford me!—Come, why delay?   Quick, for the Director's favour!   Here I can walk straight in,— no ante-chambers here! With one step I'm in the sanc- tuary—before him whose god-like piercing eye will recog- nise at once my genius.   Or must I light on competition here as well?—Should the cat— ?—   Quick, ere it is too late!"

With these last words the soliloquist was about to make straight for the Punch-and-Judy box. I had speedily recognised my friend, and determined to avert a scandal. I seized him by the arm, and span him round towards me.

" Who is it? "—he pettishly cried. He soon remembered me, quietly detached himself, and added coldly : " I might have known that it could only be *you*, that would thwart me in this step as well, the last for my salvation.—Leave me ; it may become too late."

I grasped him afresh ; but, though I was able to keep him from rushing forward to the little theatre, it was quite impossible to move him from the spot. Still, I gained the leisure to observe him closely. Great heavens, in what a condition he was! I say nothing of his dress, but of his features; the former was poor and threadbare, but the latter were terrible. The free and open look was gone; lifeless and vacant, his eye travelled to and fro; his pallid, sunken cheeks told not alone of trouble,—the hectic flush upon them told of sufferings too,—of hunger!

As I studied him with deepest sorrow, he too seemed touched, for he struggled less to tear himself away from me.

"How goes it with you, dear R . . .?" I asked with choking voice. With a mournful smile I added: "Where is your beautiful dog?"

He looked black at once. "Stolen!" was the abrupt reply.

"Not sold?" I asked again.

"Wretch," he sullenly replied, "are you also like the Englishman?"

I did not understand his meaning. "Come," I said in faltering tones—"come! take me to your house; I have much to speak with you."

"You soon will know my house without my aid," he answered, "the year is not yet up. I'm now on the high road to recognition, fortune!—Go, you do not yet believe it! What boots it to preach to the deaf? You people must *see*, to believe; very good! You soon shall see. But loose me now, if I am not to take you for my sworn foe."

I held his hands the faster. "Where do you live?" I asked. "Come, take me there! We'll have a friendly, hearty chat,—about your plans, if it must be!"

"You shall learn them as soon as they are carried out," he answered. "Quadrilles, galops! Oh, that is my forte! —You shall see and hear!—Do you see that cat?—She's to help me to fat fees!—See how sleek she is, how daintily she licks her chops! Imagine the effect when from that little mouth, between those pearly rows of teeth, the most inspired of chromatic scales well forth, accompanied by the most delicate moans and sobs in all the world! Imagine

it, dear friend! Oh, you have no fancy, you!—Leave me,
leave me!—You have no phantasy!"

I held him tighter, and implored him to conduct me to
his lodgings; without making the slightest impression,
however. His eye was fixed with anxious strain upon the
cat.

"Everything depends on her," he cried. "Fortune,
honour, fame, reside within her velvet paws. May Heaven
guide her heart, and turn on me her favour!—She looks
friendly,—yes, that's the feline nature! And she *is* friendly,
polite, polite beyond measure! But she's a cat, a false and
treacherous cat!—Wait,—*thee* at least I can rule! I have
a noble dog; he'll make thee respect me.—Victory! I've
won the day!—Where is my dog?"

He had shot forth the last few words in mad excitement,
with a piercing cry. He looked hastily round, as if seeking for his dog. His eager glance fell on the roadway.
There rode upon a splendid horse an elegant gentleman,
by his physiognomy and the peculiar cut of his clothes an
Englishman; by his side ran, proudly barking, a fine Newfoundland dog.

"Ha! my presentiment!" shrieked my friend, in a fury
of wrath at the sight. "The cursed brute! My dog; my
dog!" My strength was unavailing against the violence
with which the unhappy creature tore himself away. Like
an arrow he fled after the horseman, who happened just
then to be spurring his horse to a gallop, which the dog
accompanied with the liveliest gambols. I rushed after—
in vain! What effort of strength can compare with the
feats of a madman?—I saw the rider, the dog, and my
friend, all vanish down one of the side streets that lead to
the Faubourg du Roule. When I reached the same street,
they were gone.

Suffice it to mention that all my endeavours to track
them were fruitless.—

Alarmed, and almost driven to madness myself, I was
forced at last to give up my inquiries for the moment. But
you may readily imagine that I none the less bestirred

myself each day to find some clue to the retreat of my
unhappy friend. I sought for news in every place that
had the remotest connection with music:—nowhere the
smallest intimation! It was only in the sacred ante-chambers of the Opéra that the subordinates remembered a
pitiable apparition, which had often presented itself and
waited for an audience, but of whose name or dwelling
they naturally were ignorant. Every other path, even that
of the police, led to no surer traces; the very guardians of
the public safety seemed to have thought it needless to
worry themselves about the poor soul.

I fell into despair. Then one day, about two months
after that affair in the Champs Élysées, I received a letter
sent me in a roundabout fashion through one of my
acquaintances. I opened it with a heavy heart, and read
the brief words:

" Dear friend, come and see me die !"

The address denoted a narrow little street on Montmartre.—It was no time for tears, and I ascended the hill
of Montmartre. Following my directions, I arrived at one
of those poverty-stricken houses which are common enough
in the side-alleys of that little town. Despite its poor
exterior, this building did not fail to rear itself to a
cinquième; my unfortunate friend would appear to have
welcomed the fact, and thus I also was compelled to
mount to the same giddy height. It was worth the while,
for, on asking for my friend, I was referred to the back
attic; from this hinder side of the estimable building one
certainly forwent all outlook on the four-foot-wide magni-
ficence of the causeway, but was rewarded by the incomparably finer one on the whole of Paris.

I found my poor enthusiast propped-up on a wretched
sick-bed, drinking in this wonderful prospect. His face,
his whole body, were infinitely more haggard and emaciated
than on that day in the Champs Élysées; nevertheless the
expression of his features was far more reassuring. The
scared, wild, almost maniacal look, the uncanny fire in his
eyes, had vanished; his glance was dulled and half-extin-

guished; the dark and ghastly flecks upon his cheeks seemed quenched in a universal wasting.

Trembling, but still composed, he stretched his hand to me with the words: "Forgive me, old fellow, and take my thanks for coming."

The softness and sonority of the tone in which he uttered these few words produced on me an even more touching impression, if possible, than his appearance had already done. I pressed his hand, but could not speak for weeping.

"I think,"—went on my friend, after an affecting pause, —"it is already well over a year, since we met in that glittering Palais Royal;—I have not quite kept my word: —to become renowned within a year, was impossible to me, with the best will in the world; on the other hand it's no fault of mine that I could not write you punctually upon the year's elapse, where you must come to see me die: 'spite all my struggles, I had not yet got quite so far.— Nay, do not weep, my friend! There was a time when I must beg you not to laugh."

I tried to speak, but speech forsook me.—"Let me speak!" the dying man put in: "it is becoming easy to me, and I owe you a long account. I'm sure that I shall not be here to-morrow, so listen to my narrative to-day! 'Tis a simple tale, my friend,—most simple. In it you'll find no wondrous complications, no hair-breadth strokes of luck, no ostentatious details. Fear not that your patience will be wearied by the easiness of speech which now is granted me, and certainly might tempt me to long-windedness; for there have been days, dear old man, when I couldn't utter a sound. Listen!—When I reflect on the state in which you find me, I hold it needless to assure you that my fate has been no bright one. Nor do I altogether need to count you up the trivialities among which my enthusiasm has come to ground. Suffice it to say, that they were no *breakers*, on which I foundered!—Happy the shipwrecked who goes down in *storm*!—No: they were *quagmires* and *swamps*, in which I sank. These swamps, dear friend, surround all proud and dazzling Art-fanes, to

which we poor fools make such ardent pilgrimage, as though
they held the saving of our souls. Happy the feather-
brained ! With one successful entrechat he leaps the
quagmire. Happy the rich ! His well-trained horse needs
but one prick of the golden spur, to bear him swiftly over.
But woe to the enthusiast who, taking that swamp for a
flowery meadow, is swallowed in it past all rescue, a meal
for frogs and toads !—See, dear friend, this vermin has
devoured me ; there's not a drop of blood left in me !— —
Must I tell you how it happened ? But why ? You see
me done for ;—be content to hear that I was not vanquished on the field of battle, but—horrible to utter—*in
the Ante-chambers of Hunger I fell* !—They are something
terrible, those Ante-chambers ; and know that there are
many, very many of them in Paris,—with seats of wood or
velvet, heated and not heated, paved and unpaved !—"

"In those Ante-chambers,"—continued my friend,—" I
dreamed away a fair year of my life. I dreamt of many
wondrous mad and fabled stories from the 'Thousand-and-
one Nights," of men and beasts, of gold and offal. My
dreams were of gods and contrabassists, of jewelled snuff-
boxes and prima-donnas, of satin gowns and lovesick
lords, of chorus-girls and five-franc pieces. Between I
sometimes seemed to hear the wailing, ghost-like note of
an oboe ; that note thrilled through my every nerve, and
cut my heart. One day when I had dreamed my maddest,
and that oboe-note was tingling through me at its sharpest,
I suddenly awoke and found I had become a madman.
At least I recollect, that I had forgotten to make my usual
obeisance to the theatre-lackey as I left the anteroom,—
the reason, I may add, of my never daring to return to it ;
for *how* would the man have received me ?—With tottering
steps I left the haven of my dreams ; on the threshold of ·
the building I fell of a heap. I had stumbled over my
poor dog, who, after his wont, was ante-chambering in the
street, in waiting for his fortunate master who was allowed to
ante-chamber among men. This dog, I must tell you, had
been of the utmost service to me, for to him and his beauty

alone I owed it that now and then the lackey of the ante-
chamber would honour me with a passing glance. Alas !
with every day he lost a portion of his beauty, for hunger
gnawed his entrails too. This gave me fresh alarm, as I
clearly foresaw that the servant's favour would soon be
lost to me; already a contemptuous smile would often
purse his lips.—As said, I fell over this dog of mine.
How long I lay, I know not ; of the kicks which I may
have received from passers-by I took no notice; but at
last I was awoken by the tenderest kisses,—the warm licks
of my dear beast. I leapt to my feet, and in a lucid
interval I recognised at once my weightiest duty : to buy
the dog some food. A shrewd *Marchand d'Habits* gave
me a handful of sous for my villainous waistcoat. My dog
ate, and what he left I devoured. With *him* this answered
admirably, but I was past mending. The produce of an
heirloom, an old ring of my grandmother's, sufficed to
restore the dog to his ancient beauty; he bloomed afresh
—oh, fatal blooming !

" With my brain it grew ever darker ; I know not rightly
what took place within it,—but I remember being seized
one day by an irresistible longing to seek out the Devil.
My dog, in all his former glory, accompanied me to the
gates of the *Concerts Musard.* Did I hope to meet the
Devil there ? That also I cannot tell. I scanned the
people trooping in, and whom did I espy among them ?
The abominable *Englishman*: the same, as large as life,
and not one atom changed from when, as I related to you,
he harmed me so with Beethoven !—Fear took me ; I was
prepared to face a demon from the nether world, but never
more this phantom of the upper. O how I felt, when the
wretch also recognised *me* ! I couldn't avoid him,—the
crowd was pressing us towards each other. Involuntarily,
and quite against the customs of his countrymen, he was
compelled to fall into my arms, raised up to force myself
an exit. There he lay, wedged tight against my breast,
with its thousand torturing emotions. It was a fearful
moment ! We were soon released a little, and he shook

me off with a shade of indignation. I tried to escape; but
it still was impossible.—'Welcome, mein Herr!'—the
Briton shouted :—'I always meet you on the ways of Art!
This time we'll go to *Musard*!'—For very wrath I could
say nothing but : 'To the Devil!'—'Quite so,' he answered,
'it seems that things go devilish there!—Last Sunday I
threw off a composition, which I shall offer to Musard.
Do you know this Musard? Will you introduce me to
him?'

"My horror at this bugbear turned to speechless fear;
impelled by it, I gained the strength to free myself and
flee towards the Boulevard; my lovely dog rushed barking
after me. But in a trice the Englishman was by my side
once more, holding me, and asking in excited tones : 'Sir,
does this splendid dog belong to you?'—'Yes.'—'But it is
superb! Sir, I will pay you fifty guineas for this dog. A
dog like this, you know, is the proper thing for a gentleman, and I have already owned a number of them. Unfortunately, the beasts were all unmusical; they could not
stand my practising the horn or flute, and so they always
ran away. But I take it for granted that, as you have the
good fortune to be a musician, your dog is musical also; I
accordingly may hope that he will stop with me. Sò I
offer you fifty guineas for the beast.'—'Villain!' I cried :—
'not for the whole of Britain would I sell my friend!' So
saying, I hurried off, my dog in front. I dodged down the
back streets that led to my usual night's-lodging—It was
bright moonshine; now and then I looked furtively back :
—to my alarm, I thought I saw the Englishman's long
figure following me. I redoubled my pace, and peered
round still more anxiously; now I caught sight of the
shadow, now lost it. Panting for breath, I reached my
refuge, gave my dog to eat, and threw myself all hungry
on my rough, hard bed.—I slept long, and dreamt of
horrors. When I awoke,—my beautiful dog had vanished.
How he had got away from me, or been enticed through
the badly fastened door, to this day is a mystery to me. I
called, I hunted for him, till sobbing I fainted away.—

"You remember that I saw the faithless one again one day in the Champs Élysées;—you know what efforts I made to regain possession of him;—but you do not know that this animal recognised me, yet fled from my call like an untamed beast of the wilderness! Nevertheless I followed him and his Satanic cavalier till the latter dashed into a gateway, whose doors were slammed behind him and the dog. In my anger I thundered at the gates;—a furious bark was the answer.—Dazed and crushed, I leant against the archway,—until at last a hideous scale on the horn aroused me from my stupefaction; it reached me from the ground-floor of the mansion, and was followed by the agonised moan of a dog. Then I laughed out loud, and went my way.—"

My friend here ceased; though speech had become easy, his inward agitation taxed him terribly. It was no longer possible for him to hold himself erect in bed,—with a smothered groan he sank back.—A long pause occurred; I watched the poor fellow with painful feelings: that faint flush so peculiar to the consumptive had risen to his cheeks. He had closed his eyes, and lay as if in slumber; his breath came lightly, almost in ethereal waves.

I waited anxiously for the moment when I durst speak to him, and ask what earthly service I could render.—At last he opened his eyes once more; a dim but wondrous light was in the glance he straightway fixed on me.

"My poor friend,"—I began—"I came here with the sad desire to serve you somehow. Have you a wish, O speak it!"

With a smile he resumed: "So impatient, friend, for my last testament?—Nay, have no care; you too are mentioned in it.—But will you not first learn how it befell that your poor brother came to die? Look you, I wished my history to be known to *one* soul at the least; but I know of no one who would worry himself about me, unless it be *yourself*. ——Fear not that I am overexerting myself! 'Tis well with me and easy—no laboured breath oppresses me—the words come freely to my lips.—And see, I have little left to narrate. You can imagine that, from the point where I broke off my story, I had no more outer incidents to do with. From there begins the history of my inner life, for then I knew I soon should die. That terrible scale on the horn in the Englishman's hôtel filled me with so overpowering a weariness of life, that I there and then resolved to die. Indeed, I should not boast of that decision, for I must confess that it no longer lay entirely within my own free will. Something had cracked within my breast, that left a long and whirring sound behind; —when this died out 'twas light and well with me, as never before, and I knew my end was near. O how happy that conviction made me! How the presage of a speedy dissolution cheered me, as I suddenly perceived its work in every member of this wasted body!—Insensible to outward things, unconscious where my faltering steps were bearing me, I had gained the summit of Montmartre. Thrice welcoming the Mount of Martyrs, I resolved on it to die. I too was dying for the wholeness of my faith; I too could therefore call myself a martyr, albeit this my faith was challenged by none else—than Hunger.

"Houseless, I took this lodging, asking nothing further than this bed, and that they would send for my scores and papers, which I had stowed in a wretched hovel of the city; for, alas! I had never succeeded in pawning them. So here I lie, determined to pass away in God and pure Music. A friend will close my eyes, my effects will cover all my debts, and for a decent grave I shall not want.—Say, what more could I wish?"

At last I gave vent to my pent-up feelings.—"What!" I cried, "was it only for this last mournful service, that you could use me? Could your friend, however powerless, have helped you in nothing else? I conjure you, for my peace of mind tell me this: Was it a doubt of my friend-ship, that kept you from discovering my whereabouts and acquainting me before with your distress?"

"O don't be angry," he answered coaxingly, "don't chide me if I own that I had fallen into the stubborn belief that you

F

were my enemy! When I recognised that you were not, my brain was already in a condition that robbed me of all responsibility of will. I felt that I was no longer fit to associate with men of sense. Forgive me, and be kindlier toward me, than I have been to you!—Give me your hand, and let this debt of my poor life be cancelled!"

I could not resist, but seized his hand, and melted into tears. Yet I saw how markedly the powers of my friend were ebbing; he was now too weak to raise himself in bed; that flickering flush came ever paler to his sunken cheeks.

"A little business, dear chum," he began afresh. "Call it my last Will! For I will, in the first place: that my debts be paid. The poor people who took me in, have nursed me willingly and dunned me little; they must be paid. The same with a few other creditors, whose names you will find on that paper. I bequeath all my property in payment, there my compositions and here my diary, in which I have jotted down my musical whims and reflections. I leave it to your judgment, my experienced friend, to sell so much of these remains as will liquidate my earthly debts.—I will, in the second place: that you do not beat my dog, if you ever should meet him; I assume that, in punishment of his faithlessness, he has already suffered torments from the Englishman's horn. I forgive him!— Thirdly, I will that the history of my Paris sufferings, with omission of my name, be published as a wholesome warning to all soft fools like me.—Fourthly, I wish for a decent grave, yet without any fuss or parade; few persons suffice for my following; their names and addresses you'll find in my diary. The costs of the burial must be mustered up by you and them.—Amen!"

"Now,"—the dying man continued, after a pause occasioned by his growing weakness,—"now one last word on my belief.—I believe in God, Mozart and Beethoven, and likewise their disciples and apostles;—I believe in the Holy Spirit and the truth of the one, indivisible Art;—I believe that this Art proceeds from God, and lives within the hearts of all illumined men;—I believe that he who

once has bathed in the sublime delights of this high Art,
is consecrate to Her for ever, and never can deny Her ;—I
believe that through this Art all men are saved, and therefore each may die for Her of hunger ;—I believe that death
will give me highest happiness ;—I believe that on earth I
was a jarring discord, which will at once be perfectly resolved by death. I believe in a last judgment, which will
condemn to fearful pains all those who in this world have
dared to play the huckster with chaste Art, have violated
and dishonoured Her through evilness of heart and ribald
lust of senses ;—I believe that these will be condemned
through all eternity to hear their own vile music. I believe,
upon the other hand, that true disciples of high Art will be
transfigured in a heavenly fabric of sun-drenched fragrance
of sweet sounds, and united for eternity with the divine
fount of all Harmony.—May mine be a sentence of grace !
—Amen ! "

I could almost believe that my friend's fervent prayer
had been granted already, so heavenly a light shone in his
eye, so enraptured he remained in breathless quiet. But
his gentle, scarce palpable breathing assured me that he
yet lived on.—Softly, but quite audibly, he whispered :
" Rejoice, ye faithful ones ; the joy is great, toward which
ye journey ! "

Then he grew dumb,—the radiance of his glance was
quenched ; a smile still wreathed his lips. I closed his
eyes, and prayed God for such a death.— —

Who knows what died in this child of man, leaving no
trace behind ? Was it a Mozart,—a Beethoven ? Who
can tell, and who gainsay me when I claim that in him
there fell an artist who would have enriched the world with
his creations, had he not been forced to die too soon
of hunger ?—I ask, who will prove me the contrary ?—

None of those who followed his body. Besides myself
there were but two, a philologist and a painter ; a third
was hindered by a cold, and others had no time to spare.—
As we were modestly approaching the churchyard of
Montmartre, we noticed a beautiful dog, who anxiously

sniffed at the bier and coffin. I recognised the animal, and looked behind me ;—bolt-upright on his horse, I perceived the Englishman. He seemed unable to understand the strange behaviour of his dog, who followed the coffin into the graveyard ; he dismounted, gave the reins to his groom, and overtook us in the cemetery.

"Whom are you burying, mein Herr?" he asked me.— "The master of that dog," I gave for answer.

"Goddam!" he cried, "it is most annoying that this gentleman should have died without receiving the money for his beast. I set it aside for him, and have sought an opportunity of sending it, although this animal howls at my musical exercises like all the rest. But I will make good my omission, and devote the fifty guineas for the dog to a memorial stone, which shall be erected on the grave of the estimable gentleman!"—He left us, and mounted his horse; the dog remained beside the grave,—the Briton rode away.*

* Translator's note :—In the *Gazette Musicale* there was an additional paragraph: "Il me reste maintenant à exécuter le testament. Je publierai dans les prochains numéros de cette gazette, sous le titre de *Caprices esthétiques d'un musicien*, les differentes parties du journal du défunt, pour lesquels l'éditeur a promis de payer un prix élevé, par égard pour la destination respectable de cet argent. Les partitions qui composent le reste de sa succession sont à la disposition de MM. les directeurs d'Opéra, qui peuvent, pour cet objet, s'addresser, par lettres non affranchies, à l'exécuteur testamentaire,

RICHARD WAGNER."

3.

A HAPPY EVENING.

(Ein glücklicher Abend.)

Thus will I style this last record of earlier memories of my friend, which I believe will form an appropriate introduction to the few longer articles I now am publishing from the dead man's remains.

T was a fine Spring evening; the heat of Summer had already sent its messengers before, delicious breaths that thronged the air like sighs of love and fired our senses. We had followed the stream of people pouring toward a public garden; here an excellent orchestra was to give the first of its annual series of summer-evening concerts. It was a red-letter day. My friend R . . ., not dead in Paris yet,* was in the seventh heaven; even before the concert began, he was drunk with music: he said it was the inner harmonies that always sang and rang within him when he felt the happiness of a beautiful Spring evening.

We arrived, and took our usual places at a table beneath a great oak-tree; for careful comparison had taught us, not only that this spot was farthest from the buzzing crowd, but that here one heard the music best and most distinctly. We had always pitied the poor creatures who were compelled, or actually preferred to stay in the immediate vicinity of the orchestra, whether in or out of doors; we could never understand how they found any pleasure in *seeing* music, instead of hearing it; and yet we could account no otherwise for their rapt attention to the various movements of the band, their enthusiastic interest in the kettle-drummer when, after an anxious counting of his bars of rest, he came in at last with a rousing thwack. We were agreed that nothing is more prosaic and upsetting, than the hideous aspect of the swollen cheeks and puckered features of the wind-players, the unæsthetic grabbings of the double-bass and violoncelli, ay, even the wearisome sawing of the violin-bows, when it is a question of listening to the

* "Not dead in Paris yet" did not appear in the French. The tale was originally styled "Une soirée heureuse: Fantaisie sur la musique pittoresque," and published in the *Gazette Musicale* of Oct. 24 and Nov. 7, 1841.—Tr.

performance of fine instrumental music. For this reason
we had taken our seats where we could hear the lightest
nuance of the orchestra, without being pained by its
appearance.

The concert began : grand things were played ; among
others, Mozart's Symphony in E flat, and Beethoven's
in A.

The concert was over. Dumb, but delighted and smiling,
my friend sat facing me with folded arms. The crowd departed, group by group, with pleasant chatter ; here and
there a few tables still were occupied. The evening's
genial warmth began to yield to the colder breath of
night.

"Let's have some punch!" cried R . . ., suddenly
changing his attitude to look for a waiter.

Moods like that in which we found ourselves, are too
precious not to be maintained as long as possible. I knew
how comforting the punch would be, and eagerly chimed
in with my friend's proposition. A decent-sized bowl soon
steamed on our table, and we emptied our first glasses.

" How did you like the performance of the symphonies ? "
I asked.

"Eh ? Performance ! " exclaimed R . . . . " There are
moods in which, however critical at other times, the worst
execution of one of my favourite works would transport
me. These moods, 'tis true, are rare, and only exercise
their sweet dominion over me when my whole inner being
stands in blissful harmony with my bodily health. Then it
needs but the faintest intimation, to sound in me at once the
whole piece that answers to my full conception ; and in so
ideal a completeness, as the best orchestra in the world can
never bring it to my outward sense. In such moods my else
so scrupulous musical ear is complaisant enough to allow
even the quack of an oboe to cause me but a momentary
twinge ; with an indulgent smile I let the false note of a
trumpet graze my ear, without being torn from the blessed
feeling that cheats me into the belief that I am hearing the
most consummate execution of my favourite work. In such

a mood nothing irritates me more, than to see a well-combed dandy airing high-bred indignation at one of those musical slips that wound his pampered ear, when I know that to-morrow he will be applauding the most excruciating scale with which a popular prima donna does violence to nerves alike and soul.   Music merely ambles past the ear of these super-subtle fools; nay, often merely past their eye: for I remember noticing people who never stirred a muscle when a brass instrument really went wrong, but stopped their ears the instant they saw the wretched bandsman shake his head in shame and confusion."

"What?"—I interposed—"Must I hear you girding at people of delicate ear?   How often have I seen you raging like a madman at the faulty intonation of a singer?"

"My friend," cried R . . ., "I simply was speaking of now, of to-night.   God knows how often I have been nearly driven mad by the mistakes of a famous violinist; how often have I cursed the first of prima-donnas when she thought her tone so pure in vocalising somewhere between *mi fa sol*; eh! how often I have been unable to find the smallest consonance among the instruments of the very best-tuned orchestra.   But look you! that is on the countless days when my good spirit has departed from me, when I put on my Sunday coat and squeeze between the perfumed dames and frizzled sirs to woo back happiness into my soul through these ears of mine.   O you should feel the pains with which I then weigh every note and measure each vibration!   When my heart is dumb I'm as subtle as any of the prigs who vexed me to-day, and there are hours when a Beethoven Sonata with violin or 'cello will put me to flight.—Blessed be the god who made the Spring and Music: to-night I'm happy, I can tell you."   With that he filled our glasses again, and we drained them to the dregs.

"Need I declare,"—I began in turn,—"that I feel as happy as yourself?   Who would not be, after listening in peace and comfort to the performance of two works which seem created by the very god of high æsthetic joy?

I thought the conjunction of the Mozartian and the Beethovenian Symphony a most apt idea; I seemed to find a marked relationship between the two compositions; in both the clear human consciousness of an existence meant for rejoicing, is beautifully transfigured by the presage of a higher world beyond. The only distinction I would make, is that in Mozart's music the language of the heart is shaped to graceful longing, whereas in Beethoven's conception this longing reaches out a bolder hand to seize the Infinite. In Mozart's symphony the fulness of Feeling predominates, in Beethoven's the manly consciousness of Strength."

" It does me good to hear such views expressed about the character and meaning of such sublime instrumental works," replied my friend. " Not that I believe you have anything like exhausted their nature with your brief description; but to get to the bottom of that, to say nothing of defining it, lies just as little within the power of human speech as it resides in the nature of Music to express in clear and definite terms what belongs to no organ save the Poet's. 'Tis a great misfortune that so many people take the useless trouble to confound the musical with the poetic tongue, and endeavour to make good or replace by the one what in their narrow minds remains imperfect in the other. It is a truth for ever, that where the speech of man stops short there Music's reign begins. Nothing is more intolerable, than the mawkish scenes and anecdotes they foist upon those instrumental works. What poverty of mind and feeling it betrays, when the listener to a performance of one of Beethoven's symphonies has to keep his interest awake by imagining that the torrent of musical sounds is meant to reproduce the plot of some romance! These gentry then presume to grumble at the lofty master, when an unexpected stroke disturbs the even tenour of their little tale; they tax the composer with unclearness and inconsequence, and deplore his lack of continuity!—The idiots !"

"Never mind!" said I. "Let each man trump up scenes and fancies according to the strength of his imagination; by their aid he perhaps acquires a taste for these great musical revelations, which many would be quite unable to enjoy for themselves. At least you must admit that the number of Beethoven's admirers has gained a large accession this way, eh! that it is to be hoped the great musician's works will thereby reach a popularity they could never have attained if left to none but an ideal understanding."

"Preserve us Heaven!" R . . . exclaimed.—"Even for these sublimest sanctities of Art you ask that banal Popularity, the curse of every grand and noble thing? For *them* you would also claim the honour of their inspiring rhythms—their only temporal manifestation—being danced-to in a village-tavern?"

"You exaggerate," I calmly answered: "I do not claim for Beethoven's symphonies the vogue of street and tavern. But would you not count it a merit the more, were they in a position to give a gladder pulse to the blood in the cribbed and cabined heart of the ordinary man of the world?"

"They shall have no merit, these Symphonies!"—my friend replied, in a huff. "They exist for themselves and their own sake, not to flip the circulation of a philistine's blood. Who *can*, for his eternal welfare let him earn the merit of understanding those revelations; on them there rests no obligation to force themselves upon the understanding of cold hearts."

I filled up, and exclaimed with a laugh: "You're the same old phantast, who declines to understand me on the very point where we both are certainly agreed at bottom! So let's drop the Popularity question. But give me the pleasure of learning your own sensations when you heard the two symphonies to-night."

Like a passing cloud, the shade of irritation cleared from my friend's lowered brow. He watched the steam ascending from our punch, and smiled. "My sensations?—I felt the soft warmth of a lovely Spring evening, and imagined I was sitting with you beneath a great oak and looking up between its branches to the star-strewn heavens. I felt a thousand things besides, but them I cannot tell you * : there you have all."

"Not bad!" I remarked.—"Perhaps one of our neighbours imagined he was smoking a cigar, drinking coffee, and making eyes at a young lady in a blue dress."

"Without a doubt," R . . . pursued the sarcasm, "and the drummer apparently thought he was beating his ill-behaved children, for not having brought him his supper from town.—Capital! At the gate I saw a peasant listening in wonder and delight to the Symphony in A :—I would wager my head he understood it best of all, for you will have read in one of our musical journals a short while ago that Beethoven had nothing else in mind, when he composed this symphony, than to describe a peasant's wedding. The honest rustic will thus at once have called his wedding-day to memory, and revived its every incident : the guests' arrival and the feast, the march to church and blessing, the dance and finally the crowning joy, what bride and bridegroom shared alone."

"A good idea!" I cried, when I had finished laughing.—"But for heaven's sake tell me why you would prevent this symphony from affording the good peasant a happy hour of his own kind? Did he not feel, proportionately, the same delight as yourself when you sat beneath the oak and watched the stars of heaven through its branches?"

"There I am with you,"—my friend complacently replied, —"I would gladly let the worthy yokel recall his wedding-day when listening to the Symphony in A. But the civilised townsfolk who write in musical journals, I should like to tear the hair from their stupid heads when they foist such fudge on honest people, and rob them of all the ingenuous-

* Cf. "Wo ich erwacht, weilt' ich nicht ; doch wo ich weilte, das kann ich dir nicht sagen. . . . Ich war—wo ich von je gewesen, wohin auf je ich gehe : im weiten Reich der Welten Nacht." *Tristan*, act iii.—Tr.

ness with which they would otherwise have settled down
to hear Beethoven's symphony.—Instead of abandoning
themselves to their natural sensations, the poor deluded
people of full heart but feeble brain feel obliged to look
out for a peasant's wedding, a thing they probably have
never attended, and in lieu of which they would have been
far more disposed to imagine something quite within the
circle of their own experience."

"So you agree with me," I said, "that the nature of those
creations does not forbid their being variously interpreted,
according to the individual?"—"On the contrary," was the
answer, "I consider a stereotype interpretation altogether
inadmissible. Definitely as the musical fabric of a Beethovenian Symphony stands rounded and complete in all
artistic proportions, perfect and indivisible as it appears to
the higher sense,—just as impossible is it to reduce its
effects on the human heart to one authoritative type. This
is more or less the case with the creations of every other
art : how differently will one and the same picture or drama
affect two different human beings, nay, the heart of one
and the same individual at different times ! Yet how much
more definitely and sharply the painter or poet is bound
to draw his figures, than the instrumental composer, who,
unlike them, is not compelled to model his shapes by the
features of the daily world, but has a boundless realm at
his disposal in the kingdom of the supramundane, and to
whose hand is given the most spiritual of substances in
that of Tone ! It would be to drag the musician from this
high estate, if one tried to make him fit his inspiration to
the semblance of that daily world ; and still more would
that instrumental composer disown his mission, or expose
his weakness, who should aim at carrying the cramped
proportions of purely worldly things into the province of
his art."

"So you reject all tone-painting," I asked ?

" Everywhere," answered R . . ., "save where it either
is employed in jest, or reproduces purely musical phenomena. In the province of Jest all things are allowed,

for its nature is a certain purposed angularity, and to laugh and let laugh is a capital thing. But where tone-painting quits this region, it becomes absurd. The inspirations and incitements to an instrumental composition must be of such a kind, that they can arise in the soul of none save a musician."

" You have just said something you will have a difficulty in proving," I objected. " At bottom, I am of your opinion ; only I doubt if it is quite compatible with our unqualified admiration for the works of our great masters. Don't you think that this maxim of yours flatly contradicts a part of Beethoven's revelations ? "

" Not in the slightest : on the contrary, I hope to found my proof on Beethoven."

" Before we descend to details," I continued, "don't you feel that Mozart's conception of instrumental music far better corresponds with your assertion, than that of Beethoven ? "

" Not that I am aware," replied my friend. " Beethoven immensely enlarged the form of Symphony when he discarded the proportions of the older musical 'period,' which had attained their utmost beauty in Mozart, and followed his impatient genius with bolder but ever more conclusive freedom to regions reachable by *him* alone ; as he also knew to give these soaring flights a philosophical coherence, it is undeniable that upon the basis of the Mozartian Symphony he reared a wholly new artistic genre, which he at like time perfected in every point. But Beethoven would have been unable to achieve all this, had Mozart not previously addressed his conquering genius to the Symphony too; had his animating, idealising breath not breathed a spiritual warmth into the soulless forms and diagrams accepted until then. From here departed Beethoven, and the artist who had taken Mozart's divinely pure soul into himself could never descend from that high altitude which is true Music's sole domain."

" By all means,"—I resumed. " You will hardly deny,

however, that Mozart's music flowed from none but a musical source, that his inspiration started from an indefinite inner feeling, which, even had he had a poet's faculty, could never have been conveyed in words, but always and exclusively in tones. I am speaking of those inspirations which arise in the musician simultaneously with his melodies, with his tone-figures. Mozart's music bears the characteristic stamp of this instantaneous birth, and it is impossible to suppose that he would ever have drafted the plan of a symphony, for instance, whereof he had not all the themes, and in fact the entire structure as we know it, already in his head. On the other hand, I cannot help thinking that Beethoven first planned the order of a symphony according to a certain philosophical idea, before he left it to his phantasy to invent the musical themes."

"And how do you propose proving that?"—my friend ejaculated. "By this evening's Symphony perhaps?"

"With *that* I might find it harder," I answered,—"but is it not enough to simply name the Heroic Symphony, in support of my contention? You know, of course, that this symphony was originally meant to bear the title: 'Bonaparte.' Can you deny, then, that Beethoven was inspired and prompted to the plan of this giant work by an idea outside the realm of Music?"

"Delighted at your naming that symphony!" R . . . quickly put in. "You surely don't mean to say that the idea of a heroic force in mighty struggle for the highest, is outside the realm of Music? Or do you find that Beethoven has translated his enthusiasm for the young god of victory into such petty details as to make you think he meant this symphony for a musical bulletin of the first Italian campaign?"

"Where are you off to?"—I interposed: "Have I said anything like it?"

"It's at the back of your contention," my friend went passionately on.—"If we are to assume that Beethoven sat down to write a composition in honour of Bonaparte, we must also conclude that he would have been unable to turn out anything but one of those 'occasional' pieces which bear the stamp of still-born, one and all.* But the *Sinfonia eroica* is all the breadth of heaven from justifying such a view! No: had the master set himself a task like that, he would have fulfilled it most unsatisfactorily:— tell me, where, in what part of this composition do you find one colourable hint that the composer had his eye on a specific event in the heroic career of the young commander? What means the Funeral March, the Scherzo with the hunting-horns, the Finale with the soft emotional Andante woven in? Where is the bridge of Lodi, where the battle of Arcole, where the victory under the Pyramids, where the 18th Brumaire? Are these not incidents which no composer of our day would have let escape him, if he wanted to write a biographic Symphony on Bonaparte?—Here, however, the case was otherwise; and permit me to tell you my own idea of the gestation of this symphony.—When a musician feels prompted to sketch the smallest composition, he owes it simply to the stimulus of a feeling that usurps his whole being at the hour of conception. This mood may be brought about by an outward experience, or have risen from a secret inner spring; whether it shews itself as melancholy, joy, desire, contentment, love or hatred, in the musician it will always take a musical shape, and voice itself in tones or ever it is cast in notes. But grand, passionate and lasting emotions, dominating all our feelings and ideas for months and often half a year, these drive the musician to those vaster, more intense conceptions to which we owe, among others, the origin of a *Sinfonia eroica*. These greater moods, as deep suffering of soul or potent exaltation, may date from outer causes, for we all are men and our fate is ruled by outward circumstances; but *when* they force the musician to production, these greater moods have already turned to music

---

* In the *Gazette* there was a footnote here : "Il y a huit ans, à l'époque où cette conversation eut lieu, mon ami R . . . ne pouvait connaître la symphonie de Berlioz pour la translation des victimes de Juillet."—Tr.

in him, so that at the moment of creative inspiration it is
no longer the outer event that governs the composer, but
the musical sensation which it has begotten in him.   Now,
what phenomenon were worthier to rouse and keep alive
the sympathy, the inspiration of a genius so full of fire as
Beethoven's, than that of the youthful demigod who razed
a world to mould a new one from its ruins ?   Imagine the
musician's hero-spirit following from deed to deed, from
victory to victory, the man who ravished friend and foe to
equal wonder !   And the republican Beethoven, to boot,
who looked to that hero for the realising of his ideal
dreams of universal human good !   How his blood must
have surged, his heart glowed hot, when that glorious name
rang back to him wherever he turned to commune with his
Muse !—*His* strength must have felt incited to a like unwonted sweep, his will-of-victory spurred on to a kindred
deed of untold grandeur.   He was no General,—he was
Musician ; and in *his* domain he saw the sphere where he
could bring to pass the selfsame thing as Bonaparte in the
plains of Italy.   His musical force at highest strain bade
him conceive a work the like of which had ne'er before
been dreamt of ; he brought forth his *Sinfonia eroica*, and
knowing well to whom he owed the impulse to this giant-
work, he wrote upon its title-page the name of "Bonaparte."
And in fact is not this symphony as grand an evidence
of man's creative power, as Bonaparte's glorious victory ?
Yet I ask you if a single trait in its development has an
immediate outer connection with the fate of the hero, who
at that time had not even reached the zenith of his
destined fame ?   I am happy enough to admire in it
nothing but a gigantic monument of Art, to fortify myself
by the strength and joyous exaltation which swell my
breast on hearing it ; and leave to learned other folk to
spell out the fights of Rivoli and Marengo from its score's
mysterious hieroglyphs ! "

    The night air had grown still colder ; during this speech
 passing waiter had taken my hint to remove the punch
and warm it up again ; he now came back, and once more

the grateful beverage was steaming high before our eyes.
I filled up, and reached my hand to R . . . .

"We are at one," I said, "as ever, when it touches the
innermost questions of art. However feeble our forces, we
shouldn't deserve the name of musicians, could we fall into
such blatant errors about the nature of our art as you have
just denounced. What Music expresses is eternal, infinite,
and ideal; she expresses not the passion, love, desire, of
this or that individual in this or that condition, but Passion,
Love, Desire itself, and in such infinitely varied phases as
lie in her unique possession and are foreign and unknown
to any other tongue. Of her let each man taste according
to his strength, his faculty and mood, what taste and feel
he can!"—

"And to-night,"—my friend broke in, in full enthusiasm,
—"'tis joy I taste, the happiness, the presage of a higher
destiny, won from the wondrous revelations in which
Mozart and Beethoven have spoken to us on this glorious
Spring evening. So here's to Happiness, to Joy! Here's
to Courage, that enheartens us in fight with our fate!
Here's to Victory, gained by our higher sense over the
worthlessness of the vulgar! To Love, which crowns our
courage; to friendship, that keeps firm our Faith! To
Hope, which weds itself to our foreboding! To the day,
to the night! A cheer for the sun, a cheer for the stars!
And three cheers for Music and her high priests! Forever
be God adored and worshipped, the god of Joy and
Happiness,—the god who created Music! Amen."—

Arm-in-arm we took our journey home; we pressed
each other's hand, and not a word more did we say.

4.

ON GERMAN MUSIC.

(über deutsches Musikwesen.)

The following articles I publish from among my dead friend's papers. To me this first one seems to have been intended to win friends among the French for his Parisian undertaking, whereas its successors unmistakably betray the deterrent impressions already made on him by Paris life.

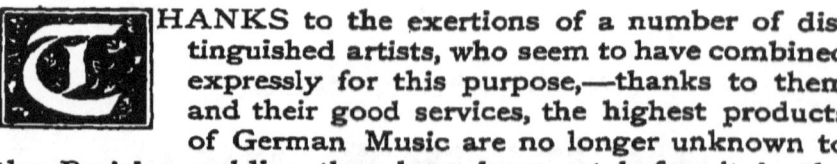

HANKS to the exertions of a number of distinguished artists, who seem to have combined expressly for this purpose,—thanks to them and their good services, the highest products of German Music are no longer unknown to the Parisian public; they have been set before it in the worthiest fashion, and received by it with the greatest enthusiasm.* People have begun to demolish the barriers which, destined perhaps to eternally sever the nations themselves, yet should never separate their arts; one may even say that through their ready acknowledgment of foreign productions the French have distinguished themselves more than the Germans, who are generally more prone to fall beneath a foreign influence than is good for the preservation of a certain self-dependence. The difference is this:—the German, not possessing the faculty of initiating a Mode, adopts it without hesitation when it comes to him from abroad; in this weakness he forgets himself, and blindly sacrifices his native judgment to the foreign gauge. But this chiefly refers to the mass of the German public; for on the other side we see the German musician by profession, perhaps from very revolt against this universal weakness of the mass, too sharply cutting off himself therefrom, and becoming one-sided in his falsely patriotic zeal and unjust in his verdict on extraterritorial wares.—It is just the reverse with the French: the mass of the French public is perfectly contented with its national products, and does not feel the least desire to extend its taste; but the higher class of music-lovers is all the broader-minded in its recognition of foreign merit; it loves to shew enthusiasm for whatever comes to it of

* Under the title of "De la Musique Allemande" this article originally appeared in the *Gazette Musicale* of July 12 and 26, 1840, forming Richard Wagner's earliest contribution to that journal.—Tr.

beautiful and unknown from abroad. This is plainly proved by the reception so quickly accorded to German Instrumental-music. Whether the Frenchman *understands* German music for all that, is another question, and one whose answer must be doubtful. Of course it would be impossible to maintain that the enthusiasm called forth by the masterly execution of a Beethoven Symphony by the orchestra of the Conservatoire is an affected one ; nevertheless it would suffice to learn the views, ideas and fancies roused in this or that enthusiast by the hearing of such a symphony, to perceive at once that the German genius has not as yet been thoroughly understood.—Let us therefore cast a more comprehensive glance upon Germany and the state of its music, to afford a clearer notion of how it should be taken.

Somebody once said : The Italian uses music for love, the Frenchman for society, but the German as science. Perhaps it would be better put : The Italian is a singer, the Frenchman a virtuoso, the German a—musician. The German has a right to be styled by the exclusive name "Musician," for of him one may say that he loves Music for herself,—not as a means of charming, of winning gold and admiration, but because he worships her as a divine and lovely art that, if he gives himself to her, becomes his one and all. The German is capable of writing music merely for himself and friend, uncaring if it will ever be executed for a public. The desire to shine by his creations but rarely seizes him, and he would be an exception if he even knew how to set about it? Before what public should he step ?—His fatherland is cut up into a number of kingdoms, electoral principalities, duchies and free towns ; he dwells, let us say, in a market-borough of some duchy ; to shine in such a borough never occurs to him, for there isn't so much as a public there ; if he is really ambitious, or compelled to support himself by his music,—he goes to the residential city of his duke ; but in this little *Residenz* there are already many good musicians,—so it is terrible uphill work to get on ; at last he makes his way; his music pleases; but in the next-door duchy not a soul has ever heard of him,—how, then, is he to begin to make a name in Germany? He tries, but grows old in the attempt, and dies; he is buried, and no one names him any more. This is pretty well the lot of hundreds; what wonder that thousands don't even bestir themselves to adopt the career of Musician? They rather choose a handicraft to earn their living, and give themselves with all the greater zest to music in their leisure hours; to refresh themselves, grow nobler by it, but not to shine. And do you suppose they make nothing but handicraft-music? No, no! Go and listen one winter-night in that little cabin: there sit a father and his three sons, at a small round table; two play the violin, a third the viola, the father the 'cello; what you hear so lovingly and deeply played, is a quartet composed by that little man who is beating time.—But he is the schoolmaster from the neighbouring hamlet, and the quartet he has composed is a lovely work of art and feeling.*—Again I say, go to that spot, and hear that author's

---

* To many a foreigner the above little picture may appear exaggerated; it is therefore particularly apropos that we read in a sketch of August Manns (*Musical Times*, March 1898) the following:

"August Friedrich Manns was born at Stolzenburg, a village near Stettin, in North Germany, March 12, 1825. His father was a glass-blower, with a pound a week and ten children, of whom August was the fifth. When the father returned from his day's work he would take down his fiddle from the wall and make music to his children. . . . At the age of six August was sent to the village school, where the day's work always commenced with a hymn sung from a figure-notation upon the ancient 'movable doh' system. In course of time the father's fiddle was augmented by another, a violoncello, and a horn, played by August's elder brothers, and later on by an old F flute, played by the future conductor of the Crystal Palace orchestra. . . . At the age of ten, August temporarily took the place of one of his brothers at the factory. . . . At the age of twelve he was sent to a school, kept by his uncle, at Torgelow, a neighbouring village. Here he became a musical pupil of Herr Tramp, the village musician. Up to this time the boy had been self-taught, and Tramp soon put him into the pathway of acquiring the proper fingering of both the flute and clarinet; but his chief instrument was the violin. As he had no means of buying an instruction book, he copied out the greater part of Rode, Kreutzer, and Baillot's book on the violin." As this quotation deals with the very decad in which Wagner was writing, it is of peculiar interest in the present connection. A few lines farther in the *Musical Times* article, we read how at fifteen young Manns was apprenticed to Urban, the town-musician of Elbing, whose

music played, and you will be dissolved to tears; for it will search your heart, and you will know what German Music is, will feel what is the German spirit.* Here was no question of giving this or that virtuoso the opportunity of earning a storm of applause by this or that brilliant passage; everything is pure and innocent, but, for that very reason, noble and sublime.—But set these glorious musicians before a full-dress audience in a crowded salon, —they are no longer the same men; their shame-faced bashfulness will not allow them raise their eyes; they will grow timid, and fear their inability to satisfy you. So they inquire by what devices other people please you, and for sheer lack of self-confidence they'll abandon their nature in shame, to pick up arts they only know by hearsay. Now they will make their fingers ache in practising gymnastics for you; those voices, which sang the lovely German *Lied* so touchingly, will make all haste to learn Italian colorature. But these passages and colorature refuse to suit them; you have heard them performed much better, and are bored by the bunglers.—And yet these bunglers are the truest artists, and in their hearts there glows a finer warmth than ever has been shed on you by those who hitherto have charmed you in your gilded salons. What then has ruined them?—They were too modest, and ashamed of their own true nature. This is the mournful chapter in the history of German Music. †

Alike the nature and the constitution of his fatherland have set the German artist iron bounds. Nature has denied him that flexibility of one chief organ which we find in the throats of the happy Italians;—political barriers obstruct him from higher publicity. The opera-composer

---

boys " were taught every instrument in the orchestra," and how "in his third year Manns played first violin in the string-band and first clarinet in the wind-band of Urban's Town-band," which confirms a general statement of Wagner's a few pages ahead.—Tr.

* "One sees that the author was young, and not yet acquainted with our elegant modern music-Germany.—The Editor" (i.e. R. Wagner in 1871).

† "It would seem that in our days this grief and shame have been happily overcome.—Ed." (i.e. R. W. in 1871).

sees himself obliged to learn an advantageous treatment of
Song from the Italians, yet to seek external stages for his
works themselves, as he can find none in Germany on which
to present himself before a nation.   So far as concerns this
latter point, you may take it that the composer who has
produced his works at Berlin, stays unknown at Vienna or
Munich for that very reason ; only from abroad, can he
succeed in attracting the whole of Germany.   Their works
are therefore like nothing more than provincial products ;
and if a whole great fatherland is too small for an artist,
how much smaller must one of its provinces be !   The
exceptional genius may soar above these limitations, but
for the most part only through the sacrifice of a certain
native self-dependence.   So that the truly characteristic
of the German always remains provincial, in a sense,
just as we have Prussian, Swabian, Austrian folk-songs, but
nowhere a German national anthem.—

This want of centralisation, albeit the reason why no
great national work of music will ever come to light, is
nevertheless the cause of Music's having preserved throughout so intimate and true a character among the Germans.
Just because there is no great Court, for instance, to gather
all that Germany possesses in the way of artistic forces, and
thrust it in one joint direction toward the highest-attain-
able goal,—just for this reason we find that every Province
has its artists who independently exert their dear-loved art.
The result is a general extension of music to the most
unlikely neighbourhoods, down to the humblest cots.   It
is surprising and astonishing, what musical forces one often
finds combined in the most insignificant towns of Germany ;
and though there is an occasional dearth of singers for the
Opera, you everywhere will find an orchestra that as a rule
can play Symphonies quite admirably.   In towns of 20,000
to 30,000 inhabitants you may count on not *one*, but two
to three well-organised bands,* not reckoning the countless

---

* " This was the actual experience of our friend at *Würzburg* in his time,
where, besides a full orchestra at the theatre, the bands of a musical society
and a seminary gave alternate performances.—Ed." (R. W. in '71).

amateurs who frequently are quite as good, if not still better-educated musicians, than the professionals. And you must know what one means by a German bandsman : it is rare indeed for the most ordinary member of an orchestra not to be able to play another instrument besides the one for which he is engaged ; you may take it as a rule that each is equally expert on at least three different instruments. But what is more,—he is commonly a composer too, and no mere empiric, but thoroughly versed in all the lore of harmony and counterpoint. Most of the members of an orchestra that plays a Beethovenian Symphony know it by heart, and their very consciousness of this gives rise to a certain presumption that often turns out badly for the performance ; for it will sometimes tempt each unit in the band to pay less heed to the ensemble, than to his individual conception.

We therefore may justly contend that Music in Germany has spread to the lowest and most unlikely social strata, nay, perhaps has here its root ; for higher, showier society in Germany must in this respect be termed a mere expansion of those humbler, narrower spheres. Maybe in these quiet unassuming families German Music finds herself at home ; and here in fact, where she is not regarded as a means of display, but as a solace to the soul, Music *is* at home. Among these simple homely hearts, without a thought of entertaining a huge mixed audience, the art quite naturally divests herself of each coquettish outward trapping, and appears in all her native charm of purity and truth. Here not the ear alone asks satisfaction, but the heart, the soul demands refreshment ; the German not merely wants to feel his music, but also to think it. Thus vanishes the craze to please the mere sensorium, and the longing for mental food steps in. It not being enough for the German to seize his music by the senses, he makes himself familiar with its inner organism, he studies music ; he learns the laws of counterpoint, to gain a clearer consciousness of what it is that drew him so resistlessly in master-works ; he goes to the root of the art, and becomes in time a tone-poet himself. This need descends from father to son, and its satisfaction thus becomes an essential part of bringing-up. All the difficulties on the scientific side of music the German learns as a child, parallel with his school-lessons, and as soon as he is at an age to think and feel for himself nothing is more natural than that he should include music in his thought and feeling, and, far from looking on its practice as an empty entertainment, religiously approach it as the holiest precinct in his life. He accordingly becomes a fanatic, and this devout and fervent *Schwärmerei*, with which he conceives and executes his music, is the chief characteristic of German Music.

Alike this bent and, perhaps, the lack of fine voices direct the German to instrumental music.—If we may take it as a general principle that every art has one particular genre that represents it at its purest and most independent, this certainly may be said to be the case with Music in its instrumental genre. In every other branch a second element combines that necessarily destroys the unity and self-dependence of the first, and yet, as we have experienced, can never raise itself to a level with it. Through what a mass of extras from the other arts must one not wade, in listening to an opera, to arrive at the real drift of the music itself! How the composer feels obliged to almost completely subordinate his art, here and there, and often to things beneath the dignity of any art. In those happy instances where the value of the services rendered by the auxiliary arts attains an equal height with the music itself, there arises indeed a quite new genre, whose classic rank and deep significance have been sufficiently acknowledged ; but it must always stay inferior to the genre of higher instrumental music, as at least the independence of the art itself is sacrificed, whereas in instrumental music the latter gains its highest scope, its most complete development.—Here, in the realm of Instrumental music, the artist, free of every foreign and confining influence, is brought the most directly within reach of Art's ideal ; here, where he has to employ the means the most peculiar to his art, he positively is bound to stay within its province.

What wonder if the earnest, deep and visionary German inclines to this particular genre of music more fondly than to any other? Here, where he can yield himself entirely to his dream-like fancies, where the individuality of a definite and bounded passion lays no chains on his imagination, where he can lose himself unhampered in the kingdom of the clouds,—here he feels free and in his native country. To realise the masterpieces of this genre of art it needs no glittering frame, no dear-paid foreign singers, no pomp of stage-accessories; a pianoforte, a violin, suffice to call awake the most enrapturing imaginations; everybody is master of one or other of these instruments, and in the smallest place there are enough to even form an orchestra capable of reproducing the mightiest and most titanic creations. And is it possible, with the most lavish aid of all the other arts, to erect a sublimer and more sumptuous building than a simple orchestra can rear from one of Beethoven's symphonies? Most surely not! The richest outward pomp can never realise what a performance of one of those master-works sets actually before us.

Instrumental music is consequently the exclusive property of the German,—it is his life, his own creation! And just that modest, bashful shyness, which constitutes a leading feature in the German character, may be a weighty reason for the thriving of this genre. It is this shamefacedness that prevents the German from parading his art, that inner halidom of his. With innate tact he feels that such a showing-off would be a desecration of his art, for it is so pure and heavenly of origin that it easily becomes defaced by worldly pomps. The German cannot impart his musical transports to the mass, but only to the most familiar circle of his friends. In that circle, however, he gives himself free rein. There he lets flow the tears of joy or grief unhindered, and therefore it is here that he becomes an artist in the fullest

meaning of the word.   If this circle is scant, it is a piano
and a pair of stringed instruments that are played on ;—
one gives a sonata, a trio or a quartet, or sings the German
four-part song.   If this familiar circle widens, the number
of instruments waxes too, and one undertakes a symphony.
—This justifies us in assuming that Instrumental-music
has issued from the heart of German family-life ; that
it is an art which can neither be understood nor estimated
by the mass of a crowded audience, but solely by the
home-like circle of the few.   A pure and noble *Schwärmerei*
is needed, to find in it that ecstasy it sheds on none but
the initiate ; and this can only be the true musician, not
the mass of an entertainment-craving public of the salon.
For everything the latter takes and greets as piquant,
brilliant episodes, is therewith quite misunderstood, and
what sprang from the inmost kernel of the noblest art is
consequently classed with tricks of empty coquetry.

We will now attempt to shew how all of German music
is founded on the selfsame basis.

The reason has already been given above, why the Vocal
genre is far less native to the Germans than that of Instrumental music.   It is not to be denied that Vocal music has
also taken a quite special direction of its own, with the
Germans, which likewise had its starting-point in the
people's needs and nature.   Yet the grandest and most
important genre of vocal music, the Dramatic, has never
attained a height and independent evolution on a par with
that of Instrumental music.   The glory of German vocal
music appeared in the Church ; the Opera was abandoned
to the Italians.   Even Catholic church-music is not at home
in Germany, but exclusively Protestant.   Again we find
the reason in the simplicity of German habits, which were
far less suited to the priestly splendour of Catholicism than
to the unpretentious ritual of the Protestant cult.   The
pomp of Catholic Divine Service was borrowed by courts
and princes from abroad, and all German Catholic church-
composers have been imitators, more or less, of the Italians.
In the older Protestant churches, however, in place of all

parade there sufficed the simple Chorale, sung by the whole congregation and accompanied on the organ. This chant, whose noble dignity and unembellished purity can only have sprung from simple and sincerely pious hearts, should and must be regarded as an exclusively German possession. In truth its very structure bears the impress of all German art ; in its short and popular melodies, many of which shew a striking likeness to other secular but always inoffensive folk-songs, one finds expressed the nation's liking for the *Lied*. The rich and forceful harmonies upon the other hand, to which the Germans set their choral melodies, evince the deep artistic feeling of the nation. Now this Chorale, in and for itself one of the worthiest events in the history of Art, must be viewed as the foundation of all Protestant church-music ; on it the Artist built, and reared the most imposing fabrics. The first expansion of the Chorale we have to recognise in the *Motet.* These compositions had the same church-songs, as the Chorale, for their basis ; they were rendered by voices alone, without accompaniment by the organ. The grandest compositions in this genre are those of *Sebastian Bach,* who must also be regarded as the greatest Protestant church-composer in general.

The Motets of this master, which filled a similar office in the ritual to that of the Chorale (saving that, in conse-quence of their great artistic difficulty, they were not delivered by the congregation, but by a special choir), are unquestionably the most perfect things we possess in independent vocal-music. Beside the richest application of a profoundly thoughtful art they shew a simple, forcible and often most poetic reading of the text in a truly Protestant sense. Moreover the perfection of their out-ward forms is so high and self-delimited, that nothing else in art excels it. But we find this genre still further magnified and widened in the great Passions and Oratorios. The Passion-music, almost exclusively the work of great Sebastian Bach, is founded on the Saviour's sufferings as told by the Evangelists ; the text is set to music, word by word ; but between the divisions of the tale are woven verses from the Church's hymns appropriate to the special subject, and at the most important passages the Chorale itself is sung by the whole assembled parish. Thus the performance of such a Passion-music became a great religious ceremony, in which artists and congregation bore an equal share. What wealth, what fulness of art, what power, radiance, and yet unostentatious purity, breathe from these unique master-works! In them is embodied the whole essence, whole spirit of the German nation; a claim the more justified, as I believe I have proved that these majestic art-creations, too, were products of the heart and habits of the German people.

Church-music therefore owed alike its origin and consummation to the people's need. A like need has never summoned up Dramatic music, with the Germans. Since its earliest rise in Italy the Opera had assumed so sensuous and ornate a character, that in this guise it could not possibly excite a need of its enjoyment in the earnest, steady-going German. Opera, with its pomps of spectacle and ballet, so very soon fell into the disrepute of a mere luxurious pastime for the Courts, that in former times, as a matter of fact, it was kept up and patronised by them alone. Naturally also, as these Courts, and especially the German ones, were so completely severed from the people, their pleasures could never become at like time those of the Folk. Hence in Germany we find the Opera practised as an altogether-foreign art-genre down almost to the end of the past century. Every court had its Italian company, no sing the operas of Italian composers; for at that time lao one dreamt of Opera being sung in any but the Italian anguage and by Italians. The German composer who aspired to write an opera, must learn the Italian tongue and mode of singing, and could hope to be applauded only when he had completely denationalised himself as artist. Nevertheless it was frequently *Germans*, who took first rank in this genre as well; for the universal tendency of which the German genius is capable made it easy to the German artist to naturalise himself on a foreign field.

We see how quickly the Germans feel their way into whatever the national idiosyncrasy of their neighbours has brought to birth, and thereby win themselves a fresh firm stand-point whence to let their innate genius spread creative wings long leagues beyond the cramping bounds of Nationality. The German genius would almost seem predestined to seek out among its neighbours what is not native to its motherland, to lift this from its narrow confines, and thus make something Universal for the world. Naturally, however, this can only be achieved by him who is not satisfied to ape a foreign nationality, but keeps his German birthright pure and undefiled; and that birthright is Purity of feeling and Chasteness of invention. Where this dowry is retained, the German may do the grandest work in any tongue and every nation, beneath all quarters of the sky.

Thus we see a German raising the Italian school of Opera to the most complete ideal at last, and bringing it, thus widened and ennobled to universality, to his own countrymen. That German, that greatest and divinest genius, was *Mozart*. In the story of the breeding, education, and life of this unique German, one may read the history of all German Art, of every German artist. His father was a musican; so he too was brought up to music, apparently with the mere idea of turning him into an honest professional who could earn his bread by what he had learnt. In tenderest childhood he was set to learn the very hardest scientific branches of his art; he naturally became their perfect master as soon as boy; a pliant, childlike mind and intensely delicate senses allowed him at like time to seize the inmost secrets of his art; but the most prodigious genius raised him high above all masters of all arts and every century. Poor all his life to the verge of penury, despising pomp and advantageous offers, even in these outward traits he bears the perfect likeness of his nation. Modest to shamefacedness, unselfish to the point of self-oblivion, he works the greatest miracles and leaves posterity the most unmeasured riches, without knowing that he did aught save yield to his creative impulse. A more affecting and inspiring figure no history of art has yet to shew.

Mozart fulfilled in its highest power all that I have said that the universality of the German genius is capable of. He made the foreign art his own, to raise it to a universal. His operas, too, were written in the Italian tongue, because it was then the only one admissible for song. But he snatched himself so entirely from all the foibles of the Italian manner, ennobled its good qualities to such a pitch, so intimately welded them with his inborn German thoroughness and strength, that at last he made a thing completely new and never pre-existing. This new creation was the fairest, most ideal flower of Dramatic music, and from that time one may date the naturalisation of Opera in Germany. Thenceforward national theatres were opened, and men wrote operas in the German tongue.

While this great epoch was in preparation, however, while Mozart and his forerunners were developing this novel genre from Italian music itself, from the other side there was evolving a popular Stage-music, through whose conjunction with the former at last arose true German Opera. This was the genre of German Singspiel, which, distant from the glare of Courts, sprang up in the people's midst and from its heart and customs. This German Singspiel, or Operetta, bears an unmistakable likeness to the older French *opéra comique*. The subjects for its texts were taken from the people's life, and mostly sketched the customs of the lower classes. They were generally of comic type, full of blunt and natural wit. The pre-eminent home of this genre was Vienna. In general it is in this Kaiser-city, that the greatest stamp of nationality has always been preserved; the gay and simple mind of its inhabitants has always been best pleased with what made straight for its mother-wit and buoyant fancy. In Vienna, where all the folk-plays had their origin, the popular Singspiel also thrived the best. The composer, indeed, would mostly restrict himself to Lieder and Ariettas;

however, one met among them many a characteristic piece
of music, for instance in the excellent "Dorfbarbier," that
was quite capable, if expanded, of making the genre more
important in time, had it not been doomed to die out
through absorption into the grander class of opera. This
notwithstanding, it had already reached a certain independent height; and one sees with astonishment that at
the very time when Mozart's Italian operas were being
translated into German, and set before the whole public
of his fatherland immediately after their first appearance,
that Operetta also took an ever ampler form, appealing to
the liveliest fancy of the Germans by an adaptation of
folk-sagas and fairy-tales.—Then came the most decisive
stroke of all: Mozart himself took up this popular line of
German Operetta, and on it based the first grand German
opera: *die Zauberflöte*. The German can never sufficiently
estimate the value of this work's appearance. Until then
a German Opera had as good as not existed; with this
work it was created. The compiler of the text-book, a
speculating Viennese Director, meant to turn out nothing
further than a right grand operetta. Thereby the work
was guaranteed a most popular exterior; a fantastic fable
was the groundwork, supernatural apparitions and a good
dose of comic element were to serve as garnish. But what
did Mozart build on this preposterous foundation? What
godlike magic breathes throughout this work, from the
most popular ballad to the sublimest hymn! What many-
sidedness, what marvellous variety! The quintessence of
every noblest bloom of art seems here to blend in one
unequalled flower. What unforced, and withal what
noble popularity in every melody, from the simplest to
the most majestic!—In fact, here genius almost took too
giant-like a stride, for at the same time as it founded
German Opera it reared its highest masterpiece, impossible
to be excelled, nay, whose very genre could not be carried
farther. True, we now see German Opera come to life, but
going backwards, or sicklying into mannerism, to the full
as quickly as it raised itself to its most perfect height.—

G

The directest imitators of Mozart, in this sense, were undoubtedly *Winter* and *Weigl*. Both joined the popular line of German Opera in the honestest fashion, and the latter in his "Schweizerfamilie," the former in his "unterbrochener Opferfest," proved how well the German opera-composer could gauge the measure of his task. Nevertheless the broader popular tendence of Mozart already loses itself in the petty, with these his copiers, and seems to say that German Opera was never to take a *national* range. The popular stamp of rhythms and melismi stiffens to a meaningless rote of borrowed flourishes and phrases, and above all, the indifferentism with which these composers approached their choice of subjects betrays how little they were fitted to give to German Opera a higher standing.

Yet we see the popular musical drama once more revive. At the time when Beethoven's all-puissant genius set open in his instrumental music the realm of daringest romance, a beam of light from out this magic sphere spread also over German Opera. It was *Weber* who breathed a fair warm life again into stage-music. In his most popular of works, the "Freischütz," he touched once more the people's heart. The German fairy-tale, the eerie saga, here brought the poet and composer into immediate touch with German folk-life ; the soulful, simple German Lied was the foundation, so that the whole was like a long-drawn moving Ballad, attired in noblest dress of breeziest romanticism, and singing the German nation's fondest fantasies at their most characteristic. And indeed both Mozart's Magic Flute and Weber's Freischütz have proved with no uncertain voice that in this sphere German Musical Drama (*opéra*) is at home, but beyond it lie stern barriers. Even Weber had to learn this, when he tried to lift German Opera above those bounds; for all its beauty of details, his "Euryanthe" must be termed a failure. Here, where Weber meant to paint the strife of great and mighty passions in a higher sphere, his strength forsook him ; his heart sank before the vastness of his task, he sought by toilsome painting-in of single features to make up for a whole that could only be drawn with bold and vigorous strokes; thus he lost his unconstraint and became in-effective.* 'Twas as if Weber knew that he here had sacrificed his own chaste nature; in his Oberon he re-turned with the sad sweet smile of death to the Muse of his former innocence.

Spohr also sought to make himself a master of the German stage, but never could arrive at Weber's popu-larity; his music lacked too much of that dramatic life which should radiate from the scene. To be sure, the products of this master must be called completely German, for they speak in deep and piercing accents to the inner heart. They entirely lack, however, that blithe and naïve element so characteristic of Weber, without which the colour of dramatic music grows too monotonous and loses all effect.

The last and most important follower of these two we recognise in *Marschner*; he touched the selfsame chords that Weber struck, and thereby swiftly gained a certain popularity. But with all his innate force, this composer was powerless to keep erect that German Opera so brilliantly revived by his predecessor, when the products of the newer French school began to make such strides in the enthusiastic welcome of the German nation. In effect, the newer French dramatic music dealt such a crushing blow at German popular Opera, that the latter may now be said to have wholly ceased to exist. Yet some further mention must be made of this last period, as it has exerted a most powerful influence on Germany, and it really seems as though the German after all would rise to be its master too.†

We can but date the commencement of this period from the advent of *Rossini*; for, with that brilliant audacity

---

* "Methinks my friend would have learnt in time to express himself more guardedly on this point.—Ed." (i.e. R. Wagner).

† Evidently referring to Meyerbeer; for the master does not appear to have realised at this epoch that the composer of the *Huguenots* was not a German, but a Jew.—Tr.

which alone could compass such a thing, he tore down all
the remnants of the old Italian school, already withered to
a meagre skeleton of empty forms.   His lustful-jovial
song went floating round the world, and its advantages—
of freshness, ease and luxury of form—were given con-
sistence by the French.   Among them the Rossinian line
gained character and a worthier look, through national
stability ; on their own feet, and sympathising with the
nation, their masters now turned out the finest work that
any folk's art-history can shew.   Their works incorporated
all the merits and character of their nation.   The delicious
chivalry of ancient France breathed out from *Boieldieu's*
glorious *Jean de Paris* ; the vivacity, the spirit, wit, the
grace of the French re-blossomed in that genre exclusively
their own, the *opéra comique*.   But its highest point was
reached by French dramatic music in *Auber's* unsurpassable " Muette de Portice " [*Masaniello*],—a national-work
such as no nation has more than one at most to boast of.
That storm of energy, that sea of emotions and passions,
painted in the most glowing tints, drenched with the most
original melodies, compact of grace and vehemence, of
charm and heroism,—is not all this the true embodiment
of latter-day French history ?   Could this astounding artwork have been fashioned by another than a Frenchman ?
There is no other word for it,—with this work the modern
French school had reached its apex, and with it the
hegemony of the civilised world.*

Small wonder, if the impressionable and impartial
German did not delay to recognise the excellence of
these products of his neighbours with unassumed enthusiasm.   For the' German, in general, can be juster than
many another nation.   Moreover these foreign imports
met a genuine need ; for it is not to be denied that the
grander genre of Dramatic music does not flourish in
Germany of itself; and apparently for the same reason
that the higher type of German play has never reached

* " Mephistopheles : ' You already speak quite like a Frenchman ! '—Ed.'"
(R. W.).

its fullest bloom. On the other hand it is more possible for the German, than for anyone else, on foreign soil to bring a national artistic epoch to its highest pitch and universal acceptation.*

As regards Dramatic music, then, we may take it that the Germans and the French at present have but one; though their works be first produced in *one* land, this is more a local than a vital difference. In any case the fact that these two nations now are stretching hands to one another, and lending forces each to each, is a preparation for one of the greatest artistic epochs. May this propitious union ne'er be loosed, for it is impossible to conceive two nations whose fraternity could bring forth grander and more fruitful results for Art, than the German and the French, since the genius of each of these two nations is fully competent to supply whatever may be lacking in the one or other.

* A longish passage appeared in the French, between this sentence and the succeeding paragraph, as follows: "Haendel et Gluck l'ont prouvé surabondamment, et de nos jours un autre Allemand, Meyerbeer, nous en offre un nouvel exemple.—Arrivé au point d'une perfection complète et absolue, le système français n'avait plus en effet d'autres progrès à espérer, que de se voir généralement adopté et de se perpétuer au même degré de splendeur ; mais c'était aussi la tâche la plus difficile à accomplir. Or, pour qu'un allemand en ait tenté l'épreuve et obtenu la gloire, il fallait sans contredit qu'il fût doué de cette bonne foi désintéressée, qui prévaut tellement chez ses compatriotes, qu'ils n'ont pas hésité à sacrifier leur propre scène lyrique pour admettre et cultiver un genre étranger, plus riche d'avenir et qui s'adresse plus directement aux sympathies universelles. En serait-il autrement quand la raison aurait anéanti la barrière des préjugés qui séparent les différents peuples, et quand tous les habitants du globe seraient d'accord pour ne plus parler qu'une seule et même langue ?"—Tr.

PERGOLESI'S "STABAT MATER." *

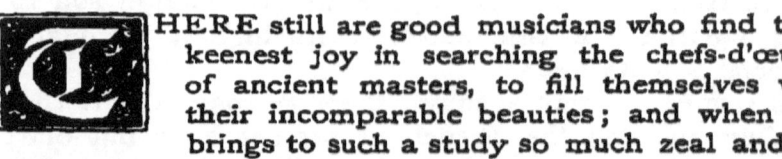HERE still are good musicians who find their keenest joy in searching the chefs-d'œuvre of ancient masters, to fill themselves with their incomparable beauties; and when one brings to such a study so much zeal and intelligence as the author of whom we are about to speak, the results deserve no less esteem and recognition than if they were original works. It would be a great mistake to ascribe to M. Lvoff the claim of having added to the perfection of the work of Pergolesi, for it is evident that his only aim has been to remind the modern school of a sublime exemplar, and to get it enrolled in the repertoire of contemporary performances. Under influence of this conviction, and in spite of all æsthetic scruples excited by this mode of secondary arrangement, it is impossible to deny the interest and importance of the publication now before us.

At an epoch like ours, when the different branches of the art of Music have taken such divergent lines, often to the point of a most abnormal transformation, it is an essential need and noble duty to ascend to primal sources for new elements of force and fecundity. But to usefully re-knit these ties of parentage with the great masters of the past, the practice of their compositions—adapted, if

* This "revue critique" of the "*Stabat Mater* de Pergolèse, arrangé pour grand orchestre avec chœurs par Alexis Lvoff, membre des Académies de Bologne et de Saint-Pétersbourg" appeared in the *Gazette Musicale* of Oct. 11, 1840. Although it is not included in the *Ges. Schr.*, having evidently been regarded by the author as simply a pot-boiler, I fancy that many of its sentences will justify my rescuing it from oblivion. Col. Alexis Lvoff, or Lwoff, was the composer of the Russian National Anthem.—Tr.

necessary, to the exigences of modern taste—will always be more efficacious than a pale and mediocre imitation of their wondrous style. In fact the last procedure offers all the danger of a retrogression, for such copiers are but too frequently inclined to reproduce in their concoctions those superannuated forms which purity of taste reproves.

The exclusive admirers of the ancient school have fallen into a vicious exaggeration, through attaching the same value to its imperfect canons as to the depth and thought revealed in its works.

Grand and noble as are those thoughts, the details of material execution shew inexperience and the gropings of a science in its infancy ; and it is impossible to call in doubt the greater perfecting of form, if not in our day, at least during the intermediary period that succeeded to this golden age of musical art.

It was with Mozart, the chief of the Idealistic school, that religious music really touched its apogee in point of structure ; and if I did not fear being misinterpreted, I should venture to express the wish that all the works of the preceding period had been transmitted to us clad in forms analogous, for the perfection of these latter would have been ample recompense for the pains of such a transformation ; nor would the difficulty have been very great, since Mozart was not too distant from the primitive epoch, and his manner still preserved its sentiment and characteristic traits. On the contrary, he has brilliantly proved how much the older masterpieces could be enhanced by a vivacity and freshness of colour, without losing aught of their intrinsic merit, so to say, and notably by his arrangement of Haendel's oratorio *The Messiah.*

We are far from blaming those who would only have Haendel's oratorio performed in a cathedral with a chorus of from three to four hundred voices, supported by organs and a quartet of stringed instruments of proportionate number, to enjoy the whole splendour and primitive energy of the composition. For the individual anxious to appreciate the historic value of Haendel's music it would no doubt be preferable to hear it rendered by such potent means,—a thing almost impossible to realise to-day for reason of one notorious circumstance, namely that Haendel himself improvised the accompaniments on the organ for the first performances of the *Messiah.* Is it not permissible to assume that the composer, unacquainted with the more perfect modern use of the 'wind,' employed the organ to produce the same effects that Mozart entrusted later to the improved wind-instruments of his day?

In any case, Mozart's instrumentation has embellished the work of Haendel in the general interest of art. It needed, in truth, the genius of a Mozart, to accomplish such a task in so complete a measure. He who undertakes a similar work to-day, can therefore do no better than adopt that for his model, without seeking to complicate its simple and natural lines; for an application of the resources of modern orchestration would be the surest means of travestying the theme and character of ancient works.

And such has been the laudable desire of M. Lvoff. An examination of his score will demonstrate that he has taken his type from the discreet instrumentation of Mozart. Three trombones, two trumpets, the drums, two clarinets and two bassoons,—such are the elements added to the original orchestra. And most frequently it is only the clarinets and bassoons that take an active part in the accompaniment, following the precedent of the bassoons and basset-horns in Mozart's *Requiem.* The greatest difficulty must have resided in the general revision of the string-quartet, as Pergolesi had written it entirely in the naïve style of olden days, limiting himself for most of the time to three parts, and sometimes even to two. Very often the complementary harmonic part was a matter of course, and one finds it hard to explain why the composer omitted to write it, thereby producing very perceptible gaps. But in other places the filling-up presented serious difficulties, especially where the melody seems to admit of only three parts, or sometimes two, and where a supplementary voice might be considered superfluous, if not harmful. Nevertheless this great obstacle has always been happily surmounted by M. Lvoff, whose general discretion is beyond all praise. The wind-instruments which he introduces, far from ever smothering or altering the original theme, serve on the contrary to throw it into higher relief. They even have a certain independent character that contributes to the effect of the ensemble, entirely after the rules adopted by Mozart, and in this regard we may particularly instance the fourth strophe, *Quæ mærebat.* Only occasionally, for example at the beginning of the first number, was it wrong, perhaps, to transfer the part of the violins to the bassoons and clarinets; not that the author has here misjudged the character of these latter instruments, but since the bass, retained for the lower strings, appears too full and too sonorous for its new superstructure.

It is astonishing, however, that the author of so conscientious a work should have let himself be once betrayed into altering the bass: namely at the commencement of the second strophe, where M. Lvoff has modified the entire phrase, greatly to the disadvantage of the original melody. No doubt he did it to avoid a passage of a certain crudity which Pergolesi had given to the part of the alto; but in our opinion there were other ways of remedying this harshness, without sacrificing the great composer's lovely bass. For the rest, it is the solitary instance, in all the work, of a change both useless and unfavourable. With scarcely another exception, we have witness of the most conscientious zeal and a highly delicate appreciation of the old chef-d'œuvre, down to tiny details of a character a trifle superannuated.

Beyond dispute the most audacious step in M. Lvoff's undertaking is the addition of choruses, since Pergolesi wrote his *Stabat* for but two voices, the one soprano and the other high contralto. Strictly speaking, it would have been better to respect the original intention of the master;

but as this introduction of choruses has in no way spoilt
the work, and as, moreover, the two original solo parts have
been preserved in their integrity, it would be impossible
to seriously blame the adaptor; in fact one must even
acknowledge that he has added to the richness of the
ensemble, for this adjunction has been effected with a
rare address and a superior understanding of the text.

Thus in the first number the intermittent fusion of the
choral with the solo voices reminds us happily of the
manner in which the two choirs are treated in Palestrina's
Stabat.   However it is principally upon the choir, that
weighs the difficulty of adding complementary parts in
the places aforesaid where Pergolesi had designed his
melody exclusively for two or three.   Here the arranger
is obliged to restrict the rôle of the chorus to three parts
at most, not to absolutely mar the original harmony and
disfigure its noble simplicity.   This is especially perceptible
in the fugal passages, such as the *Fac ut ardeat.*   Further,
the vocal theme is never in the tenor register, but devolves
exclusively on either the soprano or alto, as in the original
composition, or the bass which it was easy to extract from
the primary accompaniment.   Above all, the reviser must
have been embarrassed by the *Amen,* expressly written by
Pergolesi for two voices alone.

Apropos of No. 10, *Fac ut portem,* we must remark that
it would have been better to omit the accompaniment by
the choir, as also the concluding cadence, these two
accessories reminding one too much of modern Opera,
and ill according with the character of the sacred work.

But if we have felt it our duty to point out the reefs
presented by so rare a task, we have also to frankly avow
that the modern composer has given proof of great ability
in doubling them.   It would be impossible to praise too
much the noble aim that has governed M. Lvoff's enterprise; for if an intelligent admiration and an ardent
sympathy for so great a masterpiece alone were capable
of prompting anyone to such a labour, there also is no.
doubt that M. Lvoff took the perfect measure of its diffi-

culty and extent.   It therefore is no more than just to recognise not merely the talent, but also the courage necessary to accomplish a labour where the artist has to make complete denial of, and constantly efface himself, to let the superior genius to whom he renders loving homage shine in all his glory.

R. WAGNER.

5

THE VIRTUOSO AND THE ARTIST.*

CCORDING to an ancient legend there is somewhere an inestimable jewel whose shining light bestows forthwith, upon the favoured mortal whose glance rests on it, all gifts of mind and every joy of a contented spirit. But this treasure lies buried in unfathomed depths. The story goes, that eyes of happy mortals once were blest with superhuman power to pierce the ruins heaped above it like gateways, pillars, and misshapen fragments of a giant palace : through this chaos then there leapt to them the wondrous splendour of the magic jewel, and filled their hearts with bliss untold. Then yearning seized them to remove the pile of wreckage, to unveil to all the world the glory of the magic treasure at which the very sun would pale its fires when *its* glad rays should fill our heart with love divine, our mind with heavenly knowledge. But in vain their every effort : they could not move the inert mass that hid the wonder-stone.

Centuries passed by : the spirit of those rarest favoured ones still mirrored on the world the radiance of that starry light which once had shone upon them from the glinting jewel ; but no one could draw near itself. Yet tidings of it still existed ; there were traces, and men conceived the thought of burrowing for the wonder-stone with all the arts of mining. Shafts were sunk, levels and cross-cuts

---

* Under the title of " Du métier de Virtuose et de l'indépendance des Compositeurs : Fantaisie esthétique d'un musicien," this article appeared in the *Gazette Musicale* of Oct. 18, 1840 ; its French form, however, differs so greatly from the German of the *Ges. Schr.*, after the first page or two, that I reproduce it in its entirety on pages 123 *et seq.*—Tr.

were driven into the bowels of the earth; the most in-
genious of subterranean tactics were pursued, and one dug
afresh, cut winzes and new galleries, until at last the labyrinth
grew so confusing that all remembrance of the right direction was lost for good.   And so the whole great maze, in
whose behalf the jewel itself was finally forgotten, lay useless
quite: men gave it up.   Abandoned were adits, shafts and
raises: already they were threatening to cave in, when—so
they say—a poor miner from Salzburg came that way.   He
carefully surveyed the work of his forerunners: full of astonishment he paced the countless mazes, whose useless plan he
half surmised.   Of a sudden he feels his heart beat high for
very rapture: through a chink the jewel flashes on him; with
a glance he takes the measure of all the labyrinth: the longed-
for pathway to the wonder-stone itself grows plain; led by
its light he dives into the deepest cavern, to it, the heavenly
talisman itself.   A wondrous luminance then filled the world
with fleeting glory, and every heart was thrilled by ecstasy
untold: but the miner from Salzburg no man saw again.

Then came once more a miner, this time from Bonn in
the Siebengebirge; he wished to search in the abandoned
levels for the missing Salzburger: he lit full soon upon his
track, and so suddenly the splendour of the wonder-jewel
smote his eye, that it struck him blind.   A foaming sea of
light surged through his senses, he flung himself into the
chasm, and down the timbers crashed upon him: a fearful
din went up, as though a world had foundered.   The miner
from Bonn was never seen again.

And so, like every miner's-story, this ended—with a falling in.   Fresh ruins overlay the old; yet to this day men
shew the site of the ancient workings, and recently have
even begun to dig for the two lost miners, as kind good
people think they still might be alive.   With breathless
haste the pits are sunk afresh, and get much talked of;
the curious come from far and near, to view the spot: fragments of schist are taken away as souvenirs, and paid a
trifle for, for everyone would like to have contributed to
such a pious work; moreover one buys the life-account of

the two entombed, which a Bonn professor * has carefully drawn up, yet without being able to tell exactly how the accident occurred, which nobody knows but the Folk. And things have come to such a pass at last, that the real original legend. is clean forgotten, whilst all kinds of minor modern fables take its place, *e.g.* that quite prolific veins of gold have been discovered in the diggings, and the solidest ducats struck therefrom. Indeed there seems some truth in this; for people think less and less about the wonder-stone and those two poor miners, although the whole exploit still bears the title of a rescue-party.—

Perhaps the whole legend, with its subsequent fable, is to be understood in an allegoric sense: on that hypothesis, its meaning would soon be apparent if we took the wonder-jewel to be the *genius of Music*; the two incarcerated miners would be no less easy to divine, and the debris that covers them would lie before our feet when we gird ourselves to pierce to those enshrined elect. In truth, on whom that wonder-stone has shone in fabled dreams o' night, whose soul has felt the fire of Music in the holy hours of ecstasy,—would he fain arrest that dream, that ecstasy, *i.e.* if he would seek the tools therefor, he first of all will stumble on that heap of ruins: there he has then to dig and delve; the place is filled with gold-diggers; they pile the debris ever denser, and, would you make for the forgotten shaft, they fling down slag and cat-gold in your way. The rubble waxes high and higher, the wall grows ever thicker: sweat pours in rivers from your brow. Poor fellows! And they laugh at you.

Yet the thing may have a serious side.—

* Otto Jahn, whose Life of Mozart appeared in 1856-59, with a second edition in 1867; he also wrote for the *Grenzboten* an exhaustive review of the Complete Edition of Beethoven's works, with biographical information, re-published in his Collected Essays on Music in 1868, and was collecting materials for a minute biography of Beethoven at the time of his death in 1869. So that this clause at anyrate is an interpolation of 1870-71, having probably been represented in the original German manuscript by a reference to Schindler's biography of Beethoven, which made its first appearance in 1840; one of Wagner's Letters from Paris of 1841 (to appear in Vol. VIII.) alludes at greater length to Schindler.—Tr.

What you have written down in notes, is now to sound aloud ; you want to hear it, and let others hear it. Very good : the weightiest, nay, the ineluctable concern for you, is to get your tone-piece brought to hearing exactly as you felt it in you when you wrote it down : that is to say, the composer's intentions are to be conscientiously reproduced, so that the thoughts of his spirit may be transmitted unalloyed and undisfigured to the organs of perception. The highest merit of the executant artist, the Virtuoso, would accordingly consist in a pure and perfect reproduction of that thought of the composer's ; a reproduction only to be ensured by genuine fathering of his intentions, and consequently by total abstinence from all inventions of one's own. It follows that a performance directed by the composer in person alone can give a full account of his intentions ; nearest to him will come the man sufficiently endowed with creative power to gauge the value of observing another artist's intentions by that he sets upon his own, and it will be an advantage to him to have a certain loving pliability. After these most authorised would come such artists as make no claim to productivity, and belong to art, so to say, merely in virtue of their aptitude for making a stranger's artwork their intimate possession : these would have to be modest enough to so entirely sink their personal attributes, in whatever they may consist, that neither their defects nor their advantages should come to light in the performance ; for it is the artwork in its purest reproduction, that should step before us, in nowise the distracting individuality of the performer.

Unfortunately however, this very reasonable demand runs counter to all the conditions under which artistic products win the favour of the public. This latter's first and keenest curiosity is addressed to art-dexterity; delight in that is the only road to notice of the work itself. Who can blame the public for it ? Is it not the very tyrant whose vote we sue ? Nor would things stand so bad with this failing, did it not end by corrupting the executant artist, and make him forget at last his own true mission.

His position as vehicle of the artistic intention, nay, as virtual representative of the creative master, makes it quite peculiarly his duty to guard the earnestness and purity of Art in general: he is the intermediary of the artistic idea, which through him, in a sense, first attains to physical existence. The real dignity of the Virtuoso rests therefore solely on the dignity he is able to preserve for creative art: if he trifles and toys with this, he casts his own honour away. To be sure, 'tis small matter to him, should he not have grasped that dignity at all: though he be no artist, he yet has art-dexterities to hand: these he lets play; they do not warm, but glitter; and at night it all looks very nice.

There sits the virtuoso in the concert-hall, and entrances purely for himself: here runs, there jumps; he melts, he pines, he paws and glides, and the audience is fettered to his fingers. Go and watch the strange Sabath of such a soirée, and try to learn how you should make yourselves presentable for this assemblée; you will find that, of all that passes before your eyes and ears, you understand about as much as probably the Witches'-master there of what goes on within your soul when music wakes in you and drives you to produce. Heavens! You are to dress your music to suit this man? Impossible! At each attempt you would miserably fail. You can swing yourselves into the air, but cannot dance; a whirlwind lifts you to the clouds, but you can make no pirouette: what would you succeed in, if you took him for model? A vulgar catherine-wheel, no more,—and everyone would laugh, even if you did not get hurled from the salon.

Plainly we have nothing to do with this virtuoso. But presumably you mistook your locality. For indeed there are other virtuosi, and among them true, great artists: they owe their reputation to their moving execution of the noblest tone-works of the greatest masters; where would the public's acquaintance with these latter be slumbering, had not those eminently pre-elect arisen from out the chaos of music-makery, to shew the world

who These really were and what they did? There sticks
the placard, inviting you to such a lordly feast: one
name shines on you: *Beethoven*! Enough. Here is the
concert-room. And positively, Beethoven appears to you;
all round sit high-bred ladies, row after row of high-bred
ladies, and in a wide half-moon behind them lively gentlemen with lorgnettes in the eye. But Beethoven is there,
midst all the perfumed agony of dream-rocked elegance:
it really is Beethoven, sinewed and broad, in all his sad
omnipotence. But, who comes there with him? Great
God:—Guillaume Tell, Robert the Devil, and—who after
these? *Weber*, the tender and true! Good! And then:—
a "Galop." * O heavens! Who has once written galops
himself, who has had his stir in Potpourris, knows what a
want can drive us to it when it is a question of drawing
near to Beethoven at all costs. I took the measure of the
awful need that could drive another man to-day to Pot-
pourris and Galops, to gain the chance of preaching
Beethoven; and though I must admire the virtuoso in
this instance, I cursed all virtuosity.—So falter not, true
disciples of Art, upon the path of virtue: if a magic power
drew you to dig for the silted shaft, be not misguided by
those veins of gold; but deeper, ever deeper delve towards
the wonder-stone. My heart tells me, those buried miners
are living yet: if not, why! still believe it! What harms
you the belief?

But come, is it all mere foppery? You need the Virtuoso, and, if he's the right sort, he needs you too. So, at
least, it must once have been. For something happened,
to cause a division between the Virtuoso and the Artist.
In former times it certainly was easier to be one's own
virtuoso; but you waxed overweening, and made things
so hard for yourselves that you were obliged to turn their

* On April 20, 1840, Liszt had given a concert in the Salle Erard, playing
Beethoven's Pastoral Symphony (for two hands), a fantasia on airs from *Lucia*,
Schubert's *Serenade* and *Ave Maria*, and winding up with a *Galop Chromatique*. His *Robert le diable* fantasia would pretty certainly have figured
also, if only as encore.—Tr.

H

execution over to a man who has quite enough to do, his whole life long, to bear the other half of your labour. Indeed you should be thankful to him. He is the first to face the tyrant: if he doesn't do his business well, nobody asks about your composition, but *he* is hissed off the boards; can you be cross with him then, if, when applauded, he takes that also to himself, and does not specially return his thanks in name of the composer? Nor would that be quite what you want: you want your piece performed precisely as you thought it; the virtuoso is to add nothing to it, leave nothing from it; he is to be *your second self*. But often that is very hard: let one of you just try, for once, to sink himself so entirely in another!—

Lo there the man who certainly thinks least about himself, and to whom the personal act of pleasing has surely nothing special to bring in, the man beating time for an orchestra. He surely fancies he has bored to the very inside of the composer, ay, has drawn him on like a second skin? You won't tell me that *he* is plagued with the Upstart-devil, when he takes your tempo wrong, misunderstands your expression-marks, and drives you to desperation at listening to your own tone-piece. Yet *he* can be a virtuoso too, and tempt the public by all kinds of spicy nuances into thinking that it after all is *he* who makes the whole thing sound so nice: he finds it neat to let a loud passage be played quite soft, for a change, a fast one a wee bit slower; he will add you, here and there, a trombone-effect, or a dash of the cymbals and triangle; but his chief resource is a drastic cut, if he otherwise is not quite sure of his success. Him we must call a virtuoso of the Baton; and I fancy he's none too rare, especially in opera-houses. So we shall have to arm ourselves against him; and the best way will probably be to make sure of the real original, not second-hand virtuoso, to wit the *singer*.

Now the composer so thoroughly impregnates the Singer, that he streams from his throat as living tone. Here, one would think, no misunderstanding is possible: the Virtuoso has to pick here and there, all round him; he may

pick the wrong thing: but there, in the Singer, we sit with
our melody itself. It will be a bad job, by all means, if
we are not sitting in the right spot of him; he, too, has
picked us up from outside: have we got down as far as his
heart, or simply stuck in his throat? We were digging for
the jewel in the depths: are we caught in the toils of the
gold-veins?

The human voice, as well, is an instrument; it is rare,
and paid for dearly. How it is shaped, is the first care of
the inquisitive public, and its next *how* it is played with:
what it plays, is immaterial to the generality. The Singer
knows better: for what he sings must be so formed, as to
make it easy for him to play on his voice to great credit.
How small, in comparison, is the heed the Virtuoso has to
pay to *his* instrument: it stands ready-made; if it suffers
harm, he gets it repaired. But this priceless, wondrously
capricious instrument of the Voice? No man has quite
found out its build. Write how you will, ye composers,
but mind it is something the singer sings gladly! How
are you to set about it? Why, go to concerts, or better
still, to salons!—We don't want to write for these, but for
the theatre, the Opera,—dramatic music.—Good! Then go
to the Opera, and discover that you still are merely in the
salon, the concert-room. Here, too, it is the Virtuoso with
whom you must first come to terms. And this virtuoso,
believe me, is more perilous than all the rest; for wherever
you encounter him, he'll slip between your fingers.

Look at those most celebrated singers in the world:
from whom would you learn, if not from the artists of our
great Italian Opera, who are worshipped as positively
superhuman beings, not only by Paris, but by every capital
in the world? Here learn what really is the *art* of Song;
from them the famous singers of the French Grand Opéra
first learnt what singing means, and that it's no joke, as the
good German scrape-throats (*Gaumen-Schreihälse*) dream
when they think the thing done if their heart is in the right
place, namely seated tight upon their stomach. There you
also will meet the composers who understood how to write

for real singers : they knew that through these alone could
they arrive at recognition, eh ! existence; and as you see,
they are there, doing well, nay, honoured and glorified.
But you don't want to compose like these; your works
shall be respected; it is from them you require an impression, not from the success of the throat-feats of the
singers to whom those others owe their fortune?—Look a
little closer : have these people no passion ? Do they not
tremble and heave, as well as lisp and gurgle ? When
they sing "*Ah! Tremate!*" it sounds a little different
from your "Zittre, feiger Bösewicht!"   Have you forgotten that "*Maledetta!*" at which the best-bred audience
turned into a Methodist-meeting of niggers ?—But to you
it doesn't seem the genuine thing ? You think it a pack
of Effects, at which all reasonable men should laugh ?

However, this also is art, and one these celebrated
singers have carried very far.   With the singing-voice,
too, one may toy and juggle as one pleases; but the
game must lastly be related to some passion, for one
does not pass so altogether needlessly from rational talk
to the decidedly much louder noise of singing.   Ah ! now
you have it : the public wants an emotion it cannot get at
home, like whist or dominoes.   This, also, may have been
quite otherwise at one time : great masters found great
pupils among their singers; the tradition still lives of the
wonderful things they brought to light together, and often
is renewed by fresh experience.   Most certainly one knows
and wills that Song should also work dramatically, and
our singers therefore learn so thorough a command of
Passion that it looks as if they never left it.   And its use
is quite reduced to rule: after cooing and chirping, an
explosion makes a quite unparalleled effect; its not
being an actual matter of fact, why! that is just what
makes it art.

You still have a scruple, founded principally on your
contempt for the sickly stuff those singers sing.   Whence
springs it ? Precisely from the will of those singers, on
whose behalf it is cobbled up.   What in the world can a

true musician wish to have in common with this handiwork? But how would it stand if these fêted demigods
of the Italian Opera were to undertake a veritable artwork? Can they truly catch fire? Can they bear the
magic lightnings of that wonder-jewel's flash?

See: "Don Giovanni"! And really by Mozart! So
reads the poster for to-day. Let us go to hear and see.

And strange things happened to me, when I actually
heard "Don Juan" lately with the great Italians: it was a
chaos of every sensation in which I was trundled to and fro;
for I really found the perfect artist, but close beside him
the absurdest virtuoso, who sent him to the wall. Glorious
was *Grisi* as "Donna Anna"; unsurpassable *Lablache* as
"Leporello." The grandest, richest-gifted woman, inspired
with but one thought: to be Mozart's own "Donna Anna":
there all was warmth and tenderness, fire, passion, grief and
woe. Oh! *she* knew that the buried miner still is living,
and blessedly she fortified my own belief. But the silly
soul consumed herself for Signor *Tamburini*, the world-
most-famous barytone who sang and played "Don Juan":
the whole evening through, the man could not rid himself of
the log of wood that was tied to his legs with this fatal rôle.
I had previously once heard him in an opera of Bellini's:
there we had "*Tremate*!" "*Maledetta*," and all the Passion
of Italy rolled into one. Nothing of the sort to-day: the
brief swift pieces whizzed past him like fugitive shadows;
much airy Recitative all stiff and flat; a fish on the sands.
But it seemed that the whole audience was stranded too:
it remained so decorous that no one could trace a sign of
its usual frenzy. Perhaps a worthy mark of homage to
the true genius who swayed his wings to-night throughout
the hall? We shall see. In any case the divine *Grisi*
herself did not peculiarly entrance: nobody could quite
appreciate her secret passion for this tiresome "Don Juan."
—But there was *Lablache*, a colossus, and yet to-night a
"Leporello" every inch. How did he manage it? The
enormous bass-voice sang throughout in the clearest, most
superb of tones, and yet it was more like a chattering,

babbling, saucy laughing, hare-footed scampering; once
he absolutely piped with his voice, and yet it always
sounded full, like distant church-bells.   He neither stood
nor walked, nor did he dance; but he was always in
motion; one saw him here, there, everywhere, and yet
he never fidgeted; always on the spot, before you knew
it, wherever a fine sense of humour could scent out fun or
frolic in the situation. *Lablache* was not applauded once
in all this evening: that might be reasonable, a token of
dramatic *goût* in the audience.   But the latter seemed
really annoyed that its authorised favourite, Madame
Persiani (one's heart convulses at mere mention of that
name!), was ill at ease in the music for "Zerlina."   I
perceived that one had quite prepared oneself to be
charmed beyond all bounds with her, and whoever had
heard her a short while before in the "*Elisire d'amore*"
could not be gainsaid such a verification.   But *Mozart*
was decidedly to blame, that the charm refused to work
to-night: more sand, for such a lively fish!   Ah! what
would not audience and Persiani have given to-day, had
it been held decent to infuse a drop from that Elixir of
Love!   In effect, I gradually remarked that both sides
were bent on an excess of decency: there reigned a
unanimity which I was long in accounting for.   Why,
since to all appearance one was "classically" minded,
did the magnificent and perfect execution of that glorious
"Donna Anna" not carry everyone into that sterling
ecstasy which seemed to be the only thing proposed
to-day?   Why, as in the strictest of senses one was
ashamed of being carried away, had one come to a performance of "Don Juan" at all?   Verily the whole
evening seemed a voluntary act of penance, imposed on
oneself for some unknown reason: but to what end?
Something must really be gained by it; for such a Paris
audience will spend much, 'tis true, but always expects
a return for its money, be it only a worthless one.

This riddle also solved itself: *Rubini fired off this night
his famous trill from A to B!*   The whole thing flashed

on me. How could I have expected much from poor
"Don Ottavio," the so often mocked-at tenor-stopgap
of Don Juan? Indeed I long felt truly sorry for the so
unrivalledly adored *Rubini*, the wonder of all tenors, who
on his side went quite crossly to his Mozart-sum. There
he came, the sober, solid man, passionately dragged on
by the arm by the divine "Donna Anna," and stood with
ruffled peace of mind beside the corpse of his expected
father-in-law, who now no more could breathe his blessing
on a happy marriage. Some say that Rubini was once
a tailor, and looks just like one; I should have credited
him with more agility in that case: where he stood he
stayed, and moved no further; for he could sing, too,
without stirring a muscle; even his hand he brought but
seldom to the region of his heart. This time his singing
never touched him at all; he might fitly save his fairly
aged voice for something better than to cry out words
of comfort, already heard a thousand times, to his beloved.
That I understood, thought the man sensible, and, as he
took the same course throughout the opera whenever
"Don Ottavio" was at hand, I fancied at last it was over,
and still more anxiously inquired the meaning, the purpose of this extraordinary night of abstinence. Then
slowly came a stir: unrest, sitting-up, shrewd glances,
fan-play, all the symptoms of a sudden straining of attention in a cultured audience. "Ottavio" was left alone
on the stage; I believed he was about to make an announcement, for he came right up to the prompter's box:
but there he stayed, and listened without moving a feature
to the orchestral prelude to his *B flat* aria. This ritornel
seemed to last longer than usual; but that was a simple
illusion: the singer was merely lisping out the first ten
bars of his song so utterly inaudibly that, on my discovery that he really was giving himself the look of
singing, I thought the genial man was playing a joke.
Yet the audience kept a serious face; it knew what was
coming; for at the eleventh bar Rubini let his F swell
out with such sudden vehemence that the little recon-

ducting passage fell plump upon us like a thunderbolt,
and died away again into a murmur with the twelfth.
I could have laughed aloud, but the whole house was
still as death : a muted orchestra, an inaudible tenor ;
the sweat stood on my brow.   Something monstrous
seemed in preparation : and truly the unhearable was
now to be eclipsed by the unheard-of.   The seventeenth
bar arrived : here the singer has to hold an F for three
bars long.   What can one do with a simple F ?   Rubini
only becomes divine on the high B flat : *there* must he
get, if a night at the Italian Opera is to have any sense.
And just as the trapezist swings his bout preliminary,
so " Don Ottavio " mounts his three-barred F, two bars
of which he gives in careful but pronounced crescendo,
till at the third he snatches from the violins their trill
on A, shakes it himself with waxing vehemence, and at
the fourth bar sits in triumph on the high B flat, as if
it were nothing ; then with a brilliant roulade he plunges
down again, before all eyes, into the noiseless.   The end
had come : anything that liked might happen now.   Every
demon was unchained, and not on the stage, as at close
of the opera, but in the audience.   The riddle was solved :
this was the trick for which one had assembled, had borne
two hours of total abstinence from every wonted operatic
dainty, had pardoned Grisi and Lablache for taking such
music in earnest, and felt richly rewarded by the coming-
off of this one wondrous moment when Rubini leapt to
B flat !

A German poet once assured me that, in spite of all,
the French were the true " Greeks " of our era, and the
Parisians in particular had something Athenian about
them ; for really it was they who had the keenest sense
of " Form."   This came back to me that evening : as a
fact, this uncommonly elegant audience shewed not a
spark of interest in the stuff of our " Don Juan " ; to them
it was plainly a mere lay-figure on which the drapery of
unmixed Virtuosity had first to be hung, to give the music-
work its formal right to existence.   But *Rubini* alone

could do this properly, and so it was easy to guess why just this cold and venerable being had become the darling of the Parisians, the chartered "idol" of all cultivated friends of Song. In their predilection for this virtuosic side of things they go so far as to give it their whole æsthetic interest, while their feeling for noble warmth, nay even for manifest beauty, is more and more amazingly cooling down. Without one genuine throb they saw and heard that noble *Grisi*, the splendid woman with the soulful voice: perhaps they fancy it too realistic. But *Rubini*, the broad-built Philistine with bushy whiskers; old, with a voice grown greasy, and afraid of over-taxing it: if *he* is ranked above all others, the charm can't reside in his substance, but purely in a spiritual Form. And this form is forced upon every singer in Paris: they all sing *à la* Rubini. The rule is: be inaudible for awhile, then suddenly alarm the audience by a husbanded explosion, and immediately afterwards relapse into an effect of the ventriloquist. Mons. *Dupres* already quite obeys it: often have I hunted for the substitute, hidden somewhere beneath the podium like the mother's-voice trumpet in "Robert the Devil," that seemed to take the part of the ostensible singer at the prompter's box, who now wasn't making a sign. But that is "art." What do we blockheads know about it?—Taken all in all, that Italian performance of "Don Giovanni" has helped me to great consolation. There really are great artists among the virtuosi, or, to put it another way: even the virtuoso can be a great artist. Unfortunately they are so entangled with each other, that it is a sorrowful task to sift them out. That evening *Lablache* and the *Grisi* distressed me, while *Rubini* diverted me hugely. Is there something corruptive, then, in setting these great differences side by side? The human heart is so evil, and hebetude so very sweet! Take care how you play with the Devil! He'll come at last when you least expect him. That's what happened to Sig. Tamburini that evening, where he surely would never have dreamt it. Rubini had happily swung

DU MÉTIER DE VIRTUOSE ET DE L'IN-DÉPENDANCE DES COMPOSITEURS.

FANTAISIE ESTHÉTIQUE D'UN MUSICIEN.*

D'APRÈS une vieille légende, il existe quelque part un joyau inestimable dont l'éclat rayonnant procure soudain à l'heureux mortel qui peut fixer son regard sur lui, toutes les lumières de l'intelligence et les joies intimes d'une conscience satisfaite ; mais ce miraculeux trésor est depuis bien des siècles enfoui dans un abîme profond. Au dire de la chronique, il y eut jadis des hommes favorisés par le destin, et dont l'œil, doué d'un pouvoir surnaturel pénétrait la masse de ruines et de décombres où gisaient l'un sur l'autre entassés des portiques, des colonnades, et mille autres débris informes de gigantesques palais. C'est du sein de ce chaos que le bijou fantastique les éblouit de sa prodigieuse clarté et remplit leurs cœurs d'une extase céleste. Ils furent saisis alors d'un grand désir de soulever cet immense amas de ruines pour rendre manifeste à tous les yeux la splendeur du joyau magique qui devait faire pâlir jusqu' aux rayons du soleil, et qui survivrait non seulement à réchauffer nos organes corporels, mais encore à vivifier les fibres les plus délicates de l'âme. Mais tous leurs efforts furent vains ; ils ne purent ébranler la masse inerte sous laquelle était enseveli le précieux talisman.

Les siècles s'accumulèrent ; quelques esprits sublimes reflétèrent depuis sur le monde les rayons lumineux que la vue du trésor lointain leur avait communiqués, mais

* See footnote to page 108.—Tr.

jamais personne n'approcha du profond sanctuaire qui recélait la pierre miraculeuse. On eut l'idée d'ouvrir des mines et des conduits souterrains qui pussent, avec les procédés de l'art, faciliter la recherche du bijou mystérieux. On exécuta des travaux et des excavations admirables ; mais on poussa si loin les précautions et l'artifice, on creusa tant de galeries transversales, on ouvrit tant de mines accessoires, que par la suite des temps la confusion s'établit entre toutes ces voies divergentes, et l'on perdit définitivement dans ce labyrinthe le secret de la direction propice.

Tout cet immense travail était donc devenu inutile ; on y renonça. Les mines furent abandonnées, et déja leurs voûtes menaçaient de s'écrouler de toutes parts, quand survint un pauvre mineur qui, selon la chronique, était né à Salzbourg. Celui-ci examina attentivement l'œuvre grandiose de ses devanciers, et suivit avec une curiosité mêlée d'admiration les détours compliqués de ces tranchées innombrables. Tout-à-coup il sentit son cœur ému d'une sensation pleine de volupté, et il aperçut à une faible distance le joyau magique qui l'inondait de sa radieuse clarté. Il embrassa alors d'un coup d'œil rapide et simultanément l'ensemble du labyrinthe. Le talisman lumineux traçait devant lui la route tant désirée, et comme entraîné sur un rayon de flamme, le pauvre mineur parvint au fond de l'abîme jusqu' auprès de l'éblouissant trésor. En même temps, une émanation miraculeuse inonda la terre d'une splendeur fugitive et fit tressaillir tous les cœurs d'une joie ineffable ; mais personne ne revit plus jamais le mineur de Salzbourg.

Ce fut un autre mineur de Bonn qui conçut le premier pressentiment de cette précieuse découverte ; il se tenait à l'entrée de la mine, et il ne tarda pas à distinguer à son tour le chemin privilégié du trésor ; mais les ardents rayons projetés par celui-ci vinrent frapper sa vue si subitement qu'il en devient aveugle. Tous ses sens furent paralysés à l'aspect d'un océan de flammes crépitantes, et saisi de vertige il se précipita dans l'abîme où sa chute provoqua une ruine générale, et où retentit l'épouvantable fracas des voûtes

écroulées et des piliers démolis. Et l'on n'entendit plus
jamais parler du mineur de Bonn.

Ici se termine la légende, comme toutes les légendes de
mineur, par une catastrophe irréparable. On montre encore
la place des anciennes excavations, et, dans ces derniers
temps, on s'est occupé de déblayer plusieurs puits dans le
but de retrouver et de recueillir les cadavres des deux
pauvres mineurs. Les travaux sont poussés avec activité,
et chaque passant emporte un fragment de ce déblais en
échange d'une menue monnaie, parce que c'est une affaire
d'amour-propre que de paraître avoir participé à cette
pieuse réparation. Parfois, dit-on, l'on rencontre encore
des filons étincelants que l'on transforme par la fusion en
beaux ducats d'or; mais quant aux deux mineurs et au
joyau magique, il y a long-temps que personne n'y pense
plus.

Je ne saurais dire avec quelque certitude si cette légende
est de pure invention ou basée sur quelque fait réel; mais
elle mérite en tout cas d'être mentionnée par les applica-
tions dont cette allégorie est susceptible, car le talisman
mystérieux peut être regardé comme l'emblème du secret
magique, idéal, de l'art musical. Sur cette seule donnée,
il serait facile de découvrir une assimilation à la mine et
aux décombres. En effet, celui qu'inspire le génie de la
musique et qui éprouve le besoin de traduire en notes ses
pensées intimes, rencontrera d'abord l'amoncellement des
ruines, et parviendra peut-être ensuite dans la mine,
régulièrement creusée par l'art; mais combien peu péné-
treront jusqu' à la crypte profonde ou repose la divine
essence? Le nouvel adepte se heurtera d'abord contre
l'épaisse muraille élevée par la vanité, l'ignorance et la
routine, comme un rempart défendant l'approche du taber-
nacle sacré. Cette masse lourde et compacte effraie le
regard le moins timide, et souvent on a peine à se per-
suader que ce n'est qu'une enveloppe trompeuse qui dérobe
à l'œil le secret du beau et du vrai. Examinons de plus
près les causes de cette étrange méprise.

Toute composition musicale a besoin pour être jugée

d'être executee ; l'exécution est donc une partie importante
de l'art musical, et pour ainsi dire sa condition de vitalité
la plus essentielle. Sa première règle doit être, en conséquence, de traduire avec une fidélité scrupuleuse les
intentions du compositeur, afin de transmettre aux sens
l'inspiration de la pensée sans altération ni déchet. Le
plus grand mérite du virtuose consiste donc à se pénétrer
parfaitement de l'idée musicale du morceau qu'il exécute, et
à n'y introduire aucune modification de son cru. C'est-à-dire
qu'il n'y a vraiment d'exécution parfaite que celle dont se
charge le compositeur lui-même, et nul n'en approchera
davantage que l'individu doué tout à la fois de la faculté
créatrice et d'une organisation assez souple pour s'assimiler
en quelque façon la pensée d'autrui. Restent après cela
les artistes qui, sans prétendre au talent de l'invention,
n'ont rien à sacrifier pour saisir et pour rendre telle qu'elle
se comporte une inspiration étrangère ; car, en fait d'exécution musicale, il faudrait à la rigueur que ni les défauts ni
les qualités de l'exécutant ne pussent influencer l'auditeur,
et que le mérite seul de la composition maîtrisât toute son
attention ; d'où cette conséquence rigoureuse qu'il faut ou
bien dénier toute importance à l'exécution musicale, ou bien
lui en attribuer une tellement exagérée, qu'on la mettrait au
niveau de la conception, à la manifestation de laquelle son
concours est indispensable.

Or, il est difficile de décider s'il faut s'en prendre au
goût superficiel du public, ou bien à la vanité des virtuoses,
de cette habitude contractée avec le temps de traiter
l'exécution musicale comme une chose absolument indépendante du fond auquel elle s'appliquait. Mais il
est certain, qu'en général le public n'a pas témoigné
d'un sens critique assez profond pour apprécier à leur
juste valeur les œuvres musicales à la portée de leur idée
fondamentale. Il arriva ainsi que maintes fois le rôle
secondaire de l'exécution fut confondu avec la fonction
créatrice de la pensée, qu'on alla jusqu' à méconnaître
tout-à-fait. De leur côté, les artistes exécutants méritent le
grave reproche d'avoir abusé de cette propension vicieuse,

et d'avoir trop souvent mis tout en œuvre pour substituer
à la pensée dont ils se faisaient les interprètes, leur propre
individualité. Cette injuste prédominance accordée au
virtuose sur l'auteur de la composition, eut pour conséquence directe de faire admettre qu'en général celui-là
devait largement user du droit de modifier à son gré le
texte auquel il voulait bien prêter l'éclat de la publicité.
L'exemple fut donné par le premier virtuose qui eut la
fantaisie de surexciter l'attention et la sympathie de ses
auditeurs en mettant exclusivement en relief ses qualités
personelles. L'effet inévitable d'une semblable methode
fut donc que les ouvrages des maîtres furent tous plus où
moins défigurés, suivant que les exécutants étaient doués
d'un talent réel, ou simplement d'une certaine habileté
machinale.

Telle fut l'origine d'une tradition si fatale à l'art musical.
C'est de cette époque que datent les virtuoses à réputation.
Ceux-ci, moins pour obvier à cette altération déplorable
des ouvrages, produit d'une libre inspiration, que pour
avoir encore plus d'occasions de faire briller leurs avan-
tages, imposent aux musiciens un nouveau genre de
compositions, à savoir celui de morceaux concertants.
La condition première de leur facture consistait dans le
sacrifice de toute idée artistique et indépendante, et dans
un asservissement perpétuel à telle ou telle qualité d'organe
ou de doigté propre à chaque exécutant. L'essentiel était
d'omettre, d'annuler tout effet musical capable de maîtriser
le virtuose malgré lui ou de le rejeter momentanément sur
le second plan. Plus le public prit goût aux jouissances
superficielles attachées à ce mode d'exécution, plus les
compositions de cette nature devinrent insipides et
dépourvues de caractère. Toute fois, ce fut pour ainsi
dire un bonheur pour l'art que les virtuoses s'adonnassent
ainsi à un genre spécialement fait pour eux, car ce fut
autant gagné pour les saines productions de l'art, soustraites
par leur propre mérite à de semblables mutilations. Mais
l'abus dépassa bientôt ses premières limites ; la *virtuosité*
devint de plus en plus envahissante, et toute composition

musicale dut se résigner, pour avoir sa part des suffrages publics, à servir d'instrument et de prétexte aux expériences capricieuses des exécutants.

Dans quelle situation singulière, en effet, n'est pas tombé aujourd'hui l'art musical : le but véritable a été sacrifié à l'accessoire qui est devenu le principal but.   Ce serait déja une triste nécessité que l'obligation imposée aux compositeurs d'arranger leurs ouvrages dans l'intérêt de telle ou telle qualité spéciale de l'exécutant, mais on est allé bien plus loin.   Le musicien qui veut, aujourd'hui, conquérir la sympathie des masses, est forcé de prendre pour point de départ cet amour-propre intraitable des virtuoses, et de concilier avec une pareille servitude les miracles qu'on attend de son génie.   A la vérité, il faut rendre cette justice à l'époque actuelle, qu'elle a produit des artistes qui ont su, en dépit de cette obsession préjudiciable, donner à leur talent un développement idéal et grandiose.   Le résultat de leurs efforts a même été de purifier et d'ennoblir la fonction du virtuose.   Plusieurs de ceux-ci, en petit nombre il est vrai, et grâce à leur organisation d'élite, ont touché aux sommités de l'art, principalement dans le genre instrumental ; mais encore ont-ils dû, pour asseoir et soutenir leur réputation, se résigner à capituler avec leur conscience et à sacrifier maintes fois à la mode la pureté de leur goût.

C'est surtout dans l'exercice de la profession du chant que l'abus que nous signalons a pris un empire pernicieux. Depuis long-temps on est convenu de considérer les chanteurs Italiens comme le modèle absolu du genre ; c'est donc sur eux que porteront principalement nos remarques critiques.   Les Italiens sont habitués à s'exercer exclusivement dans la musique dramatique, et, selon nous, il serait bien préférable qu'ils donnassent carrière à leurs talents à la manière des virtuoses instrumentistes et sur l'estrade tapissée de nos salles de concerts ; car tout ce qui constitue le matériel d'un opéra, c'est-à-dire les chœurs, l'orchestre, les décors, l'action, tout cela est pour ainsi dire non avenu avec les artistes italiens. Bref, ils sont parvenus à réduire les représentations dramatiques à de simples exhibitions musicales et à asservir les compositeurs à leurs caprices les plus étranges, et ceux d'entre ces derniers qui jouissent aujourd'hui de quelque renommée, la doivent par-dessus tout à l'excès de leur complaisance et à leur servilité pour leurs ténors ou leurs *prime donne*.

Il y a sans doute dans la manière italienne une séduction particulière, et celui qui a entendu les premiers sujets du Théâtre-Italien de Paris se rend aisément compte de cette prédominance usurpée par l'exécution sur la composition elle-même ; mais le plus grand malheur dans un pareil état de choses, c'est que ces artistes merveilleux sont les seuls au monde et ne sauraient être remplacés d'aucune manière. Mais cela n'empêche pas que la fascination exercée par le succès de leur méthode fait de jour en jour plus de progrès, de telle sorte que le dommage qui en résulte ne laisse vraiment point de compensation à espérer, quelle que soit l'étendue de leur triomphe. Et la gravité de ce dommage est dans l'application du chant italien au genre de l'Opéra, car nul ne songerait à contester la valeur de leur talent de virtuoses s'ils n'exerçaient celui-ci que sur une scène appropriée et dans de justes limites. Mais ils ont annulé au théâtre tout intérêt dramatique, et ils ont persuadé à la majorité du public cette funeste illusion, que leur système satisfait suffisamment aux exigences de la musique dramatique. En effet, les chefs d'emploi de l'école italienne ne se dissimulent pas l'importance de l'action théâtrale, et leur talent incontestable leur a révélé bien des fois le secret de l'émotion dramatique dans la déclamation de certains morceaux passionnés de leurs rôles, malgré leurs efforts pour réduire ceux-ci aux proportions d'un programme de concert. Il arrive souvent que telle scène ou tel duo de leurs opéras soit connu du public avant la représentation scénique. On y a remarqué des traits admirables de vocalisation et d'effet musical, mais rien de ce qui touche à la passion et au mouvement du drame. Et quelle surprise n'éprouve-t-on pas en entendant ces jolis caprices exécutés par un premier sujet, qui leur fait subir une complète métamorphose, et féconde pour ainsi dire le néant? Tel est le secret de la perdition de la musique italienne. Car non seulement les compositeurs se croient dispensés d'inventer des thèmes caractéristiques; mais c'est, je le répète, une obligation absolue pour eux que de s'effacer constamment pour laisser tout le mérite de la création à ces virtuoses de premier ordre. Ainsi l'emploi du chanteur n'est plus de rendre et de traduire les conceptions originales du compositeur, mais de donner carrière à sa propre imagination au gré de sa fantaisie.

Ce qu'il y a d'abusif et de pernicieux dans cet échange de rôles saute bien vite aux yeux, et l'on en déplore surtout les tristes résultats, quand ces mêmes virtuoses entreprennent d'exécuter une œuvre consciencieuse et réellement indépendante. Ainsi, qu'on se rappelle l'exécution de *Don Giovanni*, et l'on sera convaincu de la réalité des griefs que nous venons d'exposer. Comparez les résultats obtenus par ces grands chanteurs luttant contre cet immortel chef d'œuvre avec l'effet qu'ils produisent dans leur répertoire habituel. Quel prodigieux assemblage de bévues! Comment donc se fait-il que ces artistes si entraînants dans les opéras de Rossini, de Bellini, et même de Donizetti, au point même de nous y faire supposer des traits de génie et des intentions dramatiques là où jamais il n'en a existé, comment ces artistes si habiles, dis-je, sont ils parvenus à rendre le merveilleux opéra de Mozart ennuyeux? Comment leur inspiration d'ordinaire si chaleureuse, a-t-elle été en cette occasion frappée de tant d'impuissance, que leur triste allure à travers ces prodiges d'harmonie les fait ressembler à des oiseaux privés d'air, ou à des poissons ravis à leur liquide élément? C'est qu'en effet ni l'air ni l'eau n'abondent dans *Don Juan*, tout plein d'un bout à l'autre de ce feu sacré allumé au joyau magique de notre légende.

Ou bien est-ce qu'en effet *Don Juan* ne serait qu'une production pâle et médiocre, et ses mélodies seraient-elles

donc trop simples pour inspirer la verve des exécutants ?
Oh! non, certes! et ces fameux virtuoses pris isolément,
sont les premiers à réfuter par leur exemple, une accusation aussi injuste. Ainsi l'admirable Lablache ne sait-il
pas donner à son rôle d'un bout à l'autre, et sans la moindre
altération égoïste, un caractère vraiment idéal ? Ses col-
lègues, à la vérité, sont loin de se montrer comme lui à la
hauteur de leur tâche, car, habitués comme ils sont à voir
leur moindre fioriture saluée par les bravos d'un public
frénétique, c'est pour eux un triste contraste que l'accueil
plein de froideur qui répond aux efforts si louables de
Lablache.

Nous touchons au point critique qui met en relief tous
les effets déplorables de ce système qui donne le pas aux
virtuoses d'opéra sur le compositeur. Mais si cet abus a
pris tant d'extension et causé tant de scandale dans une
troupe d'artistes aussi distingués, qu'on juge de ce qu'il doit
produire parmi ces virtuoses vulgaires et de bas étage qui
pululent en tous lieux ? Cependant avec des chanteurs
comme ceux du Théâtre-Italien, peut-être pourrait-on, par
une exception unique, et en raison de la rare perfection de
leur talent, pardonner à ce vice d'exécution qui n'en est
un que relativement aux textes d'une beauté suprême, et
même en adopter le résultat comme un genre d'une nouvelle
espèce. Car ce serait une erreur grave que de dénier aussi
à l'art du chanteur son indépendance propre et la faculté de
créer dans de certaines limites. Il est certain que sous le
rapport du mécanisme organique, la portée et les résultats
de la voix humaine peuvent être calculés et définis d'une
manière précise, mais en la considérant comme un élément
spirituel, et dans le ressort des émotions de l'âme, il est
difficile d'établir des règles et des démarcations rigoureuses.
Il est donc indispensable de laisser à l'exécutant, surtout
en matière de musique vocale, une certaine indépendance
personnelle ; et le compositeur qui se refuserait à une concession semblable tomberait dans l'abus à son tour en
comprimant le noble essor de l'artiste et le réduisant au
rôle servile d'un éplucheur de notes. Ce dernier défaut,

soit dit en passant, est fort commun chez les compositeurs allemands. Ils méconnaissent trop cette part d'indépendance qu'il est juste de réserver aux chanteurs. Ils les tourmentent par leurs restrictions et leur rigidité de telle sorte que très rarement l'exécution de leurs œuvres répond aux pressentiments de leur imagination.

Sans contredit le musicien qui, en composant son œuvre, sait qu'elle doit être exécutée par un chanteur en renom, a bien le droit d'écrire tel ou tel morceau de manière à faire briller les qualités prédominantes du virtuose; puisque nous voyons une réunion de gens de talent, même en sacrifiant absolument les intentions le la composition, produire un effet qui ne manque ni de pittoresque ni de séduction. Mais, nous le répétons, un pareil système ne peut réussir que dans de rares exceptions, et alors même les véritables amis de l'art regretteront toujours que l'attrait de l'exécution ne soit pas dû à une plus noble cause.

Le dommage principal résultant de l'empiétement du métier de virtuose sur la composition est surtout, comme nous l'avons déjà dit, déplorable en ce qu'il a envahi tous les genres de musique sans exception. Et rien n'est plus affligeant que de le voir régner même dans l'école de l'opéra français, qui se distinguait tellement par son caractère tranché d'indépendance. Les musiciens français ne subissent pas moins l'obligation d'accoupler à des scènes vraiment dramatiques des parties superflues uniquement destinées à faire briller le chanteur au détriment de la vérité théâtrale. Toutefois, il faut leur rendre cette justice qu'ils témoignent presque toujours d'un goût profond et d'un tact merveilleux, en ménageant autant que possible les conventions scéniques, et en intercalant, pour ainsi dire, en-dehors du drame, comme de purs accessoires, ces concessions faites à la mode dominante. C'est une sorte de capitulation polie avec les exigences dépravées du public de nos jours, et à ce titre, elle n'offrirait sans doute qu'un faible inconvénient s'il n'était à craindre que la préférence marquée des auditeurs pour ce genre de futilités n'exagérât de plus en plus la vanité des virtuoses, et n'entraînât par la suite les compositeurs, de concession à concession, à trahir irréparablement les plus sacrés interêts de l'art. Puissent-ils avoir sans cesse présent à leur souvenir l'exemple de Gluck, leur illustre prédécesseur, et se modeler sur la courageuse persévérance avec laquelle il prouva aux Piccinistes qu'il savait lutter et triompher de ses adversaires sans composer lâchement avec leurs prétentions.

R. WAGNER.

6.

THE ARTIST AND PUBLICITY.*

HEN I am alone, and the musical strings begin to stir within me, strange whirling sounds take shape of chords, until at last a melody springs forth, revealing to me the idea of my whole being ; when the heart beats time thereto in loud impatient strokes, and inspiration streams in tears immortal through the mortal eye, no longer seeing,—I often tell myself : Fool that thou art, not to bide forever by thyself, to live for these unequalled blisses, in lieu of rushing out to face that awful mass yclept the Public, to earn thee by its nothing-saying nod the fatuous authority to go on practising thy gift of composition ! † What can the most brilliant welcome of this public give thee worth a hundredth fraction of that hallowed joy which wells from thine own heart ? Why do mortals fired with a spark divine forsake their sanctuary, run breathless through the city's muddy streets, and seek in hottest haste for dull and sated men on whom to force a happiness indicible ? And what exertions, turmoils and illusions, before they can even arrive at compassing the sacrifice ! What plots and

* " Der Künstler und die Öffentlichkeit " appeared in the *Gazette Musicale* of April 1, 1841, under the title " Caprices esthétiques extraits du journal d'un musicien défunt. Le Musicien et la Publicité." After the first paragraph, however, the French again materially differs, besides bearing marks of the editorial scissors, for it is reduced to about a quarter of the usual length. In the first sentence " die als Idee mir mein ganzes Wesen offenbart " so strikingly resembles Schopenhauer's philosophy of Music that one might have taken it for an interpolation of 1871, did not the French of 1841 (i.e. thirteen years before the master read a line of Schopenhauer) give us its counterpart in " et que j'en sens jaillir enfin l'idée qui révéle tout mon être."—Tr.

† From " to earn," to the end of the sentence, did not appear in the French. —Tr.

artifices must they ply, for a good part of their life, to bring
to the ears of the crowd what it can never understand! Is
it for fear the history of Music might one fine day stand
still? Is it for that, they pluck the fairest pages from the
secret history of their heart, and snap the magic chain that
fastens sympathetic souls to one another throughout the
centuries, whilst here the only talk can be of schools and
manners? *

* As said, from this point the French diverges : " Il y a là quelque puissance
occulte et inexplicable, dont moi-même, hélas ! je subis l'influence funeste.
Plus j'y songe, moins je puis me rendre compte des motifs qui poussent les
artistes à rechercher le grand jour de la publicité.   Est-ce l'ambition, le désir
du bien-être? motifs bien puissants sans doute ; mais quel est l'homme sur
lequel ils aient prise à l'heure de l'enthousiasme ou dont ils puissent émouvoir
le génie ?   Dans la vie ordinaire, je conçois qu'on cède à ces motifs, quand il
est question d'un bon dîner, d'un article louangeur dans les journaux ; mais
jamais quand il s'agit de sacrifier les plus hautes jouissances qu'il soit donné à
l'homme de goûter.   Pour les cœurs aimants, ce pourrait bien être le désir
irrésistible de laisser s'épancher le surplus de l'enthousiasme qui les enivre
et de faire participer le monde entier à leur extase.   Malheureusement l'artiste
ne voit point le monde tel qu'il est ; il se le représente comme étant à sa
hauteur, il oublie qu'il n'est composé que de gens en fracs à la dernière mode
et en mantilles de soie.

" Ce désir immodéré et funeste de la publicité paraît être tellement vivace,
que même aux heures où l'inspiration a cessé, il continue à nous travailler le
cerveau, et c'est dans ces heures qu'il faut lui donner le nom d'ambition.   O
ambition pernicieuse, à qui nous devons tous les airs, airs variés, etc., c'est
toi qui nous enseignes à ravager systématiquement le sanctuaire de la poésie que
nous portons en nous ! c'est toi qui dans ton ironie démoniaque nous pousses à
souiller de roulades impudiques un chaste et pur accord ; à resserrer une pensée
vigoureuse et large dans un lit étroit de cadences et de niaiseries !

" O vous, *heureux infortunés*, aux joues creuses et pâles, aux yeux usés, vous
vous êtes flétris au souffle brûlant de l'étude et du travail, afin que le public vous
criât bravo ! pour l'enveloppe mensongère dont vous entouriez votre poésie dans
les moments de calcul et de réflexion prosaïque, et que vous lui arracheriez avec
joie si vous ne craigniez que votre création, si elle se montrait dans sa nudité,
ne fût obligée de fuir honteuse et éperdue devant les railleries du vulgaire.   Oh !
si vous étiez tous mes frères et mes amis, je vous ferais une proposition à l'aim-
able : je vous engagerais à faire de la musique pour votre compte, et à exercer
en même temps quelque bon métier ou à spéculer à la Bourse.   Vous seriez
alors tout-à-fait heureux et vous pourriez mener bonne et joyeuse vie.   Je veux
vous donner l'exemple ; deux heures sonnent, je vais à la Bourse ; si j'échoue
dans mes opérations, j'écrirai des quadrilles ; c'est un bon métier, qui fort
heureusement n'a rien de commun avec la musique."

With that the article ends : it was signed " Werner," but a note to the Index
of the *Gaz. Mus.* corrects the error.—Tr.

There must be some inexplicable force at work: who feels himself subjected to its power, must hold it ruinous. Certainly the first assumption to occur to one, would be that it was the bent of Genius to impart itself without regard to consequences : loud does it sound in thyself, aloud let it ring out to others! Eh, folk say 'tis the *duty* of Genius, to live for Man's pleasure; who imposed it, God alone knows! Merely it so happens that this duty never comes to consciousness, and least of all when Genius is engaged in its ownest function, of creation. But that perhaps is not the question; when it has created, it is then to feel the obligation to divest itself of the immense advantage it has above all other mortals, by surrendering its creation to them. In respect of Duty, however, Genius is the most conscienceless of beings : nothing does it bring to birth thereby, and I believe it neither regulates by that its traffic with the world. No, it abides by its nature for ever and ever : in its most foolish act it still stays Genius, and I rather fancy that at bottom of its bent to gain publicity there lies a motive of ill moral import, which again does not come to clear consciousness, but yet is serious enough to expose the very greatest artist to contemptuous treatment. In any case this passion for publicity is hard to comprehend : each experience teaches it that it is in an evil sphere, and can only hope to move a little smoothly by putting on an evil look itself. Genius,—would not all men run away from it, were it once to shew itself in its godlike nakedness as it is? Perhaps this really is its saving instinct; for nursed it not the knowledge of its purest chastity, how might it not be ravished by a ribald self-delight in its own fashionings? But the first contact with the outer world compels all genius to clothe itself. Here reads the rule: the Public wills to be amused, and thou must seek to smuggle in thine Own beneath the mantle of Amusement. Very well, we will say that Genius draws the needful act of self-denial from a feeling of duty : for Duty holds alike the command and compulsion to self-denial, self-sacrifice. Yet what duty bids a man to sacrifice his

honour, a woman her shame? For sake of these they ought
to offer up all personal welfare, if need so be. But more than
to man his honour, to woman her shame, to Genius is itself;
and if it bears the smallest wound in its own essence, compact of shame and honour in the very highest measure, then
is it nothing, absolutely nothing more.

Impossible, that Duty urges Genius to the fearful act of
self-denial whereby it makes itself away to public life. Some
dæmonic secret must lie hidden here. He, the blest, the
over-joyed, the over-rich,—goes begging. He begs for your
favour, ye victims of boredom, ye seekers after amusement,
ye vain presumptuous, ye ignorant all-wise, bad-hearted,
venal, envious reporters,—and God knows of what else thou
mayst consist, thou modern Art-public, thou institute of
Public Opinion! And what humiliations he endures!
The tortured Saint can smile transfigured: for what no
rack can ever reach, is just the hallowed soul; the wounded
warrior dragging through the shades of night may smile,
for what stays whole is his honour, his courage; the woman
smiles, who suffers shame and scorn for sake of love: for
the soul's salvation, honour, love, now first shine all transfigured in a higher glory. But Genius, that gives itself a
mark for scorn when it gives itself the air of *pleasing*?—
Happy may the world regard itself, that to it the pains of
Genius can be so relatively little known!

No! These sufferings no one seeks from sense-of-duty,
and whoever could imagine it, his duty necessarily rises from
a very different source. One's daily bread, the maintenance
of a family: most weighty motors. Only, they do not
operate in the genius. They prompt the journeyman, the
hand-worker; they may even move the man of genius to
handiwork, but they cannot spur him to create, nor even to
bring his creations to market. Yet that's the point we are
discussing, namely how to explain the impulse that drives
a man with demon force to carry just his noblest, ownest
good to open market.

Certainly a mixture of the most mysterious sort here
comes to pass, and could we ever clearly see it, 'twould

shew the spirit of the highly-gifted artist quite strictly
hovering 'twixt heaven and hell. Undoubtedly the godlike longing to impart an own interior bliss to human
hearts, is the predominant motive, and in hours of awful
stress the only strength-giver. This impulse feeds at all
times on the genius's belief in self, to which no other can
compare in vigour, and this faith again informs the artist
with that very pride which works his fall in commerce with
the miseries of earthly squalor. He feels himself free, and
in life, too, will he be it : he will have nothing in common
with his want; he will be wafted, light and quit of every
care. This may happen in fact when his genius is generally
recognised, and so the object is to bring it to acknowledgment. Though he thus appear to be ambitious (*ehrgeisig*),
he yet is not ; for he wants no honour (*Ehre*) paid him ;
but its fruit he wants, in Freedom. He only meets ambitious
men, or such as dwell content with fruits apart from honour.
How mark himself from these ? He falls into a throng
midst which he necessarily must pass for other than he
truly is. What exceptional prudence, what cautiousness
in every tiniest step, would it need for him to always walk
securely here, and ward off all misapprehension ! But he
is awkwardness personified ; confronted with the mean-
nesses of Life, he can only use the privilege of Genius to
get entangled in a constant contradiction with himself : and
so, a prey for every springe, his own prodigious gift he casts
before the swine, and squanders on the aimlessest of objects.
—In truth he merely longs for freedom to give full play to
his beneficence. To him it seems so natural a claim, that
he can never fathom why its due should be denied him : is
it not a mere question of manifesting Genius clearly to the
world ? That, he never ceases thinking, he is bound to
bring about, if not to-morrow, assuredly the next day after.
As if death were nothing ! And Bach, Mozart, Beethoven,
Weber ?—Nay, but it yet might happen !—A sad, sad
tale !—

   And with it all to be so laughable !—
   Could he only see himself, as we now see him, he must

end by laughing at his very self. And that laughter is perhaps his direst danger, for it alone can move him to begin
the frantic dance again. Yet his laughter is quite another
thing from yours : the latter is mockery, the former Pride.
For he just sees himself ; and his self-recognition, in this
infamous *quid-pro-quo* that he has tumbled into, attunes him
to that monstrous merriment of which no other man is
capable. So levity rescues him, to bear him to yet more
fearful pains. Now he credits himself with the strength to
play with even Evil : he knows that, lie as much as he
will, his truthfulness will ne'er be sullied, for he feels with
every gnaw of grief that Truth is his very soul ; and he
finds a curious consolation in the fact that not one of his lies
is believed, that he can dupe no man. Who would take him
for a jester ?—But why does he give himself the look ? The
world leaves him no other road to freedom : and this latter
(as dressed for the world's understanding) resembles little
else than—*money*. That is to with him recognition of his
genius, and for that is the whole mad game laid out.
Then he dreams : " God, if only I were so-and-so, for
instance *Meyerbeer* ! " So *Berlioz* lately dreamt of what
he would do, were he one of those unfortunates who pay
five hundred francs for the singing of a Romance not worth
five sous : then would he take the finest orchestra in the
world to the ruins of Troy, to play him the " *Sinfonia
eroica.*" *—You see, what heights the genius - beggar's

* Proof positive that at least this portion of the article was contained in the
original M.S. for the *Gazette Musicale*, as it was only two months previously (Jan.
28, 1841) that Berlioz had written in that journal : "Si j'étais riche, bien riche,
riche comme ces malheureux du siècle qui donnent cinq cents francs à un
chanteur pour une cavatine de cinq sous, . . . je partirais pour la Troade . . .
j'en ferais à peu près une solitude . . . je bâtirais un temple sonore au pied de
mont Ida, deux statues en décoreraient seules l'intérieur, et un soir, au soleil
couchant, après avoir lu Homère et parcouru les lieux qu'immortalisa son génie,
je me ferais réciter par le roi des orchestres l'autre poëme du roi des musiciens,
la symphonie héroïque de Beethoven." Is it too much to fancy that this passage of Berlioz may have sown in Wagner's mind the first seed of the " Bayreuth idea," which came to its earliest recorded expression just ten years later,
and twenty-one years after that, again, was celebrated by the crowning of a
certain foundation-stone ceremony with the performance of Beethoven's Ninth
Symphony ?—Tr.

7.

ROSSINI'S "STABAT MATER."

The account of this remarkable occurrence in the highest Paris world of music our friend despatched to Robert Schumann, who at that time was editor of the "Neue Zeitschrift für Musik" and headed the skit—signed with an inexplicable pseudonym—with the following motto :

> "Das ist am allermeisten unerquickend,
> Dass sich so breit darf machen das Unächte,
> Das Ächte selbst mit falscher Scheu umstrickend.
> RÜCKERT."

> ("Of all our evils 'tis the sorriest token
> How wide the spurious has spread its rule,
> That e'en the genuine with false shame is spoken.")

WHILE waiting for other musical treats in preparation for the glorious Paris public; while waiting for Halévy's "Maltese Knight," the "Water-carrier" of Cherubini, and finally, in the dimmest background, the "*Nonne Sanglante*" of Berlioz,—nothing so excites and captivates the interest of this fevered world of dilettanti, as —*Rossini's* piety.* Rossini is pious,—all the world is pious, and the Parisian salons have been turned into praying-cells.—It is extraordinary ! So long as this man lives, he'll always be the mode. Makes he the Mode, or makes it him ? 'Tis a ticklish problem. True, that this piety took root a long time since, especially in high society;—what time this ardour has been catered-for in Berlin by philosophic Pietism; what time the whole of Germany lays bare its heart to the musical gospel according to Felix Mendelssohn,—the Paris world of quality has no idea of being left behind. For some while past they have been getting their first quadrille-composers to write quite exquisite *Ave Marias* or *Salve Reginas*; and themselves, the duchesses and countesses, have made it their duty to study the two, or three parts of them, and edify therewith their thronging guests, groaning for very reverence and overcrowding. This glowing stress of piety had long burnt through the charming corsets of these lion-hearted duchesses and countesses, and threatened to singe the costly tulles and

* This article (to which a little editorial note was added, " From a new correspondent ") formed the 'leader' in the *N. Z. f. M* . of December 28, 1841, and was signed " H. Valentino." The quotation from Friedrich Rückert (a celebrated German poet, 1788-1866) appears to have been Schumann's own selection, for it was assigned the usual place of honour beneath the journal's superscription. The text in the *Ges. Schr.* is absolutely identical with that in the *N. Z.*—Tr.

laces which theretofore had heaved so blamelessly and un-
impassioned on their modest chests—when at last, at a
most appropriate opportunity, it kindled into vivid flame.
That opportunity was none other than the *in memoriam*
service for the Emperor Napoleon, in the chapel of the
Invalides. All the world knows that for these obsequies
the most entrancing singers of the Italian and French
Operas felt themselves impelled to render Mozart's
Requiem, and all the world may see that that was no
small matter. Above all, however, the *high* world of Paris
was quite carried away by this flash of insight : it is wont
to melt, without conditions, in presence of *Rubini's* and
Persiani's singing ; to close its fan with nerveless hand, to
sink back upon its satin mantle, to close its eyes, and lisp :
"*c'est ravissant!*" Further is it wont, when recovering
from the exhaustion of its transports, to breathe out the
yearning question : "By whom, this composition ?" For this
it really is quite requisite to know, if in one's stress to imi-
tate those singers one means to send one's gold-laced chasseur
next morning to the music-sellers, to fetch one home that
heavenly aria or that divine duet. By strict observance
of this custom the high Parisian world had come to learn
that it was *Rossini, Bellini, Donizetti*, who had provided
those intoxicating singers with the wherewithal to melt
it ; it recognised the merit of these masters, and it loved
them.

So the destiny of France would have it that, to hear the
adored *Rubini* and the bewitching *Persiani*, instead of in the
Théâtre des Italiens one must assemble beneath the dome of
the Invalides. In view of all the circumstances, the Ministry
of Public Affairs had formed the wise resolve that this time,
in lieu of Rossini's *Cenerentola, Mozart's* Requiem should
be sung ; and thus it came to pass, quite of itself, that our
dilettantist duchesses and countesses were given something
very different to hear, for once, from what they were accus-
tomed-to at the Italian Opera. With the most touching
lack of prejudice, however, they accommodated themselves
to everything : they heard Rubini and Persiani,—they

melted away; instead of their fans, they dropped their muffs; they leant back on their costly furs (for it was mortal cold in church on December 15, 1840)—and, just as at the Opera, they lisped : "*c'est ravissant!*" Next day one sends for Mozart's Requiem, and turns its first few pages over : it has plenty of *colorature*! One tries them,—but : "Good Heavens! It tastes like physic!"—"They're fugues!" "Powers above! where have we got to?" "How is it possible? This can't be the right thing!" "And yet!"—What's to be done?—One tortures oneself,—one tries,—it won't go at all!—But there's no help for it ; sacred music *must* be sung! Did not Rubini and Persiani sing sacred music?—Then kindly music-dealers, beholding the anguish of these pious ladies' hearts, rush in to the rescue : "Here you have brand-new Latin pieces by Clapisson, by Thomas, by Monpou, by Musard, &c., &c. All cut and dried for you! Made expressly for you! Here an *Ave*; there a *Salve*!"

Ah! how happy they were, the pious Paris duchesses, the fervent countesses! They all sing Latin : two soprani in thirds, with occasionally the purest fifths in all the world,—a tenor *col basso*! Their souls are calmed ; no one now need be afraid of purgatory!—

Yet,—quadrilles of Musard's, or Clapisson's, one only dances *once*,—their *Ave*! and *Salve*!, with any good grace, one can sing but *twice* at most ; that, however, is too little for the fervour of our high-class world ; it asks for edifying songs which one may sing at least fifty times over, just like the lovely operatic arias and duets of Rossini, Bellini and Donizetti. Someone had read indeed, in a theatrical report from Leipzig, that Donizetti's *Favorite* was full of old-Italian church-style ; however, the fact that this opera's church-pieces were composed to a French, and not to a Latin text, obstructed our high world from giving vent to its religious stress by singing them ; and it still remained to find the man whose church-songs one might sing with orthodox belief.

About this time it happened that *Rossini* had let nothing

be heard of him for ten long years : he sat in Bologna, ate pastry, and made wills. Among the pleadings in the recent action between Messieurs *Schlesinger* * and *Troupenas*, an inspired advocate declared that during those ten years the musical world had "moaned" beneath the silence of the giant master ; and *we* may assume that, on this occasion, the Parisian *high* world even "groaned." Nevertheless there circulated dismal rumours about the extraordinary mood the maëstro was in ; at one moment we heard that his hypogastrium was much incommoded, at another— his beloved father had died [April 29, 1839] ;—one said that he meant to turn fishmonger ; another, that he refused to hear his operas any more.   But the truth of it seems to have been, he felt penitent and meant to write church- music ; for this one relied on an old, a well-known proverb, and the fact is that Rossini evinced an invincible longing to make this proverb's second half come true, since he positively had no more need to verify its first. The earliest stimulus to carry out his expiation seems to have come to him in Spain : in Spain, where Don Juan found the amplest, choicest opportunities of 'sin, Rossini is said to have found the spur to penance.

It was on a journey which he was making with his good friend the Paris banker, Herr *Aguado* ;—they were sitting at ease in a well-appointed chariot, and admiring the beauties of Nature,—Herr Aguado was nibbling chocolate, Rossini was munching pastry.   Then it suddenly occurred to Herr Aguado that he really had robbed his compatriots more than was proper, and, smitten with remorse, he drew the chocolate from his mouth ;—not to be behind such a beautiful example, Rossini gave his teeth a rest, and confessed that all through life he had devoted too much time to pastry. Both agreed that it would well beseem their present mood to stop their chariot at the nearest cloister, and go through some fit act of penance : no sooner said than done. The Prior of the nearest monastery received the travellers like a friend : he kept a capital

* Publisher of the *Gazette Musicale.* —Tr.

cellar, excellent *Lacrymæ Christi* and other good sorts, which quite uncommonly consoled the contrite sinners. Nevertheless it struck Messrs Aguado and Rossini, as they were in the right humour, that they really had meant to undergo a penance : Herr Aguado seized his pocket-book in haste, drew out a few telling banknotes, and dedicated them to the sagacious Prior. Behind this fine example of his friend's, again, Rossini felt he must not linger,—he produced a solid quire of music-paper, and what he wrote on it post-haste was nothing less than a whole *Stabat mater* with grand orchestra ; that *Stabat* he presented to the estimable Prior. The latter gave them absolution, and they both got back into their chariot. But the worthy Prior soon was raised to lofty rank, and translated to Madrid ; where he lost no time in having the *Stabat* of his confessional child performed, and dying at the earliest opportunity. Among a thousand memorable relics, his executors found the score of that contrite *Stabat mater* ; they sold it, at not at all a bad figure, for good of the poor—and thus, from hand to hand, this much-prized composition became at last the property of a Paris music-publisher.

Now this music-publisher, deeply moved by its countless beauties, and no less touched on the other side by the growing pain of unallayed religious fervour among the high Parisian dilettanti, resolved to make his treasure public. With stealthy haste he was having the plates engraved when up there sprang another publisher, who with astounding cruelty clapped an injunction on his busy, hidden offering. That other publisher, a stiff-necked man by the name of *Troupenas*, maintained he had far better claims to the copyright of that *Stabat mater*, for his friend Rossini had pledged it to him against a huge consignment of pastry. He further averred that the work had been in his possession quite a number of years, and his only reason for not publishing it had been Rossini's wish to first provide it with a fugue or two, and a counterpoint in the seventh ; these, however, were still a hard task for the

master, as he had not quite completed his many years'
study with that end in view; nevertheless, the master of
late had gained so profound an insight into double counterpoint that his *Stabat* no longer pleased him in its present
shape, and he had decided under no conditions to lay
it thus—without fugues and such-like—before the world.*
Unfortunately Herr Troupenas' letters of authorisation
date merely from quite recent times; so that it would be
difficult for this publisher to prove his prior rights, did he
not believe he had one crushing argument, namely that so
long ago as the obsequies of the Emperor Napoleon on
December 15th, 1840, he had proposed this *Stabat* for
performance in the chapel of the Invalides.

A shriek of horror and indignation rose from every salon
of high Paris, when this latter statement was made known.
"What!" cried everyone: "A composition of Rossini's was
in existence,—it was offered you, and you Minister of Public
Affairs, you rejected it? You dared, instead, to foist on
us that hopeless Requiem by Mozart?"—In effect, the
Ministry trembled; all the more, as its uncommon popularity had made it most obnoxious to the upper classes.
It feared dismissal, an indictment for high treason, and
therefore held it opportune to spread a secret rumour that
Rossini's *Stabat mater* wouldn't at all have done for the
Emperor's obsequies as its text was concerned with quite
other things than were meet for Napoleon's shade to hear,
and so forth.—That this was merely a herring drawn across
the scent, one thought one saw at once; for one could
justly reply that not a creature understood this Latin text,
and finally—what mattered the text at all, if *Rossini's*

* According to Grove's Dictionary of Music, it was at the request of Aguado
that Rossini composed six numbers of his *Stabat Mater* in 1832 for the Spanish
Minister, Señor Valera, the work being then completed with four numbers by
Tadolini. In 1839 the heirs of Valera sold the MS. for 2,000 fr. to a Paris
publisher, at which Rossini was most indignant and instructed Troupenas to
stop the publication and performance. He then wrote the remaining four
numbers, and sold the whole to Troupenas for 6,000 fr. The first six
numbers were produced at the Salle Herz in Paris on Oct. 31, 1841; the
complete work was first performed at the Salle Ventadour, Jan. 7, 1842,
by Grisi, Albertazzi, Mario and Tamburini.—Tr.

heavenly melodies were to be sung by the most ravishing singers in the world?—

But the strife of parties round this fateful *Stabat mater* rages all the fiercer, since there is a further point involved in those awaited fugues. At last, then, is this mysterious class of composition about to be made presentable for salons of the higher dilettanti! At last, then, shall they learn the secret of that silly stuff which so racked their brains in Mozart's Requiem! At last will *they* be able, too, to boast of singing *fugues*; and these fugues will be oh! so charming and adorable, so delicate, so aërial! And these *counterpointlets*—they'll make everything else quite foolish,—they'll look like Brussels lace, and smell like patchouli!—What?—And without these fugues, without these counterpointlets, we were to have had the *Stabat*? How shameful! No, we'll wait till Herr Troupenas receives the fugues.—Heavens!—but there arrives a *Stabat*, straight from Germany! Finished, bound in a yellow cover!—There, too, are publishers who maintain they have sent baked goods to Rossini, at heavy prices! Is the bewilderment to have no end? Spain, France, Germany, all fall to blows around this *Stabat*:—Action! Fight! Tumult! Revolution! Horror!—

Then Herr *Schlesinger* decides to shed a friendly ray upon the night of trouble: he publishes a *Waltz by Rossini*. All smooth the wrinkles from their brow,—eyes beam with joy,—lips smile: ah! what lovely waltzes!—But Destiny descends:—Herr Troupenas impounds the friendly ray! That dreadful word: *Copyright*—growls through the scarce laid breezes. Action! Action! Once more, Action! And money is fetched out, to pay the best of lawyers, to get documents produced, to enter caveats.— — —O ye foolish people, have ye lost your liking for your gold? I know somebody who for five francs will make you five waltzes, each of them better than that misery of the wealthy master's!

Paris, 15th December, 1841.

＊　＊　＊

With the preceding I conclude the publication of my friend's literary remains, though they comprise several other papers that might not appear unentertaining in the feuilletonist sense of to-day. Among these were various Reports from Paris, whose flippant style I could only account for on the supposition that they were attempts of my poor friend to procure subsidies from some German journal through amusing contributions. Whether he succeeded at the time, God only knows! One thing is certain, that a bitter feeling has kept me from here reprinting for a critical posterity the Correspondence-articles dictated by his want.

Peace to his pure soul!

ON THE OVERTURE.

Über die Ouverture.

The following article originally appeared in the Gazette *Musicale of January 10, 14 and 17, 1841, under the title "De L'Ouverture." The few variants between the French and German forms I have noted* in loco.

TRANSLATOR'S NOTE.

I N earlier days a prologue preceded the play : it would appear that one had not the hardihood to snatch the spectator from his daily life and set him at one blow in presence of an ideal world ; it seemed more prudent to pave the way by an introduction whose character already belonged to the sphere of art he was to enter. This Prologue addressed itself to the spectator's imagination, invoked its aid in compassing the proposed illusion, and supplied a brief account of events supposed to have taken place before, with a summary of the action about to be represented. When the whole play was set to music, as happened in Opera, it would have been more consistent to get this prologue sung as well ; instead thereof one opened the performance with a mere orchestral prelude, which in those days could not fully answer the original purpose of the prologue, since purely instrumental music was not sufficiently matured as yet to give due character to such a task. These pieces of music appear to have had no other object than to tell the audience that singing was the order of the day. Were the weakness of the instrumental music of that epoch not in itself abundant explanation of the nature of these early overtures, one perhaps might suppose a deliberate objection to imitate the older prologue, as its sobering and undramatic tendence had been recognised ; whichever way, one thing is certain — the Overture was employed as a mere conventional bridge, not viewed as a really characteristic prelude to the drama.

A step in advance was taken when the general character of the piece itself, whether sad or merry, was hinted in its overture.* But how little these musical introductions could

* From here to the end of this paragraph the French differs a little :
' Ces ouvertures étaient courtes, consistaient souvent en un seul mouve-

be regarded as real preparers of the needful frame of mind,
we may see by Händel's overture to his *Messiah*, whose
author we should have to consider most incompetent, had
we to assume that he actually meant this tone-piece as an
Introduction in the newer sense.   In fact, the free development of the Overture, as a specifically characteristic piece
of music, was still gainsaid to those composers whose means
of lengthening a purely instrumental movement were confined to the resources of the art of counterpoint ; the com-
plex system of the " Fugue "—the only one at command for
the purpose—had to help them out with their prologues to
an oratorio or opera, and the hearer was left to decipher
the fitting mood from "dux " and " comes," augmentation
and diminution, inversion and stretto.

The great inelasticity of this form appears to have suggested the need of employing and developing the so-called
" symphony," a conglomerate of diverse types.   Here two
sections in quicker time were severed by another of slower
motion and soft expression, whereby the main opposing
characters of the drama might at least be broadly indi-
cated.   It only needed the genius of a Mozart, to create
at once a master-model in this form, such as we possess in
his symphony to the " Seraglio " ; it is impossible to hear

ment lent, et l'on peut retrouver les exemples les plus frappants de
ce mode de construction, quoique étendu considérablement, dans les
oratorios de Haendel.   Le libre développement de l'ouverture fut
paralysé par cette fâcheuse circonstance qui arrêtait les compositeurs dans
les premières périodes de la musique, à savoir l'ignorance où ils étaient
des procédés sûrs par lesquels on peut, à l'aide des hardiesses légères et
des successions de fraîches nuances, étendre un morceau de musique de
longue haleine.   Cela ne leur était guère possible qu'au moyen des finesses du
contre-point, la seule invention de ces temps qui permît à un compositeur de
dévider un thème unique en un morceau de quelque durée.   On écrivait des
fugues instrumentales ; on se perdait dans les détours de ces curieuses mons-
truosités de la spéculation artistique.   La monotonie et l'uniformité furent
les produits nets de cette direction.   Ces sortes de compositions étaient surtout
impuissantes à exprimer un caractère déterminé et individuel.   Haendel lui-
même ne paraît pas s'être aucunement soucié que l'ouverture s'accordât exactement avec la pièce ou l'oratorio.   Il est par exemple impossible de pressentir
par l'ouverture du *Messie* qu'elle doit servir d'introduction à une création aussi
fortement caractérisée, aussi sublime que l'est ce célèbre oratorio."—Tr.

this piece performed with spirit in the theatre, without obtaining a very definite notion of the character of the drama
which it introduces. However, there was still a certain
helplessness in this division into three sections, with a
separate tempo and character for each ; and the question
arose, how to weld the isolated fractions to a single
undivided whole, whose movement should be sustained
by just the contrast of those differing characteristic
motives.

The creators of this perfect form of overture were Gluck
and Mozart.

Even Gluck still contented himself at times with the
mere introductory piece of older form, simply conducting
to the first scene of the opera—as in *Iphigenia in Tauris*—
with which this musical prelude at anyrate stood mostly in
a very apt relation. Though even in his best of overtures
the master retained this character of an introduction to the
first scene, and therefore gave no independent close, he
succeeded at last in stamping on this instrumental number
itself the character of the whole succeeding drama. Gluck's
most perfect masterpiece of this description is the overture
to *Iphigenia in Aulis*. Here the master draws the main
ideas of the drama in powerful outline, and with an almost
visual distinctness. We shall return to this glorious work,
by it to demonstrate that form of overture which should
rank as the most excellent.

After Gluck, it was Mozart that gave the Overture its
true significance. Without toiling to express what music
neither can nor should express, the details and entanglements of the plot itself—which the earlier Prologue had
endeavoured to set forth—with the eye of a veritable poet
he grasped the drama's leading thought, stripped it of all
material episodes and accidentiæ, and reproduced it in
the transfiguring light of music as a passion personified in
tones, a counterpart both warranting that thought itself and
explaining the whole dramatic action to the hearer's feeling. On the other hand, there thus arose an entirely independent tone-piece, no matter whether its outward structure

was attached to the first scene of the opera or not. To most of his overtures, however, Mozart also gave the perfect musical close, for instance, those to the *Magic Flute*, to *Figaro* and *Tito*; so that it might surprise us to find him denying it to the most important of them all, the overture to *Don Giovanni*, were we not obliged to recognise in the marvellously thrilling passage of the last bars of this overture into the first scene a peculiarly pregnant termination to the introductory tone-piece of a *Don Giovanni*.

The Overture thus shaped by Gluck and Mozart became the property of Cherubini and Beethoven. Whilst Cherubini * on the whole remained faithful to the inherited type, Beethoven ended by departing from it in the very boldest manner. The former's overtures are poetical sketches of the drama's main idea, seized in its broadest features and musically reproduced in unity, concision and distinctness; this notwithstanding, we see by his overture to the *Water-Carrier* (*Deux Journées*) how even the dénouement of a stirring plot could be expressed in that form without damage to the unity of the artistic setting. Beethoven's overture to *Fidelio* (in E major) is unmistakably related to that of the *Water-Carrier*, just as the two masters approach the nearest to each other in these operas themselves. That Beethoven's impetuous genius in truth felt cramped by the limits thus drawn around it, however, we plainly perceive in several of his other overtures, above all in that to *Leonora*. Beethoven, never having obtained a fit occasion for the unfolding of his stupendous dramatic instinct, here seems to compensate himself by throwing the whole weight of his genius upon this field left open to his fancy, from pure tone-images to shape according to his inmost will the drama that he craved for; that drama which, freed from all the petty make-weights of the timid playwright, in this overture he let spring anew from a kernel magnified to

---

* The French had: "Il faut seulement remarquer que dans la manière de voir de ces deux grands compositeurs, qui ont du reste de nombreux points d'affinité, Cherubini" etc.—Tr.

giant size. One can assign no other origin to this wondrous overture to *Leonora* : far from giving us a mere musical introduction to the drama, it sets that drama more complete and movingly before us than ever happens in the broken action which ensues. This work is no longer an overture, but the mightiest of dramas in itself.

Weber cast his overtures in Beethoven's and Cherubini's mould, and though he never dared the giddy height attained by Beethoven with his *Leonora*-overture, he happily pursued the dramatic path without wandering to a toilsome painting-in of minor details in the plot. Even where his fancy bade him embrace more subsidiary motives in his musical picture than were quite consistent with the form of overture expressly chosen, he at least knew always to preserve the dramatic unity of his conception ; so that we may credit him with the invention of a new class, that of the "dramatic fantasia," whereof the overture to *Oberon* is one of the finest examples. This piece has had great influence upon the tendency of more recent composers ; in it Weber took a step that, with the truly poetic swing of his musical inventiveness, as we have seen, could but attain a brilliant success. Nevertheless it is not to be denied that the independence of purely-musical production must suffer by subordination to a dramatic thought, if that thought is not grasped in one broad trait congenial to the spirit of Music, and that the composer who would fain depict the details of an action cannot carry out his dramatic theme without breaking his musical work to atoms. As I propose to return to this point, for the moment I will content myself with the remark that the manner last described led necessarily downwards, inclining more and more towards the class of pieces branded with the name of "potpourri."

In a certain sense the history of this Potpourri begins with Spontini's overture to the *Vestale :* whatever fine and dazzling qualities one must grant this interesting tone-piece, it already shews traces of that loose and shallow mode of working-out which has become so prevalent in the operatic overtures of most composers of our age. To

forecast an opera's dramatic course, it was no longer a
question of forming a new artistic concept of the whole, its
complement and counterpart in music ; no, one culled from
here and there the most effective passages, less for their
importance than their showiness, and strung them bit ·by
bit together in a banal sequence. This was an arrangement
often even still more tellingly effected by potpourri-con-
coctors working on the same material later.* Highly
admired are the overture to *Guillaume Tell* by Rossini and
even that to *Zampa* by Herold, plainly because the public
here is much amused, and also, perhaps, because original
invention is undeniably displayed, especially in the former :
but a truly artistic ideal is no longer aimed at in such
works, and they belong, not to the history of Art, but to
that of theatrical entertainment.—

Having briefly reviewed the development of the Overture, and cited the most brilliant products of that class of
music, the question remains : To what mode of conception
and working-out shall we give the palm of fitness, and
consequently of correctness ? If we wish to avoid the
appearance of exclusiveness, an entirely definite answer is
no easy matter. Two unexampled masterpieces lie before
us, to which we must accord a like sublimity both of intention and elaboration, yet whose actual treatment and conception are totally distinct. I mean the overtures to *Don
Giovanni* and *Leonora.* In the first the drama's leading
thought is given in two main features ; their invention, as
their motion, belongs quite unmistakably to nothing but
the realm of Music. A passionate burst of arrogance
stands in conflict with the threatenings of an implacable
over-power, to which that arrogance seems destined to
submit : had Mozart but added the fearful termination of
the story, the tone-work would have lacked nothing to be

---

* This sentence was represented in the French by : "Pour un public auquel
on demandait ainsi moins de réflexion profonde, la séduction de cette manière
de procéder consistait tout à la fois dans un choix habile des motifs les plus
brillants et dans le mouvement agréable, dans le papillotage varié qui résultait
de leur arrangement.   C'est ainsi que naquirent l'ouverture si admirée de
Guillaume Tell" etc.—Tr.

regarded as a finished whole, a drama in itself; but the
master lets us merely guess the combat's outcome: in that
wonderful transition to the first scene he makes both hostile
elements bow beneath a higher will, and nothing but a
wailing sigh breathes o'er the place of battle.   Clearly and
plainly as is the opera's tragic principle depicted in this
overture, you shall not find in all the musical tissue one
single spot that could in any way be brought into direct
relation with the action's course; unless it were its introduction, borrowed from the ghost-scene—though in that
case we should have expected to meet the allusion at the
piece's end, and not at its beginning.*   No: the main body
of the overture is free from any reminiscence of the opera,
and whilst the hearer is fascinated by the purely-musical
development of the themes, his mind is given to the
changing fortunes of a deadly duel, albeit he never expects
to see it set before him in dramatic guise.

Now, that is just the radical distinction of this overture
from that to *Leonora*; while listening to the latter, we can
never ward off that feeling of breathless apprehension with
which we watch the progress of a moving action taking
place before our eyes.   In this mighty tone-piece, as said
before, Beethoven has given us a musical drama, a drama
founded on a playwright's piece, and not the mere sketch
of one of its main ideas, or even a purely preparatory introduction to the acted play: but a drama, be it said, in the
most ideal meaning of the term.†   The master's method,
so far as we here can follow it, lets us divine the depth of
that inner need which must have ruled him in conceiving
this titanic overture: his object was to condense to its
noblest unity the *one* sublime action which the dramatist
had weakened and delayed by paltry details in order to
spin out his tale; to give it a new, an ideal motion, fed
solely by its inmost springs.   This action is the deed of a
staunch and loving heart, fired by the one sublime desire
to descend as angel of salvation into the very pit of death.

* From "unless" to the end of the sentence, did not appear in the French.
—Tr.
† This last clause was absent from the French.—Tr.

One sole idea pervades the work : the freedom brought by a jubilant angel of light to suffering manhood. We are plunged into a gloomy dungeon ; no beam of day strikes through to us ; night's awful silence breaks only to the moans, the sighs, of a soul that longs from its deepest depths for freedom, freedom. As through a cranny letting in the sun's last ray, a yearning glance peers down : 'tis the glance of the angel that feels the pure air of heavenly freedom a crushing load the while its breath cannot be shared by you, close-pent within the prison's walls. Then a swift resolve inspires it, to tear down all the barriers hedging you from heaven's light : higher, higher and ever fuller swells the soul, its might redoubled by the blest resolve ; 'tis the evangel of redemption to the world.* Yet this angel is but a loving woman, its strength the puny strength of suffering humanity itself : it battles alike with hostile hindrances and its own weakness, and threatens to succumb. But the suprahuman Idea, which ever lights its soul anew, lends finally the superhuman force : one last, one utmost strain of every fibre, and the last bolt falls, the latest stone is heaved away. In floods the sunlight streams into the dungeon : " Freedom ! Freedom ! " shouts the redemptrix ; " Freedom ! Godlike freedom ! " the redeemed.

This is the Leonora-overture, *Beethoven's* poem. Here all is alive with unceasing dramatic progress, from the first yearning thought to the execution of a vast resolve.

But this work is unique of its kind, and no longer can be called an Overture, if we mean by that term a tone-piece destined for performance before the opening of a drama, merely to prepare the mind for the action's character. On the other hand, as we now are dealing, not with the musical artwork in general, but with the true vocation of the Overture in particular, this overture to *Leonora* cannot be accepted as a model, for it offers us in all-too-warm anticipation the whole completed drama in itself ; consequently it

---

* From " higher " to the end of the sentence was represented in the French by : " Semblable à un second messie, il veut accomplir l'œuvre de rédemption."—Tr.

either is un-understood or misconstrued by the hearer not already well-acquainted with the story, or, if thoroughly understood, it undoubtedly weakens the enjoyment of the explicit dramatic artwork it precedes.

Let us therefore leave this prodigious tone-work on one side, and return to the overture to *Don Giovanni*. Here we found the drama's leading thought delineated in a purely musical, but not in a dramatic shape. We un-hesitatingly declare this mode of conception and treatment to be the fittest for such pieces, above all because the musician here withdraws himself from all temptation to outstep the bounds of his specific art, i.e., to sacrifice his freedom. Moreover, the musician thus most surely attains the Overture's artistic end, to act as nothing but an ideal prologue, translating us to that higher sphere in which to prepare our minds for Drama. Yet this in nowise prevents the musical conception of the drama's main idea being given most distinct expression, and brought to a definite close ; on the contrary, the overture should form a musical artwork entire in itself.

In this sense we can point to no clearer and finer model for the Overture than that to Gluck's *Iphigenia in Aulis*, and will therefore endeavour to illustrate by this particular work our general conclusions as to the best method of con-ceiving an overture.*

Here again, as in the overture to *Don Giovanni*, it is a contest, or at least an opposition of two hostile elements, that gives the piece its movement. The plot of *Iphigenia* itself includes this pair of elements. The army of Greek heroes is assembled for a great emprise in common : under the inspiring thought of its execution, each separate human interest pales before this one great interest of the gathered mass. Now this is confronted with the special interest of preserving a human life, the rescue of a tender maiden. With what truth and distinctness of characterisation has Gluck as though personified these opposites in music ! In what sublime proportion has he measured out the two, and

* See also the special article upon this work in Vol. III.—Tr.

set them face to face in such a mode as of itself to give the conflict, and accordingly the motion! In the ponderous unison of the iron principal motive we recognise at once the mass united by a single interest, whilst in the subsequent theme that other interest, that interest of the tender suffering individual, forthwith arrests our sympathy. This solitary contrast is pursued throughout the piece, and gives into our hands the broad idea of old Greek Tragedy, for it fills us with terror and pity in turn. Thus we attain that lofty state of excitation which prepares us for a drama whose highest meaning is revealed to us already, and thus are we led to understand the ensuing action in this meaning.

May this glorious example serve as rule in future for the framing of all overtures, and demonstrate withal how much a grand simplicity in the choice of musical motives enables the musician to evoke the swiftest and the plainest understanding of his never so unwonted aims. How hard, nay, how impossible would a like success have been to Gluck himself, had he sorted out all kinds of minor motives to signal this or that occurrence of the drama's, and worked them in between these eloquent chief-motives of his overture; they here would either have been swallowed up, or have distracted and misled the attention of the musical hearer. Yet, despite this simplicity in the means employed, to sustain a longer movement it is permissible to give wider play to the drama's influence over the development of the main musical thought in its overture. Not that one should admit a motion such as dramatic action alone can supply, but merely such as lies within the nature of instrumental music. The motion of two musical themes assembled in one piece will always evince a certain leaning, a struggle toward a culmination; then a sure conclusion seems indispensable for our appeasement, as our feeling longs to cast its final vote on one or other side. As a similar combat of principles first lends to a drama its higher life, it is thus by no means contrary to the purity of music's means of effect to give its contest of tone-motives a termination in keeping with the drama's tendence. Cherubini, Beethoven, and Weber, were led by such a feeling in the conception of most of their overtures ; in that to the *Water-Carrier* this crisis is painted with the greatest definition ; the overtures to *Fidelio, Egmont, Coriolanus*, with that to the *Freischütz*, quite clearly express the issue of a strenuous fight. The point of contact with the dramatic story would accordingly reside in the character of the two main themes, as also in the motion given to them by their musical working-out. This working-out, on the other hand, would always have to spring from the purely musical import of those themes ; never should it take account of the sequence of events in the drama itself, since such a course would at once destroy the sole effectual character of a work of Tone.

In this conception of the Overture, then, the highest task would be to reproduce the characteristic idea of the drama by the intrinsic means of independent music, and to bring it to a conclusion in anticipatory agreement with the solution of the problem in the scenic play. For this purpose the composer will do well to weave into the characteristic motives of his overture certain melismic or rhythmic features which acquire importance in the dramatic action itself: not features strewn by accident amid the action, but such as intervene therein with determinant weight, and thus can lend the very overture an individual stamp—demarcations, as it were, of the special domain on which a human action runs its course. Obviously these features must be in themselves of purely musical nature, therefore such as bring the influence of the sound-world to bear upon our human life ; whereof I may cite as excellent instances the trombones of the Priests in the *Magic Flute*, the trumpet-signal in *Leonora*, and the call of the magic horn in *Oberon*.* These musical motives from the opera,

---

* In the French this sentence took the following form : " Mais on ne doit jamais perdre de vue qu'ils doivent être de source entièrement musicale et non emprunter leur signification aux paroles qui les accompagnent dans l'opéra. Le compositeur commetrait alors la faute de se sacrifier lui et l'indépendance de son art devant l'intervention d'un art étranger. Il faut, dis-je, que ces éléments soient de nature purement musicale, et je citerai comme exemples " etc.—Tr.

employed at a decisive moment in its overture, here serve
as actual points of contact of the dramatic with the musical
motion, and thus effect a happy individualisation of the
tone-piece, which in any case is meant as a suggestive
introduction to one particular dramatic story.

Now if we allow that the working-out of purely musical
elements in the overture should in so far accord with the
dramatic idea that even its issue should harmonise with
the dénouement of the scenic action, the question arises
whether the actual development of the drama or the
changes in the fortunes of its principal personages should
exert an immediate influence on the conception of the
overture, and above all on the characteristics of its close.
Certainly we could only · adjudge that influence a most
conditional exercise ; for we have found that a purely
musical conception may well embrace the drama's leading
thoughts, but not the individual fate of single persons.   In
a very weighty sense the composer plays the part of a
philosopher, who seizes nothing but the *idea* in all phenomena ; his business, as that of the great poet, lies solely
with the victory of an ·Idea ; the tragic downfall of the
hero, taken personally, does not affect him.*   From this
point of view, he holds aloof from the entanglements of
individual destinies and their attendant haps : he triumphs,
though the hero goes under.   Nowhere is this sublimest
conception more finely expressed than in the overture to
Egmont, whose closing section raises the tragic idea of the
drama to its highest dignity, and at like time gives us a
perfect piece of music of enthralling power.†   On the
other hand I know but one exception, of the first rank,

* In the French this sentence ran : "Le compositeur ne doit résoudre que la
question supérieure et philosophique de l'ouvrage, et exprimer immédiatement
le sentiment qui s'y répand et le parcourt dans toute son étendue comme un
fil conducteur.   Ce sentiment arrive-t-il dans le drame à un dénouement
victorieux, le compositeur n'a guère à s'occuper que de savoir si le héros de la
pièce remporte cette victoire, ou s'il. éprouve une fin tragique."—Tr.

† The French contained the following additional passage : "Le destin
élève [?-enlève] ici par un coup décisif le héros au triomphe.   Les derniers
accents de l'ouverture qui se montent à la sublimité de l'apothéose, rendent
parfaitement l'idée dramatique, tout en formant l'œuvre la plus musicale.   Le

Der Freischütz in Paris.
(1841.)

Of the following two articles, No. 1 appeared in the Gazette Musicale of May 23 and 30, 1841, with a note by the editor: "Bien que l'auteur de cet article professe sur la représentation du Freischütz à l'Opéra des idées contraires à celles qu'un de nos collaborateurs a déja exprimées, nous avons cru devoir accueillir son travail, parce qu'en toutes choses il est bon d'entendre les deux parties, et qu'il nous a semblé que nos lecteurs verraient avec plaisir le Freischütz considéré exclusivement sous son aspect germanique." The "contributor," herein referred to, was R. O. Spazier, the subject of whose remarks in the Gaz. Mus. of March 25, 1841, may be gathered from their title " Sur les récitatifs à ajouter à la partition du Freischütz."

The work was performed for the first time at the Grand Opéra on June 7, 1841.

Richard Wagner's second article is dated " Paris, den 20 Juni 1841," and appeared as the ' leader ' in the Dresden Abend-Zeitung of July 16, 17, 19, 20 and 21, 1841. The one article was therefore a preparation of the Paris public for the performance, the other an account of the said perform-ance transmitted to the German public.

TRANSLATOR'S NOTE.

I.

"Der Freischütz."

N the heart of the Bohemian Forest, old as the world, lies the "Wolfsschlucht"; its legend lingered till the Thirty Years War, which destroyed the last trace of German grandeur; but now, like many another boding memory, it has died out from the folk. Even at that time most men only knew the mystic gulch by hearsay: they would relate how some gamekeeper, straying on indeterminable paths through wild untrodden thickets, scarce knowing how, had come to the brink of the Wolf's-gulch. Returning, he had told of gruesome sights he there had seen, at which the hearer crossed himself and prayed the Saints to shield him from ever wandering to that region. Even on his approach the keeper had heard an eerie sound; though the wind was still, a muffled moaning swayed the branches of the ancient pines, which bowed their dark heads to and fro unbidden. Arrived at the verge, he had looked down into an abyss, whose depth his eye could never plumb: jagged reefs of rock stood high in shape of human limbs and terribly distorted faces; beside them heaps of pitch-black stones in form of giant toads and lizards; deeper down, these stones seemed living; they moved and crept and rolled in heavy, ragged masses; but under them the ground could no more be distinguished. From thence foul vapours rose incessantly, and spread a pestilential stench around; here and there they would divide, and range themselves in ranks that took the form of human beings with faces all convulsed. Upon a rotting tree-trunk in midst of all these

horrors sat an enormous owl, torpid in its day-time roost; behind it a frowning cavern, its entrance guarded by two monsters direly blent of snake and toad and lizard.   These with all the other seeming life the chasm harboured, lay in ·death-like slumber, and any movement visible was that of one plunged deep in dreams; so that the forester had dismal fears of what this odious crew might wake into at midnight.

But still more horrible than what he saw, was what he heard.   A storm that stirred nothing, and whose gusts he himself could not feel, howled over the glen, paused suddenly, as if listening to itself, and then broke out again with added fury.   Atrocious cries thronged from the pit: then a flock of countless birds of prey ascended from its bowels, spread like a pitch-black pall across the gulf, and fell back again to night.   The screeches sounded to the huntsman like the groans of souls condemned, and tore his heart with anguish never felt before: never had he heard such cries, compared to which the croak of ravens was as the song of nightingales.   And now again—deep silence: all motion ceased; only in the depths there seemed a sluggish writhing, and the owl once flapped its wings as though in dream.—

The most undaunted huntsman, the best-acquainted with the woods' nocturnal terrors, fled like a timid roe in speechless agony, and, heedless where his footsteps bore him, ran breathless to the nearest hut, the nearest cabin, to meet some human soul to whom to tell his horrible adventure, yet ne'er could find the words in which to frame it.   How ward himself from its remembrance?—

Happy the youth who bears within his heart a pious, faithful love: it alone can scare away that horror to which he deems himself foredoomed!   Is not the beloved his guardian spirit, the angel of grace that follows his every step, that shines within him and sheds content and peace upon his inner life?   Since he has loved, he is no longer the rough remorseless hunter, who revelled in the blood of his slaughtered game; his sweetheart has taught him to recognise the divine in Creation, to hear the mystic voices speaking to him from out the forest-stillness.   He often now feels seized with pity when the roe trips light and nimbly through the undergrowth ; he then fulfils his calling with reluctance, and can weep as he sees the tear-drops in the eye of the noble victim at his feet.

And yet he is bound to love the cruel sport ; for it is to his skill and certainty in firing, that he owes the right to sue the hand of his beloved.   The daughter of the Head-forester can wed with none but the successor to her father's office : to win that heirship, his "trial shot" must hit the aim on his bridal morn ; should he not then prove himself an expert marksman, should he miss, he loses forestry alike and bride.   So he now has to steel himself : hard and fast must his heart stand, if his eye is not to swerve, his hand to tremble.—Yet the closer the decisive time draws near, the more does fortune seem to plot against him.   Till then the best-skilled gunsman, it now will happen that he beats the woods for days without bringing home the smallest bag.   What evil star is dogging him ? Were it pity for his friends the wild-stock, that lames his eye and hand, how comes it that he fails when firing at that hawk, for which he has no spark of fellow-feeling ?   And why does he even miss the mark in target-practice, when it is a question of bringing his sweetheart back a silken prize to lay her anxious fears?   The old Head-forester shakes his head; the bride's anxiety is waxing every day : our keeper slinks through the woods, a prey to doleful thoughts.   He ponders his ill-luck, and tries to fathom it.   Then dawns on him the memory of that day when his fate once led him to the Wolf-glen's brink : the groans and creaking of the fir-trees, the hideous croaking of the sable swarm of birds, come back to vex his senses once again.   He believes himself the victim of a hellish power that, jealous of his happiness, has sworn his ruin.   And all he ever heard of the "wild huntsman " and his chase returns to him.   A hellish pack of hunters, horses, stags and hounds, that made night hideous with their cursed traffic of the woods.   Woe be to him who crossed their path! The human heart was all too weak to stand against the recollection of that din of weapons, bellowing of beasts, horn-calls, yelps of dogs and snorts of horses: who met the Savage Hunt, wellnigh invariably would die a short while after. The young keeper also called to mind the story of the leader of this ribald rout: a godless hunting-lord condemned to Hell, who now went forth as evil spirit, by the name of "Samiel," to win true huntsmen for his midnight revels. Oh! his comrade laughs away the legend of the Savage Hunt as moonshine, when our stripling tells him of his fears: yet it is just this wild and tricky fellow that himself awakes vague horror in him. In fact, the man is already in Samiel's clutches: he knows of secret means, of magic spells, whereby one may make certain of one's shot. He has told him that if one proceeds to a place he wots of at a given hour, and goes through certain easy incantations, one can call up spirits and bind them to one's service; if he will but follow him, he promises to get him bullets that shall hit the farthest mark at will: their name is "free-bullets," and he who uses them is called a "Freischütz" ("Free-shooter").

The youth had listened all aghast. Should he not believe in the agency of invisible spirits, when he, till then the surest marksman, could now no longer trust his gun, which never had missed his aim before? Already his peace of mind is troubled; both faith and hope within him reel. The all-important day draws near; his fortune, erewhile in his keeping, has fallen to the hands of hostile powers: with their own weapons must he vanquish them. His choice is made: where should he go, for the bullet-casting? To the Wolf's-gulch.—To the Wolf's-gulch?—At midnight?—His hair stands erect; for now he fathoms all. But he also knows that there is no alternative: Hell has him, wins he not his bride to-morrow. To give her up? Impossible! Courage alone can save him, and—courage he has. So he consents.—Yet once again he enters the Forester's house, at night-fall: pale, with a haunted look in his eye, he steps toward his beloved. The sight of that pure and pious maid to-day no longer calms him; her trust in God to him breathes scorn: who'll help him win his bride? Softly the foliage murmurs round the lonely house; a playmate seeks to cheer the troubled pair: brooding, he wildly stares into the night without. His sweetheart clasps him; her tender whispers are drowned in the awful groaning of those pitch-black firs that never leaves him, that calls him to them with the voice of death. He tears himself from the arms of his shuddering bride: to possess her, he will stake the welfare of his soul.—And out he storms: with wondrous certainty he finds the unknown track; the path seems lighted, that leads him to the pit of terror, where his comrade has already prepared the dismal work. In vain the warning spirit of his mother appears to him; the image of the bride whom he must lose to-morrow, if now he wavers, speeds him onward; he descends into the glen, and steps inside the circle of the necromantist. And Hell obeys: what the youth had dimly presaged when he saw the glen in daylight, at midnight is fulfilled. Everything awakens from its sleep of death: all stretches, stirs, and writhes; the howl becomes a roar, each groan a raving; a thousand goblins grin around the magic ring. Here must there be no flinching, or we are lost! The Wild Hunt storms over his head: his senses leave him; unconscious he sinks to the ground. How he ever awoke again?—

That night seven free-bullets were cast: six of them will hit any mark you please, beyond all fail; but the seventh belongs to him who blessed those six, and he will guide it as he pleases. The two gunsmen share: three to the bullet-moulder, four to the bride-wooer. The Prince has arrived, to direct the trial of skill: in rivalry for his favour, the Free-shooters waste their bullets on preliminary sports; it is the seventh which the bridegroom, now once more missing, takes up for the last and crowning shot. For this a white dove, just fluttering up, is given him as aim: he pulls the trigger, and his sweetheart, that moment threading through the bushes with her bridesmaids, lies bathed in blood. Samiel has claimed his wage: has he won for his Wild Hunt the luckless youth now overwhelmed by black despair?—

Thus the legend of the "Freischütz." * It seems to be the poem of those Bohemian woods themselves, whose sombre aspect lets us grasp at once how the lonesome forester would believe himself, if not the prey of a dæmonic nature-power, at least irrevocably subject to it. And that is just what constitutes the specifically German character of this and similar sagas: a character so strongly tinged by surrounding Nature, that to her we must ascribe the origin of a demonology that in other races, emancipated from a kindred influence, springs rather from the cast of their society and its prevailing religious, or so to say, its meta-physical views. Albeit terrible, this notion does not here

---

* In the foregoing account of the legend one or two quite immaterial details differ slightly from the French, but the whole setting of the present paragraph diverges sufficiently to call for quotation in full: "Telle est la tradition du *franc-tireur* (Freischütz); et, de nos jours, les chasseurs de ces contrées parlent encore de balles-franches. Cette tradition sombre, démoniaque, s'accorde parfaitement avec l'aspect solennel et mélancolique de ces formid-ables forêts de la Bohême. On comprend au premier coup d'œil le sens de ces récits populaires, quand on traverse ces solitudes, ces vallées coupées dans les rochers hérissés d'antiques sapins aux formes les plus bizarres. La tradi-tion du Freischütz porte d'ailleurs profondément l'empreinte de la nationalité allemande. Chez tout autre peuple, le diable eût été probablement de la partie; le diable est toujours en jeu partout où il arrive un malheur. Mais ce n'est que chez les Allemands que l'élément démoniaque pouvait se manifester sous des formes aussi mystiques, avec le caractère de mélancolie rêveuse; que la nature extérieure pouvait se confondre aussi intimement avec l'âme de l'homme, et produire des émotions aussi naïves et aussi touchantes. Partout ailleurs nous voyons le diable se mêler parmi la société des hommes, inspirer des sorciers et des sorcières, les abandonner au bûcher ou les sauver de la mort selon son bon plaisir; nous le voyons même revêtir le caractère de père de famille, et veiller au *salut* de son fils. Mais ces récits, le paysan le plus grossier n'y croit plus de nos jours; tandis que les contes et traditions qui ont leur origine dans les régions les plus mystérieuses de la nature et du cœur humain éveillent encore aujourd'hui les sympathies des gens instruits; ils aiment à se reporter aux jours de leur enfance où les grands arbres des sombres forêts, s'agitant au souffle de la tempête, leur paraissaient des êtres vivants, dont les voix mystérieuses étaient comme l'écho d'un monde fan-tastique."—Tr.

become downright remorseless : a gentle sadness shimmers through its awe, and the lament over Nature's lost Paradise knows how to soften the forsaken mother's vengeance. And that is just the German type. Everywhere else we see the Devil communing with men, obsessing witches and magicians, and saving or abandoning them to the stake according to his humour; we even see him figuring as father of a family, and sheltering his sons with dubious tenderness. In that the very rawest peasant no more believes to-day, because such incidents are laid too baldly in conventional life, where they quite certainly take place no longer : but happily the mystic converse of the human heart with its own surrounding Nature is not yet done away with; for in her sounding silences she speaks to it to-day just as she did a thousand years gone by, and what she told it in the days of hoary eld it understands to-day as well as ever. And so these Nature-sagas come to be the Poet's never-failing element of discourse with his folk.

But only midst this people that once shaped the legend of the " Freischütz," and still feels drawn by it, could it occur to a gifted tone-poet to compose a great musical work to a drama based thereon. If he rightly seized the keynote of the popular poem submitted to him, and if he felt the power to make his music call into full mystic life what here was hinted by a characteristic action,* he also knew that from the first mysterious accents of his overture to the ever-childlike ditty of the " Jungfernkranz " his folk would throughly understand him in its turn. And in effect, by glorifying the old folk-saga of his home the artist was ensuring himself an unparalleled success. In admiration of the accents of this pure and pregnant elegy his countrymen from North and South united, from the ad-herents of Kant's " Criticism of pure Reason " to the readers of the Vienna " Journal des Modes." The Berlin phil-

* From "if he felt" to "action " was not represented in the French. The "*Jungfernkranz*" is the " Bridal wreath" chorus sung in the third act; it will be remembered (Vol. I. p. 3) that this " Jungfernkranz " was one of the tunes that Geyer got his stepson, the seven-year-old Richard Wagner, to play to him the day before his death.—Tr.

osopher hummed : " The bridal wreath for thee we bind " ;
the Police-director repeated with enthusiasm : " Through
the woods and through the meadows " ; whilst the court-
lackey hoarsely sang : " The joy of the hunter,"—and I
myself remember having practised, as a child, a quite
diabolical turn of voice and gesture to give due rugged-
ness to " In this earthly vale of woe." The Austrian
grenadier was marched to the tune of the hunting-chorus,
Prince Metternich danced to the Ländler of the Bohemian
rustics, and the Jena students fired off the mocking-chorus at
their tutors. Here the most opposite tendencies of political
life met at one common centre : from one end of Germany
to the other the " Freischütz " was heard, sung, and danced.

And you too, ye promenaders in the Bois de Boulogne,
have trilled the music of the Freischütz : the barrel-organs
have sounded out the hunting-chorus on the boulevards ;
the Opéra Comique has not disdained the Jungfernkranz,
and the exquisite aria: " Softly sighing " has many a time
bewitched the audience in your salons.—But, do you
really understand what you are singing ?—I very much
doubt it. The grounds of my doubt are hard to explain,
most certainly not easier than this outlandish German
nature from which those strains arose ; and I almost
think I should have to begin with that " Wood," which
you surely do not know. The " Bois " is something
quite different, almost as different as your " *rêverie* " from
our susceptibility (*Empfindsamkeit*).* Indeed we are a
singular nation: " Through the woods and through the
meadows " will move us to tears, whilst we can look with
barren eyes on a fatherland split into four-and-thirty prince-
doms. Ye who only kindle into real enthusiasm when it is
a question of " *la France*," to you this certainly must seem

---

† From " The grounds of my doubt " to this point, the French again somewhat differs : " D'abord vous n'avez pas vu cette nature si étrangement
sauvage ; et puis dans la sentimentalité, dans la rêverie allemande il y a quelque
chose qui échappera toujours aux étrangers, si spirituels qu'ils puissent être."
Further, the opening of the next sentence but one, " Ye who only kindle into
real enthusiasm when it is a question of ' *la France*,' " did not appear in the
G. M.—Tr.

a weakness ; but just that weakness must you share in, if you are rightly to understand our "*durch die Wälder, durch die Auen*" ; for it is the selfsame weakness to which you owe this wonderful score of the "Freischütz," which you now desire to have exactly rendered to you,—surely with the aim of making its acquaintance in a manner that you never will.* You refuse to depart from Paris and its habits by a hair's-breadth : thither shall the Freischütz come, and present himself to you; you bid him, though, to take his ease and make himself at home ; for you wish to hear and see him as he really is, no longer in the costume of "*Robin des bois*," but openly and simple-heartedly, somewhat like the "*Postillon de Lonjumeau*" : so you say. But all this is to happen in the "*Académie royale de musique*," and that honourable institute has precepts which must make it very hard for the poor Freischütz to behave himself *sans gêne*. There stands it written : "Thou shalt dance!" This he does not ; for he is much too sore at heart, and lets the rustics twirl their sweethearts in the inn behind him. Then comes : "Thou shalt not speak, but sing Recitative" ; but here we have a dialogue of the utmost naïvety. Well, well : but from ballet-dancing and recitative-singing you absolutely cannot exempt him, for it is in the great "Grand Opéra" that he is to present himself.

There perhaps might be a simple means of meeting the difficulty,—to make an exception, for once, in favour of the glorious work. But that means you will not use, for you are only free when you wish to be ; and here, alas ! you do

---

* The last part of this sentence, with its immediate successor, took another form in the *Gazette*, pretty obviously owing to the editor's not caring to let the "aspect germanique" be too thorough : "C'est peut-être là une faiblesse, mais vous nous la pardonnerez, car c'est à elle que vous devez une admirable partition, qui mérite bien, du reste, la peine de faire un voyage, et de visiter les lieux où Samiel avait sa résidence. Un voyage à Carlsbad vous en offrirait facilement l'occasion. Si vous pensez que cela n'en vaut pas le peine, si vous ne pouvez renoncer pour une seule soirée à vos habitudes et à tout ce qui fait le charme de la vie parisienne, alors vous ne comprendrez pas le Freischütz, et pourtant vous voulez le comprendre, vous voulez l'entendre et le voir tel qu'il est ; c'est fort bien, et c'est tout juste, car vous en agissez de même avec *le Fidèle Berger*."—Tr.

M

not wish it.   You had heard of the "Wolf's-gulch" and a
devil named "Samiel," and at once the whole machinery
of Grand Opera came thronging to your mind : the rest is
naught to you.   You wanted Ballet and Recitative, and
have chosen the most original of your composers to make
the music for them.   That *him* you have chosen, honours
you, and proves that you value our master-work.   I know
no single living French musician who would understand
the score of the "Freischütz" so well as the author of the
"*Symphonie fantastique*," or be so qualified to supplement
it, were that needful.   He is a man of genius, and none
knows better than myself the resistless force of his poetic
verve ; he has a conscientious conviction that will let him
follow nothing but the imperious dictates of his talent, and
each of his Symphonies reveals the inner necessity from
which the author could not tear himself.—But my very
regard for M. *Berlioz's* eminent ability emboldens me to
lay my thoughts upon his work before him.

The score of the "Freischütz" is a perfect whole, in idea
and form alike complete in all its members.   To omit the
tiniest portion, would it not be to maim or mutilate the
master's work ?   Is it here, perhaps, a question of adapting
to the canons of our time a score arisen in the infancy of
art, of remodelling a work whose by-gone author had not
sufficiently developed it, through ignorance of the technical
means that stand at our command to-day ?   Everyone
knows that such a thing cannot be talked of ; and Mons.
Berlioz would be the first to reject such a proposal with
indignation.   No, it is a matter of bringing a perfect and
individual work into harmony with claims quite alien to it.
And how ?   A score crowned with twenty years of success,
a score in whose honour the Royal Academy of Music
means to depart for once from its otherwise so stringent
laws excluding foreign works from its repertoire, in order
to share in one of the most brilliant triumphs ever reaped
by any piece at any theatre,—such a score could not
suspend certain rules of tradition and routine ?   And one
durst not ask for it to appear in its original form, that

makes out so essential a part of its individuality ? Is that
really the sacrifice that one demands ? Or do you think
I am deluding myself? Do you believe that the ballets
and recitatives which you interpolate, will not distort the
physiognomy of Weber's work? When you replace a
naïve and often humorous dialogue by a recitative which
always dawdles in the singer's mouth, don't you think you
will efface the stamp of robust heartiness that marks the
scenes of the Bohemian rustics ? Must not the chatty confidences of the two maidens in the lonely forest-house
be shorn of their freshness and sincerity ? And however
happily these recitatives may be devised, however artistic-
ally they harmonise with the general colour of the work,
they nevertheless will mar its symmetry. It is obvious
that the German composer had a constant regard to the
dialogue : the vocal pieces are scant of length ; they must
be completely crushed by the added mass of recitatives,
and necessarily lose in sense, and therefore in effect.

In this drama, where the *Lied* has a deep sense and
such high importance, you will find none of those rushing
Ensemble-pieces, those overpowering Finales, to which
your grand operas have accustomed you. In the " Muette,"
in the " Huguenots," in " La Juive," because of the great
dimensions of the formal pieces it is essential for the
intervals to be filled by recitatives ; here spoken dialogue
would seem petty, foolish, and an utter parody. How
strange it would sound, in fact, were Masaniello suddenly to
begin to talk between the grand duet and the finale of the
second act of the " Muette "; and, after the ensemble-
number in the fourth act of the " Huguenots," if Raoul
and Valentine were to prepare themselves for the subsequent great duet by a dialogue, however choice its diction !
To be sure ; and rightly it would offend you. But what
becomes an æsthetic necessity with these operas of grand
dimensions, for the opposite reason must utterly ruin the
" Freischütz," whose vocal pieces are of far less extent. I
see in advance that, wherever the situations in the dialogue
demand dramatic emphasis, Mons. Berlioz will give free

rein to his abundant fancy; I foretell the expression of
lurid energy which he will give to the scene where Caspar
seeks to trap his youthful friend in his demonic toils,
inciting him to handsel the free-bullet, and, eager to enlist
him for the banner of Hell, addresses him the fatal
questions: "Coward! Deem'st thou this guilt does not
already lie upon thee? Deem'st thou that eagle but a
gift?" I am quite certain that at this passage a storm of
applause will reward the splendid inspirations of Mons.
Berlioz; but I am equally persuaded that, after that
recitative, Caspar's drastic arietta at the close of this act
will pass by as a piece not calling for special attention.

So you will have something quite new, quite wonderful
if you will; and we who know the Freischütz, and need
no supplemental recitatives for its understanding, shall be
pleased to see the works of Mons. *Berlioz* augmented by
a new creation, yet shall doubt whether it has aided you
to understand our "Freischütz." You will revel in a
music alternately graceful and demonic, that will charm
your ears, in turn, or make you shudder; you will hear
songs sung in marvellous perfection, that had hitherto
been given you but middlingly; a fine dramatic declama-
tion will bear you duly from one vocal number to the
next: yet, 'spite all this, you'll be annoyed at missing
many things to which you're used. The facings tacked
to *Weber's* work can only call awake in you the need of
fresh incentives to the senses, and indeed that very need
to which the works habitually presented to you with such
facings correctly correspond; your expectation will be
disappointed, however, for just this work was fashioned
by its author with quite another aim, and by no means to
comply with the requirements of the Royal Academy of
Music. Where five musicians, on our stages, take fiddle
and horn in hand before a tavern-door, and a few sturdy
peasants spin their bouncing sweethearts round and round,
you suddenly will see deployed before you all the choreo-
graphic treasures of the day; the smiling man of entrechats,
who yesternight was strutting in his lovely golden gown,

you will see receiving seriatim in his arms the elegant sylphides; and these last will strive in vain to shew to you Bohemian rustic dances; all the time you will miss their pirouettes and high-art capers: yet they will give you just enough of your accustomed pleasures to make you ask for more; to you they will recall the brilliant works of your illustrious authors, which so often have enraptured you, and at least you'll want to see a piece like "Guillaume Tell," where also figure hunters, herds, and other pretty things pertaining to a country life. After these dances, however, you will neither see nor hear another atom of the kind: in the first act you have, all told, the aria "Durch die Wälder, durch die Auen," a drinking-song of twenty bars, and in lieu of a rousing finale the singular musical sputterings of a satanic villain, which you cannot possibly accept as an aria. But I am forgetting: you will have whole scenes in recitative of such drastic musical originality as—I am convinced of it in advance—but few have ever been written; for I know how the inventive genius of your greatest instrumental composer will feel moved to add none but grand and beautiful ideas to the masterpiece he honours and admires: and for that very reason—you will not make acquaintance with the "Freischütz," and—who knows?—perhaps what you do hear of it, will even slay the wish to ever greet it in its pristine naïvety.

Yet, if it were really to step before you in its pureness and simplicity, if, instead of the intricate dances that will announce the bridesmaids' entry on your boards, you merely had the little ditty—which the Berlin philosopher so loves to hum, as I have said—and instead of these splendid recitatives you only heard the simple dialogue which every German student knows by heart, would you then acquire a genuine understanding of the "Freischütz"? Would it rouse with you that consentaneous volley of applause which the "Muette de Portici" evoked from us? Ah! I much doubt it; and perchance a similar doubt oppressed his spirit like a leaden cloud, when the Director of your Grand

Opéra* commissioned Mons. Berlioz to fit the "Freischütz" out with ballet and recitative. It is a great good-fortune that Mons. Berlioz, of all others, was entrusted with this task; certainly, out of piety towards the work and its master, no German composer would have dared to undertake it, and in France Mons. Berlioz stands alone at height of such a venture. At least we have the warranty that, down to the seemingly most trivial note, everything will be respected, nothing cut, and only so much added as is needful to comply with the requirements of the laws of the "Grand Opéra," laws ye once for all believe ye dare not overpass. And it is just this last, that gives me sad forebodings for our dear-loved "Freischütz." † Ah! Would ye, could ye, hear and see our own true "Freischütz," perhaps ye then might feel what fills me now with mournful visions, might feel it as a friendly presage of the peculiar essence of that inward contemplative spirit which is bred in the German nation as its birthright; ye would strike a friendship with that quiet trend which lures the German from the life of his great cities—all poorly copied from abroad—to Nature, to the Forest-solitude, there to revive from time to time those wonderful ur-feelings for which your very language has no words, but which those mystic tones of *Weber's* express as plainly as—your splendid trappings and narcotic arts of Opera must necessarily, alas! efface and make them indiscernible to you. And yet! Attempt it, through this strangely-laden atmosphere attempt to breathe the freshness of our woods! Only, I fear that in the best event the unnatural blend will discontent you.

* " Mons. Pillet " in the French.—Tr.

† From this point I quote the French, to the end of the article : " Ah ! si vous pouviez, si vous vouliez voir et entendre le véritable *Freischütz* allemand, peut-être seriez vous initiés à cette vie intime et méditative de l'âme qui est l'apanage de la nation allemande ; vous vous familiariseriez avec les douces et candides émotions qui vous font tour à tour désirer la présence de la bien-aimée et la solitude des bois ; peut-être comprendriez-vous cette horreur mystérieuse, ces sensations indéfinissables pour lesquelles votre langue n'a pas de nom, et que par de magnifiques décors, par des masques diaboliques, vous cherchez vainement à traduire. Dans tous les cas, cela vaut la peine d'aller à la représentation que donnera l'Académie royale de musique, et de chercher à se transporter par la pensée au milieu du monde merveilleux qui se révèle dans *le Freischütz*."—Tr.

2.

"Le Freischütz."

MY glorious German fatherland, how can I else than love thee, how fondly must I dote upon thee, were it only that from out thy soil there sprang the "Freischütz"! Needs must I love the German Folk that loves the "Freischütz," that eke to-day believes the marvels of its most naïve Saga, that e'en to-day, in full-grown manhood, still feels those sweet mysterious thrills which made its heart beat fast in youth! Ah! thou adorable German reverie; thou *Schwärmerei* of woods and gloaming, of stars, of moon, of village-bells when chiming seven at eve! Happy he who understands you, can feel, believe, can dream and lose himself with you! How dear it is to me, that *I*, too, am a German!—

This, and much more I ne'er can tell, came piercing lately through my heart, as though 'twere stabbed by gladness; I felt a burning wound, which ploughed its way up to the brain, yet in place of blood—it made the most ecstatic tears to flow. What it was that dealt this dagger-thrust of bliss, and how it came about,—*that* I can tell no soul in all this great, this splendid Paris; for here the folk are mostly Frenchmen, and the French are a merry nation, full of quip and quirk : right sure, they'd only wax the merrier, and cut more quips and better quirks, were I to tell them *what* it was that dealt me that divinely healing blow.

But you, my gifted German countrymen, you will not laugh; you'll understand me when I tell you :—it was a passage in the "Freischütz." 'Twas where the rustic lads had taken their lasses by the hand, and waltzed them off to the tavern ; the forest swain sat lonely at the table in the open—downcast and brooding on his evil luck ;—the evening shades grew darker yet and darker, and faintly from the distance came the blithe dance-music of the horns. —I wept when I saw and heard all this, and my neighbours in the Paris Opéra believed I had come by a grave misfortune.   When I had wiped away my tears I polished up my glasses, and resolved to write about the "Freischütz" [for the *Abend-Zeitung*—orig.].   In course of the performance the French took pains to furnish me with a mass of stuff for my projected article ; but, properly to master it, you must let me go logically to work, as the French are so uncommonly fond of doing, and begin at the beginning.—

Without doubt you know well enough, my favoured German countrymen, that no folk on earth is so perfect in itself as not to need, upon occasion, to adopt the good things of another ; you know it, and can speak from personal experience.   So it came to pass, one day, that the most perfect nation upon earth—for everyone knows that the French at least consider themselves as such—took it into its head to follow the general custom, and see, for once in a way, what its respected neighbours had really got to offer in exchange for all the thousand glorious things which, year in year out, it had nursed the generous habit of showering so richly on them.   The French had heard that the "Freischütz" was a first-class thing, and therefore resolved to make a trial of its quality. . Indeed, they called to mind a piece with charming music which had been played to them about three-hundred times, and which people said was taken from that "Freischütz."   One called it "*Robin des bois*," and assured them that French Culture had done its best to make the thing both logical and tasty ; so that they could not but believe—especially as it had had a great success—that whatever was good in this "*Robin des bois*" must be set to the credit of French art, and hence that they really had only heard and seen a French piece with a handful of nice foreign couplets mixed in ; ergo, that it still remained for them to make a genuine acquaintance with the German national-product. On the whole, they were not far wrong in this belief. Wherefore the Director of the Grand Opéra, as the supreme representative of the French art-will, decided to let his singers study and present the "Freischütz" as large as life ; apparently with the object of shewing the Germans that in Paris, too, one had some sense of justice.

True, there is another version of this Paris Freischütz-saga : folk say that a simple publisher's speculation afforded the poetic stimulus, and that the astute Director embraced it the more willingly as his exchequer had been brought into such terribly low water through the everlasting failures of the solidest French composer-banks, that he thought good to raise a despairing loan from a house whose credit stood so high as the German "Freischütz." Whatever the rights of the case may be, the usual stock of high-flown phrases was to be expected as a matter of course ; one was bound to talk of a brilliant homage which one thought it only fitting to accord a foreign masterpiece,—that goes without saying ; and, as it is our bounden duty to yield an unconditional belief to the French whenever they parade their fanatical unselfishness, let us take it for absolutely granted that this is the authentic tale.— —It was resolved, then, to give the "Freischütz" *as it is*, chiefly because one could not give its "*Robin des bois*" arrangement—that being the property of the Opéra Comique—and because, on the other hand, the extraordinary success of that arrangement had proved there must be something splendid at back of this Freischütz, namely silver, gold, and banknotes galore. The Director determined to embark on a voyage of discovery after these excellent objects, and constituted the magnates of his realm a discovery-council to help him heave to light the treasure.

The discovery-council held a sitting ; but the first thing it discovered, was the difficulty of making the clumsy foreign Freischütz presentable at the court of the very grand Opéra.

A terrible shock :—there was no logic in the text ; moreover it was German, so that no one, to say nothing of a Frenchman, could possibly understand it.   Both these disagreeables one decided to amend, by selecting an *Italian* to translate the un-logical *German* book into *French.*   This, at any rate, was a happy thought ; the main affair, however, the question of title, neither the Italian nor the Frenchman could settle satisfactorily.   "*Il franco arciero*" was really too Italian,* and "*Franc-tireur*" might have been intelligible to a German, perchance, but never to a Frenchman. , So one hit on the expedient of calling it "*Le Freischutz*" ; whereby one at least had the advantage of avoiding all possibility of being misunderstood.

As soon as one had come to terms about the title and Herr Pacini was commissioned to translate the textbook into French, also to supply it with as much logic as possible, the Statutes of the Grand Opéra announced themselves with stiff-necked majesty.   One well-dressed giant rose to his feet, and bade : "*Let there be dance* ! "—Everyone was horrified, for, hunt as one would in the score of the Freischütz, nowhere was an *air de danse* to be found.   The distress was great ; no one knew after which passage, in this hopeless music, one was to introduce the man with the golden-yellow satin suit, and the two ladies with the long legs and short skirts.   Surely not to the beat of the common *Ländler*, which lay between one's finger and thumb just before the air of Max ?   Perhaps after the huntsman's chorus, or the air : "Wie nahte mir der Schlummer " ?— It was enough to make a man despair !   Yet dancing must somehow or other be done, and the "Freischütz" must obtain a ballet-number, however much one had made up one's mind to give it no otherwise than "as it is."   But

* This title was used, however, for the Italian performance at Covent Garden Theatre, March 16, 1850, the recitatives being then supplied by Costa.—Tr.

one rose superior to all scruples of conscience when one suddenly remembered that Weber himself, of course, had written an "Invitation to the Dance"; * who could raise the smallest objection to one's accepting the selfsame master's invitation ?—Everyone embraced, for very joy :— things seemed like going right at last.

Then up there sprang another giant Statute, and said : " *Ye shall not speak* ! "—The unhappy council of discovery had clean forgotten that the singers of this Freischütz have quite as much to say as to sing, and fell into a fresh despair. Each man stared glum and gloomily at space ; the Director questioned Fate, as to whatever was to become of this *original* representation of the Freischütz ? Here there was no way out to find ;—the recitatives from " Euryanthe " would not fit in at all ; otherwise one might have eked it out with them, just as one had helped oneself to the "Invitation to the Dance." A bold game must here be played, and the dialogue turned into Recitative itself.— Since there was no *Italian* handy, to compose these recitatives as well ; since, moreover, the *Spaniards* are troubling themselves mighty little with music just now, and the *English* were too busy with their Corn-bill to be able to take up the composition of recitatives for a *German* Freischütz,—one naturally must choose a Frenchman ; and as Herr Berlioz already had written a deal of droll, eccentric music, so in the belief of the discovery-council no one could be more fit than *he*, to add a dash of extra music to this droll, original Freischütz.

Herr Berlioz congratulated the "Freischütz" on having fallen into his hands ; for he knew it and was fond of it, and also knew that under *his* operations it would suffer the least disfigurement. With the conscientiousness of a true artist, he resolved to alter not one note of Weber's score, to omit nothing, neither anything to add, but what the Director and his discovery-council had thought needful in

---

* Berlioz employed this piece (orchestrated by himself) and some dance-tunes from Weber's *Preciosa* for a " divertissement " added to the " fête du tire " in the third act.—Tr.

compliance with the tyrannic statutes of the Opéra. He felt that, so far as possible, the same honour must be shewn this opera as we in Germany bestow, for instance, on "*Fra Diavolo*" and the "*Domino Noir*," which we reproduce in their entire original shape, neither adding Bach-ian fugues and eight-voiced motets, nor omitting intellectual couplets such as: "Hé! to and fro, Postilion of Lonjumeau!" *

However, despite my knowledge that our beloved Freischütz was in the best French hands, I could not clear my German heart of grave misgivings as to the outcome of the undertaking. It was impossible for me to believe that the selfsame Frenchmen who knew no means, in all the world, to admit our Freischütz to their stage in its own original shape, would be able to take it in and understand it when brought before their eye and ear externally distorted. Therefore, in a burst of patriotic zeal, I resolved to tell the Paris public my views anent the proposition, and got an article printed in which I spoke my mind without reserve or fear. Before all, I thought it well to acquaint the French somewhat more minutely with the nature of the Freischütz legend. So far as in me lay, I explained to them the meaning of a "*franc-tireur*"; what one was to understand by a "*balle-franche*"; what sort of affair was a *Jungfernkranz*; in short—all those things which every child at school, with us, has at his fingers' ends. With these I threw in some remarks about the Bohemian woods and the German dreamery; for no Frenchman can conceive a German without woods and dreaming,—a circumstance which stood me here in excellent stead. I went on, however, to express my anxieties; pointing out to the public the injurious effect of the male dancer in the suit of golden-yellow satin, and the two ladies with the

---

* "So schön und froh, Postillon von Lonjumeau!"—In this case Wagner has brought matters up to date in his 1871 edition;—Adam's *Postillon de Lonjumeau* being even yet a favourite on the German stage. The original "couplet" chosen, was "O kommt zum treuen Schäfer, kehret ein!" ("Approach your faithful shepherd, hither turn!"), from the German version of Adam's *Le fidèle Berger* (Paris, 1838), the title of that work then filling the place now taken by "*Fra Diavolo*."—Tr.

long legs and short petticoats—upon the simple structure
of the original work. Above all, I prepared it for the
harm that would be sure to arise from the many exceedingly short pieces of the original opera being lost among
the recitatives, which necessarily must take up a disproportionate amount of time, thus damaging the impression
of those airs and songs; to say nothing of the misfortune
that the crisp, and often naïve dialogue of the German
book must part with all its meaning and life under the
very best musical treatment.—I thus did what I thought
needful to vindicate our national property *in advance*, in
the wellnigh inevitable event of a failure of the forthcoming
experiment.

—Everyone was against my opinion; I was cried down and
told that I over-estimated the Freischütz' claims to originality. Unhappily, however, my prophecy was almost literally
fulfilled. After the performance, many people admitted
that I was right; but others maintained that our Freischütz
was good for nothing. I am convinced that these latter are
in the wrong;—but, to account for their horrible dictum,
to gain some faint idea of how these people could come by
the notion that the Freischütz was a piece of rubbish, one
necessarily must have also heard and seen its performance
at the theatre of the *Académie royale de Musique.*—

To Herr Berlioz it had not been possible to secure the
Opéra's best singers for the rôles in the Freischütz: he,
the public, and the work itself, were forced to put up with
the second class of that creation; and suffice it to say, that
even the *first* is not worth much. The singers of the
second class are children of darkness, and very often
laughed to scorn. Everybody is aware that that is not
conducive to a good general effect, even with French
operas; with our glorious *Freischütz*—in which there
already is so much to tickle the national predisposition
of the French—this second variety of singer made an
amusing effect, no doubt, but scarcely an inspiring one.
For my own part I laughed a good deal, even when the

French kept serious; for when I had finally arrived at the conviction that I was seeing God knows what—only *not* my beloved Freischütz—I cast all pious scruples to the winds and laughed more crazily than any of my neighbours, save just at the beginning, at the place where, as already said, I wept.

Taking things all round, one may safely assume that the whole personnel of the Paris Grand Opéra was *dreaming*:—for that my unlucky article may have to bear some part of blame, as I had directed the public to woods and dreamery. To me it appeared that my hint had been laid to heart and carried out with terrible punctiliousness;—of woods the scene-painters naturally had not been stingy, so that there seemed nothing left for the singers but to give their whole mind to the dreamery. Beyond this, they whined a deal at times, and *Samiel* even shivered. This shivering of Samiel's I necessarily must discuss at once, for it was the point where all my scruples melted to a beneficial mirth.

Samiel was a slim young man, of about five-and-twenty years; he wore a lovely Spanish costume, above which he had thrown a black-crape mantle. The expression of his face was highly interesting, much helped, no doubt, by his beautiful whiskers; for the rest, he was of a merry, sprightly temper, and played with great skill the rôle of a Paris detective. Bending forward, with finger to mouth, he kept drawing near to Max all through that unfortunate young huntsman's aria with charming caution, as though to catch what Max was singing,—for the matter of that, a very hard thing to accomplish, for even the public, in spite of its textbooks, was often in doubt as to whether he was singing Italian or French. Once, at the point where Max had travelled to the brink of the footlights in order to put his mad question to Fate, Samiel came so close upon his heels that he actually took in the word "*dieu*," shot out with overwhelming force; this word seems to have made a most disagreeable impression upon him, however, for hardly had he grasped it than he felt impelled to execute a shivering scene the like of which I never saw before, not even at a French theatre. All the world knows to what perfection the French actors and actresses have brought the art of shivering; but Samiel's performance made all the rest mere child's-play.—The stage of the Grand Opéra, as you will readily believe, is very broad and very deep; so that you may imagine what a stretch of road there lay, from Max's position at the extreme left of the footlights to the extreme right background, for Samiel to cover with a perpetual shivering of his hands, legs, head and trunk, after he had heard that—to him—so distressing word. He had trembled himself away for a considerable time, and yet had only reached the middle of the stage; in view of the terrible exertion this manœuvre must have cost him, it was therefore to be feared that he would drop before he reached his shelter in the background. On French stages, however, nothing occurs without full calculation; here, too, the manager had reckoned up the loss of Samiel's strength, and given his order to the machinist to drag the Wild Hunter down into a trap. This order was strictly carried out, and at the very nick of time; a flash of lightning, which momentarily took the place of Samiel, did its part in rounding off the whole effect; and we had the satisfaction of supposing that the godless shiverer would find time and succour in his subterranean quarters, to recover from his unexampled fatigue.

Max gave decided preference to the dreamy side of his character. Beneficial as this was to the general conception of his rôle, at times he pushed his reverie a little bit too far: he would often forget even the key in which the orchestra was playing after Weber's wise prescription; in the fixity of his hallucination he took his notes a trifle deeper, whereby his rendering evoked a weird effect, no doubt, but in nowise a consoling one. In his aria he therefore wandered mournfully among the "woods and meadows," —one may say, he overdid alike the dreamy wandering and his lowering of pitch.

His comrade *Caspar*, on the contrary, was blithe and

unconcerned, notwithstanding that he presented a most mystic appearance,—for his good-natured demeanour was not at all well suited to his particularly mournful face ; moreover, nothing could have been more melancholy than his gait. The truth is, the singer of " Caspar " had been hitherto wont to take part in the Chorus—an occupation so conducive to the development of public spirit; since he is of uncommonly lengthy make of body, he had always let that precious feeling for equality prevail on him to bring his towering proportions into better harmony with the corporeal ensemble of his colleagues. Without great inconvenience, however, he scarcely could shorten himself by his *head* ; so he chose to effect the wholesome abridgment through a peculiar zigzag bowing-inwards of his knees. Owing to these self-denying efforts, the ensemble of the Chorus— except where it was bad—had always answered admirably : in the part of Caspar, too, this ingrained habit of self-sacrifice came in most handy to our singer ; for, as I have already explained, together with the lugubrious cast of his physiognomy it held the balance, so profitable to the character of this shady scoundrel, against the actor's native bonhomie. At least it seemed so to the French ; for, however much the gait and mien of Caspar roused their mirth, they were quite convinced that this all was as it should be, and that the singer was doing his faithful best to comply with the requirements of his rôle.

Towards the end of the opera, it became clear to them that Caspar was really in league with the Devil :—who could doubt it when witnessing the extraordinary, the unwonted death, or rather burial of the abandoned fellow ? After Caspar had been struck by that shot, so inexplicably illogical to the French mind, he had, as everyone knows, to receive a further visit from Samiel ; the wretch cursed God and all the world, according to the usage of the situation ; but, seeing that he so far forgot himself as to pay even Samiel the honour of a curse, that person took it in such bad part that he carried him off at once beneath the stage ; a proceeding which not only upset the Chorus, who suddenly

lost sight of Caspar, but painfully perplexed the Prince
himself, who confessedly had intended to have the villain
thrown into the Wolf's-gulch. Nevertheless both Prince
and Chorus drew themselves out of the affair with all the
Frenchman's presence of mind by making believe as though
nothing unlooked-for had happened; they let the thing go
its own way, and revenged themselves for Caspar's pre-
mature retirement by giving him the benefit of some well-
deserved revilings, as funeral oration.

Moreover the Prince and his court were just the people
to inspire respect; both were dressed in oriental style, and
their costumes told one that the Prince was ruler over a
remarkably extensive kingdom. He himself, with a few
of the magnates of his realm, wore Turkish garments,
whence one saw that he was Sultan, or, at the smallest,
Pasha of Egypt; the remainder of his court, however,
together with his very numerous body-guard, was clad
à la Chinese, which plainly told one that the sovereignty
of its master stretched from Constantinople to Pekin at
the least; but, since all the other characters were scrupu-
lously clothed Bohemian-wise, there was nothing left but
to imagine that the mighty Sultan had advanced his
borders north-westward also, as far as Prague and Teplitz. Yet everyone knows that, even at time of their
most brilliant conquests, the Turks never pushed farther
than to the gates of Vienna; so that we necessarily must
incline to the belief, either that the costume-cutter of the
Grand Opéra is in possession of secret historical documents, giving him a better acquaintance than ourselves
with the victories of the Turkish people, or that he wil-
fully or unwittingly transferred the story of our Freischütz
from Bohemia to Hungary: in favour of which latter
theory one certainly cannot adduce the unmistakably
Bohemian, and not *Hungarian*, costume of the peasants
and huntsmen, but rather the historic fact that Hungary
once really bore the Turkish Sultan's yoke. In any case
the idea was romantic, in a measure even oriental; moreover it made a good moral impression, to see the ruler of

all the Mussulmans entering into such unbiassed and truly Christian confidences with a hermit; he thereby read all Christian powers a lesson, to behave with like humanity towards Mohammedans and Jews.

But let us leave these details of the performance; were I to tell you everything that contributed to turn my patriotic discontentment to convulsive mirth, I should have a long, and to you a fatiguing, story to get through. Allow me, therefore, to confine myself henceforward to the broader aspect of the conception and execution of our Paris Freischütz.—

Beforehand I had feared that, beyond the evil of their necessarily too great extent, the recitatives of Herr Berlioz would more particularly impair the whole through their composer's giving rein to his impetuous productiveness on many a tempting occasion, and thus allowing them a too great self-assertion. At the performance—strange that I should have to say it—I found to my *regret* that Herr Berlioz had completely renounced all ambitious designs in the framing of these recitatives, and taken the greatest pains to place his labours in the background. To my *regret*, as said, I discovered this; because not only is the Freischütz thus *disfigured*, as was to be foreseen in any event, but at like time made intolerably *wearisome*. It was an especially unfortunate impression to make upon the French, for whom, and whom alone, Herr Berlioz' work was really reckoned. To us Germans, of course, it would often have given a twinge of pain, to sit and hear the outbursts of applause that undoubtedly would have accompanied the recitatives of Herr Berlioz if, laying aside his modesty, he had yielded to ambitious inspirations; but at anyrate those outbursts would have done good service to the Freischütz, in the sense of its Paris production,—it would have livened up the French a little, and they would not after all have found our countryman himself a bore. However, the opposite effect resulted: for what they robbed of the romantic opera's true crisp outline these recitatives gave no recompense, and they contributed their full share to the public's despair by preparing it the terriblest of tortures, a boundless ennui.

The manner in which these recitatives were *sung*, added no little to the blame attaching to them; every singer thought needful to play *Norma* or *Mosé*; the whole way through, they treated us to portamentos, tremolos, and such-like dainty morsels.

This came out the most painfully in the scene between Agatha and Annette. *Agatha*, who all the time imagined she was playing Donizetti's "*Favorite*" with the slaughtered innocence, wept copiously for its loss, stared gloomily before her, and once or twice had spasms; to add to the effect, they had given her a (by all means original-) Bohemian costume, all made of lace and satin, whilst Annette appeared in a coquettish ball-dress. Annette seemed to have a dim idea that she was to represent a cheerful character; but naïve mirth is quite as unknown to the ladies of France, as coquetry to ours. The stupidest Annchen we ever see on German boards, when singing: "Comes a smart young fellow wooing," takes the ends of her skirt in either hand, and trips to Agathe, perking her head up where proper, and casting down her eyes where needful. But this was clean impossible to the Annette of Paris; from beginning to end, she preferred to remain on one spot and coquet with the box of the "dandies"; a piece of behaviour that thoroughly fulfilled her own conception of the German damsel's character. The French didn't find anything remarkable in it;—no more did I.—

But the place where the hopeless statute, forbidding the singers of the Paris Opéra to speak, exerted its most disastrous influence, was the scene of the Wolf's-gulch; everything that Weber had given Kaspar and Max to say, in this melodrama, had here of course to be sung, thereby causing a delay beyond all bearing. The French were peculiarly enraged by this: to them the whole "Devil's-kitchen," as they called it, was inexplicable rubbish; but to see such an unconscionable time expended on it, quite passed their patience. Had they only been treated to a little excitement, or some amusing apparitions; had a chain of sprites and sylphides formed the circle, instead of those tedious dead-men's skulls; in place of the lazy owl that flapped its wings—had some buxom ballerina flung her tarletan and legs; or at the least had open-minded nuns concerned themselves with the seduction of the phlegmatic young forester, the Parisians perhaps would have known where they were. But nothing of the sort took place, and even Caspar, whose mind should have been fully occupied with his bullet - moulding, went through an agony of impatience at the extraordinary dearth of goings - on. I myself was not much easier; when I observed the peevish humour of the audience round me, I breathed a silent prayer to all the saints, that they would move the manager to fetch out some-thing from his stock-in-trade.

It was therefore with undisguised delight that, after the *first* bullet had been cast, Caspar and I noticed an un-expected fizzle break out among the bushes, vanish as quick as thought, but leave behind, alas! a most un-pleasant smell. This beginning was at anyrate sufficient to wake our hopes, which stayed unfulfilled, however, at the *second* bullet. So Caspar called forth bullet number *three* in great suspense; I shared his tension,—again nothing happened; we blushed for this laziness of Samiel's, and hid our faces. But the *fourth* bullet must really be moulded, and to our immense satisfaction, besides two bats that skimmed across the mystic circle, we saw some jack-o'-lanthorns dancing in the air, which unfortunately put the melancholy Max to great perplexity by their too much pressingness. So we came to bullet number *five* with the most brilliant prospects, for now or never must the *Wild Hunt* appear. As a fact, it did not keep us waiting:—upon a mountain, six shoes above the heads of the two foresters, four naked children, mysticly illumed, shewed forth; they carried bows and arrows, and were therefore held by most for Cupids; after a little dumb-crambo, a kind of cancan, they rushed off to the wings.

Much the same sort of performance was given by a lion, a wolf and a bear, as well as four more boys who also came on naked and went with bows and arrows the way of the Wild Hunt.—

Thrilling as these shows had been, yet Caspar and I could have wished that after the *sixth* bullet the · thrill should be carried still farther; but here the manager thought wise to make a pause, evidently to give time to the ladies in the boxes to recover from their fright. When I witnessed what happened after the *seventh* bullet, I saw that this pause had been one of preparation, for without it the sequel could never have brought about the intended weird effect. Upon the bridge leading over the waterfall three men appeared in mantles of a startling black; the same thing happened in the foreground, and just where Max was standing. The poor man must have taken his guests for undertakers, since their appearance so annoyed him that he could only throw himself full-length upon the ground. So ended the terrors of the Wolf's-gulch.*

I perceive that again I have strayed into a record of details; once for all to bar that tempting path, I will therefore tell you absolutely nothing more about the Paris performance of the Freischütz, but occupy myself solely with the public and its verdict on our national work.

The average Parisian is wont to regard the representations at the Grand Opéra as above reproach, for he knows no establishment where he could see an opera better given; these people, therefore, could be of no other opinion than that they had seen the " Freischütz " thoroughly well performed, at anyrate better than on any stage of Germany. Hence they haven't the slightest inclination to blame the performers for anything which they found dull and foolish

---

* It is easy to see that the author then mistook the character of the Paris Grand Opéra, making it beneath its dignity to deal with what it calls " *Féeries* " and abandons to the Boulevard-theatres. On the occasion of the performance of "Tannhäuser" I suffered no less myself from this lemureness, than the Freischütz had to bear with in its day.—Ed. (i.e. R. Wagner in the 1871 edition.)

in this Freischütz ; no, they simply have come to the conclusion that, taken broadly, what for the Germans may be
a masterpiece, for *them* is simply a mass of rubbish.   In
this opinion they are above all confirmed by the memory
of " *Robin des bois* " : that arrangement of the Freischütz
had made a remarkable hit, as already mentioned, and,
seeing that a like honour has not fallen to the original
work, people naturally are persuaded that the transcription
was a vast improvement on it.   As a matter of fact, that
transcription had the advantage of not possessing the
terribly long recitatives of Herr Berlioz to counteract
the effect of Weber's pieces ; moreover, the author of
" *Robin des Bois* " had been lucky enough to import some
logic into the plot.

By this " logic " there hangs a curious tale.   Just as the
French have drilled their language by the strictest rules of
logic, so they demand their observance in all that is spoken
in that language.   I have heard Frenchmen who, for that
matter, had been highly pleased with even this performance
of the *Freischütz*, but always came back to the one fatal
point, that *there wasn't an ounce of logic in it*.   To myself
it had never occurred, in all my life, to make logical
researches in the Freischütz ; so I asked them what sort of
affair was really at stake ?   Then I learnt that the logical
French temper had been particularly put out by *the number
of the Devil's-bullets*.   Why,—they asked,—why *seven* bullets ?   Why this never-heard extravagance ?   Would not
three have been ample ?   Three is a very good number to
count, and use, in any circumstance.   How on earth, in *one*
short act, is one conveniently to introduce the employment
of seven bullets ?   It would need at least five whole acts,
to solve this problem lucidly, and even then one would be
faced with the difficulty of having to get rid of *several*
bullets in *one* act.   For, to tell the truth—as everyone
must see—to have a pouchful of such Devil's-ammunition
is no laughing matter ; how contrary to all common sense
must it be, then, for two young sportsmen to squander *six*
of these bullets on one fine morning with such crying

levity, and so entirely without rhyme or reason, knowing, as well they must, that unpleasantness would arise when they came to the *seventh* !

In the same strain they exclaimed against the 'catastrophe,' with unsuppressed disgust. " How is it conceivable "—said one—" that a shot, aimed at a pigeon, can at the same time slay a bride, apparently, and a good-for-nothing huntsman actually ? We admit the possibility of a bullet missing a pigeon and hitting a man,—such accidents do occur, alas !—But how a bride and all the bystanders can believe, for full five minutes, that *she* was hit as well—that passes all conceivability ! Moreover this shot is void of all dramatic truth :—how much more logical it would be for the young huntsman, in despair at a *bad shot*, to wish to put the last free-bullet through his brains, —the bride runs up, and tries to snatch the pistol from him,—it goes off, but the bullet steers above the huntsman—thanks to the bride's interference—and lays dead the godless comrade, placed behind him in the direct line of fire ! There you would have your *logic* ! "

My brain began to reel :—of such obvious truisms I had never even dreamt, but always taken the Freischütz for gospel, with all his want of logic.—There one sees what uncommonly clever chaps the Frenchmen are ! They see the Freischütz just one solitary time, and at once can prove you that we Germans have languished five-and-twenty years in hideous delusion about his logic ! We hapless creatures, who have all along believed that a shot fired off at an eagle at seven in the evening could cause the fall of a family-portrait in a shooting-box at least two and a quarter miles off !—

Logic is the consuming passion of the French, and they settle all their verdicts by its rules. Not one of the mutually-conflicting criticisms in the journals is found wanting, on this occasion, in the most logical grounds for its opinion, how difficult soe'er the exegesis must have been ; seeing that one paper, for instance, maintains that the Freischütz is grey, another that beyond denial it is

green.   The best arrangement has been that of Herr
Berlioz, in the *Journal des débats* ; in his article upon the
" Freischütz " he does not forget to say a few pretty things
about Weber and his masterpiece itself, which acquire a
peculiar sanctity through his speaking in the selfsame
pretty terms about the performance.   For that matter it
is only natural, as we know that the reporter himself had
furnished the musical *mise en scène* ; he thus was bound to
pay the Freischütz' representatives a compliment for the
trouble they had given themselves, under his direction,
with the rehearsing of an opera so much against their
taste.   But Herr Berlioz displays his genuine modesty by
not hinting one word, in all his article, as to the value
of his recitatives.   All the world was touched, when in a
subsequent number of the same journal Herr Berlioz'
colleague, Jules Janin, most friendlily took up the office of
discussing the Freischütz-performance, but made it the
occasion of saying absolutely nothing save a valiant word
of praise about the recitatives of his journalistic brother.
There was no one here who did not hold this covenant
between the two colleagues for reasonable and in accordance with the rules of Paris logic.

Other journals have other modes of applying their special
points of logic ; those in opposition to the Director of the
Grand Opéra naturally can do no else than give a plainer
verdict on the poor performance, though they try to make
it still more forcible by *at like time* leaving not a single
unpulled hair on our Freischütz himself.

The most logical of all, however, is the emission of the
Charivari :—the author of this article wishes the directorate
of the Grand Opéra joy of having *given shelter* to a masterpiece of German art *after that work had been disowned by
the compatriots of its creator and banished from its country's
soil.*

Coming to *this* passage, my patience at last gives out.
I have been laughing so far, and had reason to do the
same about the *Charivari* article ; but there are points

where one's laughter stops short, however much matter be left for it. Shall I tell you, my German fellow-country-men, what has moved me *not* to laugh at the last-named article? Hear, then: it is the *anger* at seeing myself unable to find in any shade of journal in this great metropolis of uncommonly free France either acceptance for a vigorous rebuttal of that stupid slander, or for any sort of exposure of the failings in the *Paris* Freischütz !— For the French permit thrust and riposte between parties alone; *then* they make no bones about stripping each other of the last rag of honour or reason. But the calmest and most reasonable explanation or éclaircissement, once it is addressed to *all* parties alike, must never and never come under their eyes. In such a case they mutually dissemble what they know and what they don't know, concealing it beneath their mawkish Logic, and are mighty proud of knowing naught of anything in all the world but precisely what they *choose to.*

So is it. These *spirituel* Frenchmen lack not only the ability, but positively the will, to step beyond the limits of their inherited ideas about the good and beautiful, were it even for curiosity's sake. Of course I am saying nothing new, for there is nothing new to say about them, as, despite their yearly changing Mode, they never can grow *new.* But I must lay the oft-told story anew to your hearts, since there has been a notion forming for some little time among us, that between Germans and French, especially in artistic taste, an approximation was taking place. This idea has arisen, no doubt, from our having heard that the French were translating "Goethe" and playing Beethoven's Symphonies quite masterly. Both things have taken, and are taking place; that's true enough: but to-day I inform you that they also have given the Freischütz. Exactly as much as *this* has done toward a rapprochement of the two nations, have Goethe and Beethoven accomplished,—not an iota more; and that is less than nothing, for the " Freischütz " has eminently contributed to estranging the French from the Germans again.

We must harbour no illusions here; on many a point the French will forever stay foreign to us, however much we two may wear the same cravats and swallow-tails.

Whenever, for a thousand possible reasons, we attempt to approach them closer, we are obliged at once to cast away a good portion of our own best qualities: in this it is impossible to cheat the French, to make them believe by externals that we are turning out French music, if the whole inner sentiment is not modelled on what they call their "logic." The last is a very tough job, and anyone who speaks from experience can certify that it takes a double dose of nationality and patriotism, to keep one's inner kernel whole amid the French exactions. No greater pleasure can one therefore feel, than to set the French with their redoubtable logic beneath the light, upon occasion; but it's no easy matter, for they're wide-awake as none besides, and their douanes are rigidly shut against all foreign imports; at least the customs-toll is mighty high, and it costs some pains to raise it.

On the contrary, how over-upright and good-natured are we Germans, when with hospitable diligence we search the lauded masterpieces of our neighbour-folk for any tasty morsel; nay, even lift the tasteless out as foreign rarity, and carry it to the apothecary to make a plaister for our nether parts, all ruined by much sitting! Ye guess not that these drugs are fit at most for ridding bugs and fleas, and the Parisian knows his wares too well to put even *thus* much trust in them; whence it happens that so huge a host of vermin swarms in France's proud metropolis.

O, how compassionate and kind ye are to the miseries which the French themselves have lost a taste for! Do ye know that through that angel-virtue ye have become a butt to this laughter-lusting people? Know ye what tales they tell, to make you foolish in the eyes of the Parisian world?—They tell how one of them, in May or April of this very year, paid a visit to the Court-theatre of Berlin or Vienna, and the people there were giving "Fra Diavolo" or "Zampa." Every Frenchman who hears tell of it con-

cludes, in power of his logic, that ye are the most taste-
forsaken people in the world, and dies of laughter.

Not long ago I witnessed such a laughing-fit; since I
already had laughed too much at other things, I did not
this time join in, but clenched my fist and swore an oath.
Whoever cares to know what I then swore, shall hear it in
good season ; *were I more than me, were I one of those happy
ones whom Schiller sings in his hexameters, ye should hear at
once the oath I swore when the Frenchmen laughed at your
piety toward Zampa and Fra Diavolo.**

What?—We, the favoured nation to whom God let a
Mozart and *Beethoven* be born, were fashioned for the
laughing-stock of Paris salons?—In truth we serve that
purpose, and deserve it; the emptiest head on the Boulevard des Italiens has a right to laugh at us, for we bring it
on ourselves.—I make it no reproach to us, that we are able
to appreciate the merits of French art; for this one circumstance it is, that lifts us heaven-high above the French.
Happy we, that we can value everything the outland sends
us, down to the last farthing of its worth! This priceless
gift has been bestowed on us Germans by an all-kind
Heaven; for without it no universal genius, like Mozart,
could ever have been born among us, and through it we
are able to forgive his scoff to everyone who makes merry
over us. But for all that, it lies in the ordinance of Nature
that there are times of war, as times of peace ; so, would
ye in some warlike time take vengeance on the French, ye
could not punish them more bitterly than by one day sending back per extra-post the envoys of their holy spirit,
their " Fra Diavolo " and " Zampa," their " Fidèle Berger "
—and whatever other Christian names they bear.† Be
sure that, should the Frenchmen be compelled once more
to hear the sermons of these inspired teachers, they would

---

* These words were not italicised (or rather, spaced) in the *Abendzeitung.*—
Tr.

† Poor friend, how wroth thou waxest at these " Christian " names ! Hadst
thou but lived to see our day,—yes, the new great day of victory over France,
—what wouldst thou say of us, on seeing what names thy hated emissaries bear
at last !—R. Wagner [1871].

HALÉVY'S "REINE DE CHYPRE."

Bericht
über eine neue Pariser Oper.

("La Reine de Chypre" von Halévy.)

The following "Report" on Halévy's Reine de Chypre
*(first perf. Dec. 22, 1841) originally formed the leading
article in the Dresden* Abend-Zeitung *of Jan. 26, 27, 28
and 29, 1842. For further particulars see preface to the
present volume.*

TRANSLATOR'S NOTE.

WHAT an important affair is a French Grand-opera! Its first appearance on the Paris stage is an event of incalculable consequence: passion, rivalry, enthusiasm, curiosity, speculation, art-interest and commercial instinct, all rise thereat, gleam, glow, beam, gape, laugh, cry, reckon, hope and fear. Though we leave the poet, composer, scene-painter, machinist, ballet-master, dancers, singers, ay, even the public itself on one side for the moment, we come full tilt on the Director:— what is this 'first night' not to him! He has had to spend 40,000 francs hard cash on the mounting of this opera, so he naturally is all agog to see what he will gain thereby, or whether he will not even lose his whole investment. Though in all his life he may have never contracted the bad habit of biting his nails, sheer humanity would pardon him for unconsciously falling into it of a sudden at the third scene of the fourth act.—Who is *that*, with the black hair and never-resting eye? He is full at once of nervousness and admiration, peers into his neighbour's features for the effect of the last aria, and at the self-same instant praises up its glorious theme:—'tis no other than the music-publisher, who already has paid the composer 30,000 francs down for the new score.*—Do you see the young musician there, with pale cheeks and a devouring look in the eyes? With breathless haste he listens to the performance, gulps down the outcome of each single number: is it enthusiasm, or jealousy? Ah, 'tis the care for daily bread: for, if the new opera proves a success, he has reason to hope that that publisher will give him orders for "fantasias" and "*airs variés*" on its "favourite melodies."—In the highest balcony that man with the critically-outstretched ear fulfils the office of

* Maurice Schlesinger, whilst the "young musician" is the author.—Tr.

transplanting popular morsels to the countless barrel-organs of the town:—he is just taking note of the aria of the dying King. — There you see the deputies or plenipotentiaries of the Provincial theatres : with rapt attention they are studying the trappings of the grand procession and the relative proportion of paid claqueurs to the amateur enthusiasts.

In nebulous distance, in the romantic semi-shade of oak-groves and Italian cellars, my ardent-patriotic eye spies serious ruminating men in black dress-coats and brown paletots:—who are these, who so sedulously clap their glasses to their lifeless eyes? Are they not just complaining of the backwardness of the German Bund and French Government in not yet laying railways from all points of Germany to the very parterre of the Grand Opéra in Paris, to enable them to snap up in a moment *that* which brings them peace and comfort, brand-new Parisian operas?—O, I know you.   At a hurried computation there are two-and-fifty of you: ye are German Theatre-Directors !—

My welcome to your excellencies ! You have re-transferred me to my beloved Fatherland, and that on a night, amid a surrounding, before a spectacle, which lie a thousand miles and more away—so far, so far, that fears have often seized me lest my severance were final ! But ye, O ye are the levellers of all the world ! Ye hurl down mountains from the path, to bring Parisian vaudevilles to our Professors ! Ye dry up the free German Rhine, to bring a "Glass of Water" * out of France ! Surely *ye* will yet lay railways to transport whole grand Parisian operas, with all their festal marches, flying dancers, traps and machines, entire into your slips !—And we Germans have no enterprise?— —

Of this, and much more like it, I obtained a glimpse and notion lately, upon attending the first performance of the " Queen of Cyprus." Marvellous ! I heard *French*

---

* Scribe's " *Un verre d'eau*," referred to in Wagner's letter of Dec. 23, 1841, to the same journal.—Tr.

verses and *French* music,—I saw *Venetian* poniards and
spies of the Council of Ten, I breathed the balmy air of
Cyprus, and fancied I was drinking its incendent wine,—
yet between it all I never could escape the well-fed,
grinning face of one of those Fifty-two! Was it the
excessively shiny ebon hair of that spectre, that riveted
my recreant eye, or was it the triumphant look upon its
features, which seemed to cry to me: " I shall be the
first again, you will see, to give this opera in Germany " ?
—'Twas a horrible vision, and I'm not quite rid of it yet,
now that I am taking up my pen to write you my sober
and calm opinion of Halévy's new opera. To free myself
entirely from its influence, I therefore deem best to make
straight for that ghost with the well-oiled jet-black hair,
and speak an earnest word with it.—Why, spectre, giv'st
thou honest folk no peace, when they attend the first
performance of a new work at the Paris Grand Opéra?
Why appear at the head of those two-and-fifty, and
transfer me at a blow from Cyprus to the common
German trading-city ? — Because I am a German? —
Frenchmen, I admit, would not believe in thee. But
that does not suffice me. Get thee hence, and never let
thy face be seen again at the Opéra! What is't to thee
and the likes of thee? How should it trouble thee, what
the Parisians get their fellow-countrymen to write, play,
sing, compose for them?—Thou pull'st a lamentably
serious face, as if thou wouldst persuade me that with
all thy retinue in silk and velvet thou'dst pine and starve,
were folk to limit thee to what *thy* fellow-countrymen
imagine and compose.—What! So poor dar'st thou rate
thy countrymen? Speak out! Why giv'st thou no new
German operas ? — " Because they're tedious." — Why
tedious ?—" Because our best composers can never get
other than stupid texts."—There I hit the nail at last;—
I'll let my spectre go, and dwell upon the chapter
of "*bad opera-texts*," which in truth is a serious and distressing chapter, a chapter of the want and woe of
hundreds.

o

A not unmeritorious German composer, Herr D.,* lately met me with a complaint of his great text-want; he had let it go the length of costing money, and offered a prize for good German libretti: not long ago he received quite a pile of them,—he read through one after the other with a shudder, and laid them by uncomforted. — Another musician comes hither from Germany expressly to spend his money and the diplomatic influence of his Court on arriving at a real French text, which he wishes, when translated, to compose for Germany.—From Munich I hear that Kapellmeister *Lachner* has actually arrived at last at succeeding with an opera, since the Court-theatre there had not grudged 1,500 francs to M. de *Saint-Georges* for writing him a text-book.† Great heavens! Messieurs Poets and Composers, more openly your weakness could not be proclaimed! And yet, only take a good look at the thing! Is it so superlatively hard a matter, to write a good libretto? Take a hint how to make it quite simple. First of all you must have *poesy* within you, and your *heart* in the right place: then, as you are such omnivorous readers of books old and new, it cannot but occur that your whole heart will go out to this or that event or story, — that you can read no farther, that suddenly you see miraculous impassioned shapes alive before you, you feel their pulses beat, and hear their joyful hymns and mournful ditties. Having got so far, it will be impossible for you to do aught else than seize your pen and draft a glowing drama that must stir and lift the breast of all men; such a drama you only further need to commit to one of those well-schooled, emotional musicians of whom our Germany at all times has so many: *him* will your drama next inspire, and what his inspiration shapes in common aim with you will be the *finest opera* in the world.

But that requires a gift of *poesy* and the deepest, subtlest

* Presumably Heinrich Dorn.—Tr.
† In the *Abend-Zeitung* it was "3,000 francs," and "*der brave Lachner.*"
—Tr.

feeling; so if there be folk among you who have never meddled with these excellent things, at the very least they will have *knack* (Geschick), for Knack is indispensable to the cobbler's and the saddler's hand-work, and therefore also to that of the opera-text-maker. Well, if you have knack you must go read journals, novels, books, imprimis the great book of *history* * : you'll not have long to seek before you find a half or whole page that tells you of some strange event you never knew before, or had not yet experienced. Then ponder this event a little ; draw three or even five bold lines across it, which you may call *acts* if you please ; give to each of these acts a measured share of the action ; make this interesting,—(surely nothing is easier than that !)—here let a marriage be suddenly broken off,—there the lover carry off his sweetheart,—here strike a young cavalier half dead, there let a senator's daughter be crowned Queen, and finally hurl the intriguer out of the window ;—trim up with golden cups of poison, secret doors in the arras, hidden spies and all that sort of entertaining thing,—and before one can turn one's wrist you'll have an operatic text as good as *any* for whose sake German musicians besiege Parisian text-makers, and above all—precisely as fine as the text of the "Queen of Cyprus."

If, however, you unfortunately haven't even *knack*, why ! do what you will,—write criticisms, smoke cigars, and go to bed early ;—but write our unlucky composers no opera-books : for, clever as you are, you yet are in terrible error about this business. You imagine, to wit, that before you can write an opera-text something extraordinary must occur. to you : there in place of men—so you think—all kinds of clouds and flowers must appear, or—if nothing but men will come to your mind, namely barons, officers, knights, hang-dogs and countesses, at least they must all behave as clouds and flowers, or it will be impossible to let them *sing*. Your chief concern is therefore to banish all

* A little pun on " *Geschick* "—" skill " or " knack "—and " *Geschichte* "—" history."—Tr.

action, at least to never let your characters transact when they have once been primed for singing: for music, all must be *lyric, unboundedly lyric*, almost *nothing-saying*:— only then, you believe, can the musician set his melodies and modulations going with due unction! And if it is clean impossible to avoid all action for three hours long, you can see no other remedy than to let your people say in downright German prose at last that one has slain the other, the son has found his father, but the police have arrested the lot of them. Again, you generally have the misfortune to fall upon subjects that refuse to fit those admirably lyric spurts at all. What, for instance, is an operatic Lieutenant or Major to say and sing, when rustics set a-thrashing him? Nothing else, to be sure, than "Jott's schwere Noth!"—which indeed would sound quite pointed and dramatic ;—but instead of it you let him sing God-knows-what silly stuff about "the finger of fate," "the will of the gods," and—should a young lady be near —of "love" and "dove," which most certainly has never occurred to a Prussian Major in all his life.

If you only knew how sensible it would be to give no seeming thought to the composer, but simply do your best to write a feeling *drama* scene by scene! For that's the way to make it possible for the musician, too, to write *dramatic* music ; a thing you stubbornly deny him now.— As to the verses, one certainly may take it as a rule, that *good* are better than *bad*: but you will do extremely wrong, to make too much of them ; for the musician often cannot use your choicest lines at all, and, to give his music fluence and expression, feels bound to dislocate your costliest rhythms and bury your finest rhymes.

Now, to shew you plainly how, even without the gift of *poesy*, and simply by going to work with some *knack*, one may turn out an opera-text that in the hands of a talented composer not only will generally interest and excite, but also satisfy in a certain sense, I will epitomise the *text of the* "*Reine de Chypre*," contrived by Herr St. Georges, and hope thereby to prove that the French are really no magicians.

Herr St. Georges had read in the book of History that in the latter half of the fifteenth century, with predatory designs on the island of *Cyprus*—then ruled by monarchs of the French house of *Lusignan*—, *Venice* hypocritically took the part of a prince of that house, whose right to the throne was disputed by his family; how it helped him to his crown, and sought to saddle him with its baneful influence by giving him for wife *Catarina*, daughter of the Venetian senator *Andreas Cornaro*. This King died soon thereafter, and, as is generally supposed, by Venetian poison; for on the night of his death conspiracies came to a head, to rob the royal widow of the regency over her little son ; Catarina's obstinate refusal to give up the reins of government, however, together with her spirited resistance, this time frustrated Venice' plan.—Here is a first-rate action-of-State,—no one can deny it. Now let us see how Herr *St. Georges* has used this historical find for a five-act *lyric* drama.

The first act plays at Venice, in the palace of the senator *Andreas Cornaro* ; he is on the point of marrying his daughter *Catarina* to a French knight, Herr Düprez— I meant to say, *Gerard de Coucy*. Gerard and Catarina love each other, and mutually re-express it in a fairly long duet;—the good Senator is rejoiced at their love, and blesses it :—enters a man in red robes, with a black scarf; Cornaro recognises him as a member of the *Council of Ten*, shudders, and sends the lovers from the room. *Moncenigo*, as the marplot is called, acquaints the senator with the Council's decision to marry Catarina to the King of Cyprus, and informs Andreas that nothing is more urgent than for him to revoke his word to the French knight and fall in with this royal marriage, or pay by death for disobedience to Venice's commands. He grants the senator an hour for reflection, which the latter expends on gloomy thoughts. Meanwhile the wedding-feast begins; Venetian lords and French knights—the friends of Gerard —appear as guests; only the senator keeps away; in his stead, however, a handsome slim young man finds oppor-

tunity to perform a much admired *pas de trois* with two of
his excessively short-skirted lady friends ; this comes to an
end when the unhappy father enters and informs all present
that the wedding will not take place, since he withdraws
his word to Gerard.   Universal consternation : questions,
entreaties, cries, threats, alternate : Gerard's friends accuse
the Senator of breaking his pledge, the Venetian lords
defend him, the disappointed bridegroom raves, the poor
bride faints, and the curtain falls.—What more could you
ask of a first act ?—

The second act transports us into Catarina's oratory,
which does not forget, however, to open its great windows
on the Grand Canal ; the moon shines, and gondoliers are
singing.   The inconsolable patrician-daughter is fingering
a prayer-book, and finds a few lines from her lover inside,
telling her that at midnight he will come to carry her off ;
at which she rejoices exceedingly.   She is waiting for the
knight already, when her down-bent father enters, excuses
himself to his daughter, and implores her, for his comfort
and her own, to consent to the union with Cyprus's King :
highly as he tints the merits of this match, he is quite
unable to incline her to his wish, and leaves the room with
a mourning heart.   But, scarcely is Catarina alone once
more, than the quiet of her oratory is disturbed again : she
hears her name called.   I am sure you know from Victor
Hugo's " Tyrant of Padua " how that infamous *Council of
Ten* had secret doors and passages in the house of every
Venetian of any standing, unknown to the tenants themselves, by which to send their spies at will into the very
heart of the best-guarded palaces, there to carry out their
treacheries.   Now such a door and such a secret passage
open on one of the walls of the young lady's oratory, and
he who steps out of it is no less a personage than *Signor
Moncenigo*, member of the Council of Ten.   He tersely
explains to the terrified damsel that, as soon as her lover
presents himself, she is to assure him *she loves him no
longer* and feels consumedly attracted by the crown of
Cyprus :—her *only* way of saving his life.   She asks, who

means to murder him? He opens the secret door; with
the words, "These hands!" he shews her quite a company
of dagger-twitching villains, and withdraws into the passage.
—Midnight strikes:—the lover appears, his wretched sweetheart dares not rush to meet him. Imagine what a situation
for a duet! The cavalier gently urging to flight,—the ina-
morata half-fainting for fright, eavesdropped and shadowed
by assassins. His reproaches of her seeming coldness are
driving her to let out the truth,—when that awful door
just opens, once, in warning to her; another time, still
visible to her alone, Signor Moncenigo himself steps forth,
with menacing gestures:—in despair she at last cries out
to the knight that she by no means loves him any more,
and wishes to be Queen of Cyprus. What Gerard answers,
is easy to conceive: after a little astonishment at the
bluntness of his beloved, he acquaints her with his hatred,
his contempt; she suffers fearfully and threatens to swoon
away, as indeed she does in the end when her hoodwinked
lover rushes off with a most painful "*adieu pour jamais!*"
Moncenigo and the murderers come out, and bear away
the fainting girl, to pack her off to Cyprus.—That's quite
Venetian, and in nowise uninteresting.

Herr St. Georges now gives us a free passage to Cyprus,
which the third act shews in all its glory:—we are in a
"Casino" of *Nicosia*; a thousand torches light the luscious
night, enchanted groves and leafy bosquets frame the scene;
—here Cypriot gentlemen are seated, there Venetian;—
voluptuous ladies mingle in the feast, in goblets sparkles
priceless wine,—one plays, one sings, one dances;—'tis
enough to cheer one's heart, to be a witness. Signor
Moncenigo does not fail to put in an appearance: Venice
and its Council of Ten are omnipresent. Here, too, he
finds his work cut out. He is informed that a suspicious
figure, the very image of Sir Gerard de Coucy, has been
seen about; promptly he makes up his mind to decree the
wretch's murder, as he might easily be cause of great un-
pleasantnesses here. In fact, as soon as the motley party
has dispersed, we hear the French knight's cry for help

quite near us ; sword-clatterings follow, and finally the cut-throats' flight. Gerard appears with a stranger knight, whom he thanks for the timely aid that saved him from assassins' poniards ; the unknown—none other than *Jacques Lusignan*, the King of Cyprus himself—protests that he has merely done his knightly duty, but declines to divulge his name, contenting himself with calling *France* his father-land.   Gerard is charmed to have met a fellow-countryman, Lusignan equally so :—" *Vive la France, the lovely land*!" rings out from either's lips ;—knightly friendship is plighted. The pair indulge in polite cross-questionings ; one un-burdens his griefs to the other, as discreetly as possible : Lusignan describes himself as a poor exile, compelled to uphold his rights in a foreign country ; Gerard confesses that he is brought to Cyprus by great sorrow and the passion to revenge himself on the despoiler of his happiness. Both promise mutual support, swear succour and fidelity. Then cannons sound from the harbour :—the Queen's vessel is approaching Cyprus !   Lusignan breathes deep for joy and rapture : his good star is in the ascendant !—Gerard, plunged into quite other feelings by the thunder of the guns, bemoans disloyalty and thirsts for vengeance !—

Thus we reach the fourth act : great festivities, and pomp unrivalled !   We are at the port, awaiting with the shouting mob the Queen's arrival :—her ship draws near, she steps on costly carpets to the land ; Lusignan, as King, comes from the castle to meet her,—artillery-salvoes, pealing bells, blare of trumpets, accompany the gorgeous train to the cathedral.—The stage is deserted when he appears, the miserable Gerard, brooding over the attainment of his vengeance : he knows that he is rushing on inevitable death ; nevertheless he will avenge himself, then suffer any shameful end.   He seeks admission to the church, but is driven back by the returning cortège ; he takes his stand in a niche of the castle-wall, in wait for the King, and when Catarina approaches at the latter's hand Gerard hurls him-self upon him with bare dagger.   At once he recognises his countryman and rescuer : horrified at his attempt, he totters back, but the guards arrest him. The infuriated mob demands his blood; the King, amazed and horrified, accuses him of broken troth: "Me, thy deliverer from murderous hands, thou fain wouldst slaughter?"—However, he waves aside the panting crowd, and gives Gerard to the hands of Cypriot justice.

The fifth act plays two years later. The strict historic interval is *four* years; but Herr St. Georges has displayed great knack in shortening such a tiresome pause by its half. The King, grown old before his time, lies stricken with a lingering mortal illness. Catarina, resigned to her lot, and filled with esteem for her husband, watches by the sick-bed. Lusignan thanks her for her kindness and fidelity, and reveals to her his knowledge of her earlier relations with Gerard; for the latter, secretly saved by him from death at the block, in gratitude had told him all, and *he*, far from chiding his wife for it, was moved to admiration of her loyalty and steadfastness, and wished her happiness when liberated from the fetters which his coming death would soon dissolve.—A Maltese knight, with pressing matters for the King, is announced: Lusignan gives orders for him to be led before the Queen [in the throne-room]; for he feels that his last hour is drawing nigh, and wishes to commit to his wife the regency for his infant son. The Maltese Knight, none other than Gerard de Coucy, enters and is received by the Queen: this brings about a painful scene, —sad memories are reawakened. Gerard cannot resist upbraiding her afresh with faithlessness, but Catarina disarms his taunts by relating the terrible circumstances which had *forced* her to declare she no more loved him. Gerard, assuaged, proceeds to tell the Queen his business:—he has been informed by the Senator, now dead of remorse, that Lusignan is dying of slow poison, which Venice, angered at the King's incomplaisance and unexpected love of independence, has had administered to him; in return for Lusignan's magnanimous behaviour toward him, he has come to acquaint him with the fiendish plot, and, if possible, to save him. "*Too late!*" thunders out the surreptitiously

admitted Moncenigo. "No man now can save the King;
he is succumbing at this moment to the penalty that Venice,
wroth at the defiance he dared to wage against her influence,
has put upon him! And thou, Catarina,—an thou valuest
thy life,—Venice bids thee lay the reins of government
within her hand."—"Never!" cries the indignant Queen:
"For my son will I reign, and to avenge my husband!"—
"On whom dost thou rely, then, thus to beard us?"—"On
my people, to whom this very hour I'll publish Venice'
barefaced treason!"—"No one will believe thee, for *I'll*
proclaim that, in adult'rous commune with that knight o'er
there, thou'st wrought thy husband's death. Say, who'll
deny it?"—"I!"—cries the King, already deemed dead,
entering pale and cramped with ghastly tortures, having
braced his last expiring strength to creep to the doorway
of the chamber and take in Moncenigo's shameless speech.
—This situation is of extraordinary effectiveness.—The
King declares that he will spend his life's last moments on
foiling Venice's most vile designs and assuring the people
of his consort's innocence. Moncenigo, undaunted, makes
a signal from the window with his scarf,—cannon-shots and
uproar are heard: too late the traitor is seized by the Royal
Guard. Everyone rushes to the fray, to quell the Venetian
rebellion; Gerard, rejoiced at the thought of rendering
Lusignan a service, drives the Venetians out of the arsenal
by aid of his knights: Catarina sets herself at the head of
the people, whom she swiftly has filled with enthusiasm:
Venice is defeated, and the dying King commits his luckless crown to the hands of his wife. She takes her little
son upon her arm, though, regardless of Herr St. Georges'
kind reduction, he quite historically has thriven to a bonny
boy of three years old at least; the people swear allegiance,
and the Maltese Knight, remembering his order's vow, bids
farewell to his early love for ever.—

Now who will deny that this is an opera-text one
scarcely could better, under circumstances? Here is a plot
that rivets the spectator from act to act, excites and enter-

tains, touching—where required, appalling—where occasion
suits,—offering the composer a hundred opportunities of
bringing all his aptitudes and talents into light.

And yet it would occur to no one, to style this text an
artwork: above all, the honoured author has decidedly
failed in that gift we call *poesy*: here nothing springs from
a higher spiritual idea, no inner swirl has carried the writer
away, no glowing inspiration lifted him from out himself.
He has seized the first historic fact that came to hand;
without caring for any special idea at bottom, his choice fell
on *this* because professional experience told him that an
adaptation of this story would offer ground for all those
favourite and strong Effects which form the stock-in-trade
of the Parisian playwrights of to-day, effects they all have
used a thousand times before. And such is the nature of
this entire opera :—every scene both interests and enter-
tains, but none is able to arouse *enthusiasm* for a moment,
or set our higher powers in swing. Yet Herr St. Georges
is shrewd enough to know that a note of enthusiasm must
here and there be introduced; even in the "Queen of
Cyprus" he has not omitted to win the heart of his
audience by an appeal to its sympathies: he makes use
of the circumstance that Gerard and Lusignan, who meet
in Cyprus by hazard, are *Frenchmen*, and lets them ventilate
enthusiasm for their country—"fair France,"—which could
not stay without effect, as the Paris public consists of
Frenchmen for the most part. And there is the further
advantage that, with trifling pains, this scene can be
adapted to the patriotism of any nation. If one plays
this opera at *Munich* for instance, all one need do is to
turn Venice into *Russia*, Cyprus into *Greece*, make Jacques
Lusignan *King Otto*, the knight Gerard a Bavarian *cavalry-
officer* on half pay; in that duet one then can quite
appropriately sing "*my fair Bavaria*," and the desired
enthusiasm will not be wanting. In fact I am curious to
know if Herr St. Georges has not made this arrangement
himself in Lachner's "Catarina Cornaro" for Munich.

So you see, respected German opera-text-makers, how

extremely easy it is to get quite admirable subjects, heap interest on interest in them, eh! even conjure up a species of enthusiasm, without more trouble to yourselves than the acquisition of a little Knack. And you have one advantage over the French, namely a far freer theatrical *censorship*. You, for instance, could let Venetian machinations break out in Cyprus without alarm, though *here* they had much to contend with, as the French Government at first feared allusions to recent riots at Toulouse. This by the way,— but you may gather from the "Reine de Chypre" that you have only to take the first likely historical subject, dress it out with all manner of family or society episodes, such as weddings, elopements, duels and so forth, to give a talented musician ample opportunity to let his gift of dramatic composition shine on every facet and entertain an audience most attractively for four or five hours at a stretch.

In this Herr Halévy has fully succeeded; his music is decorous, feeling, in many places even most effective.[*] There is a grace I had never suspected in Halévy's talent in the many charming vocal passages for which the text affords abundant scope, and I was struck above all by a great endeavour at simplicity in the treatment of the whole. It would be of high importance to our time, were this endeavour to proceed from the Paris Grand Opéra at an epoch when our German operatic composers have just begun to hanker after the French luxury and pomp; we then should have nothing more than to turn half-way back, to anticipate the French at least in this reactionary movement. Halévy has successfully striven for simplicity, however, in none but the vocal portion of his opera, from which he has banished all those pernicious fireworks and intolerable prima-donna-flourishes that (to the great delight of illustrious Paris amateurs) had flowed from the scores of Donizetti & Co. into the pen of many a clever composer of French Opera. Far less has it succeeded in his instru-

---

[*] In the *Abendzeitung*, for "anständig" ("decorous") stood "edel" ("noble"), and for "most effective" stood "neu und erhebungsvoll" ("new and elevating").—Tr.

mental portion. If—God knows why!—we are to give up the modern use of the brass, we necessarily must also quit the method of composing which that use has led to ; but in truth the notion of dramatic music peculiar to Halévy, for example, is to be regarded much rather as an advance, than a retreat; and its predominant *historic* tendence—if I may be allowed the term—might be considered a good basis from which to arrive at the solution of problems perhaps not even broached as yet. It is not to be disputed that this Historic character fully admits of an *intelligent* employment of the brass, especially the modern instruments, as we know from Halévy's own *Juive* for instance ; and if this talented composer has allowed himself to be scared away from their further use, perhaps through witnessing the hideous abuse of this mode of instrumentation by the newer Italian opera-makers and Parisian quadrille-composers, he at any rate is in an error at total variance with the retention of his mode of composing. For, and I repeat it, in his latest work Halévy has not abandoned his earlier conception of dramatic music; and hence it comes that passages occur, especially in the first two acts, whose character demands their instrumenting altogether otherwise, i.e. more "modernly," to produce the effect most certainly intended : hereby he has fallen into the fault of asking from clarinets and oboes, for instance, an effect to be expected of nothing but horns and ventil-trumpets ; and thus it comes, that these passages give one the impression of a thorough schoolboy's instrumentation. In course of the opera, however, the composer has cast his whim to the winds, and instruments according to his nature. Apart from this point (after all, but a minor one), in general the later acts are more effective than the earlier : in every number one lights on great beauties, and in this respect the last act merits special mention, as the *composer* has really known to imbue it with a high-poetic flavour : the dying King thereby acquires a touching, an affecting import, and truly harrowing is the effect of a *quartet* belonging to that situation which I already termed fine when speaking of the text. A certain dread sublimity, transfigured by a breath of elegy, is generally a characteristic trait in Halévy's better, his heart-derived productions.

To sum up in brief: if this opera does not reach the level of "*La Juive*," it certainly is not attributable to any falling-off in the creative force of the *composer*, but simply to the absence of a grand, enthralling, or generally awe-compelling poetic idea in the *book*, such as actually is present in that "*Juive.*" That notwithstanding, the Parisian Grand Opéra may congratulate itself on the birth of this work.*

Rejoice, then, honoured *two-and-fifty*! You receive once more a babe that costs you not a farthing's worth of labour-pains. And should the time come round when ye must fondle strapping German children in your arms, don't growl at me for having called them into being; for, though I cannot doubt that my present discoveries and counsels in the matter of operatic text-craft will instantly cause our German dramatists to write the best librettos in the world for our composers, I had no idea of harming you in purse and business, but rather conceived the rosy hope of opening up to you a perhaps more *glorious* source of revenue. Of that rest assured!—

Paris, December 31, 1841.

---

* In the *Abendzeitung* this sentence was continued by "for it is decidedly the best that has appeared on its boards since Meyerbeer's 'Huguenots.' "—Tr.

AUTHOR'S INTRODUCTION

TO

VOLUME II. OF THE GESAMMELTE SCHRIFTEN.

(1871.)

THE history of the origin of the works collected in this second volume I must reserve for a future occasion, as I narrated it at length a few years after the Dresden period to which they belong, and that in a manner and from a standpoint which too plainly bear the character of that somewhat later epoch, not to demand enrolment with the writings of the latter time.* The order of arrangement of the present contents will of itself give the reader a glimpse into that origin. Preponderant are the dramatic poems,† to one of which is also attached a special study (on the "Wibelungen"). Further, what interrupt their earlier course are memories of occurrences within the province of my artistic functions as Dresden Kapellmeister. What broke the latter off so suddenly, is sufficiently in- dicated for the present in the character of the essay printed at this volume's close, a draft of reorganisation for the Dresden Court-theatre, and especially in its pre- fatory account of the fate of my attempt to get it sanctioned. Abrupt as must seem the fall from the ideal sphere of productivity into the highly realistic one of a counting-up of salaries and so forth, I finally con- quered my own doubt of the propriety of publishing this work in the present connexion upon recognising that my subsequent and apparently eccentric statements of the relation of our Art to our ruling Publicity‡ might be viewed as the mere lucubrations of an overstrung, in any case a thoroughly unpractical man, who could take no account of the reality of Life and its relations. In the publication of this almost wearisomely detailed work it consequently has been my object to help to contravene

---

* See Volume I. of the present series, pages 316 *et seq.*—Tr.
† *Tannhäuser, Lohengrin* and *Siegfried's Tod.*—Tr.
‡ "Art and Revolution" etc., see Vols. I. and II.—Tr.

the usual prejudice of unimaginative men, who are only too willing to deem the fanciful, productive artist, their so-called "genius," entirely unpractical and incapable of taking the actuality of things in cold blood. To teach these people, who are productive in nothing and never get a truly practical idea themselves, what bunglers they are in their praxis; and to prove to them how miserably they waste and uselessly expend the very means wherewith the most Expedient and Significant could be accomplished, so soon as a right understanding had been drawn from the inmost essence of the matter,—it was difficult for me to resist this attraction at the time, even though I dared not flatter myself that I should find acceptance for either my instruction or my proof. That my efforts in this sense were doomed to stay resultless, and my useless toil be looked upon with smiling scorn,— this could but teach me, in my turn, that however rightly I might understand my matter, I still was in grave error as regards the "world." In what that error consisted, I surely have no need to point out here: who thoroughly has grasped it, well may smile upon the world no less than he is smiled at when he tries to teach it.

However, the case is conceivable that some day an earnest demand for instruction by true experts might issue from those regions themselves: I then should be curious to know how, after deliberate perusal, a work such as this of my own from the year 1849 could be rejected as unpractical. Without any anticipation of living to see that phenomenon, nevertheless I believe I must lay my work complete before the kindly reader if I seriously desire to make him thoroughly acquainted with me.

So much in apology, should such be needful!

Bericht

über die Heimbringung der sterblichen Überreste

Karl Maria von Weber's

aus London nach Dresden.

(Aus meinen Lebenserinnerungen ausgezogen.)

————————

The "*Report on the home-bringing of the mortal remains of Karl Maria von Weber from London to Dresden,*" extracted by Wagner from his often-mentioned "*Memoirs*" (as stated in the parenthetic note), immediately follows the poem of the Tannhäuser *drama in Vol. ii. of the* Gesammelte Schriften. *Weber's coffin was received in Dresden on the evening of December 14, 1844, and interred on the succeeding day.*

The first impetus to the movement would seem to have come from an anonymous letter in the Gazette Musicale *of January 21, 1841, whose writer describes his visit to the Moorfields Chapel in Finsbury Circus, and his difficulty in discovering Weber's resting-place there:* "*Deux enfants de chœur vinrent à moi pour s'informer du but de ma visite. Le nom de Weber leur était inconnu.*" *They descended to the crypt:* "*je vis les cercueils noirs posés en couches irrégulières les uns sur les autres . . . Enfin le sacristain de l'église vint se joindre à nous ; il nous aida dans nos recherches, qui n'en furent pas plus fructueuses. Déjà je me résignais et me disposais à remonter, lorsqu'un de mes jeunes guides, après avoir longtemps couru de cercueil en cercueil et essuyé la poussière qui recouvrait les inscriptions, s'écria tout-à-coup :——I have found him ; here it is, Carl-Maria Von Weber . . . Le cercueil dans lequel sont renfermés les restes du grand compositeur ressemble exactement à une grande botte de violon ; il est là confondu avec tout le vulgaire des morts que chaque jour entasse autour de lui. Quand l'enceinte sera devenue trop petite, on s'en débarrassera d'une façon ou de l'autre. Peut-être si le hasard ne m'avait conduit en son dernier séjour, dans quelque temps d'ici ses restes. auraient disparu pour toujours dans la* fosse commune."

In the Gazette *again a note appears on March 21, 1841, to the effect that* "*the artists of the Dresden Royal Kapelle*

have resolved to transport the body of Weber from London.
A part of the expenses has already been covered by a sub-
scription among the artists of the Kapelle and many persons
in every class of society. To provide the balance, a public
concert will be given next month in the Dresden Catholic
church" etc. Whether this was the "concert" referred to by
Wagner below, it is difficult to say ; in any case the Com-
mittee formed in 1841 appears to have very soon dissolved,
as Glasenapp informs us, and the matter was falling back
into oblivion when Richard Wagner took it up, somewhere
about the beginning of 1844.

TRANSLATOR'S NOTE.

REPORT.

 BEAUTIFUL and. earnest incident reacted
on the mood in which I was already finishing
the composition of "Tannhäuser" at the end
of the dying year, and profitably neutralised
the various distractions rising from my outward intercourse. It was the ultimate conveyance, in
December 1844, of the mortal remains of *Karl Maria von
Weber* from London to Dresden. Some years before, a
Committee had been formed to agitate for this removal.
A traveller had made known the fact that the modest
coffin which sheltered Weber's ashes was stowed in such
an out-of-the-way corner of St Paul's church in London,*
that it was to be feared it would soon be past discovery.
My energetic friend Professor *Löwe* had profited by this
news to rouse the Liedertafel, of which he was the passionately active president, to undertake the transference of
Weber's remains. The concert of male singers, given for
the purpose of raising the necessary funds, had had a

* For which read " Moorfields Chapel " (dedicated to St. Mary),—see
opposite page.—Tr.

relatively great success ; folk were pressing for the Theatre
to follow suit, when an obstinate resistance was encountered
in high quarters.   The Dresden General-Direction signified
to the Committee that the King held religious scruples
against the proposed disturbance of a dead man's rest.
One could scarcely credit the motive alleged, yet could not
well contest it ; and so the new era of my appointment as
Kapellmeister was made the plea for obtaining my advocacy
of the plan.   I assented with great alacrity, and allowed
myself to be placed on the Committee ; an artistic authority,
the Director of the Cabinet of Antiques, Herr Hofrath
Schulz, was added to our number, together with a banker ;
the agitation was actively commenced afresh ; appeals were
issued in all directions ; exhaustive plans were drafted, and
above all, numberless sittings took place.   But here again
I fell into antagonism with my chief, Herr *von Lüttichau* :
he certainly would have gladly forbidden me to have anything to do with the thing, under pretext of the Royal
Will, had it been possible, and had not previous experiences
taught him, as the people say (and with them Herr *von
Lüttichau*), that there was "a hair in that broth" when
served to me.   As in any case the King's objection to the
undertaking was not so definitely meant, and my chief
could scarcely help seeing that this Royal Will could not
have hindered its prosecution on a private path ; whilst on
the other hand it would bring the Court into bad odour if
the Royal Theatre, to which *Weber* had once belonged,
were to play the sulking enemy,—Herr *von Lüttichau*
rather sought by pleasantries to turn me from my intervention, without which, as he argued, the affair would
surely never come about.   He represented how invidious
it would be, to pay such extravagant honour to the
memory of precisely *Weber*, when the deceased *Morlacchi*
had served the Royal Kapelle so much longer, yet nobody
proposed to fetch his ashes back from Italy.   To what
consequences might it not lead?   He put the case that
Reissiger were shortly to die on a trip to the baths ; his
widow then might demand, with just as much right as

Frau *von Weber* now, that the body of her husband should be brought home with hymn and chant. I tried to reassure him on this point; though I didn't succeed in making clear to him the difference he had overlooked, yet I managed to convince him that the thing must now pursue its course, especially as the Berlin Court-theatre had already announced a benefit-performance in support of our object. That performance—instigated by *Meyerbeer*, to whom my committee had addressed itself—took place with a representation of "Euryanthe," and brought us in the handsome contribution of full 2,000 thalers [about £300]. Some minor theatres followed; so that the Dresden Court-theatre could now no longer lag behind, and we soon were able to hand our banker a sufficient sum to defray the expenses of transport and provide a seemly vault with a suitable tombstone, and still retain a nucleus for Weber's statue to be erected later. The older of the immortal master's orphaned sons made the journey himself to London, to bring back his father's ashes. The body was brought by ship, up the Elbe, to the Dresden landing-stage, here first to be restored to German soil. This transference was to take place in the evening, by torchlight and in solemn train; I had undertaken to provide the mourning music then to be performed. I compiled it from two motives of "Euryanthe"; that portion of the overture which represents the spirit vision I made conduct into the cavatina of Euryanthe, "*hier dicht am Quell*,"— also quite unchanged, though transposed to B flat,—and ended with the transfiguration of that first motive, as it recurs at the close of the opera. This quite appropriate symphonic piece I expressly orchestrated for 80 picked wind-instruments, taking particular care only to use their smoothest registers, however great the volume; in the section taken from the overture I replaced the tremolo of the violas by twenty stopped trumpets in the gentlest *piano*; and even at the rehearsal in the theatre the whole thing struck so deep a chord in our memory of Weber that not only was Frau *Schröder-Devrient*—who was present at the

time, and at anyrate was a personal friend of Weber's—
most profoundly touched, but I could not help admitting to
myself that I never had wrought out anything so completely answering to its aim. No less successful was the
music's execution in the open street when the cortège took
its way: as the extremely slow tempo, accentuated by
no plain rhythmic landmarks, was bound to offer peculiar
difficulties, I had had the stage completely cleared at
the rehearsal, to gain the necessary room to let the
bandsmen march around me in a circle while they played
the piece, already duly practised. I was assured by
witnesses who watched the cortège passing, from their
windows, that the impression of solemnity had been
unspeakably sublime.

After we had laid the coffin in the little mortuary chapel
of the Catholic cemetery in the Friedrichstadt, where it was
silently and reverently welcomed by Frau Devrient with a
wreath, on the following morning was carried out its solemn
lowering into the vault prepared for its reception. To myself and the other president of the committee, Herr Hofrath
Schulz, the honour of delivering a funeral oration had been
allotted. Quite recently a singularly touching subject had
been furnished me by the death of the lamented master's
second son, *Alexander von Weber*, shortly before this re-
interment. His mother was so terribly shattered by the
unexpected bereavement of this thriving youth that, had
our undertaking not already gone too far, we should almost
have seen ourselves compelled to give it up; for in this
fresh so awful loss the widow seemed disposed to recognise
the voice of Heaven indignant at the vanity of wishing to
disturb the ashes of one so long deceased. As the public,
in its prevalent temper, had manifested symptoms of a
like belief, I held it my peculiar duty to place this side of
our endeavour in its proper light; and after my successful
vindication I was assured on all hands that not a word of
that was heard again. Herewith I made a strange experience, as it was the first time in my life that I had ever had
to pronounce a ceremonial speech in public. Since then,

whenever I have had to hold forth, I have always spoken *ex tempore*; this first time, however, if only to give my speech the needful terseness, I had written it out and learnt it by heart. As the subject and my setting of it entirely filled my mind, I was so certain of my memory that I had taken no thought for any kind of artificial aid; thus it came that I set my brother *Albert*—who was standing near me at the ceremony—in great alarm for a moment, and he told me afterwards that, for all his emotion, he had cursed me for not having supplied him with the manuscript to prompt me. It was this way: on beginning my speech in clear full tones, for an instant I was so strongly affected by the almost terrifying impression made upon me by my own voice, its timbre and accent, that in an absolute trance I seemed to *see* myself, exactly as I *heard* myself, before the breathless-listening crowd; in this projection of myself I fell into a magnetised expectance of the event that was about to pass before me, precisely as if I were not myself the very being who was standing here and had to speak. Not the smallest fright, or even embarrassment, occurred to me; merely, after an appropriate cadence there followed so disproportionately long a pause, that those who saw me standing with my eyes transfixed were puzzled what to make of me. Only my own long silence and the voiceless hush around me, reminded me that here I had not to hearken, but to speak; at once I resumed, and delivered my speech to the end with such fluency that the famous actor *Emil Devrient* assured me that he had been amazingly impressed by the incident, not only as mourner at the most affecting burial, but in particular as dramatic orator. The ceremony ended with the singing of a poem written and composed by myself for male voices, which, notwithstanding its great difficulty, was admirably rendered under the lead of our best opera-singers. Herr von Lüttichau, who attended this rite, at all events declared to me that he had now been convinced and persuaded of the rightness of the undertaking.

The whole issue of my labours was consoling to my

inmost heart; and had anything been lacking to it, the sincerest thanks of *Weber's* widow, whom I visited on my return from the church-yard, contributed to scatter every cloud. For me it had a deep significance, that I whom *Weber's* living presence had won so passionately for music in my earliest childhood, and who later had been so sorely stricken by the tidings of his death, in man's estate should now have entered into immediate personal contact with him through this second burial. From the tenour of my intercourse with living masters of the art of Tone, and the experiences I made of them, one may judge at what a fount my yearning for familiar commune with the Masters had to brace itself. It was not consoling, to look from *Weber's* grave towards his living followers; yet the hopelessness of that outlook was only with time to come to my full consciousness.

SPEECH AT WEBER'S LAST RESTING-PLACE.

ERE rest thee then! Here be the unassuming spot that holds for us thy dear-loved relics! And had they flaunted there midst vaults of princes, within the proudest minster of a haughty nation, we dared to hope thou'dst liefer choose a modest grave in German soil for thy last resting-place.—For thou wast none of those chill seekers after fame, who own no fatherland, to whom that plot of earth is dearest where ambition finds the rankest soil in which to thrive.—Was it a fate that drove thee whither Genius itself must bring itself to market, thou turn'dst thy yearning gaze betimes towards the hearth of home, towards the modest country nook where, seated with thy loving wife, thy heart welled song on song. "Ah! were I once more with you, dear ones!"—this was the latest sigh, for sure, wherewith thou pass'dst from life.

Wast *thou* so fond a dreamer, then who shall blame us that we felt alike toward *thee*; if, laying thy fair dreams to heart, we nursed the silent wish to have thee back once more in our dear homeland? That *Schwärmerei* of thine: with all the power of sympathy, it made of thee the darling of thy folk! Ne'er has a *German-er* musician lived, than thou. Where'er thy genius bore thee, to whatsoever distant realms of floating fancy, it stayed forever linked by thousand tendrils to the German people's heart; that heart with which it wept and laughed, a child believing in the tales and legends told it of its country. Eh! 'twas this childlikeness that led thy manhood's spirit, the guardian angel that preserved it ever chaste and pure; and in that chasteness lay thy individual stamp. As thou maintain'dst that shining virtue ever spotless, thou needest naught to ponder, naught invent—thou neededst but to feel, and straightway hadst thou found the font original. Thou kept'st it till thy death, this highest virtue; thou couldst not cast it off or barter it, that fairest heirloom of thy German birth; thou never couldst betray us!—And lo! the Briton may yield thee justice, the Frenchman admiration; but the German alone can *love* thee. His thou art; a beauteous day amid his life, a warm drop of his own blood, a morsel of his heart—and who shall blame us if we wished thine ashes, too, should mingle with his earth, should form a portion of dear German soil?

Upbraid us not, ye men who so misprised the nature of the German, that heart which dotes on what it loves. Was it dotage bade us claim the precious coil of our dear Weber, then was it that same *Schwärmerei* that makes us so akin to him, the phantasy whence sprang the glorious blossoms of his genius, for whose sweet sake the world admires, and we, we love him.

And so, dear Weber, 'tis love that prompts us to a work of love, when thee—who never sought'st for admiration, but solely love—we snatch from eyes of admiration and bring to arms of love. From out the world, which thou bedazzledst, we lead thee back into thy country, the bosom of thy family! Ask the hero who went out to victory, what most rejoiced him after glorious days upon the field of honour? For sure, the threshold of the father-house, where wife and child await him. And see! we have no need to speak in images: thy wife, thy children wait for thee in very truth. Soon shalt thou feel above this resting-place the tread of thy fond wife, who long—so long!—had waited for thy coming back, and now, beside her darling son, weeps hottest love-tears for the home-sped friend of her true heart. To the world of the living, she belongs—and thee, become a blessed spirit, no more can she greet thee face to face; but God hath sent an envoy forth to greet thee eye to eye on thy return, to bear thee tidings of thy dear ones' everlasting love. Thy youngest son was chosen for that office, to knit the bond 'twixt living and

deceased; an angel of light he hovers now between you,
conveying messages of love from each to each.

Where now is death? Where life? Where both join
hands in bond so wondrous fair, there is the seed of life
eternal.—Let us as well, thou dear departed, commingle in
that bond! Then shall we know no longer death, no more
decay, but only flower-time and harvest. The stone that
closes on thy earthly shell shall then become for us the
desert rock from which the man of might once smote
sweet waters; to farthest ages shall it pour a glorious
stream of ever-quickened, e'er-creative life.

Great Fountain of all being, grant that we prove ever
mindful, ever worthy of this bond!

CHANT

AFTER THE ENTOMBMENT.

YE favour'd of this hour, uplift your voices,
This hour whose solemn peace ye all attest !
To mind commit what now our heart rejoices,
To words and tones the joy that swells our breast !
No longer mourns the shrouded German Mother,
Our German Earth, bereft of her dear son ;
No longer yearns for our beloved brother
Across the sea, in distant Albion :—
She's taken him anew into her womb
Whom once she bore in all his tender bloom.

Here, where the tears of grief were dumbly flowing,
Where love with sobs its dearest still requites,
Here was there knit a bond of hope e'er-growing
That us to him, the shining one, unites :
Ye fellows of that bond, come journey hither,
Here greet as pilgrims of one faith and race ;
Bring here the fairest flowers, that ne'er can wither,
The flowers of lealty to this noble place :
For here rests he, midst faithful hearts and fond,
Who sheds the dew of blessing on our bond.

BEETHOVEN'S CHORAL SYMPHONY
AT DRESDEN, 1846.

Bericht über die Aufführung

der neunten Symphonie von Beethoven

im Jahre 1846 in Dresden

(aus meinen Lebenserinnerungen ausgezogen)

nebst

Programm dazu.

"Report on the performance of Beethoven's Ninth Symphony at Dresden in the year 1846, together with a Programme."

The "Report," as stated in the German title, is an extract from Richard Wagner's "Memoirs," written between the years 1866 and 1871.

The "Programme" was subsequently used at the Carlsruhe Musical Festival of October 1853, conducted by Franz Liszt; within a month or two thereafter it was reprinted by "Hoplit" (Richard Pohl) in a pamphlet entitled "Das Karlsruher Musikfest im Oktober 1853" (Leipzig, 1853), together with the "Programmes" of the Tannhäuser and Lohengrin overtures, already given in Volume III.

TRANSLATOR'S NOTE.

REPORT.

Y chief undertaking this winter consisted in an extremely careful preparation of *Beethoven's Ninth Symphony* for performance on Palm-Sunday in the Spring. This performance brought me into many a conflict, and had most fruitful influence on my whole future evolution. Its outer history was as follows. The Royal *Kapelle* (band) had but one opportunity a-year, outside the Church and Opera, of figuring independently in a major musical performance: in behalf of the Pension-fund for its widows and orphans the so-called Old Opera-house was ceded each Palm-Sunday for a performance, originally of none but oratorios. To make it more attractive, a Symphony was eventually added to the Oratorio. As we Kapellmeisters (Reissiger and myself) had arranged to take these works in turn, the "Symphony" for Palm-Sunday of the year 1846 happened to fall to me. I had a great longing for the Ninth; and my choice was backed by the outward circumstance, that this work was as good as totally unknown in Dresden. When the orchestral committee in charge of the Pension-fund came to hear of this, they were so seized with fright that they sought an audience of our General-Director *von Lüttichau*, to beg him use his supreme authority to bend me from my purpose. The grounds they adduced, were that the Pension-fund would suffer from a choice of this symphony, as it stood in ill repute here and assuredly would keep the public from the concert. Some years ago, they also said, this Ninth Symphony had been given by *Reissiger* at a charity-concert with a disastrous failure, frankly admitted by the conductor himself. In fact it needed all my zeal and every conceivable argument, to overcome the scruples of our chief in the

Q   241

first place. With the orchestral committee there was nothing else for me to do than break off all relations for the moment, as I heard that they were filling the town with their complaints about my recklessness. To shame their outcry, I determined to prepare the public for the performance—in which I still persisted—and the work itself in such a fashion that the notice roused at least should bring about a particularly large attendance, and thus insure the treasury against the boded loss.* Hence the Ninth Symphony became in every possible respect my point of honour, to whose success my every power was strained. The committee objected to the expense of obtaining the orchestral parts: I borrowed them from the Leipzig Concert-union.—How I felt, to see and con those cryptic pages for the first time since my earliest youth, when I had spent the vigils of the night on copying out this score, whose look had plunged me then into a mystic reverie! Just as in that uncertain Paris time the hearing of a rehearsal of the first three movements by the incomparable orchestra of the Conservatoire had suddenly transported me, across whole years of aberration, to a wonderful communion with those days of youth, and exercised a magic force upon the fertilising of my inner aspirations, so now that last resounding memory mysteriously took life in me anew, when I saw with my own eyes again what in that earliest time of all had stayed but mystic eye-work for me. I had passed through much since then, through much that lay unuttered in my deepest heart and urged me now to earnest meditation, to a wellnigh desperate questioning of my destiny and fate. What I dared not speak out to myself, was the knowledge of the utter hollowness of my artistic and civic existence, in a walk of life where I could only view myself as a stranger without one faintest prospect. Now that despair, which I had sought to dissemble from my friends, was turned to bright elation by this symphony. It is impossible that the work of a master should ever have seized the pupil's heart

* See footnote to next page.—Tr.

with such enthralling power, as mine was seized by the first movement of this symphony. Whoever had caught me poring the open score to contrive its means of execution, or heard my fits of sobs and moaning, would certainly have asked if this was meet behaviour for a Royal-Saxon Kapellmeister! Happily I was spared such visits by our orchestral committee and their First Kapellmeister, or any other gentlemen at home in classic music.

My first step was to draft a kind of Programme, after the precedent of the Book-of-words for choral pieces; a guide to an emotional understanding of the work—not directed to a critical analysis, but purely to react upon the hearer's feeling. This Programme, in which I was immensely assisted by famous passages from Goethe's "Faust," was well received not only at the time in Dresden, but later on at other places. Further, I anonymously inserted all sorts of brief enthusiastic jottings in the Dresden *Anzeiger*,* to interest the public in a work which, people told me, was "in disgrace" at Dresden. My efforts even on this outward side were so thoroughly successful that, not only did the receipts exceed anything taken in previous years, but the committee regularly employed the remaining years of my stay in Dresden to ensure an equally substantial sum by repetition of this symphony.

As to the artistic side of the performance, I provided for an expressive rendering on the part of the orchestra by marking in the band-parts themselves everything I deemed needful for a drastic bringing out of nuances. In particular I took careful advantage of the local custom of doubling the 'wind' at grand musical performances, which formerly had been used in the clumsy style of giving the "piano" phrases to one set of instruments, the forte-

* In the third edition of his *Leben Richard Wagner's* Glasenapp tells us that these unsigned "jottings" appeared on March 26 and 31, and April 2, 1846—Palm Sunday falling on April 5. They were inserted at Wagner's own expense, as the Anzeiger appears to have flourished on the singular system of taking money for whatever literary matter its contributors might choose to send in.—Tr.

passages to both. As an instance of my pains to secure distinctness I may cite a passage of the second movement, at first in C, where the whole of the strings maintain the principal rhythmic figure, in a unison of three octaves, against the second theme allotted to the weak wood-wind: "*fortissimo*" being prescribed for the whole orchestra, carry it out as you will, the melody of the wood-wind is completely lost in what really is nothing but a string-accompaniment, and as good as never heard at all. As no letter-piety in the world could induce me to sacrifice the master's true intention to his erroneous marks, I here allowed the strings to give a mere suggestion of strength, instead of actual fortissimo, until they take up the extension of the new theme in alternation with the wind: on the other hand I made the doubled wind exert the utmost force, with the result that their motive was heard distinctly for the first time—as I believe—since the creation of this symphony. I proceeded in a similar way throughout, to ensure the greatest definition in the dynamics of the orchestra. Many a brain has been racked, for instance, by the *fugato* in 6/8 time after the choral verse: "Froh wie seine Sonnen fliegen," in the "*alla marcia*" section of the symphony: taking my cue from the preceding strophe, which seems encouraging to fight and victory, I read this fugato as an actual battle-piece in joyous earnest, and had it played throughout in fiery tempo and with the utmost strain of force. On the day after the first performance I had the satisfaction of receiving a visit from Musikdirektor Anacker of Freiberg, who came to confess that he had till then been one of my antagonists, but since this performance he must number himself with my implicit friends: what had completely won him over—as he told me—was just that reading and delivery of this fugato.—Further, I paid great attention to the unusual recitative-like passage for the violoncelli and contrabassi at the beginning of the last movement, which once had brought such great humiliation on my old friend Pohlenz. Considering the excellence of our contrabassists, in particular, I felt justified in making for the highest perfection here. In course of twelve special rehearsals, which I devoted to the instruments concerned alone, we succeeded in arriving at a phrasing that sounded almost spontaneous, and bringing out the most striking expression alike of feeling tenderness and puissant energy. —From the very commencement I had recognised that the possibility of making this symphony a truly popular success depended on an ideal victory over the extraordinary difficulties in the *choruses.* I saw that claims were here advanced, such as could only be met by a large and enthusiastic mass of singers. The first thing therefore, was to secure myself an exceptionally strong chorus; beyond the usual reinforcement of our theatre-choir by the somewhat feeble *Dreissig'sche Singakademie,* after conquering circumstantial difficulties I engaged the Kreuz-school choir with its splendid boy-voices, as also the choir of the Dresden Seminary, equally well-versed in sacred music. At our countless rehearsals I sought to spur these three-hundred singers to a veritable ecstasy, in my own fashion; for instance I succeeded in proving to the basses that the famous passage "*Seid umschlungen, Millionen,*" and particularly the "*Brüder, über'm Sternenzelt muss ein guter Vater wohnen,*" could not be sung in the ordinary way at all, but must be *shouted out* as if in highest transport. I set them the example of such a rapture that I really believe I brought them all into a quite unwonted state, and would not desist till I no longer could hear my own voice above the others, but felt as if submerged in the warm sea of tone.—The barytone recitative: "Freunde, nicht diese Töne," which may be termed almost impossible on account of its unusual difficulties, I had the great delight of getting rendered with superb expression by *Mitterwurser,* after that mode of mutual inspiration we already knew so well.—Moreover I took the precaution of having the platform completely rebuilt, to ensure a good acoustic effect for the orchestra, which I now disposed on an entirely new system. As one may imagine, it was a particularly hard job to extort the costs of this; yet I gained my point, and through an altogether new construction of the podium we were able to concentrate the whole orchestra in the middle, surrounded by a steep amphitheatre of seats for the numerous choir of singers; of extraordinary advantage to the massive effect of the choruses, this lent the finely-balanced orchestra great energy and precision in the purely symphonic movements.

Even at the full rehearsal the hall was crowded. My colleague thereupon committed the incredible folly of intriguing against the symphony among the audience, and drawing attenton to *Beethoven's* lamentable eccentricity; Herr *Gade* on the other hand—coming from Leipzig, where he then was conducting the Gewandhaus-concerts—after this full rehearsal assured me, among other things, that he would gladly have paid the entrance-fee twice over, to hear that recitative of the basses once again. Herr *Hiller* found that I had gone too far in modifying the tempo; how he meant this, I discovered later from his own conducting of spirited orchestral works. Beyond all dispute, however, the general success exceeded every expectation, and especially with non-musicians: among the latter I remember the philologist Dr *Köchly*, who approached me to confess that he had for the first time been able to follow a symphonic work from beginning to end with intelligent interest.

For my own part, this occasion fed the comfortable feeling of force and faculty to carry to a successful issue what I meant in earnest.

PROGRAMME.

CONSIDERING the great difficulty presented by a first hearing of this extraordinarily important tone-work to those who have not yet had the opportunity of making its close and intimate acquaintance ; and seeing that a by no means insignificant portion of the audience will probably be found in that position, it well may seem permissible to furnish, not so much a help to absolute understanding of Beethoven's masterpiece—since that could come from nothing save an inner intuition—as hints in explanation of its artistic scheme : for in view of its as yet unimitated novelty, this last might easily escape the less-prepared and therefore readily-bewildered hearer. Though it must be admitted that the essence of higher Instrumental-music consists in its uttering in tones a thing unspeakable in words, we believe we may distantly approach the solution of an unachievable task by calling certain lines of our great poet *Goethe* to our aid ; words that, albeit standing in no manner of direct connection with Beethoven's work, and in nowise exhausting the meaning of his purely musical creation, yet so sublimely express the higher human moods at bottom of it that in the worst event, of an inability truly to understand the music, one might content oneself with treasuring up these thoughts, and thus at least not quit its hearing with a heart entirely unmoved.

FIRST MOVEMENT.

The first movement appears to be founded on a titanic struggle of the soul, athirst for Joy, against the veto of that hostile power which rears itself 'twixt us and earthly happiness. The great chief-theme, which steps before us at one stride as if disrobing from a spectral shroud, might

THIRD MOVEMENT.

How differently these tones address our heart! How pure, how heavenly the strain wherewith they calm our wrath, allay the soul's despairing anguish, and turn its turbulence to gentle melancholy! It is as if a memory were awakened, the memory of purest happiness from early days :

Sonst stürzte sich der Himmelsliebe Kuss	In days long gone, e'er rained on me the kiss
Auf mich herab, in ernster Sabbathstille,	Of Heaven's love in sabbath's solemn quiet ;
Da klang so ahnungsvoll des Glockentones Fülle,	The pealing church-bells rang aloud the sweetest fiat,
Und ein Gebet war brünstiger Genuss.	And prayer to me was ecstasy of bliss.

With this memory we reach again that tender yearning so beautifully expressed in this movement's second theme, to which we might appropriately apply these other lines of Goethe's :

Ein unbegreiflich holdes Sehnen	A fathomless enraptured yearning
Trieb mich durch Wald und Wiesen hinzugeh'n,	Drove me through woods afar from mortal eyes,
Und unter tausend heissen Thränen	And midst a flood of tear-drops burning
Fühlt ich mir eine Welt entsteh'n.	I felt a world around me rise.

It appears as the yearning of love, and in turn is answered by that hope-inspiring, soothing first theme—this time in a somewhat livelier dress ; so that with the second theme's return it seems to us that Love and Hope came arm-in-arm to wield their whole persuasive force upon our troubled spirit.

Was sucht ihr, mächtig und gelind,	Why seek me out, ye tones from Heaven,
Ihr Himmelstöne, mich am Staube ?	Why shower your potent blessings on the dust ?
Klingt dort umher, wo weiche Menschen sind.	Go sound where men are made of softer metal.

Thus the still-quivering heart appears to waive aside their solace : but their gentle might is stronger than our already-yielding pride ; conquered, we throw ourselves into the arms of these sweet messengers of purest happiness :

O tönet fort, ihr süssen Himmelslieder,	Sound on, thou soothing-sweet angelic strain :
Die Thräne quillt, die Erde hat mich wieder.	My tears find vent, earth welcomes me again.

Ay, the wounded heart is healing; it plucks up strength, and mans itself to high resolve—as we gather from the wellnigh triumphal passage toward the movement's close. This exaltation is not yet free from all reaction of the outlived storm ; but each recurrence of our former grief is met at once by fresh exertion of that gracious spell, till finally the lightning ceases, the routed tempest rolls away.

FOURTH MOVEMENT.

The transition from the third to the fourth movement—which begins as with a shriek of horror—we again may fairly characterise by Goethe's words :

Aber ach ! schon fühl' ich bei dem besten Willen	Ah me ! howe'er I hold my spirit willing,
Befriedigung noch nicht aus dem Busen quillen !	I feel no balm from out my bosom rilling.
Welch' holder Wahn,—doch ach, ein Wähnen nur !	A beauteous dream—but ah, the cheat of sight !
Wo fass' ich dich, unendliche Natur ?	Where seize I thee, O Nature infinite?
Euch Brüste, wo ? Ihr Quellen alles Lebens,	Ye milky paps, ye founts of all life's main,
An denen Himmel sowie Erde hängt,	To you both earth and heaven cling
Dahin die welke Brust sich drängt.—	To cool their parching at your spring.
Ihr quellt, ihr tränkt, und schmacht' ich so vergebens ?	Ye well, ye drench, and I must thirst in vain?

With this opening of the last movement Beethoven's music takes on a more definitely *speaking* character: it quits the mould of purely instrumental music, observed in all the three preceding movements, the mode of infinite, indefinite expression ; * the musical poem is urging toward

---

* *Tieck*, regarding this character of Instrumental-music from his own standpoint, was moved to the following dictum : "At deepest bottom of these Symphonies we hear insatiate Desire forever hieing forth and turning back into itself, that unspeakable longing which nowhere finds fulfilment and throws itself in wasting passion on the stream of madness, battles with every tone, now overwhelmed, now conquering shouts from out the waves, and seeking rescue sinks still deeper."—It almost seems as if Beethoven had been prompted

·a crisis, a crisis only to be voiced in human speech. It is wonderful how the master makes the arrival of Man's voice and tongue a positive necessity, by this awe-inspiring recitative of the bass-strings; almost breaking the bounds of absolute music already, it stems the tumult of the other instruments with its virile eloquence, insisting on decision, and passes at last into a song-like theme whose simple stately flow bears with it, one by one, the other instruments, until it swells into a mighty flood. This seems to be the ultimate attempt to phrase by instrumental means alone a stable, sure, unruffled joy : but the rebel rout appears incapable of that restriction ; like a raging sea it heaps its waves, sinks back, and once again, yet louder than before, the wild chaotic yell of unslaked passion storms our ear. Then a human voice, with the clear, sure utterance of articulate words, confronts the din of instruments ; and we know not at which to wonder most, the boldness of the inspiration, or the naïvety of the master who lets that voice address the instruments as follows :

| *Ihr Freunde, nicht diese Töne! Son-dern lasst uns angenehmere anstimmen und freudenvollere!* | No, friends, not tones like these! But let us sing a strain more cheerful and agreeable ! |

With these words Light breaks on Chaos ; a sure and definite mode of utterance is won, in which, supported by the conquered element of instrumental music, we now may hear expressed with clearness what boon it is the agonising quest of Joy shall find as highest, lasting happiness.

| *Freude, schöner Götterfunken,*
  Tochter aus Elysium,
Wir betreten Feuertrunken,
  Himmlische, dein Heiligthum.
Deine Zauber binden wieder,
  Was die Mode streng getheilt,
Alle Menschen werden Brüder,
  Wo dein sanfter Flügel weilt. | Joy, thou fairest of immortals,
  Daughter of Elysium,
Fired by thee we pass the portals
  Leading to thy halidom.
Thy dear spell rebinds together
  What the mode had dared divide ;
Man in man regains his brother
  Where thy fost'ring wings abide. |

---

by a similar consciousness of the nature of instrumental-music, in the conception of this symphony.—R. Wagner.

Wem der grosse Wurf gelungen,
  Eines Freundes Freund zu sein,
Wer ein holdes Weib errungen,
  Mische seinen Jubel ein !
Ja,—wer auch nur Eine Seele
  Sein nennt auf dem Erdenrund !
Und wer's nie gekonnt', der stehle
  Weinend sich aus diesem Bund !

Who the joy hath learnt, to gain him
  Friend of his to be his friend ;
Who a loving wife hath ta'en him,
  Gladsome cry to ours shall lend !
Yea—who but can claim one being
  For his own on all earth's strand.
He who dares not, let him fleeing
  Slink with sobs from out our band.

Freude trinken alle Wesen
  An den Brüsten der Natur ;
Alle Guten, alle Bösen
  Folgen ihrer Rosenspur !
Küsse gab sie uns und Reben,
  Einen Freund, geprüft im Tod !
Wollust ward dem Wurm gegeben,
  Und der Cherub steht vor Gott !—

Joy is dew'd on all creation
  From great Nature's mother-breast,
Good and bad in ev'ry nation
  Cull her roses, east and west.
Wine and kisses hath she given,
  One prov'd friend where death erst trod ;
E'en the worm to joy is thriven,
  And the Cherub stands 'fore God.

Warlike sounds draw nigh : we believe we see a troop of striplings marching past, their blithe heroic mood expressed in the words :

Froh, wie seine Sonnen fliegen
  Durch des Himmels prächt'gen Plan,
Laufet, Brüder, eure Bahn,
Freudig, wie ein Held zum Siegen.

Glad as there his suns are leading
  Swift their course through fields of blue,
  Onward brothers stout and true,
Hero-like to vict'ry speeding.

This leads to a brilliant contest, expressed by instruments alone : we see the youths rush valiantly into the fight, whose victor's spoil is *Joy* ; and once again we feel impelled to quote from Goethe :

Nur der verdient sich Freiheit wie das
  Leben,
Der täglich sie erobern muss.

But he may claim his due in life and freedom,
  Who battles for it day by day.

The battle, whose issue we never had doubted, is now fought out ; the labours of the day are crowned with the smile of Joy, of Joy that shouts in consciousness of happiness *achieved* anew :

Freude, schöner Götterfunken,
  Tochter aus Elysium,
Wir betreten Feuertrunken,
  Himmlische, dein Heiligthum.
Deine Zauber binden wieder
  Was die Mode streng getheilt,
Alle Menschen werden Brüder,
  Wo dein sanfter Flügel weilt.

Joy, thou fairest of immortals,
  Daughter of Elysium,
Fired by thee we pass the portals
  Leading to thy halidom.
Thy blest magic binds together
  What the mode had dared divide ;
Man in man regains his brother
  Where thy fost'ring wings abide.

In the transport of Joy a vow of *Universal Brotherhood* leaps from the overflowing breast; uplifted in spirit, we turn from embracing the whole human race to the great Creator of Nature, whose beatific Being we consciously attest,—ay, in a moment of sublimest ecstasy, we dream we see between the cloven skies :

Seid umschlungen, Millionen !	Hand to hand, earth's happy millions !
Diesen Kuss der ganzen Welt !	To the world this kiss be sent !
Brüder, über'm Sternenzelt	Brothers o'er heav'n's starry tent
Muss ein lieber Vater wohnen !	Sure our Father dwells 'mid billions.
Ihr stürzt nieder, Millionen ?	To your knees, ye countless millions ?
Ahnest du den Schöpfer, Welt ?	Knowest thy Creator, world ?
Such' ihn über'm Sternenzelt	Seek him where heav'n's tent is furl'd,
Über Sternen muss er wohnen !	Throned among his starry billions.

And now it is as if a revelation had confirmed us in the blest belief that *every human soul is made for Joy*. With all the force of strong conviction we cry to one another :

Seid umschlungen, Millionen !	Hand to hand, earth's happy millions !
Diesen Kuss der ganzen Welt !	This fond kiss to all the world !

and :

Freude, schöner Götterfunken,	Joy, thou fairest of immortals,
Tochter aus Elysium,	Daughter of Elysium,
Wir betreten feuertrunken,	Fired by thee we pass the portals
Himmlische, dein Heiligthum.	Leading to thy halidom.

With God to consecrate our *universal love*, we now dare taste the *purest* joy.   Not merely in the throes of awe, but gladdened by a blissful truth revealed to us, we now may answer the question :

Ihr stürzt nieder, Millionen ?	To your knees, ye favour'd millions ?
Ahnest du den Schöpfer, Welt ?	Knowest thy Creator, world ?

with :

Such' ihn über'm Sternenzelt !	Seek him where the stars are strewn !
Brüder, über'm Sternenzelt	Brothers, o'er the starry dome
Muss ein lieber Vater wohnen !	Surely dwells a loving Father !

In intimate possession of our granted happiness, of childhood's buoyancy regained, we give ourselves henceforth to its enjoyment. Ah ! we have been re-given innocence of heart, and softly Joy outspreads its wings of blessing o'er our heads:

Freude, Tochter aus Elysium,	Joy, thou daughter of Elysium !
Deine Zauber binden wieder	Thy sweet spell rebinds together
Was die Mode streng getheilt,	What the Mode had dared divide;
Alle Menschen werden Brüder,	Man in man regains his brother
Wo dein sanfter Flügel weilt.	Where thy fost'ring wings abide.

To the gentle happiness of joy succeeds its jubilation: —we clasp the whole world to our breast; shouts and laughter fill the air, like thunder from the clouds, the roaring of the sea; whose everlasting tides and healing shocks lend life to earth, and keep life sweet, for the *joy* of Man to whom God gave the earth as home of *happiness*:

Seid umschlungen, Millionen !	Hand to hand, ye countless millions !
Diesen Kuss der ganzen Welt !	To the world this kiss be sent !
Brüder, über'm Sternenzelt	Brothers, o'er the starry tent
Muss ein lieber Vater wohnen !	Our Father dwells 'mid joyful billions.
Freude ! Freude, schöner Götterfunken !	Joy, blest joy ! thou brightest spark of godhood !

THE WIBELUNGEN.

WORLD-HISTORY AS TOLD IN SAGA.

(Summer 1848.)

Die Wibelungen.

Weltgeschichte aus der Saga.

(Sommer 1848.)

* * *

In the stimulating recent past I too was occupied with the rewakening of *Frederick the Red-beard,* so longed for by so many, and strove with added zeal to satisfy an earlier wish to use my feeble breath to breathe poetic life into the hero-Kaiser for our acting stage. The outcome of the studies by which I sought to master my subject I have embodied in the following work: though its details may contain nothing new to the researcher or student of that branch of literature, yet their allocation and employment seemed interesting enough to some of my friends to justify the printing of the little sketch. I consented the more readily, as this prelude will remain the only fruit of my labours on the stuff itself; labours which themselves impelled me to abandon my dramatic plan, for reasons that will not escape the attentive reader.

The Ur-Kinghood.*

THEIR coming from the East has lingered in the memory of European peoples down to farthest times : Sagas preserved this recollection, however much disfigured. The maintenance of the Kingly power among the different nations, its restriction to one favoured race, the fidelity with which it was accorded solely to that race even in the latter's deepest degeneracy,—must have had a deep foundation in the people's consciousness : it rested on the memory of the Asiatic ur-home, on the origin of folk-stems in the Family, and on the might of the family's Head, the Stem-father "sprung from the Gods."

To gain a concrete idea of this, we must think of that ur-Folk somewhat as follows.—

At the epoch which most Sagas call the " Sint-Fluth " or Great Deluge, when our earth's Northern hemisphere was about as much covered by water as now is the Southern,† the largest island of this northern world-sea

---

* *Die Wibelungen* originally appeared as a pamphlet, issued by Wigand of Leipzig at the end of 1849, evidently with the prefatory note on the opposite page. In Wagner's *Letters to Uhlig* we read under date Sep. 16, 1849, " Up to now I have only been able to scribble in a common-room, and to this circumstance you must attribute my compliance with your wish that I should get my Wibelistic essay ready for publication. In fair-copying it, however, I have made a good many alterations ; so that it perhaps may interest you to compare the accompanying manuscript with the older version, when I would direct your particular attention to chapters 3 and 12, dealing with real property, in which you will find an abundant use of the material." —The " material " would seem to be the late events in Dresden, possibly also some work of Feuerbach's that Wagner had recently been reading, for chapter 3 bears strong evidence of the Feuerbachian cast of sentence, and I find that this is the same letter to which I referred in my Preface to Vol. I.—which see. —Tr.

† This hypothesis, I have lately been assured, is not quite tenable.—Ed. [i.e. R. Wagner, 1871.]

would have been the highest mountain-range of Asia, the so-called Indian Caucasus: upon this island, i.e. these mountains, we have to seek the cradle of the present Asiatic peoples, as also of those who wandered forth to Europe. Here is the ancestral seat of all religions, of every tongue, of all these nations' Kinghood.

But the Ur-kinghood is the Patriarchate: the father was the bringer-up and teacher of his children; to them his discipline and doctrine seemed the power and wisdom of a higher being, and the larger grew the family, the more prolific in collateral branches, the more peculiar and divine must seem to it the mould of its original head, to whom it owed not only its body, but also all its spiritual life and customs. As this Head laid down both discipline and doctrine, in him the royal and priestly powers united of themselves, and his authority was bound to grow in measure as the family became a Stem, above all in degree as his original might descended to his body's heirs direct: as the stem became accustomed to behold in these its chieftains, at last the long-deceased Stem-father, from whom that undisputed honour flowed, was certain to appear a god himself, or at least the earthly avatar of an ideal god; and this idea in turn, enshrined by age, could only serve to perpetuate the fame of that ur-race whose most immediate scions formed the chieftains of the day.*

Now, when the waters retreated from the northern hemisphere to flood the southern once again, and the earth thus took its present guise, the teeming population of that mountain-isle descended to the new-found valleys, the gradually emerging plains. What brought about the hardening of the Patriarchate to a Monarchic despotism among the races dwelling in the broad and fruitful plains of Asia, has been sufficiently set forth: the races wandering farther westwards, and reaching Europe in the end,

* For the use of the prefix "ur" I must refer the reader to my footnote to Vol. I. p. 169. When translating that volume I felt somewhat timid as regards the introduction of a neologism, but now that I find the prefix very widely adopted by learned translators, I am emboldened to employ it more frequently, albeit merely about half as often as it occurs in the original.—Tr.

commenced a livelier and freer evolution. Constant war and want in rawer climes and regions brought forth betimes the feeling and consciousness of the racial unit's independence, with its immediate result in the formation of the Commune. Every head-of-a-family exerted his power over his nearest of kin in similar fashion as the Stem-head claimed the right of ancient usage over the whole stem : in the bond of all the heads of families the king thus found his counterpart, and finally his limitation. The weightiest point, however, was that the king soon lost his priestly office, i.e. the first interpreting of God's decree —the sight of God—since this was now fulfilled for his immediate clan by every single head-of-family with the same authority as the Ur-father had fulfilled it for his family. The King accordingly was left with little more than the application and execution of the god's decree, as rendered by the members of the commune, in the equal interest of all and pursuant to the customs of the tribe. But the more the voice of the community was busied with ideas of worldly Right, i.e. with Property and the Individual's right to its enjoyment, the more that Sight of God—which originally had ranked as an essentially higher prerogative of the Stem-father—would pass to a personal verdict in matters of worldly dispute, and consequently the religious element of the patriarchate would dwindle more and more. Only to the person of the King and his immediate kinsmen, would the feeling of the stem still cleave : he was the visible point-of-union of all its members ; in him they saw the successor to the Ur-father of the widely-branching fellowship, and in each member of his family the purest of that blood whence the whole Folk had sprung. Though even this idea grew dim in time, yet awe and honour of the royal stem abode the deeper in the people's heart the more incomprehensible to it the reason for original distinction of this house, of which the sole unchanged tradition said that from no other must its kings be chosen. This relation we find in almost all the stems that wandered into Europe, and plainly recognise its bear-

ing on the tribal kings of Greek pre-history ; but it mani-
fests itself the clearest in the German stems, and above
all in the ancient royal lineage of the *Franks*, in which,
under the name of the "Wibelingen" or "Gibelinen," an ur-
old royal claim advanced to the demand of world-dominion.

The Frankish royal race makes its first appearance in
history under the name of "Merovingians" ("*Merwingen*") :
we know that, even in the deepest degeneration of this
race, it never occurred to the Franks to choose their kings
from any other ; every male member of this family was competent to rule ; could men not tolerate the vices of the one,
they sided with the other, but never left the family itself;
and this at a time of such corruption of the national code
by willing acceptance of the Romanic taint that almost
every bond of noble wont was loosed, so that the Folk
indeed could hardly have been recognised without its
Royal race. 'Twas as if the people knew that, sans this
royal stem, it would cease to be the Folk of Franks.
The idea of the inalienable title of this race must therefore have been as deeply rooted, as it needed centuries
of fearful struggles to root it out when it had reached
its highest ideal meaning, and with its death begin a
wholly new ordainment of the world. We refer to the
going-under of the "Ghibelines."

The Nibelungen.

The ceaseless strain of men and races toward never-
compassed goals will mostly find a clearer explanation
in their Ur- and Stem-sagas than can be gathered from
their entrance into naked History, which tells us but the
consequences of their essential attributes. If we read tl
Stem-saga of the Frankish royal race aright, we fir
therein an explanation of its historic deeds past anythir
obtainable on other paths of scrutiny.

Unquestionably the *Saga of the Nibelungen* is the birth

right of the Frankish stem. Research has shewn the basis of this saga, too, to be of religio-mythic nature: its deepest meaning was the ur-conscience of the Frankish stem, the soul of its royal race, under whatsoever name the primal Asiatic highlands may first have seen that race arise.—

For the moment we will neglect the oldest meaning of the myth, in which we shall recognise *Siegfried* as God of Light or Sun-god: to prepare ourselves for its connection with history, we now will merely take the saga where it clothes itself with the more human garb of ancient herodom. Here we find Siegfried as the winner of the *Nibelung's Hoard* and with it might unmeasurable. This Hoard, and the might in it residing, becomes the immovable centre round which all further shaping of the saga now revolves: the whole strife and struggle is aimed at this Hoard of the Nibelungen, as the epitome of earthly power, and he who owns it, who governs by it, either is or becomes a Nibelung.

Now the Franks, whom we first meet in history in the region of the Lower Rhine, have a royal race in which appears the name "Nibelung"; especially among its purest scions, who even before the time of Chlodwig were ousted by a kinsman, Merwig [5th cent.], but regained the kingship later as Pipingen or Karlingen [Pepins or Carlovingians]. Let this suffice for the present, to shew, if not the genealogic, at least the mythical identity of the Frankish royal family with those Nibelungen of the saga; which has adopted unmistakable features from the history of this stem into its later, more historical development, where the focus still remains possession of that Hoard, the cynosure of earthly rule.—

After the founding of their reign in Roman Gallia, the Frankish Kings attacked and overthrew the other German national stems, the Allemani, Bavarians, Thuringians and Saxons · that the latter henceforth bore the relation of subjects to the Franks, and though their tribal usages were mostly left them, they had to suffer the indignity of being totally robbed of their royal races, so far as these had not already disappeared; this loss brought home to them the full extent of their dependence, and in the deprivation of its symbol they mourned the downfall of their native freedom. Though the heroic lustre of Karl the Great [Charlemagne]—in whose might the germ of the Nibelungen-hoard appeared to reach its fullest force —diverted for some time the German stems' deep discontent, and made them gradually forget the fame of their own dynasties, yet never did their loathing vanish quite away; under Karl's successors it leapt so strongly back to life, that the division of the great Reich, and the severance therefrom of stricter Germany, must be mainly attributed to the struggle of the downtrod German stems for freedom from the Frankish rule. A total severance from that royal Stem of Rulers, however, was not to take place before still later times ; for though the purely German stems were now united in one independent kingdom, yet the bond of this union of earlier autonomous and severed national stems consisted ever in the Kingly function, and this could only be arrogated by a member of that Frankish ur-race. The whole inner movement of Germany therefore made for independence of the separate stems under new derivatives of old stemraces, and through annulment of the unifying royal power exerted by that hated foreign race.

With the death of the last male Karling in Germany we consequently are brought to the point when a total sundering of the German stems almost arrived, and would surely have arrived in full, had there still existed any plainer vestiges of the ur-old royal races of the single stems. The German Church in the person of its virtual patriarch, the Archbishop of Mainz, then saved the (always tottering) unity of the Reich by delivering the royal authority to Duke Konrad von Franken, who likewise sprang on the female side from the ancient race of kings : only the weakness of his rule, again, brought the inevitable reaction to a final head, as shewn in the attempt to choose a king from among the strongest of the earlier subject, but now no longer manageable German folk-stems.

In the choice of the Saxon Duke *Heinrich*, however, and as if for hallowing it, the consideration may have counted, that his race also was allied by marriage with the Karlingen. But what a resistance the whole new Saxon royal-house had constantly to combat, is evident from the mere fact that the Franks and Lothringians, i.e. those peoples who numbered themselves with the originally ruling stem, would never recognise as lawful King the scion of a folk once conquered by them, whilst the other German stems felt just as little called to pay allegiance to a king imposed upon them by a stem no higher than their own, and equally subjected by the Franks in former times. Otto I. was the first to subdue the whole of Germany, and chiefly through his rousing against the violent and proud hostility of the strictly Frankish stems the national feeling of the Allemani and Bavarians—German stems once trodden down by them —so that the combination of their interests with his kingly interest supplied the force to crush the old Frankish pretensions. The consolidation of his sovereignty, however, appears to have been no little helped by his attainment of the Romish Cæsarate, renewed in former days by Karl the Great; for this conferred on him the lustre of the old Frank ruling-stem, compelling a respect not yet extinct. As if his family had plainly seen this, his successors made incessant journeys to Rome and Italy; to return with that halo of reverence so evidently meant to veil their native lineage in oblivion and translate them to the rank of that ur-race alone equipped for rule. They thus had won the "Hoard" and turned to "Nibelungen."

The century of kingship of the Saxon house, however, forms a relatively short interregnum in the infinitely longer empire of the Frankish stem; for after extinction of the Saxon house the royal power returned to a scion of that Frankish stem, Konrad the Salier,—in whom, again, a female kinship with the Karlingen was proved and taken in view,—and remained with it until the downfall of the "Ghibelines." The choice of Lothar of Saxony, between the extinction of the male Frankish stem and its continuation by descendants on the distaff side, the Hohenstaufen, may be deemed a mere reactionary attempt, and this time of little durability; still more so, the later choice of the Guelph Otto IV. Only with the beheading of young Konrad at Naples can one view the ur-old royal race of the "Wibelingen" as totally extinct; strictly speaking, we must recognise that after him there were no more German Kings, and still less Kaisers, in the high ideal import of that dignity indwelling in the Wibelingen.

Wibelingen or Wibelungen.

The name *Wibelingen*, designating the Kaiser-party in opposition to the *Welfen*, is of frequent occurrence, especially in Italy, where the two opponents gained their ideal scope; upon a closer search, however, we find how utterly impossible it is to explain these highly significant names by *historical* documents. And this is natural: bare History scarcely ever offers us, and always incompletely, the material for a judgment of the inmost (so to say, instinctive) motives of the ceaseless struggles of whole folks and races; that we must seek in Religion and Saga, where we mostly shall find it in convincing clearness.

Religion and Saga are the pregnant products of the people's insight into the nature of things and men. From of old the Folk has had the inimitable faculty of seizing its own essence according to the Generic idea, and plainly reproducing it in plastic personification. The Gods and Heroes of its religion and saga are the concrete personalities in which the Spirit of the Folk portrays its essence to itself: however sharp the individuality of these personages, their content (*Inhalt*) is of most universal, wide-embracing type, and therefore lends these shapes a strangely lasting lease of life ; as every new direction of the people's nature can be gradually imparted to them, they are always in the mood to suit it. Hence the Folk is thoroughly sincere and truthful in its stories and inventions, whereas the learned historian who holds by the mere pragmatic surface of events, without regard to the direct expression of the people's bond of solidarity,* is pedantically untrue because unable to understand the very subject of his work with mind and heart, and therefore is driven, without his knowing it, to arbitrary subjective speculations. The Folk alone understands the Folk, because each day and hour it does and consummates in truth what of its very essence it both can and should ; whereas its learned schoolmaster cudgels his head in vain to comprehend what the Folk does purely of itself.

If—to prove the truthfulness of the people's insight with reference to our present case—instead of a history of Lords and Princes we had a Folk-history, we certainly should also find there how the German peoples always knew a name for that wondrous Frankish race of Kings which filled them all with awe and reverence of a higher type ; a name we find again in history at last, Italianly disguised as "*Ghibelini.*" That this name applied not only to the Hohenstaufen in Italy, but already to their forerunners in Germany, the Frankish Kaisers, is historically attested by Otto von Freisingen : the current form of this name in the Upper Germany of his time was "*Wibelingen*" or "*Wibelungen.*" Now this title would entirely conform with the name of the chief heroes of the ur-Frank stem-saga, as also with the demonstrably frequent family-name among the Franks, of Nibeling, if the change of the initial letter N to W could be accounted for. The linguistic difficulty here is met with ease, if we rightly weigh the origin of just that consonantal change ; this

* " Das Volk ist somit in seinem Dichten und Schaffen durchaus genial und wahrhaftig, wogegen der gelehrte Geschichtsschreiber, der sich nur an die pragmatische Oberfläche der Vorfallenheiten hält, ohne das Band der wesenhaften Volksallgemeinheit nach dem unmittelbaren Ausdrucke desselben zu erfassen," etc.—

lay in the people's mouth, which, following the German
idiom's native bent, made a Stabreim of the two opposing
parties, Welfs and Nibelungs, and gave the preference to
the party of the German folk-stems by placing first the
name of the "Welfen" and making that of the foes of
their independence come after it as rhyme. " *Welfen* und
Wibelungen " the Folk will long have known and named
or ever it occurred to learned chroniclers to plague themselves with the derivation of these, to them, recondite
popular nicknames.   The Italian people, likewise standing
nearer to the Welfs in their feud against the Kaisers,
adopted these names from the German folk-mouth, and
turned them quite according to their dialect to " Guelphi "
and " Ghibelini."   But the learned agony of Bishop Otto
of Freisingen inspired him to derive the title of the
Kaiser-party from the name of a wholly indifferent
hamlet, Waiblingen—a charming trait that plainly proves
how fit are clever folk to understand phenomena of world-
historic import, such as these immortal names in the
people's mouth !   The Swabian Folk knew better who the
" Wibelungen " were, for it called the *Nibelungen* so, and
from the time of the ascendence of its native blood-related
Welfs.

If we borrow from the Folk its conviction of the identity
of this name with that of the ur-old Frankish dynasty, the
consequences for an exact and intimate understanding of
this race's wondrous strivings and ambitions, as also of the
doings of its physical and spiritual opponents, in Folk and
Church, are so incalculable that its light alone will let us
look into the mainsprings of one of the most eventful
periods of world-historic evolution with clearer eye and
fuller heart than our dry-as-dust chronicles ever can give
us ; for in that mighty Nibelungen-saga we are shewn as if
the embryo of a plant, whose natural conditions of growth,
of flower-time and death, are in it certainly foretold to the
attentive observer.

So let us embrace that conviction : and we cannot do so
with a stronger confidence than it inspired in the popular

mind of the Middle Ages coeval with that race's deeds; a confidence that survived to the poetic literature of the Hohenstaufen period, where we may plainly distinguish in the Christian-chivalrous poems the Welfian element become at last a churchly one, in the newly-furbished Nibelungenlieder that utterly contrasting Wibelingian principle with its often still ur-pagan cut.

The Welfen.

Before proceeding to a minuter examination of the point last touched, it is requisite to define more closely the direct opponents of the Wibelingen, the party of the *Welfen*. In the German language " Welfe " means sucklings, at first of dogs, and then of quadrupeds in general. The notion of pure descent and nurture at the mother's breast was easily conjoined to this, and in the poetic people's-mouth a "whelp" would soon be tantamount to a pure-bred son, born and suckled by the lawful mother.

In the times of the Karlingen, at its ancient Swabian stem-seat there enters history a race in which the name of *Welf* is handed down to farthest generations. It is a Welf who first arrests the eye of History by declining to accept enfeoffments from Frankish kings; as he could not stop his sons from entering relations partly connubial and partly feudal with the Karlings, the old father left his lands in deep disgust and withdrew into the wilderness, to be no witness of his race's shame.

If the dry chronicles of that time thought good to record this trait, to them so unimportant, we certainly may assume that it was far more actively embraced and spread abroad by the people of the downtrod German stem; for this incident, whose like may have often occurred before, expressed with energy the proud yet suffering self-consciousness of all the German stems as against the ruling tribe. Welf may thus have been acclaimed a "true whelp," a genuine son of the genuine stem-mother; and,

with the constantly increasing wealth and honour of his
race, it might easily end in the people's viewing the name
Welf as synonymous with German tribal independence
against the feared but ne'er-beloved Frankish sovereignty.

In Swabia, their ancestral seat, the Welfs at last beheld
in the advancement of the petty Hohenstaufen through
intermarriage with the Frankish Kaisers and arrival at
the dignity of Swabian, and thereafter Frankish Dukes,
a fresh shame put upon them ; and King Lothar used
their natural embitterment against this race as chief means
of resistance to the Wibelungen, who openly impugned his
royal right.   He increased the power of the Welfs to a
degree unknown before by granting them the two duke-
doms of Saxony and Bavaria at the same date, and only
through the great assistance thus obtained was it possible
for him to assert his kingship against the clamour of the
Wibelungen, ay, so to humble them that they themselves
held it not unadvisable to found a future stronghold among
the German stems by intermarriage with the Welfs.
Repeatedly did the possession of the major part of
Germany devolve on the Welfen, and though his Wibeling
predecessors had deemed expedient to withdraw it from
them, Friedrich I. appears to have seen in the recognition
of such an estate itself the surest means of reconcilement
with an invincible National party and lastingly laying the
hatred of ages ; in a sense, he pacified them by material
possession, the less disturbedly to realise his own ideal of
the Kaiserdom, which he had grasped as none before.

What part is to be ascribed to the Welfs in the final
foundering of the Wibelingen, and with them of the
stricter German monarchy, is plainly told in history : the
latter half of the thirteenth century shews us the fulfilled
reaction of the narrower national spirit of the German
stems, in their thirst for independence, against the royal
yoke originally imposed upon all by the Franks.   That
these stems themselves were almost entirely disbanded
till then, is to be explained, among other things, by their
having lost their royal families as result of their first

subjection to the Franks; their other noble houses, the nearest of kin to the former, could therefore more easily make themselves absolute (directly holding from the Reich,—*reichsunmittelbar*) under the shelter and pretext of inherited imperial fiefs, and thus induce the thorough disgregation of the stems in whose broader national-interest the fight against the supremacy of the Wibelungen had first been waged. The ultimately successful reaction was therefore founded less upon an actual triumph of the stems, than on the collapse of the central kingly power undermined from of old by that fight. That it did not take place in the sense of the Folk, but in the interest of lords who were splitting up the folk-stems, is thus the ugly feature in this historical occurrence, however much that issue lay appointed by the nature of the existing historic elements themselves. Yet we may call everything related hereto the "Welfic" principle (devoid of any stem-saga), in opposition to that of the Wibelungen, which developed into nothing less than a claim to world-dominion.

The Nibelungen-hoard in the Frankish Royal race.

Clearly to grasp the inner relation of the Nibelungen-saga to the historical significance of the Frankish Kingship, let us once more turn back, and at somewhat greater length, to a consideration of the historic doings of this ancient princely race.

In what state of inner dissolution of their tribal system the Frankish stems at last arrived at their historic seat, the present Netherlands, cannot be strictly ascertained. We at first distinguish Salic and Ripuarian Franks; and not merely this distinction, but also the fact that larger districts (*Gaue*) had their independent Princes, makes it obvious that the original Stem-kingship had suffered a strongly democratic devolution through the rovings and most varied partings, as also the later re-uniting of branch-races. One thing is certain, that only from the

hey stretched its physical significance to ever fuller width
>y constant conquest and addition to the royal might, and
he latter more especially by a systematic rooting-out of
ill the blood-relations of their house.

One of the sons of Chlojo was saved, however; his
descendants fled to Austrasia, regained the Nibelgau,
:stablished themselves at Nivella, and finally re-appeared
n history as the "Pipingen," a name unquestionably given
:hem by the hearty sympathy of the Folk with the fate of
:hose little sons of Chlojo, and hereditarily accepted in
due gratitude for this people's helping and protecting love.
For these it was reserved, after recovery of the Nibelungen-
hoard, to raise the material value of the worldly power
upbuilt thereon to its uttermost pitch: Karl the Great,
whose predecessor had entirely set aside at last the puffed-
up and degenerate race of the Merwingen, gained and
governed the whole German world, together with the
former West-Roman Empire so far as German peoples
dwelt therein; he accordingly might deem himself de
facto successor to the rights of the Roman Cæsars, and
claim their confirmation by the Romish Pontiff.

Arrived at this high stand-point, we now must prepare ourselves for a survey of the world's condition at that time, and
indeed in the sense of the mighty Nibelung himself; for this
is the point from whence the historic import of that often-
mentioned Frankish saga is to be taken more clearly in eye.

When Karl the Great looked down from the height of
his West-Roman Kaiser-throne upon the world he knew,
the first thing to strike him, must have been that solely in
himself and family had the German ur-Kingship survived:
all the royal races of the German stems related to him,
so far as language proved a common origin, had passed
away or been destroyed by subjugation, and he thus might
deem himself the only representative and lawful heir of
German Ur-Kinghood. This state of affairs would very
naturally lead him and his nearest kin, the Franks, to regard
themselves as the peculiarly-privileged, the oldest and
most imperishable stem-race of all the German nation, and

S

eventually to find an ideal right to that pretension in their primitive stem-saga.   In that stem-saga, as in every ur-old saga of like kind, an originally religious core is plainly visible.   Though we left that kernel on one side at its earliest mentioning, it now is time to view it closer.

Origin and evolution of the Nibelungen-myth.

Man receives his first impressions from surrounding Nature, and none of her phenomena will have reacted on him so forcibly from the beginning, as that which seemed to him to form the first condition of the existence, or at least of his knowledge, of everything contained in Creation : and this is *Light, the Day, the Sun.* Thanks, and finally worship, would be paid this element the first ; the more so, as its opposite, Darkness, Night, seemed joyless, hence unfriendly and fear-compelling.   Now, as man drew all his joy and animation from the light, it soon would come to mean the very fount of Being: it became the begetter, the father, the god ; the breaking of day out of night at last appeared to him the victory of Light over Darkness, of Warmth over Cold, and so forth ; and this idea may have been the first to breed in man a moral consciousness and lead him to distinction of the useful and the harmful, the friendly and hostile, Good and Bad.

So far, at anyrate, this earliest nature-impression must be regarded as the common basis of all Religions of every people.   In the individualising of these general ideas derived from physical observation, however, is to be sought the gradually-conspicuous cleavage of religions according to the character of different nations.   Now the stem-saga of the Franks has the high pre-eminence that, in keeping with the stem's peculiarity, it developed more and more from this beginning to historic life, whereas a similar growth of the religious myth into a genealogic saga is nowhere to be found among the other German stems : in exact degree as these lagged behind in active influence on history, did their stem-sagas stop short at the religious myth (superlatively the case with the Scandinavians), or get lost in wholly undeveloped fragments at the first shock with historic nations more alive.

At the farthest point to which we can trace it, the Frank stem-saga shews the individualised Light or Sun-god, who conquers and lays low the monster of ur-Chaotic night :— this is the original meaning of *Siegfried's fight with the Dragon*, a fight like that Apollo fought against the dragon Python. Yet, as Day succumbs to Night again, as Summer in the end must yield to Winter, Siegfried too is slain at last: so the god became man, and as a mortal man he fills our soul with fresh and stronger sympathy; for, a sacrifice to his deed of blessing us, he wakes the moral motive of Revenge, i.e. the longing to avenge his death upon his murderer, and thus renew his deed. The ur-old fight is now continued by ourselves, and its changeful issue is just the same as that eternal alternation of day and night, summer and winter,—and lastly of the human race itself, in ceaseless sway from life to death, from triumph to defeat, from joy to grief, and thus perennially rejuvenating in itself the active consciousness of the immortal fund of Man and Nature. The quintessence of this constant motion, thus of Life, at last in " *Wuotan* " (Zeus) found expression as the chiefest God, the Father and Pervader of the All. Though his nature marked him as the highest god, and as such he needs.must take the place of father to the other deities, yet was he nowise an historically older god, but sprang into existence from man's later, higher consciousness of self; consequently he is more abstract than the older Nature-god, whilst the latter is more corporeal and, so to phrase it, more personally inborn in man.

If this may pass as a general statement of the evolutionary path of Saga, and finally of History, from the ur-Myth, our next concern will be that weighty point in the fashioning of the Franks' stem-saga which gave this race its quite specific physiognomy,—to wit, the *Hoard*.

In the religious mythos of the Scandinavians the term

Nifelheim, i.e. Nibel = Nebelheim [the Home of Haze]
comes down to us as designation of the (subterranean)
sojourn of the Night-spirits, " Schwarzalben," in opposition
to the heavenly dwelling of the " Asen " and " Lichtalben "
["Light-elves "]. These Black-elves, " Niflûngar," children
of Night and Death, burrow the earth, find out its inner
treasures, smelt and smith its ore : golden gear and keen-
edged weapons are their work. Now we find the name
of "Nibelungen," their treasures, arms and trinkets, again
in the Frankish stem-saga, but with the distinction that
the idea originally shared by all the German stems has
here evolved to ethical historic import.

When Light vanquished Darkness, when Siegfried slew
the Nibelungen-dragon, he further won as victor's spoil the
Nibelungen-hoard it guarded. But the possession of this
Hoard—whose properties increase his might beyond all
measure, since he thereby rules the Nibelungen—is also
reason of his death : for the dragon's heir now plots to win
it back. This heir despatches him by stealth, as night the
day, and drags him down into the gloomy realm of Death :
Siegfried thus becomes himself a Nibelung. Though doomed
to death by acquisition of the Hoard, each sequent genera-
tion strives to seize it : its inmost essence drives it on, as
with necessity of Nature, as day has ever to dethrone the
night anew. For in the Hoard there lies withal the secret
of all earthly might : *it is the Earth itself with all its splendour, which in joyous shining of the Sun at dawn of day we
recognise as our possession to enjoy, when Night, that held its
ghostly, gloomy dragon's-wings spread fearsomely above the
world's rich stores, has finally been routed.*

If we look closer at this Hoard, *the Nibelungen's special
work,* in it we recognise at first the metal bowels of the
earth, and next what is prepared therefrom : arms, ruler's-
ring, and stores of gold. So that Hoard included in itself
the means of gaining and insuring mastery, as also the one
Talisman of Rule : the hero-god who won it first, and thus
became a Nibelung partly through his power and partly
through his death, left as heirloom to his race the active

right to claim the Hoard: to avenge the slain and keep or win the Hoard afresh, this stress makes out the soul of all the race; by this it may be recognised throughout the saga, and above all in its history, that race of the Nibelungen-Franken.

Now, should it be thought too daring to assume that even in the ur-home of the German tribes that wondrous race once reigned above them all, or, if the other German stems have sprung from it, that at their head it once had ruled all other peoples on that Asiatic mountain-isle, at least a later phase is irrefutable,—that it actually governed all the German stems in Europe, and at their head, as we soon shall see, both claimed and strove for the dominion of every nation in the world. That deeply innate stress, now stronger and now weaker, this race of Kings appears to have referred in every age to its prime origin ; and Karl the Great knew perfectly what he was doing, and why, when he had all songs of the stem-saga most care-fully collected and transcribed: he knew they would confirm the Folk's belief in the ur-old right of his dynasty.

The rank of Romish Kaiser and the Roman stem-saga.

The sovereign-instinct of the Nibelungen, till then more brutal in its satisfaction, was led at last by Karl the Great towards an ideal aim : this psychologic moment (*der hierzu anregende Moment*) must be sought in Karl's assumption of the *Roman Cæsardom*.

If we cast a glance upon the extra-German world, so far as it lay bare to Karl the Great, we find the selfsame kingless plight as with the subject German stems. The Romanic nations ruled by Karl had long since lost their royal races through the Romans; the Slavonic nations, little valued in themselves and destined for a more or less thorough Germanising, had never won for their ruling races, now also falling to decay, a recognition equal to the German's. Rome alone retained historic claim to rule, and that to rule the world ; that world-dominion had been exerted by the Cæsars in the name of a people, not of an ur-old royal race, but nevertheless in form of Monarchy. These Cæsars, in latter days capriciously selected first from this, then that component of the brew of nations, had never had to prove a racial right to the highest sovereignty in all the world. The deep corruption, impotence, and shameful foundering of this Roman Cæsarate —propped up at last by nothing but the German mercenaries, who had possession of the Roman Empire long years before its actual extinction—had certainly not faded from the memory of its Frankish conquerors. Yet, for all the personal weakness and depravity of the emperors known to the Germans, a deep awe and reverence of that rank under whose authority this highly-cultured Roman world was ruled had been implanted in the minds of the barbaric intruders, and there had stayed until these later times. And in that feeling there might lurk, not only respect for a higher culture, but also an old remembrance of the first brush of the German peoples with the Romans, who under *Julius Cæsar* once had reared a strong and lasting dam against their restless inroads.

Already German warriors had hunted Gauls and Celts, with hardly a stand, over the Alps and across the Rhine ; the conquest of the whole of Gallia was easily within their grasp, when suddenly in Julius Cæsar they encountered a force unknown to them before. Beating them back, vanquishing and partly subjugating them, this supernal captain must have made an indelible impression on the Germans ; and confirmed was their deep awe of him when they later learnt how all the Roman world had bent to him, how his patronymic " Cæsar " had been hallowed to the title of the highest earthly might, whilst he himself had been translated to the Gods from whom his race had sprung.

This divine descent was grounded on an ur-old Roman saga, according to which the Romans issued from a primordial race that, coming once from Asia, had settled on the banks of the Tiber and Arno. The quick of the religious halidom committed to the offspring of this race indisputably made out for ages the weightiest heritage of the Roman nation : in it reposed the force that bound and knit this active people ; the " sacra " in the keeping of the oldest, immemorially-allied patrician families, compelled the heterogeneous masses of plebeians to obedience. Deep awe and veneration of the holy things, whose sense enjoined a vigorous abstemiousness (as practised by the sorely-tried ur-father), make out the oldest, inconceivably effective laws whereby the headstrong folk was governed ; and the "*pontifex maximus*"—the unchanging successor of Numa, the moral founder of the Roman State—was the virtual (spiritual) king of the Romans. Actual Kings, i.e. hereditary holders of the highest worldly rulership, are unknown in Roman history : the banished Tarquins were Etruscan conquerors ; in their expulsion we have less to recognise a political act of insurrection against the royal power, than the old stem-races' national act of shaking-off a foreign yoke.

Now, when the plebs was no longer to be held in check by these stern and spiritually-armoured ancient races ; when through constant warfare and privation it had made its strength so irresistible that, to avoid a destructive discharge thereof against the inmost core of the Roman State-system, it must be loosed upon the outer world in conquest, then, and still more as result of this world-conquest, the last bond of ancient customs slowly snapped, and religion dropped into its utter opposite through the most material worldlifying : dominion of the world, enslavement of its peoples—no more dominion of the inner man, subdual of his egoistic animal passions—was henceforth Rome's religion. The Pontificate, though it still stood outward token of the ancient Rome, passed over to the worldly Imperator as his weightiest attribute, significantly enough ; and the first man to combine both powers was just that Julius Cæsar, whose race was lauded as the very oldest emigrant from Asia. Troja (*Ilion*), so

said the old stem-saga now ripened to historic consciousness, was that sacred town of Asia whence the Julian
(*Ilian*) race had sprung : during the destruction of his
father-town by the united Hellenic stems Æneas, son of
a goddess, had rescued the holiest relic (the Palladium)
preserved in this ur-people's city, and brought it safe to
Italy: from him descend the primal Roman races, and
most directly of them all the Julian; from him, through
the possession of that ur-folk's halidom, was said to date
the core of Romandom, their old religion.

Trojan descent of the Franks.

How full of meaning is the historically-attested fact that,
shortly after the foundation of their rule in Roman Gallia,
the Franks gave themselves out as likewise *sprung from
Troy*. The chronicle-historian gives a pitying smile to
such a stale conceit, which cannot hold a grain of truth.
But he whose purpose is to vindicate the deeds of men
and races by their inmost views and impulses, will find it
of the highest moment to note what they *believed*, or tried
to make others believe, about themselves. And no feature
can be of more striking historic importance, than this
naïve utterance of the Franks' belief in their ur-right to
rule, upon their entry on that Roman world whose culture
and whose past inspired them with reverence, yet to rule
which they were proud enough to base their right directly
on the principles of classic Romandom itself. So they,
too, sprang from Troy; in fact it was their royal race that
governed once in Troy. For one of their ancient stem-
kings, *Pharamond*, was none other than *Priamus*, the very
head of the Trojan royal family, who after the destruction
of the city, so they said, had journeyed into distant parts
with a remnant of his people. The first point for us to
notice here, is that the naming of towns or transformation
of their names by an addendum, as also the poetic adaptations of the Trojan War and incidents allied therewith in

vogue until the later Middle Ages, afford sufficient evidence of the wide spread and lasting influence of this new saga. Whether it was in all respects as new as it looks, and does not contain a germ far older than its new disguisal in the Græco-Roman dress,—this certainly is worth inquiry.

The legend of an ur-old town or castle, built by the earliest human races and circled with Cyclopean walls to guard their holiest fetish, we find with almost every nation of the world, and especially with those of whom we may assume that they spread westward from those ur-hills of Asia. Did the archetype of these fabled cities not actually once exist in these peoples' earliest home? Surely there was one oldest, first walled city, which held in it the oldest and most venerable race, the well-spring of all patriarchism, i.e. of Kinghood joined with Priesthood. The farther did the stems move westward from their ancient home, the holier would grow their memory of that ur-town ; it became to them a city of the Gods, the Asgard of the Scandinavians, the Asciburg of the related Germans. On their Olympos we find again among the Greeks the dwelling of the Gods ; before the Romans'· Capitol, no less, it may originally have hovered.

Certain it is, that wherever the stems, now grown to nations, made their abiding home, there that ur-town was copied in reality : to it, the new stem-seat of the ruling oldest race of Kings and Priests, the sanctity of the primordial city was gradually transferred ; and the farther did the races journey from it in its turn, and build again, the more accountably would wax the glamour of this new stem-city also. Very naturally, however, with the freer evolution of these branch-communities, and their growing sense of self-reliance, the desire for independence would arise ; and in.exact degree as the ancient ruling-race, that governed from the new stem-city, endeavoured to imprint its sovereignty on the offshoot communes, or cities, and met their stiffening recusance with added tyranny. The first national Wars of Independence were therefore those waged by Colonies against the Mother-cities ; and so

obstinate must have grown their enmity, that nothing less
than the destruction of the old stem-city, with the extirpa-
tion or total banishment of the hereditary ruling-race, could
still the hate of the epigoni or lay their fears of fresh
oppression.   All the greater historic nations that followed
in each other's footsteps from the Indian Caucasus to the
Mediterranean Sea know such a holy city, copied from the
ur-old city of the Gods on earth, as also its destruction by
new generations : very probably they even nursed the
memory of an ur-old war of earliest races against the eldest
ruling-race in that Gods'-city of their hoariest home, and of
that town's destruction : this may have been, in fact, the
first general tussle for the Nibelung's Hoard.

Nothing do we know of great Mother-cities founded by
our German stems on that Ur-town's model in their long
North-westward wandering, which was finally arrested by
the German Ocean and the sword of Julius Cæsar.   On
the other hand, the memory of the Gods'-city in their
oldest home itself had lingered with them; and, un-per-
petuated to the eye by material reproduction, it had settled
to the more abstract notion of a Gods'-abode in Asgard.
Not till we come to their new and stabler home, our present
Germany, do we meet with signs of Asenburgs.

Different had been the evolution of the peoples thrusting
South-westwards, among whose Hellenic stems the last
distinct remembrance, of their united fight-for-independence
against the Priamids and the razing of Troy, as the most
signal outset of a new historic life, had almost totally
extinguished every other memory.   Now, as the Romans,
after a closer acquaintance with the historic stem-saga of
the Hellenes, had held themselves completely justified in
linking on the dim remembrances of their forefathers'
descent from Asia to that sharp-cut myth of the better-
cultured nation (as if to represent their subjugation of the
Greeks as a reprisal for the destruction of Troy), just so
did the Franks lay hand on it, perhaps with no less title,
when they came to know the legend and its sequel.   If
the German memories were less distinct, at least they were

still older, for they clung directly to the earliest home, the burg (Etzel-, i.e. Asci-burg) in which was stored the Nibel-ungen-hoard once won by their Stem-god and left to them and their strong arm; thus the burg whence they had once already ruled all kindred folks and races. The Grecian Troy became for them that cradle city, and the King of immemorial right, dislodged therefrom, in them revived his ancient privilege.

At last confronted with the history of the South-west wanderers, must not his race regard its wondrous preserva-tion as a token of the gods' eternal preference? All peoples now descended from the races that had waged a patricidal war against the oldest royal race in the cradle-home, and, victorious then, had forced this race to journey toward the raw inhospitable North while they fenced in the fertile South for leisurely expansion,—all these the Franks found *kingless*. Long since extinct and rooted out, were the oldest tribes in which these stems had erst known Kings; a last Greek Stem-King, the Macedonian *Alexander* —offspring of Achilles, that foremost vanquisher of Troy—, had un-kinged the whole southern Orient itself, up to the cradle of mankind in central Asia, as if in last fulfilment of that earliest patricidal war: with him his race expired too, and from that time none had rule except unrightful raiders of the royal power, who all had finally succumbed beneath the weight of *Julian Rome*.

After extinction of the Julian race even the Roman Emperors were arbitrarily elected, in any case not racially legitimate, dictators: their empire, or ever they them-selves became aware of it, had long since ceased to be a "Roman" empire; as from of old it had only been bound up by force, and a force maintained through well-nigh naught but armies, so, now that the Romanic nations were completely degenerated and effeminate, these armies were formed of almost none but hired troops of German origin. Hence, gradually renouncing all material worldly might, after long estrangement from itself the Roman spirit necessarily turned back upon itself, to its ur-nature;

and thus, adopting Christianity, it gave birth to a new development, the Roman Catholic Church: the Imperator again became all Pontifex, Cæsar again Numa, in new peculiarity of import. Now the *Pontifex maximus*, or *Pope*, was approached by the full-blooded representative of Ur-world-Kinghood, *Karl the Great*: the bearers of the oldest Kinghood and the oldest Priesthood, dissevered since the razing of that cradle city (according to the Trojan saga: the *royal Priamos* and the *pious Æneas*) met after centuries of parting, and touched as body and spirit of mankind.

Joyful was their meeting: nothing should ever part them more; the one should give the other troth and shelter: the Pontifex crowned the Cæsar, and to the nations preached obedience toward their lawful King; the Kaiser installed the Priest of God in his supreme pastorate, in whose exercise he undertook to shield him with the arm of worldly strength against all caitiffs.

Now, if this king was de facto master of the West-Roman empire, and might the thought of the ur-kingly title of his race awake in him the claim to perfect sovereignty of the world, in the Kaisership he gained still stronger title to that claim, especially through his entrustment with the shelter of that Christian Church which was to span the world. For the further development of that majestic world-relation, however, it is most important to remark that this spiritual title set up no altogether novel claim of the Frankish royal race, but simply woke to plainer terms a claim ingenerate in the germ of the Frankish stem-saga, though veiled till then in dimmer consciousness.

Material and Ideal contents of the Nibelungen-Hoard.

With Karl the Great the often-cited ur-old myth attains its most material confirmation in a grand harmonious juncture of world-history. Thenceforward in exact degree as its real embodiment dissolved and fell to pieces, its essential *ideal* content was to mount to such a point that, entirely divested of the Real, the pure Idea steps plainly formulated into History, and finally withdraws therefrom to pass, even as to its outward garment, completely back to Saga.

Whereas in the century after Karl the Great, under his more and more incompetent successors, the actual kingdom and the sovereignty over subject peoples had crumbled up and lost in power, all the atrocities of the Karlings sprang from one root-instinct common to them all, the longing for sole possession of the Nibelungen-hoard, i.e. of rule supreme. Since Karl the Great this seemed to need confirming by the Kaisership, and he who won the Kaiser-throne believed himself the true possessor of the Hoard, whatever the diminution of its worldly wealth (in landed property). The Kaiserhood, with the supreme authority to it alone attaching, was thus invested with a more and more ideal meaning; and during the period of total defeat of the Frankish ruling-stem, when the Saxon Otto seemed to be restoring the real Cæsarate of Karl the Great in fresh conjunction with Rome, its *ideal* aspect would appear to have come to ever clearer consciousness in the mind of that old stem. The Franks and their ducal race of one blood with the Karlingen, thinking of the saga, may have told themselves something like this: "What though the real possession of the land is torn from us, and once more we're thrown upon ourselves,—can we but regain the Imperial rank, for which we'll never cease to strive, with it we win again our ancient title to mastery of the world; and then we'll know to ply it better than these usurpers of the Hoard, who do not even understand its use."

In effect, as soon as the Frankish stem regained the Kaiserdom, the world-question hinging on that dignity advanced to an ever more important stage, and that through its relation with the Church.

In measure as the worldly power had lost in real estate

and approached a more ideal development, the originally purely ideal Church had attained to worldly possession. Each party seemed to comprehend that, for its perfect establishment, it must draw into itself what had lain at first without it; and so from both sides the original antithesis was mounting to an open fight for exclusive world-dominion. Through the growing consciousness of both parties to this more and more stubborn fight, of the prize at stake for winning or retaining, the Kaiser at last was forced to the necessity of acquiring the spiritual dominion of the world, if he meant to safeguard his material title ;— the Pope, on the other hand, must annihilate these material claims, or rather take them to himself, if he meant to remain or become the actual governor and overseer of the World-Church.

The resultant demands of the Pope were insofar grounded upon Christian Reason (*Vernunft*) as he felt bound to adjudge to Spirit the power over Body, consequently to God's Vicar on earth the supremacy over His creatures. The Kaiser, on the contrary, saw that his prime concern was to prove his power and claims quite independent of any hallowing or ratifying, to say nothing of bestowal, by the Pope; and for this he found what he deemed a perfect title in the old belief of his stem-race in their origin.

In its earliest form, the stem-saga of the Nibelungen went back to the memory of a divine Ur-father, not only of the Franks, but perhaps of all the nations issued from the Asiatic home. Very naturally in this Ur-father, as we find with every patriarchal system, the royal and priestly powers had been combined as one and the same authority. The later severance of these powers would rank in any case as consequence of a dissension in the race, or, had the priestly power devolved on all the fathers of the commune, in them at most could it be recognised, but never in an upstart Priest opponent to the King; for the fulfilment of the priestly office, so far as it was to be assigned to one sole person for them all, could fall to no one but the King, as Father of the racial whole. That there was no need for those ur-old notions to be sacrificed in toto on the conversion to Christianity, not only is proved by facts, but may be deduced with little pains from the essential content of the old traditions. The abstract Highest God of the Germans, Wuotan, did not really need to yield place to the God of the Christians ; rather could he be completely identified with him : merely the physical trappings with which the various stems had clothed him in accordance with their idiosyncrasy, their dwelling-place and climate, were to be stripped off; the universal attributes ascribed to him, for the rest, completely answered those allotted to the Christian's God. And Christianity has been unable to our day to extirpate the elementary or local Nature-gods : quite recent legends of the Folk, and a wealth of still-prevailing superstitions, attest this in our nineteenth century.

But that one native Stem-god, from whom the races all immediately derived their earthly being, was certainly the last to be given up : for in him was found the striking likeness to Christ himself, the Son of God, that he too died, was mourned and avenged,—as we still avenge Christ on the Jews of to-day. Fidelity and attachment were transferred to Christus all the easier, as one recognised in him the Stem-god once again ; and if Christ, as Son of God, was father (at least the spiritual) of *all* men, that harmonised the better and more conclusively with the divine Stem-father of the Franks, who thought themselves indeed the oldest race and parent of all others. Christianity therefore, with their incomplete and physical understanding of it, would rather strengthen the Franks in their national faith, particularly against the Roman Church, than make them falter ; and in rejoinder to this vital obstinacy of the Wibelingian superstition, we see the natural instinct of the Church attacking with almost a mortal dread this last, but sturdiest survival of paganism in the deeply hated race.

The "Ghibeline" Kaiserdom and Friedrich I.

Now it is highly noteworthy that the stress toward Ideal vindication of their claims becomes more pronounced in the Wibelingen or Wibelungen (to name them with the historic folk-mouth) in measure as their blood departs from immediate kinship with the ur-old ruling race. If in Karl the Great the drift of blood was still at height of its ancestral strength, in the Hohenstaufian *Friedrich I.* we see almost nothing but the ideal stress : it had become at last the very soul of the Imperial entity, that could find less and less legitimation in its blood and real estate, and therefore sought it in the Idea.

Under the last two Kaisers of the Frankish ducal race of the Salier the great fight with the Church had begun in deadly earnest. Heinrich V., previously supported by the Church against his hapless father, had scarcely reached the rank of Kaiser than he felt the fateful craving to renew his father's wrestle with the Church, and, as if the only means of combating her claims, to extend his title over her as well: he must have divined that the Kaiser were impossible, should his world-dominion not include dominion of the Church herself. It is characteristic, on the other hand, that the interim non-Wibelingian Kaiser Lothar adopted an attitude of peaceful submission to the Church : he did not fathom what the Kaiser-rank implied; *his* claims did not extend to world-dominion,—those were the heirloom of the Wibelingen, the old-legitimist contenders for the Hoard. But clearly and plainly as none before, great *Friedrich I.* took up the heir-idea in its sublimest sense. The whole inner and outer depravation of the world appeared to him the necessary consequence of the weakness and incompleteness with which the Kaiser's power had been exerted thitherto : the material might, already in sorry case, must be perfectly amended by the Kaiser's ideal dignity; and that could only come to pass when its extreme pretensions were enforced. The ideal lines of the great fabric that rose before Friedrich's energetic soul may · be drawn (in the freer mode of speech allowed to-day) somewhat as follows :—

"In the German Folk survives the oldest lawful race of Kings in all the world : it issues from a son of God, called by his nearest kinsmen *Siegfried*, but *Christ* by the remaining nations of the earth ; for the welfare of his race, and the peoples of the earth derived therefrom, he wrought a deed most glorious, and for that deed's sake suffered death. The nearest heirs of his great deed, and of the power won thereby, are the 'Nibelungen,' to whom the earth belongs in name and for the happiness of every nation. The Germans are the oldest nation, their blue-blood King is a 'Nibelung,' and at their head he claims world-rulership. There can therefore exist no right to any sort of possession or enjoyment, in all this world, that does not emanate from him and need its hallowing by his feoffment or sanction : all property or usufruct not bestowed or sanctioned by the Kaiser is lawless in itself, and counts as robbery ; for the Kaiser enfiefs and sanctions for the good, possession or enjoyment, of *all*, whereas the unit's self-seized gain is a theft from all.—In the German Folk the Kaiser grants these feoffments or confirmations himself; for all other nations their Kings and Princes are attorneys of the Kaiser, from whom all earthly sovereignty originally flows, as the planets and their moons receive their radiance from the sun.—Thus too the Kaiser delegates the high-priestly power, originally no less pertaining to him than the earthly might, to the Pope of Rome : the latter has to exercise the Sight-of-God in his name, and to acquaint him with the God's-decree, that he may execute the Heavenly Will in name of God upon the earth. The Pope accordingly is the Kaiser's most important officer, and the weightier his office, the more does it behove the Kaiser to keep strict watch that the Pope exerts it in the meaning of the Kaiser, i.e. for the peace and healing of all nations upon earth."—

No lower must we reckon Friedrich's estimate of his rank supreme, his right divine, if we are properly to judge the motives brought to clearest daylight in his actions.

T

We see him in the first place making firm the base of his material might by composing the territorial strife in Germany through reconcilement with his relatives the Welfen, and compelling the princes of bordering peoples, in particular the Danes, Poles and Hungarians, to accept their lands in fee from him. Thus fortified he fared to Italy, and, as arbiter over the Lombards in the Roncalian Diet, for the first time published to the world a systematic digest of the Kaiser's claims; in which, for all the influence of Imperial Roman principles, we recognise the strictest consequences of the aforesaid view of his authority: his Imperial Right was here extended even to the grant of air and water.

No less determined were his claims against and over the Church herself, after an initial period of reserve. A disputed Papal election gave him the opportunity of exerting his supreme right: with strict observance of what he deemed fit priestly forms, he had the election scrutinised, deposed the Pope who seemed to him at fault, and installed the vindicated rival in his place.

Every trait of Friedrich's, every undertaking, each decree, bears most indisputable witness to the energetic congruence with which he ever strove to realise his high ideal. The unwavering firmness with which he opposed the no less obstinate Pope Alexander III., the almost superhuman rigour—in a Kaiser by no means prone to cruelty by nature—with which he doomed to overthrow the equally undaunted Milan, are incorporate moments of the grand Idea informing him.

Two mighty foes, however, stood up against the heaven-storming World-king; the first at starting-point of his material power, in the German landed system,—the second at the terminus of his ideal endeavour, the Catholic Church established in the conscience of Romanic peoples in particular. Both foes joined forces with a third, on which the Kaiser, in a sense, himself had first bestowed its consciousness: the *instinct of freedom in the Lombard communes.*

If the earliest resistance of the German stems had had its origin in the thirst for freedom from their Frankish rulers, that bent had gradually passed over from the shattered tribal fellowships to the lords who snatched these fragments to themselves: although the effort of these princes had all the evil attributes of selfish lust-of-mastery, yet their longing for its independent satisfaction might rank in their eyes as a fight for freedom, however less exalted it must seem in ours. The bent-to-freedom of the Church was more ideal by far, more universal: in Christian terminology it might count as struggle of the soul for liberation from the fetters of the sensual world, and undoubtedly it passed for such in the minds of her greatest chiefs; she had been forced to share too deeply in the world's material taste of might, however, and her ultimate victory could therefore be gained through nothing but the ruin of her inmost soul.

But the spirit of freedom shews out the purest in the Lombard townships, and precisely (alas! almost solely) in their decisive fights with Friedrich. These fights are insofar the most remarkable event of a critical historic period, as in them, for the first time in the history of the world, the spirit of ur-human freedom embodied in the Burgher-commune girds up itself to a fight for life and death with an old established, all-embracing sovereignty. Athens' fight against the Persians was patriotic opposition to a huge monarchic piracy: all similar famous deeds of single townships, until the time of the Lombardians, bear the selfsame character of defence of ancient *racial* independence against a foreign conqueror. Now, this ancestral freedom, that cleaves to the root of a nationality till then untroubled, was in nowise present with the Lombard communes: history has seen the population of these cities, compounded of all nations and bare of any old tradition, fall shameful victim to the greed of every conqueror; through a thousand years of total impotence, in these cities lived no nation, i.e. no race with any consciousness of its earliest origin: in them dwelt merely *men*, men led by the need of mutual insurance of an undisturbed prosperity to an ever plainer evolution of the principle of Society, and its realisement through the Commune (*Gemeinde*).

This novel principle, devoid of racial lore or chronicle arising purely of and for itself, owes its historic origin to the population of the Lombard cities, who, imperfectly as they could understand and turn it to a lasting good, yet evolved themselves thereby from deepest feebleness to agents of the highest force;—and if its entry into history is to count as the spark that leaps from the stone, then Friedrich is the steel that struck it from the stone.

Friedrich, the representative of the last racial Ur-Folk-Kinghood, in mightiest fulfilment of his indeviable destiny, struck from the stone of manhood the spark before whose splendour he himself must pale. The *Pope* launched his ban, the *Welf Heinrich* forsook his king in his direst want,—but the sword of the *Lombard band of brothers* smote the imperial warrior with the terrible rout at Lignano.

Ascent of the Ideal content of the Hoard into the "Holy Grail."

The World-ruler recognised from whence his deepest wound had come, and who it was that cried his world-plan final halt. *It was the spirit of free Manhood loosed from the nature-soil of race*, that had faced him in this Lombard Bond. He made short work of both the older foes : to the High-priest he gave his hand,—he fell with crushing force upon the selfish Guelphs ; and so, once more arrived at summit of his power and undisputed might,—*he spake the Lombards free, and struck with them a lasting peace.*

At Mainz he gathered his whole Reich around him ; * all his feudatories, from the first to the last, he fain would

---

* It is impossible not to recognise how much of the idea of this Friedrich I. has passed into Wagner's Wotan.—Tr.

greet once more: the clergy and the laity surrounded him; from every land Kings sent ambassadors with precious gifts, in homage to his Kaiser-might. But *Palestine* sent forth to him the cry to save the Holy Tomb.—To the land of morning Friedrich turned his gaze: a force resistless drew him on toward Asia, to the cradle of the nations, to the place where God begat the father of all Men. Wondrous legends had he heard of a lordly country deep in Asia, in farthest India,—of an ur-divine Priest-King who governed there a pure and happy people, immortal through the nurture of a wonder-working relic called "*the Holy Grail.*" —Might he there regain the lost Sight-of-God, now garbled by ambitious priests in Rome according to their pleasure?—

The old hero girt him up; with splendid retinue of war he marched through Greece: he might have conquered it, —what booted that?—unresting he was drawn to farthest Asia. There on tempestuous field he broke the power of the Saracens; unchallenged lay the promised land before him; he could not wait for the construction of a flying bridge, but urged impatient Eastwards,—on horse he plunged into the stream: none saw him in this life again.

Since then, the legend went that once the *Keeper of the Grail* had really brought the holy relic to the Occident; great wonders had he here performed: in the Netherlands, the Nibelungen's ancient seat, a Knight of the Grail had appeared, but vanished when asked forbidden tidings of his origin;—then was the Grail conducted back by its old guardian to the distant morning-land;—in a castle on a lofty mount in India it now was kept once more.

In truth the legend of the Holy Grail, significantly enough, makes its entry on the world at the very time when the Kaiserhood attained its more ideal direction, and the Nibelung's Hoard accordingly was losing more and more in material worth, to yield to a higher spiritual content. The spiritual ascension of the Hoard into the Grail was accomplished in the German conscience, and

the Grail, at least in the meaning lent it by German poets,
must rank as the Ideal representative or follower of the
Nibelungen-Hoard ; it, too, had sprung from Asia, from
the ur-home of mankind; God had guided it to men as
paragon of holiness.

It is of the first importance that its Keeper was priest
and king alike, that is, a Master (*Oberhaupt*) of all Spiritual
Knighthood, such as was introduced from the Orient in
the twelfth century. So this Master was in truth none
other than the Kaiser, from whom all Chivalry proceeded ;
and thus the real and ideal world-supremacy, the union of
the highest kinghood and priesthood, seemed completely
attained in the Kaiser.

The quest of the Grail henceforth replaces the struggle
for the Nibelungen-Hoard, and as the occidental world,
unsatisfied within, reached out past Rome and Pope to
find its place of healing in the tomb of the Redeemer at
Jerusalem,—as, unsatisfied even there, it cast its yearning gaze, half spiritual half physical, still farther toward
the East to find the primal shrine of manhood,—so the
Grail was said to have withdrawn from out the ribald
West to the pure, chaste, reachless birth-land of all
nations.—

To pass the ur-old Nibelungen-saga in review, we see
it springing like a spiritual germ from an oldest race's
earliest glance at Nature (*Naturanschauung*) ; we see this
germ develop to a mighty plant on ever more material
soil, especially in the Historic evolution of the saga, so
that in Karl the Great it seems to thrust its knotty fibres
deep into the actual earth ; till finally in the Wibelingian
Kaiserdom of Friedrich I. we see this plant unfold its
fairest flower to the light : with him the flower faded ;
in his grandson Friedrich II., the highest mind of all
the Kaisers, the wondrous perfume of the dying bloom
spread like a lovely fairy-spell through all the world of
West and East ; till with the grandson of the last-named
Kaiser, the youthful Konrad, the leafless withered stem

was torn with all its roots and fibres from the ground, and stamped to dust.

Historic residue of the Material content of the Hoard, in "Real Property."

A shriek of horror rang through every country when the head of Konrad fell in Naples to the blows of that *Charles d' Anjou* who in every lineament presents the perfect archetype of all post-Wibelingian Kinghood. He sprang from the oldest of the newer royal races : in France the Capets had long succeeded to the last French Carlovingian. Hugo Capet's origin was well beknown ; everybody knew what his race had been before, and how he arrived at the throne : cunning, policy, and violence at a pinch, were the tools of him and his successors, compounding for the right they lacked in the people's eyes. These Capets, in all their later branches, were the pattern for the modern King- and Prince-hood : in no belief in ur-racial descent could it seek foundation for its claims ; of every prince the world, coeval and posterior, knew by what mere grant, at what purchase-price, or through what deed of violence, he had attained to power, and by what art or means he must contrive to keep it.

With the foundering of the Wibelungen, mankind had been torn from the last fibre whereby it still hung, in a sense, to its racial-natural origin. The Hoard of the Nibelungen had evaporated to the realm of Poetry and the Idea ; merely an earthly precipitate remained as its dregs : *real property*.

In the Nibelungen-myth we found expressed by all the generations who devised, developed and enacted it, an uncommonly clear idea of the *nature of property, of ownership*. If in the oldest religious view the Hoard appeared to be the splendour of the Earth laid bare to all by daylight, we later see it take more compact form as the hero's might-conferring booty, won as guerdon of the bravest, most astounding deed from a vanquished odious adversary. This Hoard, this talisman of might, 'tis true, is henceforth claimed as with hereditary right by the descendants of that godlike hero ; yet it has this foremost characteristic, that it is never gained afresh in lazy peace, by simple contract, but only through a deed akin to that of its first winner.   Moreover, this constantly-repeated deed of heritage has all the moral meaning of vendetta, of retribution for the murder of a kinsman : so we see blood, passion, love, hate, in short—both physically and spiritually— purely-human springs and motives at work in the winning of the Hoard ; man restless and suffering, man doomed to conscious death by his own deed, his victory, and most by his possession, at the head of all ideas of the root-relation of acquirement.—These views, which honoured *Man* as focus of all power, entirely corresponded with the mode of treating property in actual life.   If in earliest antiquity there certainly prevailed the simplest and most natural principle of all, namely that the measure of possession or enjoyment must be meted by man's Need, among conquering nations with excess of goods the strength and prowess of the best-famed fighters became as naturally the measure-giving Subject to the Object of more enjoyable and richer spoils.   In the historic *Feudal system*, so long as it retained its pristine purity, we see this heroic-human principle still plainly voiced : the grant of a fief was merely to this one particular human being who had earned the right to claim reward for some decisive deed, some weighty service.   From the moment when a fief became *hereditary*, the man, his personal excellence, his acts and deeds, lost value,—which passed over to his property : hereditary possession, no longer personal virtue, now gave their standing to his heirs, and the resulting deeper and deeper depreciation of Man, against the higher and higher appreciation of Property, at last took body in the most contra-human institutions, such as those of Primogeniture ; from which, in strange perversity, the later Noble drew all conceit and arrogance, without reflecting that by deriving his worth from a stiffened family-possession he was openly disowning any actual *human nobleness.*

So—after the fall of the heroic-human Wibelungen—this hereditary ownership, then property *in general, de facto possession,* became the title for all rights existing or to be acquired ; and Property gave Man that right which man had theretofore conveyed to property.   It was this dreg of the vanished Nibelungen-Hoard, then, that the sobered German lords had kept them : though the Kaiser might soar to the highest peak of the Idea, what clung there to the ground below, the Duchies, Palatinates, Marks and Counties, all ranks and offices enfeoffed by the Kaiser, in the hands of his utterly un-idealistic vassals condensed to mere *possession, property.*   Possession now was consequently *Right,* and upright was it kept by all Established and Approved being henceforth drawn from that one right on a more and more elaborate system.   He who had a share in property, or managed to acquire one, *from that instant* ranked as a natural pillar of the State (*der öffentlichen Macht*).   But this also must be hallowed : what the most glorious Kaisers had claimed in good faith as their ideal title to rule the world, these practical gentry now applied to their possessions ; the old divine ur-right was arrogated to himself by every former crown-official ; the God's-decree was expounded by Justinian's Roman Rights, and, to the bewilderment of property-enslaved mankind, transcribed in Latin law-books.   Kaisers were still appointed, though directly after the downfall of the Wibelungen their rank had already been hawked to the highest bidder ; no sooner were they chosen, than to work they set to "*acquire*" a goodly family-seat "by grace of God," as one henceforth styled the forcible appropriation or nibbling-off of districts. Grown wiser, one gladly left the World-dominion to dear God, who behaved by far more leniently and humanely to the actually-reigning most selfish and depraved vulgarity of the Sons of the Holy Roman Empire than erewhile the old heathen Nibelung warriors, who for any act of mean-

THE NIBELUNGEN-MYTH.

AS SKETCH FOR A DRAMA.

(Summer 1848.)

Der Nibelungen-Mythus.

Als Entwurf zu einem Drama.

(1848.)

ROM the womb of Night and Death was spawned a race that dwells in Nibelheim (Nebelheim), i.e. in gloomy subterranean clefts and caverns: *Nibelungen* are they called; with restless nimbleness they burrow through the bowels of the earth, like worms in a dead body; they smelt and smith hard metals. The pure and noble Rhine-gold *Alberich* seized, divorced it from the waters' depth, and wrought therefrom with cunning art a ring that lent him rulership of all his race, the Nibelungen: so he became their master, forced them to work for him alone, and amassed the priceless *Nibelungen-Hoard*, whose greatest treasure is the Tarnhelm, conferring power to take on any shape at will, a work that Alberich compelled his own brother Reigin (Mime = Eugel) to weld for him. Thus armoured, Alberich made for mastery of the world and all that it contains.

The race of *Giants*, boastful, violent, ur-begotten, is troubled in its savage ease: their monstrous strength, their simple mother-wit, no longer are a match for Alberich's crafty plans of conquest: alarmed they see the Nibelungen forging wondrous weapons, that one day in the hands of human heroes shall cause the Giants' downfall.—This strife is taken advantage of by the race of *Gods*, now waxing to supremacy. *Wotan* bargains with the Giants to build the Gods a Burg from whence to rule the world in peace and order; their building finished, the Giants ask the Nibelungen-Hoard in payment. The utmost cunning of the Gods succeeds in trapping Alberich; he must ransom his life with the Hoard; the Ring alone he strives to keep:— the Gods, well knowing that in it resides the secret of all Alberich's power, extort from him the Ring as well: then he curses it; it shall be the ruin of all who possess it. Wotan delivers the Hoard to the Giants, but means to keep the Ring as warrant of his sovereignty: the Giants

defy him, and Wotan yields to the counsel of the three
Fates (Norns), who warn him of the downfall of the
Gods themselves.

Now the Giants have the Hoard and Ring safe-kept by
a monstrous Worm in the Gnita- (Neid-) Haide [the
Grove of Grudge]. Through the Ring the Nibelungs
remain in thraldom, Alberich and all. But the Giants
do not understand to use their might; their dullard minds
are satisfied with having bound the Nibelungen. So the
Worm lies on the Hoard since untold ages, in inert dread-
fulness : before the lustre of the new race of Gods the
Giants' race fades down and stiffens into impotence ;
wretched and tricksy, the Nibelungen go their way of
fruitless labour. Alberich broods without cease on the
means of gaining back the Ring.

In high emprise the Gods have planned the world, bound
down the elements by prudent laws, and devoted themselves to most careful nurture of the Human race. Their
strength stands over all. Yet the peace by which they
have arrived at mastery does not repose on reconcilement :
by violence and cunning was it wrought. The object of
their higher ordering of the world is moral consciousness :
but the wrong they fight attaches to themselves. From
the depths of Nibelheim the conscience of their guilt cries
up to them : for the bondage of the Nibelungen is not
broken ; merely the lordship has been reft from Alberich,
and not for any higher end, but the soul, the freedom of
the Nibelungen lies buried uselessly beneath the belly of
an idle Worm : Alberich thus has justice in his plaints
against the Gods. Wotan himself, however, cannot undo
the wrong without committing yet another : only a free
Will, independent of the Gods themselves, and able to
assume and expiate itself the burden of all guilt, can loose
the spell ; and in Man the Gods perceive the faculty of
such free-will. In Man they therefore seek to plant their
own divinity, to raise his strength so high that, in full
knowledge of that strength, he may rid him of the Gods'
protection, to do of his free will what his own mind in-

spires. So the Gods bring up Man for this high destiny, to be the canceller of their own guilt; and their aim would be attained even if in this human creation they should perforce annul themselves, that is, must part with their immediate influence through freedom of man's conscience. Stout human races, fruited by the seed divine, already flourish: in strife and fight they steel their strength; Wotan's Wish-maids shelter them as Shield-maids, as *Walküren* lead the slain-in-fight to Walhall, where the heroes live again a glorious life of jousts in Wotan's company. But not yet is the rightful hero born, in whom his self-reliant strength shall reach full consciousness, enabling him with the free-willed penalty of death before his eyes to call his boldest deed his own. In the race of the *Wälsungen* this hero at last shall come to birth: a barren union is fertilised by Wotan through one of Holda's apples, which he gives the wedded pair to eat: twins, *Siegmund* and *Sieglinde* (brother and sister), spring from the marriage. Siegmund takes a wife, Sieglinde weds a man (Hunding); but both their marriages prove sterile: to beget a genuine Wälsung, brother and sister wed each other. Hunding, Sieglinde's husband, learns of the crime, casts off his wife, and goes out to fight with Siegmund. *Brünnhild*, the Walküre, shields Siegmund counter to Wotan's commands, who had doomed him to fall in expiation of the crime; already Siegmund, under Brünnhild's shield, is drawing sword for the death-blow at Hunding—the sword that Wotan himself once had given him—when the god receives the blow upon his spear, which breaks the weapon in two pieces. Siegmund falls. Brünnhild is punished by Wotan for her disobedience: he strikes her from the roll of the Walküren, and banishes her to a rock, where the divine virgin is to wed the man who finds and wakes her from the sleep in which Wotan plunges her; she pleads for mercy, that Wotan will ring the rock with terrors of fire, and so ensure that none save the bravest of heroes may win her.—After long gestation the outcast Sieglinde gives birth in the forest to

Siegfried (he who brings Peace through Victory): Reigin (*Mime*), Alberich's brother, upon hearing her cries, has issued from a cleft and aided her: after the travail Sieglinde dies, first telling Reigin of her fate and committing the babe to his care. Reigin brings up Siegfried, teaches him smithery, and brings him the two pieces of the broken sword, from which, under Mime's directions, Siegfried forges the sword Balmung. Then Mime prompts the lad to slay the Worm, in proof of his gratitude. Siegfried first wishes to avenge his father's murder: he fares out, falls upon Hunding, and kills him: only thereafter does he execute the wish of Mime, attacks and slays the Giant-worm. His fingers burning from the Worm's hot blood, he puts them to his mouth to cool them; involuntarily he tastes the blood, and understands at once the language of the woodbirds singing round him. They praise Siegfried for his glorious deed, direct him to the Nibelungen-hoard in the cave of the Worm, and warn him against Mime, who has merely used him as an instrument to gain the Hoard, and therefore seeks his life. Siegfried thereon slays Mime, and takes the Ring and Tarnhelm from the Hoard: he hears the birds again, who counsel him to win the crown of women, Brünnhild. So Siegfried sets forth, reaches Brunnhild's mountain, pierces the billowing flames, and wakes her; in Siegfried she joyfully acclaims the highest hero of the Wälsung-stem, and gives herself to him: he marries her with Alberich's ring, which he places on her finger. When the longing spurs him to new deeds, she gives him lessons in her secret lore, warns him of the dangers of deceit and treachery: they swear each other vows, and Siegfried speeds forth.

A second hero-stem, sprung likewise from the Gods, is that of the *Gibichungen* on the Rhine: there now bloom *Gunther* and *Gudrun*, his sister. Their mother, Grimhild, was once overpowered by Alberich, and bore him an unlawful son, *Hagen*. As the hopes and wishes of the Gods repose on Siegfried, so Alberich sets his hope of gaining back the Ring on his hero-offspring Hagen. Hagen is sallow, glum and serious; his features are prematurely hardened; he looks older than he is. Already in his childhood Alberich had taught him mystic lore and knowledge of his father's fate, inciting him to struggle for the Ring: he is strong and masterful; yet to Alberich he seems not strong enough to slay the Giant-worm. Since Alberich has lost his power, he could not stop his brother Mime when the latter sought to gain the Hoard through Siegfried: but Hagen shall compass Siegfried's ruin, and win the Ring from his dead body. Toward Gunther and Gudrun Hagen is reticent,—they fear him, but prize his foresight and experience: the secret of some marvellous descent of Hagen's, and that he is not his lawful brother, is known to Gunther: he calls him once an Elf-son.

Gunther is being apprised by Hagen that Brünnhild is the woman most worth desire, and excited to long for her possession, when Siegfried speeds along the Rhine to the seat of the Gibichungs. Gudrun, inflamed to love by the praises he has showered on Siegfried, at Hagen's bidding welcomes Siegfried with a drink prepared by Hagen's art, of such potence that it makes Siegfried forget his adventure with Brünnhild and marriage to her. Siegfried desires Gudrun for wife: Gunther consents, on condition that he helps him win Brünnhild. Siegfried agrees: they strike blood-brothership and swear each other oaths, from which Hagen holds aloof.—Siegfried and Gunther set out, and arrive at Brünnhild's rocky fastness: Gunther remains behind in the boat; Siegfried for the first and only time exerts his power as Ruler of the Nibelungen, by putting on the Tarnhelm and thereby taking Gunther's form and look; thus masked, he passes through the flames to Brünnhild. Already robbed by Siegfried of her maidhood, she has lost alike her superhuman strength, and all her runecraft has she made away to Siegfried—who does not use it; she is powerless as any mortal woman, and can only offer lame resistance to the new, audacious wooer; he tears from her the Ring—by which she is now to be wedded to Gunther—, and forces her into the cavern,

U

where he sleeps the night with her, though to her astonishment he lays his sword between them. On the morrow, he brings her to the boat, where he lets the real Gunther take his place unnoticed by her side, and transports himself in a trice to the Gibichenburg through power of the Tarnhelm. Gunther reaches his home along the Rhine, with Brünnhild following him in downcast silence: Siegfried, at Gudrun's side, and Hagen receive the voyagers.—Brünnhild is aghast when she beholds Siegfried as Gudrun's husband : his cold civility to her amazes her ; as he motions her back to Gunther, she recognises the Ring on his finger : she suspects the imposture played upon her, and demands the ring, for it belongs not to him, but to Gunther who received it from her : he refuses it. She bids Gunther claim the ring from Siegfried : Gunther is confused, and hesitates. Brünnhild : So it was Siegfried that had the ring from her ? Siegfried, recognising the Ring : "From no woman I had it ; my right arm won it from the Giant-worm ; through it am I the Nibelungen's lord, and to none will I cede its might." Hagen steps between them, and asks Brünnhild if she is certain about the Ring ? If it be hers, then Siegfried gained it by deceit, and it can belong to no one but her husband, Gunther. Brünnhild loudly denounces the trick played on her ; the most dreadful thirst for vengeance upon Siegfried fills her. She cries to Gunther that he has been duped by Siegfried : "Not to thee—to this man am I wed ; he won my favour." —Siegfried charges her with shamelessness : Faithful had he been to his blood-brothership,—his sword he laid between Brünnhilde and himself:—he calls on her to bear him witness.—Purposely, and thinking only of his ruin, she will not understand him.—The clansmen and Gudrun conjure Siegfried to clear himself of the accusation, if he can. Siegfried swears solemn oaths in confirmation of his word. Brünnhild taxes him with perjury : All the oaths he swore to her and Gunther, has he broken : now he forswears himself, to lend corroboration to a lie. Everyone is in the utmost commotion. Siegfried calls Gunther to stop his wife from shamefully slandering her own and husband's honour: he withdraws with Gudrun to the inner hall.—Gunther, in deepest shame and terrible dejection, has seated himself at the side, with hidden face: Brünn-hild, racked by the horrors of an inner storm, is approached by Hagen. He offers himself as venger of her honour: she mocks him, as powerless to cope with Siegfried: One look from his glittering eye, which shone upon her even through that mask, would scatter Hagen's courage. Hagen: He well knows Siegfried's awful strength, but she will tell him how he may be vanquished? So she who once had hallowed Siegfried, and armed him by mysteri-ous spells against all wounding, now counsels Hagen to attack him from behind; for, knowing that the hero ne'er would turn his back upon the foe, she had left it from the blessing.—Gunther must be made a party to the plot. They call upon him to avenge his honour: Brünnhild covers him with reproaches for his cowardice and trickery; Gunther admits his fault, and the necessity of ending his shame by Siegfried's death; but he shrinks from com-mitting a breach of blood-brotherhood. Brünnhild bitterly taunts him: What crimes have not been wreaked on her? Hagen inflames him by the prospect of gaining the Nibelung's Ring, which Siegfried certainly will never part with until death. Gunther consents; Hagen proposes a hunt for the morrow, when Siegfried shall be set upon, and perhaps his murder even concealed from Gudrun; for Gunther was concerned for her sake: Brünnhilde's lust-of-vengeance is sharpened by her jealousy of Gudrun. So Siegfried's murder is decided by the three.—Siegfried and Gudrun, festally attired, appear in the hall, and bid them to the sacrificial rites and wedding ceremony. The con-spirators feigningly obey: Siegfried and Gudrun rejoice at the show of peace restored.

Next morning Siegfried strays into a lonely gully by the Rhine, in pursuit of quarry. Three mermaids dart up from the stream: they are soothsaying Daughters of the waters' bed, whence Alberich once had snatched the gleaming

Rhine-gold to smite from it the fateful Ring: the curse and power of that Ring would be destroyed, were it re-given to the waters, and thus resolved into its pure original element. The Daughters hanker for the Ring, and beg it of Siegfried, who refuses it. (Guiltless, he has taken the guilt of the Gods upon him, and atones their wrong through his defiance, his self-dependence.) They prophesy evil, and tell him of the curse attaching to the ring: Let him cast it in the river, or he must die to-day. Siegfried: "Ye glib-tongued women shall not cheat me of my might: the curse and your threats I count not worth a hair. What my courage bids me, is my being's law; and what I do of mine own mind, so is it set for me to do: call ye this curse or blessing, it I obey and strive not counter to my strength." The three Daughters: "Wouldst thou outvie the Gods?" Siegfried: "Shew me the chance of mastering the Gods, and I must work my main to vanquish them. I know three wiser women than you three; they wot where once the Gods will strive in bitter fearing. Well for the Gods, if they take heed that then I battle *with* them. So laugh I at your threats: the ring stays mine, and thus I cast my life behind me." (He lifts a clod of earth, and hurls it backwards over his head.)—The Daughters scoff at Sieg-fried, who weens himself as strong and wise as he is blind and bond-slave. "Oaths has he broken, and knows it not: a boon far higher than the Ring he's lost, and knows it not: runes and spells were taught to him, and he's forgot them. Fare thee well, Siegfried! A lordly wife we know; e'en to-day will she possess the Ring, when thou art slaughtered. To her! She'll lend us better hearing."—Siegfried, laughing, gazes after them as they move away singing. He shouts: "To Gudrun were I not true, one of you three had ensnared me!" He hears his hunting-comrades drawing nearer, and winds his horn: the hunts-men—Gunther and Hagen at their head—assemble round Siegfried. The midday meal is eaten: Siegfried, in the highest spirits, mocks at his own unfruitful chase: But water-game had come his way, for whose capture he was not equipped, alack! or he'd have brought his comrades three wild water-birds that told him he must die to-day. Hagen takes up the jest, as they drink: Does he really know the song and speech of birds, then?—Gunther is sad and silent. Siegfried seeks to enliven him, and sings him songs about his youth: his adventure with Mime, the slaying of the Worm, and how he came to understand birdlanguage. The train of recollection brings him back the counsel of the birds to seek Brünnhilde, who was fated for him; how he stormed the flaming rock and wakened Brünnhild. Remembrance rises more and more distinct. Two ravens suddenly fly past his head. Hagen interrupts him: "What do these ravens tell thee?" Siegfried springs to his feet. Hagen: "*I* rede them; they haste to herald thee to Wotan." He hurls his spear at Siegfried's back. Gunther, guessing from Siegfried's tale the true connection of the inexplicable scene with Brünnhilde, and suddenly divining Siegfried's innocence, had thrown himself on Hagen's arm to rescue Siegfried, but without being able to stay the blow. Siegfried raises his shield, to crush Hagen with it; his strength fails him, and he falls of a heap. Hagen has departed; Gunther and the clansmen stand round Siegfried, in sympathetic awe; he lifts his shining eyes once more: "Brünnhild, Brünnhild! Radiant child of Wotan! How dazzling bright I see thee nearing me! With holy smile thou saddlest thy horse, that paces through the air dew-dripping: to me thou steer'st its course; here is there Lot to choose (*Wal su küren*)! Happy me thou chos'st for husband, now lead me to Walhall, that in honour of all heroes I may drink All-father's mead, pledged me by thee, thou shining Wish-maid! Brünnhild, Brünnhild! Greeting!" He dies. The men uplift the corpse upon his shield, and solemnly bear it over the rocky heights, Gunther in front.

In the Hall of the Gibichungs, whose forecourt extends at the back to the bank of the Rhine, the corpse is set down: Hagen has called out Gudrun; with strident tones he tells her that a savage boar had gored her husband.—Gudrun falls horrified on Siegfried's body: she rates her brother with the murder; Gunther points to Hagen: He was the savage boar, the murderer of Siegfried. Hagen: "So be it; an I have slain him, whom no other dared to, whatso was his is my fair booty. The ring is mine!" Gunther confronts him: "Shameless Elf-son, the ring is mine, assigned to me by Brünnhild: ye all, ye heard it."—Hagen and Gunther fight: Gunther falls. Hagen tries to wrench the Ring from the body,—it lifts its hand aloft in menace; Hagen staggers back, aghast; Gudrun cries aloud in her sorrow;—then Brünnhild enters solemnly: "Cease your laments, your idle rage! Here stands his wife, whom ye all betrayed. My right I claim, for what must be is done!" —Gudrun: "Ah, wicked one! 'Twas thou who brought us ruin." Brünnhild: "Poor soul, have peace! Wert but his wanton: his wife am I, to whom he swore or e'er he saw thee." Gudrun: "Woe's me! Accursed Hagen, what badest thou me, with the drink that filched her husband to me? For now I know that only through the drink did he forget Brünnhilde." Brünnhild: "O he was pure! Ne'er oaths were more loyally held, than by him. No, Hagen has not *slain* him; for Wotan has he marked him out, to whom I thus conduct him. And I, too, have atoned; pure and free am I: for he, the glorious one alone, o'erpowered me." She directs a pile of logs to be erected on the shore, to burn Siegfried's corpse to ashes: no horse, no vassal shall be sacrificed with him; she alone will give her body in his honour to the Gods. First she takes possession of her heritage; the Tarnhelm shall be burnt with her: the Ring she puts upon her finger. "Thou froward hero, how thou held'st me banned! All my rune-lore I bewrayed to thee, a mortal, and so went widowed of my wisdom; thou usedst it not, thou trustedst in thyself alone: but now that thou must yield it up through death, my knowledge comes to me again, and this Ring's runes I rede. The ur-law's runes, too, know I now, the Norns' old saying! Hear then, ye mighty Gods, your guilt is quit: thank him, the hero, who took your guilt upon him! To mine own hand he gave

The " Kapelle," or Court-band, had its origin in a so-called " Kantorei" founded by Kurfürst Moritz of Saxony in 1548. Its Tercentenary Festival took place on Sep. 22, 1848; the celebration began with a concert, at which, besides an overture by Richard Wagner's colleague Reissiger, the second half of the first act of Lohengrin *(from the hero's entry) was given for the first time, in cantata-form. The concert was followed by a banquet in the hall of the Harmonie-Gesellschaft, when, after the usual official toasts, Wagner's speech was delivered, apparently impromptu. It will be noticed that this " Toast" was subsequent to the drafting of the plan of theatre-reform.*

TRANSLATOR'S NOTE.

HE era spanned to-day by the existence of our Kapelle is of the most unwonted moment : the three centuries of life of this art-institute cover that period which historians call the Third in World-history, commencing with the epoch of the Reformation and continuing to the present day ; it is the period of the human spirit's evolution to ever more distinct self-consciousness : in it that spirit has sought with surer tools to grasp its destiny, to probe the natural necessity of all existing forms of being upon earth. An art-institute that has grown-up in and with this period, cannot have stayed a stranger to the spirit of that evolution : the influence of the era will have stamped and moulded it. And so we find : to the spirit of Protestant piety that seized all hearts 300 years ago, this institution owes its origin ; a Prince who bore the sword in bold emprise for Protestant in dependence, at like time founded at his Court the institute whereby that spirit was to find its art-expression.—As years rolled on, nothing could have more conduced to its advancement, than the gradual spread of taste for Art at the Court of Dresden : it drew the institution nearer to a worldly mission, constantly improved its organism to that end, and, where it served for pleasure and enjoyment, assembled ever more superb artistic forces in it. Now, it is a laudable feature in the love of artistic pleasure, to willingly let others share in its enjoyment : our delight is heightened in the company of many ; to this feeling we owe it, that a wider and wider participation by the general public has rather been encouraged, than merely yielded to. So that this splendid institute now belongs almost exclusively to Public life, and a beloved, art-devoted Prince equips it with especial view to this broader sphere of action.

With the growth of everything, the several members of

315

this art-body have grown as well ; if in the beginning it
was possible to regard Instrumental-music as a mere
appurtenance of Vocal-music, the Masters of German
Music in particular have given the instrumental orchestra
so high a function, that this department of the institute
must needs be cultivated as an essentially self-dependent
body : through the Theatre on the other hand, Vocal-
music had evolved to so entirely novel a complexity, that
it must at last be almost completely severed from that
body, and committed to a special tutelage.   Thus, now
that after three-hundred years we have arrived at a goal
practically opposite to the starting-point, in celebrating
a Jubilee of the Kapelle we to-day mean almost nothing
but its Orchestra.   Let us abide by that for the present,
and ask :

*Is the institute a worthy bearer of the Spirit of German
Music, unfolded to so high a prime, that spirit which stirs
the Present with the mighty breath of Beethoven ?*

With full and joyful heart I cry : Ay, ay !   It is.—
And if it stands so wholly on the summit of the times,
it has fulfilled its task till now.   All praise and thanks
to those who have so staunchly kept and nursed this
institute,—they have done good service in the cause of
Art.

No fairer likeness can I find for such a guise as that in
which this institute now shews itself, than : It is a *man* !—
A man in the full intention of the word, arrived at that
puissant stage of his development where he can look
back with understanding on his past, i.e. the evolution of
his faculties, and proceed with active consciousness of his
vocation in the present.   Now, the child of the Present is
the Future, and the clearer and more steadily man looks
toward that, the more purposefully will he employ the
present.   Man's purpose is to act usefully, and his activity
will be then completely useful, when he lets it operate in
unceasing accord with his best and highest faculty ; has

he learnt nothing beyond the hewing of stones, let him
hew stones,—but, can he rear fair edifices, then let him
leave the hewing of stones to those who know no other
trade, and delight the world with the fair buildings he
erects : only by his acting in accordance with his highest
faculty, will he also be useful in his walk of life. But
above all, is he useful, when he *forms* and educates ; thereby
he guarantees himself a lasting operation in the Future :
and here the Present has the justest claim on him ; for
the higher the type of his abilities and acquirements, the
less were they lent him for himself alone, but in trust for
all to whom he can impart them.—The institute to which
I have applied this simile, as the most perfect and precious
of its kind in all the Fatherland, should be of as much
use to the musical art of the Fatherland as ever it can :
this it first attains by its performances, which should always
stand in the worthiest possible harmony with its ability ;
next, by its laying itself open, with ever greater interest
and furtherance, to the art-production of the Fatherland ;
and finally, by its becoming the radiating-point of highest
musical culture for the whole Fatherland. If these fair
destinies are more and more perfectly fulfilled by the
institute, if its great usefulness is consequently brought
to the. knowledge of the whole Fatherland more clearly
every day, then the time and tempest that could harm its
permanence in any way can never come to pass.

In conclusion I return to my " man," to drink him a
hearty good health. If he is to live up to the level
of his destiny, he must be hale and blithe: therefore if
we find one ailing member in him, be it merely a lame
finger, we must cure him till he is perfectly sound.
But if he is to feel quite whole and well, the man requires a *wife*, i.e. the Instrumental Orchestra requires
an equally healthy Vocal Institute entrusted to its
keeping: this I call a woman, since we all know that
the existing Orchestra has issued from the womb of a
Choir.

So a long, a happy, and an honoured life to this fair

In his Life of Wagner *Herr C. F. Glasenapp reproduces a letter of the master's (now in the possession of Mons. Alfred Bovet) dated May 16, 1848, and addressed to the Minister of the Interior:* " *In the interest of an institute whose fate is now in the balance, I permit myself the most respectful plea for an exhaustive hearing. My paper will occupy an hour in reading, and the question therefore is whether it will be possible for you to accord that hour to me* to-morrow *(Wednesday) evening, or at latest in the course of Thursday? In that case I would most humbly beg you to induce State-Minister Herr Dr von Pfordten to attend the audience granted me, as I am not quite certain to which department of the Cabinet the matter to be broached by me belongs in fact, and would therefore like to leave that point to the de-cision of the Ministers both of the Interior and of Public Worship* (Cultus). *In any case the matter is so urgent, at this juncture, that I hold it my duty to implore the honour of a speedy answer." The interview accordingly took place, with the results related in the following pages.*

In his Letters to Uhlig *we find the author proposing to publish his " Reorganisation " draft in pamphlet-form in 1850, and writing a fairly long preface to the work, dated the 18th of September of that year: in that preface he refers, among other reasons for the plan, to the rumoured resignation of the General-Director (von Lüttichau) on completion of his twenty-fifth year of office, but adds, " Things still remain on their old footing . . . only my court-uniform is pulled off: one arm was sticking in it when I drafted that reform, and my not having been rid of the whole thing is the principal fault in the paper: the stiff trimmings hampered me while writing."*

Various motives, however, forbade the publication at that time; consequently the work did not appear in print until its inclusion in Vol ii. of the Ges. Schr.

TRANSLATOR'S NOTE.

HE publication of the following somewhat lengthy work may prove a weariness to many a reader ; for, even should he be willing to follow all my movements, he will this time find himself lost with me on a rather stubbly field, where it even comes to the counting of figures. Perhaps, however, it will touch him to see me driven to the necessity of seeking welfare for my art on such a field, and he will not grudge me recognition of the pains I already took so long ago to win that art a worthy foothold in the State itself. In any case it may interest some few to hear about the incitation to this work, and more especially its fate.

It was in the years 1848 to 1849, when all men's minds seemed bent upon *reform*, that I formed my own ideas as to how the Theatre and Music might be benefited by that spirit. But the special stimulus to work out these thoughts to a complete draft of reorganisation for the Dresden Court-theatre was supplied me by my observation of the temper in which the newly-elected Radical Chamber of Deputies, in the Kingdom of Saxony, was minded to examine the Royal Civil List : it had come to my ears that among other things the subvention for the Court-theatre, as a luxurious place of entertainment, was to be eliminated. I therefore resolved to approach the Minister of the Interior, to whose care all art-establishments in the land were committed, and place him in a proper position to reply to the proposal of the Deputies, inasmuch as he could admit the justice of their strictures on the present working of the theatre, but also teach them how a theatre might very well be made deserving of exceptional support by the State. So that my plan was, not merely to rescue the theatre, but at like time to conduct it to a noble sphere of action under shelter and inspection by the State. The Minister, the upright *Martin*

X

Oberländer, seemed to fall in with my idea; but he could promise me little success if I made a point of having the draft submitted to the Chamber by the Government, as he feared the whole affair would find small favour at Court: people there would only scent an inroad on their privileges, as for instance the proposal to have no more courtiers in the berth of Intendant, and would never consent to take the initiative in such a measure.—While I was hesitating, in consequence, whether I should go so far as to entrust to one of the Deputies the motion for transferring the theatre from the King's Civil List to the State-budget, the political catastrophe of May 1849 arrived, and put an end to every thorough-going project of Reform for many a year.

When I subsequently obtained the return of my manuscript from Herr Oberländer, I gathered from various notes on its margin that my draft had been received with scorn in those circles to which the Minister had thought it his duty to communicate it. At anyrate I recognised that the fear of damage to the theatre from the side of the Deputies, which had moved me to my project, was considered altogether groundless in those circles, as one already knew better how such-like attacks would be dealt with.

With the Theatre, as well, things were to stay as they were.—

That I henceforth sought a broader base for my ideas, and preferred to league myself with Chaos, rather than with the Established, will not escape the reader of the third volume of this collection [Vol. I. English]; through a long series of years, however, he will find me constantly returning to this one device of culture, to give the Theatre a worthy standing, and perhaps will be surprised at the endurance with which I always strove to bend the accident of local circumstances to its practical illustration. That it never met with any notice, will perchance astonish him again.—

After this exordium I now present my draft itself.

N the art of the Theatre the other arts converge, in greater or less degree, to so immediate an impression as none of them is able to produce alone. Its essence is association, with complete retention of the rights of the individual. —Its extraordinary effect upon the taste and manners of a nation has been actively recognised by leaders of the State at different epochs, and in France the State's direct protection has supplied it with an organisation which has furthered its productivity to such a point that French theatric art must be considered paramount in Europe to this day.—In Germany this art has always been in straits between the nation's higher intellectual need and the lower question of material existence. After isolated attempts to decide this conflict in a worthy manner, among which that of Kaiser Joseph II. was the noblest, ever since the memorable epoch of the Vienna Congress the Princes of Germany have held it their common duty to place the theatre in their Residences under their immediate guardianship:—the art's material side has consequently thriven on its rich provision from the royal coffers; but the decisive circumstance that to the head of affairs one summoned courtiers about whom one never asked whether they had any special knowledge of theatric art, has been of serious detriment to its intellectual interest. The higher intellectual assistance of the nation was necessarily excluded from an institute whose governing authority was irresponsible to the nation: the Intendant has been responsible to the Prince alone; in the Prince's personal taste, and more particularly in the degree of his sympathy with the Theatre, has lain the only guarantee for the spirit and conduct of an art-institute which claims, as no other, to be the expression of the higher intellectual activity of the whole nation.—

Every ill that this could lead to, has punctually appeared; for all the increase to their outward brilliance, the inward hollowness and demoralising aimlessness of stage-performances, taken in the bulk, have reached such a pitch that the nation has come to look disdainfully upon the Theatre as nothing but a costly place of entertainment, and to-day one often hears the question, How in times of harass can such an idle institution have the right to claim subvention from the Civil List?

This overt doubt suffices of itself to shew how far the Theatre has lagged behind its higher duty, and how important it is to lose no time in insuring the fulfilment of that duty against all harmful influences. That insurance can only be furnished by the entire nation itself, through the institute's being handed over to its full and free co-operation, and consequently declared a *National Theatre*: —the guardianship of the Theatre's highest ethical law must be assigned to the supreme *responsible* authority in the land; this authority is the *Ministry of Cultus*.*

If we seek to frame the State's supreme requirement of the Theatre in one brief sentence, as yet we cannot find a finer definition than this of Kaiser Joseph's:

" *The Theatre should have no other purpose, than to work for the ennobling of taste and manners.*" †

The responsibility for constant maintenance of this principle should therefore be undertaken by the Minister; —but that responsibility can only rest in his power when he *includes in the organisation of the theatre the full, free partnership of the intellectual and moral forces of the nation*, so that *he*, in turn, makes the nation responsible for itself. It is therefore the Minister's earliest duty, to call such an organisation to life; we believe that the following proposals would furnish a perfectly suitable one, and its immediate practical execution would retain the subvention at the figure at present ear-marked for the Dresden

---

* The Ministry of Public Worship and Instruction.—Tr.

† Or "morals" (" *Sitten* "). This motto is also quoted in Vol. III., p. 365, " The Vienna Opera-house."—Tr.

Court-theatre on the Civil List of His Majesty the King.

We begin with the *existing Court-theatre at Dresden.* This should be henceforth styled :

German National-theatre at Dresden.

The members of this Theatre are :

I. Directly operative : the *Actors* and *Singers,*

II. Indirectly operative : the *Stage-poets* and *Composers* of the land.

Organisation of the German National-theatre.

I. The Actors and Dramatic Singers form the directly active personnel of the National-theatre. For the purpose of performance they are supported, in the first place, by the Theatre-master and the other practical assistants. Every one of them is engaged and discharged by the Director exclusively, and their salaries fixed by free agreement between themselves and him. Their sustenance in old age, or in case of incapacitation, they mutually insure by constant contribution to a Sustentation-fund, such as already exists :—a uniform arrangement for all the German National-theatres is to be aimed at. The entire active personnel is subject to the orders of the Director and the Regisseurs by him appointed.

Actors and Singers &c.

II. In indirect relation with the theatre stand the Dramatic Poets and Composers : the creations of their art are the life-blood of the Theatre :—they should therefore be assigned a voice in its management in ratio to their general participation in the Theatre, especially as it is *they* who have to be the chief conservers of the one root-principle laid down.

Union of Dramatic Poets and Composers.

All the playwrights and composers of the fatherland should therefore form themselves into a Union, which they might fortify, according to their judgment, by the admission of writers and musicians not directly working for the stage, so as to represent in themselves the full artistic and scientific vigour of the nation. This Union will spread its branches throughout the land, in ·every town where there is a sufficient number of writers and musicians to constitute a Branch-society.

The natural task of the larger Union is to watch over the preservation of the *æsthetic, ethical,* and *national* purity of the National-theatre ; *criticism* accordingly, which hitherto has been ranged outside and therefore counter to the institute, will now be exercised from within and in the *common* interest. Under the most comprehensive criticism of all the intellect in the land the theatrical presentments to be set before the public shall be so far purged of the defects of experimental speculation that, after the closest estimate of extant faculties, the *perfect* artwork is offered forthwith to common enjoyment, and the public thus at once assumes its true unbiassed attitude towards the artwork, i.e. is able to express its approbation according to its own free judgment. (The immoral trade of the theatrical Reporter will be hereby done away with.)

Question of Honoraria. The Union, moreover, acquires a voice in the institute through defending the material interests of dramatic literature ; it therefore has to advocate the right of playwrights and composers to a share in the receipts of their intellectual products when brought to light by the actors and singers :—in agreement with the Directors of the National-theatres it has to fix the rate of this share, as also the mode of levying it.

Committee. The Union should therefore elect a Committee of consultation, first of all for the capital, as the seat of the chief National-theatre, to confer with the Director. For all interests in common with the Union of Poets and Composers the Director is to have the assistance of another Committee, chosen from and by the members of the active stage-personnel, and equal in number to the Committee of the Union of Poets &c. It will be left to each of these bodies to decide in what manner, and for what length of time, they will appoint their representatives. In this Combined Committee resolutions will be carried by a majority ; should there be a tie, the Director has a casting-vote ; the side dissatisfied with the result has the right of appeal to the Minister, who, as responsible to the entire land, gives a definite decision. Every Member of Committee has the right of motion : motions counter to an order of the Director's require the support of a fourth of the Combined Committee : in case of a majority of votes against him, he must either give way, or appeal to the Minister. In this Combined Committee dramatic works proposed for performance, in particular, shall be discussed and criticised : as to the question of acceptance or rejection of a piece submitted, the Combined Committee

Jury. constitutes itself a Jury, and decides by a majority. In it the national interest of German Art is to be considered above all else : works of Foreign Art shall only be admitted to performance after a vote by the majority of the Combined Committee, and only in adaptations such as appear to it consistent with, and worthy of German Art.

The members of the Committee of the Playwrights and Composers' Union have free admission to the theatre, also every member of the Union who has written a piece already brought to hearing on the stage.

The Director. *The Director of the National-theatre is elected by a majority of all the members of the active Stage-personnel and the Union of native Poets and Composers ;* the Combined Committee has to nominate the candidates, the Minister to ratify the general vote. He receives a fixed salary, which he settles with the Minister after election: if his demands exceed the sum deemed fitting by the Minister, the latter has to make it a ground for disputing the election; and only when the same choice is repeated with full knowledge of this circumstance, may the Minister desist from his objection.

His appointment is assured to him for life; he himself is at liberty to lay down the Directorship and return to his former position; his provision for old age, or in case of incapacitation, follows the law applying to Servants of the State: incapacitation may be asserted either by himself, or by the Combined Committee of the Theatre, and submitted to the decision of a majority of all the members of the Stage-personnel and the Union of Poets and Composers.

The Director has to determine the appointment and dismissal *Inner Management.* by contract of the whole active Stage-personnel, as also the salaries by agreement with those concerned. He selects the Regisseurs, and all the officials whom he considers needful in support of the active personnel. He determines the repertory and the order in which the pieces accepted by the Combined Committee are to appear and be repeated. He dictates the casting of rôles and parts, with the respective employment of the actors or singers. He arranges for the stage-mounting, and how much it is to cost. The Managerial Council *Managerial Council.* (*Verwaltungsrath*) assigned to him for this inner function consists of the Regisseurs, or, for the Opera, the Regisseurs and Musical Conductors, on the one side, on the other of members of the active personnel; the number of those officers appointed by the Director to be equalled by that of the members chosen or re-elected yearly by the stage-personnel itself. Though every member of this Council has an equal vote, the Director has a casting-vote: motions against a decision of the Director's are to be put in the *Combined Committee* in the mode set forth above.

The finances of the theatre are managed by officers appointed and *Treasury.* dismissable by the Director, in any case sworn in; towards the Minister he binds himself by oath to use his best endeavours to secure the most suitable employment both of the contribution furnished by the State and of the ordinary receipts.—He manages the treasury so that any surplus from good theatric years is saved to cover eventual deficits in bad years. His general principle is to *pay his way* with the subvention and the easily-calculable total of receipts, which can certainly be done by *suitable* disbursement, such as is only possible, again, to a person thoroughly acquainted with a theatre's *true* needs.

In case of the Director's absence he appoints his own deputy, on whom he devolves his full authority. In the event of his death the Combined Committee at once appoints a Provisional Director;

the latest term for a new regular election is to be fixed by the Minister
with a view to hastening it.

Branch-theatres.

The question now arises : In what position stand the other towns
of Saxony towards the Capital, with regard to their share in the
Theatre ?

To the State-subvention every province of the land contributes its
proportion :—to what extent does it also share in enjoyment ? Might
not each town demand to have a similar institute within its walls
"for ennobling the taste and manners" of its inhabitants ?—The answer
is simple :—If the utmost perfection is to be striven for in such an
institute, of its nature it must be concentrated on one point, not
dispersed over many. Were the sum already set aside to be split
into a subvention for all, or even the more important towns of the
land, it would nowhere suffice to give such theatres the relief needful
to make them independent of the necessity of speculating on the less-
cultured, and therefore to be cultivated, taste of the broader mass ;
hence the country's allowance would be squandered to no purpose.
It can only be of true use to the land and its intellectual interests,
when it is expended on the maintenance of a chief-institute that
represents the national honour. The home of this institute must be
the Capital of the country, which is alike the seat of Government ;
were it only for the obvious reason, that the largest and most
frequented city alone can provide that ample support in the way
of entrance-money without which the State-subvention would not
nearly suffice for the theatre. Every Saxon, so far as he sympathises
with the honour of Art, has therefore to pin his pride to the flourishing
of the National-theatre in Dresden ; each visit to the capital will
offer him the opportunity of sharing the artistic honour of his fatherland in return for a small fee paid down for entrance to the theatre,
and consequently of obtaining at little cost an enjoyment which can
only be offered him in equal fulness through his renouncing its like in

The Leipzig Theatre.

his own provincial town. However, there is one other city of Saxony,
the only one besides the capital, that has hitherto maintained a standing theatre, and thus evinced the power of providing itself with the
pleasures of the stage out of its own purse : this is *Leipzig*. Till now
the Leipzig theatre has subsisted solely on the interest shewn it by that
city : but, among much good work in course of years, there has at all
times appeared an ill inseparable from the doings of a theatre which
has to find in its takings its only means of sustenance : the demands
of higher ethics and intelligence can never be successfully enforced
upon a private speculatorwhose only inducement to risk his money in
such a venture is the prospect of gain, which he feels entitled to ensure
by any means that he thinks fit.—Now, if the State adopts the aforesaid

maxim for the Theatre in general, and insists on compliance therewith, it must needs be powerless where it does not assist withal in furnishing the means to ward off present evils.—In the case just named, can the Saxon State command the private speculator to conduct his theatre exclusively upon those higher lines ? Can it, in a word, forbid the performance of trivial farces and the like, while these ensure him the attendance of the crowd ?—If it cannot, then ought it to compel Leipzig to support a theatre out of its own purse to maintain the principle the State has recognised, especially as Leipzig will already be contributing its quota to the chief National-theatre ? No ! To assert its power here as well, the State must also—subsidise. 'This it can do by allotting to Leipzig, for the present, a portion of the main subvention. If the Royal Court-theatre has hitherto been set down for 40,000 thalers * on the Civil List, henceforth the National-theatre at Dresden would have to do with 30,000 thalers, while Leipzig would receive a yearly grant of 10,000 thlr., its theatre be declared a *National theatre, with the same organisation as the Dresden one,* and its management be likewise placed under the responsibility of the Ministry. An inventory would have to be taken in concert with the city, and the lesser subsidy be made more valuable by the promise that Dresden shall send good and inexpensive actors to Leipzig from the Stage-school to be founded in the former city (as detailed below). The proviso that the same organisation shall be given to the national-theatre at Leipzig as to that in Dresden makes it unnecessary to go any farther into its future constitution, for the difference will merely consist in a comparative restriction of outlay, altering nothing in the principle.

None of the other Provincial towns has hitherto been able to support The Pro a standing theatre, even in the humblest fashion. *Chemnitz* itself could vincial towns. only offer good receipts in the winter months at most. These towns could therefore advance no manner of claim to a National-theatre, as they would be in no position to supplement the allowance by the indispensable factor of receipts. Their share in the country's National Theatre must accordingly be confined to the occasion of a visit to the capital or Leipzig.

Directors of acting-companies, however, have at all times obtained Travelling concessions from the Saxon Government to scour the country : these companies. troupes have made longer or shorter visits to the provincial towns, and consequently brought them into immediate acquaintance with the Theatre. How extremely defective these relations of the Theatre to the Public were bound to fall out ; how injurious to taste, and still

---

* As sums of money based on the " thaler " are of frequent mention in the following pages, I may give the formula for approximately converting thalers into pounds sterling : add one half of the total, and strike off the last cipher.— the thaler being equal to about 3s. ; thus 40,000 thlr. is equivalent to £6,000. —Tr.

more to morals, these strolling companies have always been ; how deeply they have depressed the estimation of the Actor's status, even now when it is being made so extravagantly much of in some quarters, —all this has been so forcibly set forth in the newly-published book of *Eduard Devrient* : "A History of German Acting," that we here need merely refer to that.   The State *cannot* tolerate these companies any longer, were it only that in their regard it is unable to watch over the Theatre's chief principle : "to work for the ennoblement of taste and manners."   It is therefore to be urged upon the Government neither to grant nor to renew any more such concessions, and either to cancel at once or give notice to those already current, not even grudging sacrifices in compensation to those concerned ; for the greatest incon-sistency must be laid at its door, were it strenuously to maintain that needful principle for the chief cities of the land, and yet abet the provinces in flouting it.   As these towns ought to be fully recompensed for the loss of their former so-called pleasures, however, and provided with the enjoyment of far better stage-performances, perhaps in exact measure and number as before, we shall return to this question after specifying our plans for the foundation of a Stage-school.

Institution of a Stage-school.

Even from a purely economic point of view, the Theatre has hitherto behaved most foolishly in having done nothing, or nothing adequate, to provide itself with the necessary generator of its artistic material : the discovery of suitable and useful talents has heretofore been left to chance ; as nothing was attempted for their training anywhere, they were rare, therefore costly, and the Virtuoso proper almost priceless.

So it came to pass that true culture was no longer expected of actors : a little talent, but above all, an acquired routine, sufficed. Hence the inner contempt, still nursed among the intelligent classes of the nation, for the Actor and especially the Singer.   This state of things, so detrimental to the Theatre both spiritually and materi-ally, should be remedied for all time by the institution and suitable organisation of a Stage-school : without any further cost worth mentioning, such a school can be embodied as an integral member in the organisation of a *properly endowed* Chief National-theatre, upon the following lines :

Organisation of the School.

Every half-year the Ministry will announce throughout the land that lads who have attained at least their 16th, and girls their 14th year, may apply for reception into the Stage-school at Dresden ; the parents or other relatives of the young people, so soon as these have been accepted, have to undertake their maintenance in a decent and becoming fashion for three years long at Dresden ; instruction and every means of developing their aptitudes will be given them gratis, and after three years, should they meanwhile have displayed decided talent, they will also be assured a sufficient livelihood.   Young people of highly-pronounced ability, who can be proved to have no means of paying for a three-years' stay in Dresden, will have their maintenance provided by relief from a floating fund.

The Teaching-staff will be formed as follows : Teachers.

From among the members of the active stage-personnel of the two theatres the Director chooses teachers of the art of acting, who have to give instruction to their respective pupils in the practice of their art, in return for a fixed addition to their salary.

A dancing-master, who must also understand the art of fencing, will be appointed by the Director to attend to the pupils' bodily training.

(What concerns their musical education, and especially the art of singing, we shall deal with when we come to the Kapelle.)

Further : by the Union of Poets and Writers, and from among its members, there shall be named a teacher of æsthetics, dramatic art and poetry, who will receive a regular appointment as such at the National-theatre, and be paid from its treasury. It is for the Union to deter-mine whether his appointment shall be for life, or temporary and interchangeable. This teacher has to give free lectures to the whole active personnel of the theatre upon every subject in any way con-nected with the stage, such as art, literature, history &c., with especial view to the intellectual development of the pupils of the art of acting, who will also attend these lectures : according to the Director's judg-ment, pupils will also be assigned to him for private instruction.

The applicant for admission to the School is at once subjected to a preliminary examination, followed by either acceptance or rejection ; in the former case the pupil enters the *third class*, and receives *elementary instruction* in every branch of the arts of acting and singing. At the end of the first half-year he is again examined in presence of the whole staff of teachers : should his aptitudes awake no reasonable hopes, he is sent back to his friends with the recom-mendation of some other calling : if better promise is shewn, he enters a fresh half-yearly term, and passes upon completion of the first year of tuition into the *second class*. Acceptance
and classifica
tion of the
pupils.

In the *second class* the pupil still pursues a course of suitable in-struction, but is at like time made acquainted with the practice of what he has learnt, on a *trial-stage* : with the stage itself he should also be familiarised according to his abilities, either by taking part in the chorus, as a supernumerary, or even, should it seem advisable, in minor speaking parts. In this class he has to remain for two full years ; only in case of quite exceptional talent, and after the half-yearly examinations have proved unusually rapid progress, might he pass into the first class at an earlier date.

By the time the pupil reaches the *first class* he must have developed his skill as a practical actor, on the trial-stage, so far as to be able to execute to the teachers' satisfaction every major or minor rôle or singing-part, appropriate to his individuality, in a circle of dramatic works that do not overstep the stage at which his powers of conception have arrived in general. If this faculty has *not* yet appeared in him, and if the Chorus-director agrees, he passes straight into the actual choir, with the proper salary. Only if he does not seem competent for even that, and no other post is vacant at the theatre that would suit his capacity and at like time meet his inclination, must he be finally dismissed.

Now, as nothing is so requisite for the certainty and self-reliance of the young actor who has reached this same first class, as the testing of his work before a genuine audience, not merely one composed of his familiar teachers, the question arises : How to procure him this public audience ?—since the public of the capital has the right to demand, not the mere experiments of artistic training, but their utmost finished results. The young actor would therefore be relegated to the minor theatres ; these theatres, however, must likewise stand under the control of the Director of the Chief-theatre, if the influence of the School is still to be exerted on the pupil. This will be most suitably attained, if the withdrawn concessions for touring the provincial towns be made over in toto to the Director of the chief theatre : he would then have to form either one or two troupes, as need required, in which many a lesser talent, instead of being discharged, or a veteran not sufficiently disabled to admit of pensioning, but who is beginning to be a hindrance to the higher interests of the principal stages, might be usefully disposed of for the present. He would entrust these troupes to the conduct of Regisseurs or Directors of his own choice, enrolling with them the pupils of the first class according to their capability, so as to let them commence their career as practical actors or singers on well-managed provincial stages. The pupils of the first class would thus at once be drawing a salary, which had best be fixed at a uniform figure for them all. The surplus to be anticipated from these branch-undertakings, with any skilful management, can be devoted to a fund for altogether destitute young people, as already suggested when speaking of the acceptance of pupils.

The Director, or one of his deputies, will personally inspect the pupils' work at the provincial theatres as often as possible, convince himself of the maturity of individual talents, and fill up vacancies in the personnel of the National-theatre by definitive engagement of those found fit. This advantage, of obtaining good performers from the institute at a moderate cost, will stand open to the National-theatre at Leipzig also, so that both the National-theatres of the land will supply themselves from this Stage-school. The Directors of the two National-theatres have to agree between themselves as to the appointment of each pupil, according to their need.

If a pupil of the first class receives an offer of engagement from a Engagement theatre outside the country, he is to report it to the Director : should of the pupils. there be no similar position vacant for him at either of the two National-theatres at the moment, and no prospect of the like within six months, the pupil is to receive permission to accept the offer, so that there may be no idea of purchase or trade in human beings attaching to the institution. On the other hand, in the event of there being no single talent in the first class of pupils available to fill a gap arising in the personnel, the Directors of both National-theatres shall be at equal liberty to supply their need from an outlying theatre.

The advantage of these arrangements to the Theatre and its art is past disputing :—the *Theaterinstitut* will become an organic whole for the entire Saxon fatherland, a whole that renews and evolves itself from out itself, ensuring to the Actor's rank the most complete respect and parity with that of every other citizen of State, because its root-conditions rest on those of broadest culture.—

A special advantage accrues to the higher ethical aim of the State itself from its being able to demand that aim of every section of the whole ; its powerlessness over the self-supporting provincial stages is done away with, and in this respect the important point is to be taken in eye, that the Director of the chief theatre has a completely free hand to allow no performances to be set before the public of the provinces but such as have been approved by the intelligence of the land—here represented by the Combined Committee—as answering to the higher principle of dramatic art. He will permit the branch-companies to practise, in the first place, none but good pieces, in the second and a most important one, none but such as are within their range and capabilities, and harmonious to the modest frames of smaller stages ; whereas one now can take no step against that utter ruin of taste and manners consequent on operas and pieces calculated for the colossal dimensions of the largest Parisian theatres, for instance, being attempted with the most miserable mutilations, the most deficient personnel, and on the least appropriate boards.

The higher aim of Art will thus be rightly seized and applied to the smallest juncture, and the entire fatherland accordingly ensured a fitting share in the National Theatre, to all the nation's intellectual forces a full and free co-operation in it, and thereby a reasonable foundation laid for its most purposeful development in keeping with the nation's faculty and will.

With reference to the provincial theatres it is to be added that, as (1) the organisation in their regard cannot enter life until a first class of pupils shall have been formed as far as necessary, and (2) it would throw too many people out of work, were the current concessions to be withdrawn of a sudden,—such concessions may continue till they gradually run out, but with an extreme limit of four to five years, after which every one of them must be cancelled. It would be best to acquaint their holders with this decision at once, especially as in the present agitated times these concessions can offer but small advantage in themselves, and most of the companies—particularly in view of the summer—are on the point of breaking up.

First of all, however, the Minister appoints a Director of the Dresden National-theatre, with the commission to call the new organisation to life in measure and as gradually as to him appears expedient.

With the proposed organisation of a German National-theatre for the Kingdom of Saxony it is quite impossible that serious evils and abuses should endure for long, unless they were rooted in the incapacity or ill-will of the whole nation itself: such an inconceivable contingency no legislation in the world could cure. Wherefore any minuter code or prescript, beyond those needful for the organisation itself, would be quite superfluous. One further point alone we hold of such importance, that it should be decided in advance: this is *the number* of the stage-performances.

In Dresden it has latterly been the custom to open the theatre on every evening in the week—thus, seven times a-week. The consequent damage to the spirit and quality of the performances is unmistakable, if one reflects that representations of never so popular pieces cannot be repeated at brief intervals with a theatre-public of limited size and variety ;—accordingly, that only a constant change of pieces and their genres can attract the public to the theatre in sufficient numbers ;—with the result that almost the entire programme for a week has to be composed of different and differently-fashioned pieces: a requirement which excludes all possibility of adequate preparation, and with it all responsibility for finished execution. If in theory this great evil is surmountable, all practice has proved the reverse. It has happened that, with this excessive number of performances in every week, obstacles have stood in the way of this or that intended work, and, to comply with the convention, so-called 'scratch-perform-ances' have taken place, as a rule of such a quality that they quite disgust the audience with the theatre for a time, whilst they gravely injure the artistic interest by fostering the idea of its all being nothing but journeyman-work.

Although this evil has been fully admitted by the existing Management, the rejoinder has been, in the main : that Dresden had too many visitors, and others, who would never know what to do with themselves on an evening when there was no theatre. In our opinion this reply involves the bitterest condemnation of the prevailing estimate of the Theatre. So, only when people don't know what to do with a tiresome evening, will they go to the theatre ? In effect, with a large section of the public this view has become a habit, and the Theatre accordingly has sunk to a mere source of entertainment, a pastime as surrogate for playing cards and so forth. If we did not start with a far higher and worthier opinion of the Theatre, and seek to bring it to common acceptance, we fail to see by what right we could ever demand the active support of the nation for this institute. Our view, as already set forth, is a nobler one ; we claim the fullest and keenest interest of the whole nation for an artistic establishment that combines all the arts with the object of ennobling taste and manners. This interest of the public's must be active, energetic,—not slack and superficially attracted. Were it solely for that reason, we must never dream of shewing ourselves in a journeyman light, never set before it representations that have issued from the customary fix': no, every one must bear the stamp of utmost possible finish, that Art may constantly assert its rank and dignity. This is the first thing to be attained by *limiting* the number of so-called play-nights.—But still other grounds may be adduced : if the Theatre is to retain the nation's lively and continual interest, it must not trifle with that interest by bidding-in the public day by day ; it must voluntarily stand aside on certain evenings of the week, which should be relinquished to the citizen for his share in the deliberation of the common weal, to the family for its enjoyment of itself, as also to the other unmixed arts, those of independent vocal and instrumental music in particular, for their performances. Thus will the Theatre and its retainers enter a harmonious relation with the State.

It is completely erroneous, to assume that the receipts must suffer from a reduction in the number of play-nights: —a few good returns per week scarcely compensate for the many bad ones inevitable with a plethora of play-nights. If the interest of the public is confined to a smaller number of performances, it also will devote a keener sympathy to these: the knowledge that one can enjoy a certain pleasure every night, blunts the longing for it. It will, and must inevitably be proved that *five* good performances a-week, for instance, are better attended and bring in more than seven middling ones, among them some quite bad. One unconditional gain will be a saving in the daily costs, and consequently a reduction in the regular yearly outlay.

Wherefore it should be decreed in advance, that the play-nights at the National-theatre in Dresden be reduced from seven per week to five at most, and proportionately for Leipzig.

The Musical Institute.

IN direct alliance with the Theatre stands the musical
Kapelle.

This institute, originally founded (as its name "Kapelle"
tells us) for glorifying the Service of God with a musical
rite, was put to its first worldly purpose by employment
to assist in amusing the Court at princely festivals and
the like; chief among these amusements, in earlier days,
was the Italian Opera. In course of time the function of
the institute became more and more a secular one, and its
enjoyment was thrown open to the public, so that with the
final erection of the Court-theatre it has been devoted for
the principal part to that: true, that the Kapelle has to
furnish the musical service in Church as extensively as
before, and it is under this heading that it is scheduled on
the Civil List of His Majesty the King; by far the greater
portion of its duties, however, now accrues to the Theatre,
in which the orchestra for plays and operas is supplied
exclusively by it. Its use for the private entertainment of
the Court has thus, of course, been limited in the extreme;
of late the Kapelle has merely had to provide a portion of
the entertainment on New Year's day during the Royal
banquet, and on the second day of Easter at a Court-
festival, whilst on various evenings, particularly in the
winter, single virtuosi from the Kapelle have been summoned to the Palace. The enjoyment of the doings of
the institute has thus been made over almost exclusively
to publicity, and for the major portion they consist in
its co-operation at the performances of the theatre, as
also in grand concerts: its original destination for the
Church is now confined to maintaining the *number* of
services; their *spirit* has suffered grave mischief, particu_
larly through the vocal branch of the Kapelle having

Y   357

been almost entirely neglected, a matter to which we propose to return.

Amid such circumstances it is pre-eminently the instrumental branch of the Kapelle, the *Orchestra* proper, that has flourished : it is it, that has upheld the honour of the whole institute, and ensured it the nation's esteem. Its maintenance and due development would therefore be founded not only on the utmost interest of Art, but also on a national wish. Yet the question is, whether the sum allotted yearly to the maintenance of the Kapelle on the Civil List could not be employed more aimfully than hitherto, to make thereof a musical institute in whose organism every department of Absolute Music should be included and equally represented ; further, that should contain within itself its fount of renovation and development, and finally, should be of service to the cause of Music in the entire Saxon fatherland? The solution of this weighty problem has certainly been neglected hitherto, nay, the problem itself not even recognised ; and, in the same degree as with the Theatre, this evil reposes on the fact that to the supreme control of this institute the self-same court-official has been appointed until now, an officer in whom no special artistic knowledge was presupposed,—without which knowledge, even with the most upright and admirable will for the best, the true Best for Art itself can never be discovered.

For the number of the members of such a musical institute the present need is to be fixed as an enduring standard, especially as it is dictated by the accommodation in the art-localities themselves ; the requirements from the several parts of the organism are to be strictly settled once for all ; the relative expenditure upon them constitutes the Estimate (*Etat*), which is also determined in advance,—so that nothing will remain for the Management, but to arrange the filling of the estimate as best subserves the ends of *art*; for this *no man can be qualified, but he to whom the artistic conduct of the institute is committed with full responsibility for its doings*; and that is the Kapellmeister (or Musical Conductor), just as in the theatre it is the Director who has gained professional experience from the stage itself. His responsibility for the institute, however, must be solidly founded; and that will be reached the surest through a constitutional organisation thereof. The organisation of the institute must hence be taken first in eye, and after ascertaining how the yearly income can be best devoted to the harmonious constitution of a perfect whole, it will be easier to name the independent parts whose representatives should themselves combine to sustain a good artistic spirit.—

At every performance, whether in the Church, the Theatre or Concert-room, the instrumental Orchestra is brought into more or less direct connection with the vocal Choir : for the Church we shall shew that, according to all ideas of a becoming Church-music, the orchestra has even to recede before the choir. Now, this very important member of the musical institute, how is it constituted at present ? *The Choir.*

For service in Church the Kapelle-fund pays a number of singers who are engaged from the operatic company according to whether they are of the Catholic confession : it is to be remarked that the very requirement of this confession-of-faith makes the selection difficult and limited, and further, that the benefit of a church-wage has frequently been given to singers who already were half invalided for Opera, or to such whose demands were too heavy for the theatrical treasury to meet without assistance, but with the silent understanding that as long as the singer's voice was of strength for the stage it was not to be claimed by the Church. The number of these so-called "soloists" was reinforced by five to six Catholic stage-choristers, so that the total of men's voices comes at present to fourteen. The female voices, soprano and alto, are represented by ten to twelve boys from the Catholic free-school in this city (mostly recruited for this purpose from Bohemia), who are drilled by an "instructor." In former times Italian castrati were engaged as soprano and alto soloists, but now have vanished before the moral sense of the age. These 24 to 26 singers, who by no means make out a choral Institute for reason of their very heterogeneous nature, are accompanied in church by an orchestra of 50 strong : completely overbalancing the singers, this orchestra unites with them to execute compositions penned by local Kapellmeister from the time of the past century to the beginning of the present ; compositions belonging for the most part to a style in which (obsolete) worldly virtuosity predominates, whilst churchly reverence, with few exceptions, is hardly represented at all. Having *Church-singers.*

Stage-choir.

mentioned this in passing, let us state that the aforesaid singers form the only vocal institute incorporated with the Kapelle.

The Stage-choir has lately been the subject of a new solicitude.* Thirty years back, especially with nothing but an Italian Opera, so little importance was attached to the choir that it was represented by a mere handful of choristers. Since the advent of certain German, and particularly of the modern French Grand operas, however, its higher importance has been gradually acknowledged, and concessions made from time to time to artistic demands for its strengthening. Steps have also been taken in quite recent days to emancipate the chorus-singer, in respect of wages and provision for the future, from a state of deepest degradation. The demands upon the chorister, compared with the dramatic singer or the member of the orchestra, from whom individual artistic attainments are likewise expected, are certainly of humbler nature : it is enough for him to have a voice of average quality, an unobjectionable exterior, and diligence. His successful employment in indistinguishable combination with his numerous colleagues is mainly the duty of the Chorus-director, who trains him for this purpose. Nevertheless the State neither can nor ought to tolerate his being turned into a slave for the object of its higher pleasures ; and that he both has been and is, when, with his time so fully occupied as to make every other means of livelihood impossible to him, his wages scarce suffice for the common necessaries of life, and his provision for infirmity can only in the rarest cases be commended to the bounty of the King. Some care has been devoted to this question of late, but not as yet sufficient. Above all, moreover, the artistic condition of the Chorus is not what it should be : in its co-operation with the orchestra of the Kapelle it is at a decided disadvantage in point of strength, and its artistic training is not yet adequately provided by an organised Chorus-school. These evils make their presence felt in Opera, and particularly in the Concert-room.

Endowment of a Choral-institute.

According to the latest figures the expenditure from the stage-treasury upon the choir and Choir-director amounts to 8,000 thlr. ; to this must be added the payment of an auxiliary chorus of military singers, requisitioned for most of our operas, which brings the total to

* To Wagner's old friend the Chorus-master W. Fischer; see Vol. III. pp. 148 *et seq.* : " His achievements as choir-conductor form a red letter in the calendar of Art. . . . How often have I had to deplore the poor fellow, when he could only answer my reckless demands with his own despair : his good singers were upon the sick list; the best, resigned for refusal of increased salary ; the remainder tired out by excessive work, or detained to act as supers in the play-rehearsals. Yet he was a man of resource . . . and the thing succeeded, God knows how." On page 344 *inf.* Fischer is again alluded to, re the "hunting up" of ancient church-composers.—Tr.

about 10,000 thlr. If we therefore fix 10,000 thlr. as the sum which *must* in any case be paid by the Dresden theatre for a good choir, we once for all may take these 10,000 thlr. as a standing allotment from the subvention for the Theatre ; if on the other hand we draw from the Kapelle-estimate the 5,000 thlr. at present spent on the Church-choir, we obtain 15,000 thlr. in all ; and that is ample, according to our calculations, to endow a Choral-institute that would fill a worthy place beside the Orchestra of the Kapelle in Church, in Theatre and Concert-room.

The feasibility of this plan depends, in the first place, on the discontinuance of the existing institute for church-singing : we therefore must devote a few more words to that.

If Catholic Church-music is to justify its retention in the Hofkirche at *Dresden*, considering the spirit of the times, it must recover its wellnigh lost distinction of religious inwardness and sublimity. In the 16th century Pope Marcellus meant to banish music from the Church entirely, because its prevalent scholastic-speculative trend was a menace to the piety and inwardness of religious expression : *Palestrina* saved Church-music from the ban, by restoring it to that expression ; his works, with those of his pupils and the immediately succeeding century, form the flower and paragon of Catholic church-music: *they are written exclusively for men's voices.* The first step towards the downfall of true Catholic church-music was the introduction of orchestral instruments therein : through them and their ever freer and more independent application a sensuousness has been imposed on the religious expression that not only has proved a most serious check to it, but also has had the most mischievous influence upon the vocal part itself: the virtuosity of the instrumentalist ended by challenging the singer to rival it, and soon the worldly taste of Opera completely invaded the Church: certain passages of the sacred text, such as *Christe eleison*, became standing subjects for operatic arias, and singers trained to the Italian mode were bidden into church for their delivery.—`

To the age in which this altogether perverse and irreligious tendence assumed the upper hand, belongs the establishment of a Catholic Court-service in Dresden : from this centre has the music of our Catholic Court-church expanded, along this worldly line has it developed. Through the importation of expensive singers, particularly Castrati, the composer was set the task of shewing off their talents ; and all the compositions that make out our available store for the service of God, with single exceptions strewn here and there among the separate numbers, belong to this style that has now been rightly recognised as bad in taste and positively insulting to a sound religious spirit.   If we add, that the circumstances which prompted those compositions exist no more in Dresden ; that those singers, and especially the castrati, are no longer with us ; therefore, that the pieces reckoned for their vocal virtuosity have now to be rendered by singers to whom it is totally alien, the parts for the castrati being gabbled through by boys : the unnatural-ness, and often the abomination, of retaining such a style' of music will be apparent.—An immediate remedy might be, to introduce a few women-singers into church, to take the place of the castrati : further, carefully to select the repertory from such compositions as lean the least towards that bad direction.   For, since the time when Church-music lost its purity through the intrusion of orchestral instru-ments, the greatest musicians of their age have neverthe-less composed church-pieces of supreme artistic value in themselves.   These masterworks, however, do not belong to that pure ecclesiastic style which there are so many grounds for considering it high time to restore ; they are artworks of Absolute Music, built on a religious basis indeed, but far more fitted for performance at Spiritual Concerts than during Divine Service in the church itself, particularly on account of their excessive length, which quite forbids the rendering of the works of a Cherubini, Beethoven and so forth, during the Mass.   But, were we even to renounce the full purity of church-music, and adapt these masterpieces of composition for use in the Catholic Court-church by cuts, for instance, the quarters for our choir itself would offer an insuperable obstacle. The space allotted us for seating the band and choir could not be sufficiently enlarged to give accommodation to a number of singers proportionate to the necessary strength of the orchestra (an unconditional necessity with these compositions) without a total reconstruction, involving a disturbance of the architectural proportions of the whole nave. Yet the *human voice, the immediate bearer of the Sacred Word,* and not the instrumental finery, or even trivial fiddlery of most of our present church-pieces, *must take the precedence in church*; and if church-music is wholly to return to its original purity, *vocal music alone* must Vocal music represent it again. For the only necessary accompani- alone. ment the genius of Christianity invented a becoming instrument, which holds its undisputed place in all our churches; this is the *organ*, which most ingeniously unites a great variety of tone-expression, but of its very nature excludes all virtuosic flourishes, and cannot draw an outwardly disturbing notice to itself by sensuous charms. The space allotted us in the present Catholic Court-church is admirably adapted for installing a strong choir of singers, in lieu of the band, and their effect in this build- ing would be uncommonly fine and impressive; for its acoustics are of the greatest advantage to the more tranquil motion of the human voice, whereas the busier vibrations from the instruments often jar upon the ear, and therefore spoil an understanding of the music, since the unusually powerful echo confuses them and makes a discord.

Two initial obstacles stand in the way of introducing purely vocal Introduction music into our Catholic Court-church. The first, removable at once of females and by a decision of the authorities, consists in the prohibition of females, Protestants —who are absolutely necessary for establishing a good and powerful church. chorus,—as also in the impossibility of recruiting the personnel from any but members of the Catholic communion. We are proposing nothing but the *restoration of a truly elevating, a religious church- music*: the Catholic clergy can have no conceivable grounds for doing other than encourage this effort in every way. Women are already allowed to take part in church-singing in many Catholic lands: were there a special scruple in the case of Dresden, on the ground that in so preponderantly Protestant a city the pomp of Catholic divine-service already attracts a merely curious crowd to the church, and would do so still more if females took part in it,—one might reply that, as the female sex is not prevented from visiting the nave itself out of pure curiosity, there could be no objection to seating it in the raised position of the choir, and moreover it could be hidden from distinct sight by a grille enclosing the chorus; it should be a sufficient guarantee, however, that the famous virtuosi of the Opera will not be employed in Church, on principle, as the occasional "soli" will be of such a nature that so-called chorus-leaders will be fully competent for their simple rendering.—The requirement of a confession of Catholic faith from every member of the choir, in an almost purely Protestant country, could hardly be deemed insuperable by the Catholic clergy of to-day, were it only that most of the children of the fatherland would be thereby debarred from education at this choral institute.   To overcome this scruple, however, it will suffice to agree that the stricter *ceremonial-singing* shall be furnished by a number of Catholic members of the choir.

The second obstacle, only to be overcome in course of time, consists in the dearth of purely vocal pieces for the church.   That can only be remedied step by step, and the following might be the method :—

Already a number of appropriate compositions by Palestrina and his followers are being hunted up : the Kapellmeisters will be commissioned to restore the lost traditions of their rendering according to their own artistic judgment, consequently to restore these works to their full freshness and warmth of religious expression, as has been proved quite feasible, and to see to their rehearsal in this sense.—From a fund to be discussed below, *prizes* will be offered to all the composers in the fatherland and Germany for good church-compositions in purely vocal score, and at like time for the discovery of older music and its revisal with suitable marks of expression.—Until such time as the repertory has become large and varied enough to supply every need in an ecclesiastic year, the existing state of church-music will have to be maintained, with merely an occasional substitution of services of unmixed vocal music with an increased choir ; but in measure as the store of vocal compositions waxes, and the present contracts with church-singers expire one by one, alike the compositions now in use and the co-operation of the orchestra will entirely disappear from the church, yielding place at last to purely vocal music.   In larger Spiritual Concerts, on the other hand, the orchestra in union with the full choir will be able to do sufficient to set the masterpieces of mixed church-music before the public as an independent order ; so that with this new arrangement only the *bad*, but not the *good*, creations of this class will vanish.—

The Choral-institute, thus raised to be a worthy member of the whole, will be organised as follows.—

The number of choristers must be regulated on the principle that it shall somewhat exceed that of the instruments in the orchestra with which they co-operate: it has been proved that an orchestra can easily cope with a chorus even twice as strong as itself. Allowing for an improvement in the present rate of wages, the yearly sum of 15,000 thlr. would be employed on 70 chorus-singers, the Choir-director, his substitutes and so on, in the following fashion : *Arrangement of the Choral-institute.*

As the requirements from a good chorus-singer are of modest nature, it is to be assumed that the Saxon fatherland, and even Dresden by itself, will offer a sufficient supply of available talent : the Choral-institute should therefore be filled and renewed in the main from natives of the fatherland. To this end the institute must undertake the duty of ensuring its future prosperity by conferring instruction. At the same time as the notices for the Stage-school, then, invitations to join the Chorus-school will be published half-yearly. Young people applying for admission, the lads not under 16, the girls not under 14, as before, have to declare at once whether they wish to be trained for the chorus alone, or also for the theatre. In the latter case they will be. submitted to an examination of their aptitudes in that respect ;—should these not be deemed sufficient, the. Choir-director has to judge the applicant's fitness to become a chorus-singer by a special examination : if this is satisfactory, the applicant is permitted to enter the Chorus-school exclusively ; however, even the choral scholars will be accorded the right of applying for a renewed trial of any talents they may have since developed for the Play, or the higher art of Dramatic Song, at the half-yearly examinations of the pupils of the Stage-school.—Moreover every pupil of the Stage-school, who has any competence of voice, is to share the course of instruction in the Chorus-school : this concerns even the more talented pupils, whose ability has marked them for the higher walks of Dramatic Song, as experience teaches how important is the practice of systematic choral singing for the nurture and invigoration of musical gifts. *Chorus-school.*

This presumably somewhat large body of scholars and participators in the Chorus-school will be divided into two classes, corresponding with the third and second classes of the Stage-school. In the third class of the Stage-, or the second of the Chorus-school, the pupils will receive free elementary instruction in music and singing, in general, from the Choir-director or his substitutes for a whole year : by the dancing, fencing, and drill masters their bodily training will be promoted ; they will also be admitted to the general rehearsals of the Chorus proper.—In the first class of the Chorus-, or the second of the Stage-school, they will already be called to take part in the larger

choir in Church, Theatre and Concert-room, at grand performances.
At half-yearly examinations their progress will be repeatedly tested :
after proof of total unfitness, at any such examination, they may yet
be discharged and sent home to their friends with the recommendation of another career.—From among the more advanced in this first
class of the Chorus-school the actual Chorus is to be replenished as
need demands.   The National-theatre at Leipzig is to be directed to
draw its supply of choristers exclusively from the first class of the
Dresden Chorus-school, in order to ensure a paid appointment as
speedily and to as many pupils as possible : they will also furnish the
requisite chorus-singers for the one or two branch-companies, it being
understood, of course, that their appointment (whether here or there)
will follow the order of merit.   Outlying theatres will be allowed to
engage them, providing no appointment at either of the two National-
theatres can be promised within half a year.   Every chorister already
actually appointed may still announce himself for the half-yearly
examinations of the Stage-school, so that, in case of latent faculties
having since developed in him, he may not be cut off from the possibility of maturing them, and consequently of pursuing a more brilliant
career than that of the Chorister.

Provision for old age shall be secured to the members of the
Choral-institute in the following fashion :

The Chorus-director, on the advent of infirmity, will be pensioned
according to the law for Civil Servants, and receive his pension from
the fund for invalided members of the Kapelle, as heretofore has been
the case with the precentor [?—"*Ceremoniensänger*"] and instructor
of the boys ; the same applies to the church-singers, whose pensions
no longer will burden the Civil List, with the new organisation.

If a Chorus-singer loses his voice to such a degree that his further
co-operation would be useless or injurious to the working of the choir,
his provision is to be arranged for in the first instance by his receiving
(according to his position in active service, whether at the chief
National-theatre in Dresden, or in one of the subsidiary companies
for the provinces) a different post of equal emolument, or next
below his present rate ; therefore all positions suitable for chorus-
singers, male or female, must be reserved exclusively for them.
However, if 1) the transferred chorister proves unequal to the new
duties assigned him, 2) no post is vacant for him at the time of his
invaliding as chorus-singer, or 3) he declares his preference for the
smaller income of a pension, to retaining his present rate of wages
or a trifle under in return for undertaking other duties,—he is then to
be provided for, according to a fixed scale, from a fund to be founded
and kept up in the following manner.

1) In course of every year a performance is to be given at the
theatre for the benefit of the Pension-fund : to this performance

the Director will devote the production of a new opera, on a day of the week on which no stage-representation takes place in ordinary.

2) For the same purpose a concert-performance shall be given every year, at which the Orchestra is to support the Chorus.

3) According to the annual requirements of the fund, the Chorus is authorised to institute performances of purely vocal music.

The members of the Choral-institute choose from among themselves a Committee to manage this fund. The Chorus-director, on his side, is pledged to keep strict watch that choristers become unfit for choral singing shall not remain a mischief to the artistic standing of the institute,—he therefore has to propose and insist on their transference or pensioning in good season. For this he is responsible to the chief musical authority of the institute.

We now return to the Instrumental-orchestra of the Kapelle. According to the figures for 1848 the Civil List expenditure upon this principal branch of the institute, inclusive of the salary to the Generaldirektor, the Kapell- and Konzertmeister, the Musikdirektor, the organists, accessists and servants, the yearly outlay on purchase and repair of instruments, and the sum devoted to gratuities,—thus, without the cost of the church-choir,—amounts to considerably over 40,000 thlr. The precept on the Civil List is consequently exceeded in no small degree. Our task would therefore be, *to improve the institute to the utmost, and yet reduce the expenditure to its original estimate.*

The number of bandsmen deemed needful of late years has been based on the number and arduousness of the duties expected from them. At present, beyond 60 so-called "wirkliche Kammermusiker," there are 20 Accessists with an annual wage of 150 thlr. each. In view of the size of the localities in which the performances take place, this number was absolutely necessary to cope with the number of duties demanded : the latter consist in over 200 church-services and daily occupation at the theatre, where from 3 to 4 operas have been given weekly, besides the provision of an orchestra for the entr'acte music at every play. Then in summer there have often been double representations, in the city and at the summer-theatre, the orchestra frequently being required at the one place for a grand 'opera, at the other for a singspiel ; an excessive number of rehearsals was entailed by these clashing performances and their ceaseless change. So that the aforesaid number of bandsmen was no more than barely sufficient, with an orchestra that had constantly to be divided into two.

A state of affairs which has involved such overtaxing of our musical forces, counter to the best interest of art, both should and will be done

Orchestra.

Ratio of the number of duties.

Future limition of duti

away with by the new organisation of the National-theatre. Henceforward the number of so-called play-nights will be reduced to 5 a-
week : of these days 2, in very rare cases 3 at most, will be devoted
to Opera ; whilst the music between the acts of a play, it is to be
hoped, will be entirely dispensed with, for the following reasons.—

The necessity of having music after the fall of the
curtain at end of a play-act is to be justified on no artistic
ground : rather is it a mere habit dating from the accident
of ancient custom, whose retention is injurious to the culture
of Art in every respect.

To correspond with the intended impression of an act
just finished at the Play, the music should at least have
been expressly written for it; yet no repertory of entr'acte-
music can consist of anything but pieces divided into the
highly general categories of serious and gay,—a distinction
wholly insufficient here.   People at various times have
given themselves the most inconceivable trouble to com-
pile appropriate entr'acte music, and always have failed.
Now, what artistic end can this music serve, if it never
and nowhere has reached the end suggested?   It is to
entertain the audience in the pauses.   But an audience
which has met to see a good play, to follow the development and portrayal of characters and situations peculiar
to the Actor's art, desires no music, to say nothing of such
as simply spoils its pleasure.   It is the mentally passive,
merely superficially-excited portion of the audience, which
one does not trust oneself to leave to inward meditation
or outward comment on the impression just received, that
this music is meant to delude about the length of the
pauses : what an ignoble task for Art !   But, according to
all experience, the deception doesn't even succeed : with a
lengthier entr'acte the necessary repetition of single movements in the music-piece exasperates the audience by the
added tedium of this means of distraction, so that the wait
often seems longer than it really is.   The livelier portion
of the audience derides and mocks this music when it arrests
attention by its importunity or dulness, but deliberately or
involuntarily stops its ears to it as a rule.   Now judge the

effect which these evils combine to produce on the bandsmen! The sleepy, older bandsman grows still sleepier at
such performances, the younger, fiercer one feels a positive
hell-torment in being bound thereto.   To have to cast his
beloved art before an audience either talking aloud or
yawning, must enrage him to begin with, *demoralise* him
to end with.   For the honour of music, the honour of the
play, and finally the honour of the public, this arrangement
must be discontinued; we all must pluck up strength to
break with such a vicious habit, for in the long run *it* is
blamable that music really written to enhance the effect of
a particular play passes by with no impression, nay, without even attracting the needful notice, as we have always
found the case here with Beethoven's splendid music to
Egmont.   How much higher will be the effect of such
music on these rare occasions at the play, when the public
shall have not been made indifferent by everlasting strum-
mings, and therefore shall prick up its ears as to something
quite out of the common!

*The customary play-music will therefore disappear in
future.—*

The little theatre at the Linkisches Bad has of late been provided
by the General-management of the Court-theatre with representations
in course of the summer, simply because it would otherwise have been
let by its owner to an outside company, whose competition one feared.
Even for reason of its little space and the disproportionate expenditure, the receipts from such performances could never equal what
would have been taken in the city: but owing to the so-called
double-shift there commonly arose most reprehensible collisions,
which, coupled with the general character of the representations at
the Summer-theatre, could only demoralise the spirit of the whole
institute.   The Director of the National-theatre will henceforth spare
its personnel all part in these performances, and for the summer
months he will allot the stage at the Linkisches Bad to one of our
touring-companies, whose director he himself appoints, whose conduct
he supervises, and in which he has previously incorporated pupils of
the first class of the Stage-school: this will at like time afford him
the easiest opportunity of convincing himself on the spot of the young
people's achievements and progress.

The *Link-
isches Bad*

The modest band required by this troupe for singspiels and operettas will also support its representations at the Linkisches Bad, a band to whose formation we propose to return later on. *But the orchestra of the Kapelle will have nothing more to do with these performances.*

As we are proposing gradually to do away entirely with the Orchestra's co-operation in church, it would be left with only the 2, or at utmost 3 performances per week in the theatre ; and even though we add to these a certain number of concerts in course of the year, the arduousness of its duties will be so reduced as to remove all necessity of maintaining a body that can be divided into two at a pinch. If this was hitherto the first necessity to keep in eye, henceforth the only aim can be to form a *single* well-poised orchestra to take over every duty, so far as expedient, in its entirety ; for without undue exaction one may demand that each of its members shall undertake an opera twice a-week, with the needful rehearsals, and also hold himself in readiness for a third performance, perhaps a simpler singspiel with music of its own. Now, the mere fact of the orchestra being composed of the same musicians, at all its functions, will contribute to an artistic finish such as never could be fully attained before. The wind-instruments in particular have hitherto been doubled in our Kapelle, since the duties could not possibly be met by a single pair : the constantly varying combination of the wind-choir from the different sets of players has in many cases been most injurious to a perfect refinement of artistic rendering, especially through the inequality of pitch. A perfect execution can only be compassed when all the bandsmen grow up as into one indivisible body.

The size of the space in which the orchestra has to perform, and the teachings of experience as to the necessary proportions of its several groups, afford the figure for the requisite strength of the whole. In our playhouse the following quota of instruments has proved needful for operas on the grander scale :

20 violins, 6 violas, 6 violoncelli, 4 to 5 double-basses, 2 to 3 flutes, 2 to 3 oboes (incl. cor anglais), 2 to 3 clarinets (incl. bass-clarinet), 2 to 3 bassoons, 4 horns, 2 to 3 trumpets, 3 trombones, 1 pair of drums.

To satisfy the aforesaid needs of an onerous and highly varied service, for each of the wind-instruments (with exception of the trombones) another desk was added ; further, for the flute, oboe, clarinet and bassoon, *one* "accessist," for the horn of late, owing to the pressure of circumstances, as many as *three*, at 150 thlr. yearly. For the violins on the other hand only 18 (including the two Konzertmeister), for the violas 5, and the violoncelli also 5, musicians were actually appointed ; extra wants were supplied by 6 to 7 accessists for the violin, 3 for the viola, 2 for the 'cello, and 1 for the double-bass.

The make-shift institution of "accessists" cannot be justified, The Ac-
cessists. especially in view of their rate of wages : exactly the same duties are demanded of them as of a fully-appointed bandsman, yet they are paid but half the wage of the lowest Kammermusikus ; had these people issued from a school belonging to our Orchestra, and consequently owed their free instruction to the institute, it might have been no more than reasonable to expect them to repay their obligation by supporting it *gratis* at special performances as soon as they were sufficiently advanced ; for which, again, they would have been compensated by the reversion of appointments in the band itself. Hitherto, however, a vacancy among the accessists has had to be advertised far and wide, to get musicians to apply for it : then from the provincial towns of the fatherland, or beyond, would come musicians young and old who owed their education to a Town-musician or the like : at their examination we generally had to bewail a serious lack of good training, and consequently to pay the penalty for having done nothing to train young musicians at an institute which possesses in itself the ablest artists upon every instrument.

When at last a well-formed talent was found and chosen, its owner was assigned the post of Accessist at a yearly wage of 150 thlr., with no consideration whether for such a pittance a stranger could remove to Dresden from the provinces, or even from abroad, and maintain himself decently through a length of years (we have known cases where they extended to 15). As we were bound to choose none but the *best* of the applicants, it often would happen that he was already of maturer age, or married and saddled with children, so that the greatest misery ensued ; for the undeniable chance of obtaining a speedy appointment in the ranks of actual Kapellists would always tempt a man to accept such a post.—This institution, as composed at present, must therefore be abolished in the interest both of art and of humanity :—with the new organisation we shall no longer *need* it.

For if we do away in future with the fourth desks for the wind, as Future com-
position of the
Orchestra. superfluous with the plan now mooted, and if we add these desks to the strings, besides the two Konzertmeister we shall obtain

20 desks for the violin	instead of the present 16
6 „ „ viola	„ „ „ 5
6 „ „ violoncello	„ „ „ 5*

These, with the 3 desks for each of the wood-instruments, the 4 for the horn, the 3 for the trumpet and trombone, etc., offer the proper

---

* The line for the double-bass appears to have dropped out of the original. By adding 5 for that instrument, we get 37 for the strings ; these with 3 for the flute, 3 oboes, 3 clarinets, 3 bassoons, 4 horns, 3 trumpets, 3 trombones and 1 for the drums, make 60 desks in all.—Tr.

strength for a self-included orchestra, which, with a not excessive service, has no need of accessists, but can be supplemented from a first class of pupils on special occasions.

Allowing for a moderate improvement upon the present scale, the salaries for these 60 posts would be best arranged as follows :

10 desks at 600 thlr.				making 6000 thlr.	
10	,,	500	,,	,, 5000	,,
10	,,	450	,,	,, 4500	,,
10	,,	400	,,	,, 4000	,,
10	,,	350	,,	,, 3500	,,
10	,,	300	,,	,, 3000	,,

Up to the level of 450 thlr., these figures should be reached at an equal rate of progress by every bandsman, no matter for what instrument he is engaged, according to the length of time he has been appointed ; whereby the great injustice will be obviated, that, however excellent the bandsman, he remains too long at a lower wage for simple reason that no vacancy has occurred in his group of instruments, whereas a younger and perhaps less-skilled performer on another instrument has a rapid rise of salary through accident of place. However, to meet the legitimate claims of more talented individuals, and thus to retain the best of artists for every single instrument of its class, the following proviso should be made :

The 600 *thlr. places* shall be allotted according to special merit to 2 violinists, 1 viola-player, 1 violoncellist, 1 contrabassist, 1 flautist, 1 oboist, 1 clarinetist, 1 bassoon-player and 1 cornist. The 500 thlr. places are likewise reserved for these instruments, with the exception that one trumpeter also may attain to one of them.—

To the above total of 26,000 thlr. must be added

the salary for a harp-player,	300 thlr.
,, ,, ,, an organist,	600 ,,
,, ,, ,, his substitute,	400 ,,
Further, for a Konzertmeister,	1500 . ,,
,, ,, his deputy,	1000 ,,
,, ,, a Musikdirektor,	1200 ,,
,, ,, the servants,	1000 ,,

32,000 thlr.

At the head of the whole musical institute, as we began by shewing, there can only stand the officer entrusted with its artistic conduct, and therefore with sole responsibility for the spirit of its work : this is the

Kapellmeister, who assumes at once the musical direction and managerial inspection. He consequently receives the salary of 2000 thlr. hitherto paid to the Generaldirektor, and to assist him in the musical command a single Musikdirektor suffices : the second Kapellmeister's post thus vanishes in future, as superfluous and detrimental to the unity of artistic and managerial control.

The grand total of salaries would accordingly amount to 34,000 thlr. The still-remaining 1000 thlr. will be employed on the maintenance and provision of necessary instruments, as also on the purchase of scores and parts for the concerts of the Kapelle : these music-sheets will form in time a library, which, like every other public library, should be open to the use of the whole fatherland, and especially of the pupils of the Dresden music-school.

But as probably no more than half that sum will be required for this purpose, the annual balance shall be devoted to the prizes for good vocal church-compositions already referred to : when the immediate need of such compositions shall have been satisfied, prizes shall be offered for other musical works, non-dramatic however. The estimate of 40,000 thlr. would thus be filled, if we include the 5000 thlr. for the choral institute. *Prizes.*

In the frequent cases of emergency the members of the Kapelle have hitherto been left to appeal for gratuities, and the like, to the bounty of His Majesty the King : a fund specially set aside for this purpose had to answer the need, though never adequately. Neither such a fund, nor such appeals, should continue any longer. In full compensation, the Kapelle might be once for all accorded the right of instituting concerts on its own behalf; the receipts of the theatre would in nowise be diminished, as henceforward it is to be open for only five nights in the week, leaving blank days on which the interest of no one will be affected. The fixing of the number of such concerts shall be left to the free judgment of the Kapelle, having regard to both the artistic and the material profit to be drawn therefrom,—however, in view of the rank of such concerts, as also of the harm to the orchestra's employment in the theatre that would arise from an excessive number, it must be stipulated that in the six winter-months they shall not amount to more than 12, i.e. 2 per month. As to the application of the revenue from these concerts the Kapelle shall likewise decide for itself; it will arrange with the Chorus what share shall fall to it for its co-operation, and the Chorus in turn will appoint a committee to dispose of that share to its best advantage. The Orchestra's first care will be to assist necessitous individuals of its body from the net returns, and then to distribute the balance among its members according as it shall determine. A precisely similar arrangement maintains the admirable spirit of the exemplary *Concerts.*

To make this splendid institute of obvious use to musical art in the entire fatherland, the affiliation thereto of a music-school must be deemed essential. Hitherto the education of musicians has been left in Dresden to mere private tuition and the willingness of single artists. At Leipzig, since the past few years, a so-called Conservatorium for Music has been established * on a legacy of one of its citizens, and further endowed by the Government. Now, this Leipzig institute can only thrive to full prosperity, and truly benefit the whole land, when it is removed to Dresden and incorporated with the most important musical institute of the country, namely the Kapelle. Additions to the more considerable salaries of our best instrumental artists would gain for this school the services of the most famous virtuosi of Germany without excessive cost, whilst our excellent orchestra would furnish the best model and school for the more proficient pupil : in union with the Stage-school the ample means of the National-theatre in Dresden would contribute to a high perfection of the art-school to be thus expanded. This conservatorium, henceforth embracing a school for Stage, for Orchestra and Chorus, would accordingly be made the national centre of all that sphere of artistic education ; its forces would operate more energetically through combination : thus, for instance, the Leipzig Conservatorium is unable to afford an adequate salary for the appointment of a good singing-master, such a rarity at present ; in union with the Dresden Stage-school, and in view of the benefit of such a teacher to the theatre itself, the needful salary could be very well allowed. But a further decisive advantage would accrue, in the provision for pupils matured into young artists : pupils of the first class of the Orchestra-school who had already reinforced our band at larger concert-performances, and thus had practice in the best orchestral playing, would be quite the most suitable for filling any vacancies in the orchestra itself ; the Leipzig orchestra will also recruit itself from them, in the same way as with the pupils of our Stage- and Chorus-school. Anyone too impecunious to wait for an appointment in one of these two orchestras would be employed at first in a band of the provincial troupes, but without forfeiting his chance of returning to one of the two chief orchestras at a fitting opportunity.

We must refrain at present from going farther into the organisation of such an Orchestra-school, as that can only be settled in agreement with the Leipzig Conservatorium. But the mutual advantage to both chief cities, the use of this association to the whole land, springs to the eye ; and should Leipzig hesitate to recognise it, one would only have to reply that that city will now be compensated by the creation of a subsidised National-theatre, whilst its free scholarships founded

* By Mendelssohn in 1843.—Tr.

on the Blümner bequest will be reserved for it upon the transference of the Conservatorium to the capital.

The balance between the public functions of the two cities might accordingly be thus adjusted: *Leipzig* is the centre of *scientific* education for the country through its *University*; *Dresden* the focus of *artistic* education through the union of the Conservatorium with the national Institute for Drama and Music on the one hand, on the other through its Academy of the Plastic Arts.

The Ministry should therefore be earnestly solicited to effect a removal of the Conservatorium to Dresden in friendly agreement with the town of Leipzig.

The nation's full free partnership in this institute, how-ever, must extend to its artistic doings. In a scarcely less degree than Dramatic art, is Music able to work on taste, ay, also upon *manners*: the first point will be disputed by no one, even in our day; but a direct relation to morality has not as yet been generally ascribed to Music, in fact it has even been judged as morally quite harmless. That is not so. Could an effeminate and frivolous taste remain without influence on a man's morality? Both go hand in hand, and act reciprocally upon each other: not to refer to the Spartans, who forbade a certain type of music as injurious to morals,—let us think back to our own immediate past; with tolerable certainty we may contend that those inspired by *Beethoven's* music have been more active and energetic citizens-of-State than those bewitched by Rossini, Bellini and Donizetti, a class consisting for the most part of rich and lordly do-nothings. A speaking proof is further afforded by Paris: anyone might have observed during the last [? couple of] decads that in exact degree as the morals of Parisian society have rushed into that unexampled corruption, its music has foundered in a sphere of frivolous taste; one has only to hear the latest compositions of an Auber, Adam and so on, and to compare them with the odious dances performed in Paris at the time of Carnival, to perceive a terrible connection. If this rather proves that Morals operate on Music, yet the

(margin note: Ethical relation of Music to State.)

the State's affair to apply to this art, as well, that demand addressed by Kaiser Joseph to the Theatre : " that it shall work for the ennobling of taste *and* manners."   One of the Ministers must assume responsibility for the maintenance of this principle; and that he can only do, again, when he includes the nation's full free partnership in the organisation of this institute too, so that here also the more intelligent section shall watch over that principle in the people's interest.   .

A Union of all the composers in the fatherland should therefore form itself, to be strengthened according to its judgment by the admission of musical theorists and even purely practical executants.   To this Union will be committed the watching of that principle from its own standpoint.   From its members it chooses a Committee, in the first instance for Dresden, which has to represent in particular the interests of younger and newer composers as regards the institute. The Director of the institute, the Kapellmeister, has to fortify himself in his conferences with this committee by an equally numerous Committee of active members of the Orchestra, elected by the latter.

In this Combined Committee a majority decides, and in case of an equal division of votes the Director : the dissatisfied party has right of appeal to the Minister.   To *this* combined committee the musical section of the combined Theatre-committee has to address itself, for one thing, should it happen to be in the minority on a question involving that supreme principle in the acceptance or rejection of an opera, and to insist on an association of the two combined committees for the purpose of settling the point.

Further, this Combined Committee [of musicians] has to discuss the musical works of newer composers and their admissibility for performance at concerts : in the matter of acceptance or rejection it has to constitute itself a jury.   Its particular duty will therefore be to draw to light the works of new and still unknown composers, so as to procure them all conceivable furtherance according to desert.   One day a-month will therefore be appointed, on which the orchestra makes trial of the works of such composers before the full Committee : the pieces to be admitted to such rehearsals are previously to be determined by the latter body.   Thus it will no longer happen that young composers can never get that proper hearing of their own creations so supremely important for their further progress : if they merit it, they will now be also sure of having their products brought to the ear of the public itself at the concerts.

If an artist wishes to hold a concert on his own account, he first must ask the Combined Committee for the orchestra's support; should he obtain its consent, the proposal is to be laid before the assembled orchestra, which decides the question by a majority of votes : its co-operation is then given gratis.

The Minister on the other hand has the right, whenever consistent with their ordinary duties, to dispose of the orchestra and chorus in pursuance of some public end.

Motions counter to an order of the Director (Kapellmeister) are to be put in this Combined Committee, but only when supported by a fourth of its members ; the Director then has either to abide by the vote of the majority, or to appeal to the Minister, who decides according to the fundamental principle.

The members of the Composers' Committee receive free admittance to all these concerts, as also every member of the Union who has already had one of his compositions performed thereat.

The Director (or Kapellmeister) is elected by all the active members Inner of the Orchestra and all the members of the Union of Composers : Management the Combined Committee proposes the candidate, and his election is decided by a majority; the Minister has to ratify the choice. His salary is settled once for all, his appointment is for life. Upon the advent of incapacitation, asserted either by himself or by the Combined Committee, and confirmed by a majority of the electoral body, he is to be pensioned according to the law for State-servants, as heretofore. He has the right of conducting all the performances of the musical institute ; according to his judgment, he transfers a portion of them to the Musikdirektor. He has to decree the employment of the musical forces from the artistic standpoint, also to fix the strength of the orchestra and chorus in particular cases. He has to keep watch that, while the principle of an increase of wages according to length of service up to the 450 thlr. rate is strictly observed, the higher posts are filled in sole accordance with the above proviso in respect of talent and the particular class of instrument. He has to decide the engagement of members of the orchestra, and to keep strict watch that invalided bandsmen do not become a mischief to the orchestra's artistic status, but are pensioned according to the law for servants of the State, as heretofore.

The Managing Council associated with him for the above purposes Managing consists of the Musikdirektor and the two Konzertmeister, reinforced Council. by three members of the orchestra elected annually by a majority of that body. In this Council all questions touching the management are decided by a majority,—the Director, however, has a casting-vote. The artistic conduct of public performances belongs unconditionally to him, and against his arrangements in their regard, as also against his decision in the Council, motions can only be put in the *Combined* Committee in the mode aforesaid, which at like time opens out a

recourse to the Minister. The candidate for the vacant posts of
Musikdirektor and Konzertmeister is proposed by the Managing
Council to the assembled active members of the orchestra, who decide
by a majority : the election has to be ratified by the Minister, who in
general may call each choice in question, and has to withdraw his
objection only when the selfsame choice is repeated after information
of his grounds against it.

The Kapellmeister is the immediate bond of union between the
orchestral and choral institutes and the management of the theatre.
The Director of the Theatre has to look exclusively to him for the
working of those two institutes in the interest of the stage-performances,
and for all neglect, disturbance or carelessness in the so-called theatre-
service the Kapellmeister is responsible to him.   In the fullest interest
of the Kapellmeister himself, this responsibility for the actions of the
theatre is naturally grounded on his being also responsible for the
artistic actions of its singing personnel. The Kapellmeister, who has
to conduct the special practice of the singers even without the attendance of the orchestra, is therefore an ex officio member of the Managerial Council of the Theatre : in the matter of casting the vocal parts,
and consequently of the fit employment of the singers, his voice must
carry a determinant weight with the Director, although the definite
decision will rest with the latter alone.   In mutual conferences upon
this point the Kapellmeister is assisted by the Musikdirektor : both
officers, or at the least the Kapellmeister, therefore form the non-elected
allies of the Director in the Committee combined from active members
of the Theatre and the Union of Playwrights and Composers.

This new organisation can only be called to full life very gradually : the
present constitution of the orchestra can only be brought into the state
deemed needful for the future by the elimination of those concerned in
lapse of time.   That, however, will probably keep pretty even pace
with the reduction of duties (especially for the church) and the formation of an auxiliary class of pupils.   The present over-expenditure for
the Kapelle will therefore continue to burden the Civil List until the
reorganisation approaches completion : when a salary falls in, for
instance, its proceeds must be employed in the first place to better the
present organisation ; and the fourth desks of the wind must be retained
till all existing accessists have been promoted to the actual Kapelle.
Wherefore the task of commencing to introduce the new constitution
at once, so far as possible, might be entrusted to one of the two present
Kapellmeister.

The question remains, whether it might not lead to regrettable collisions, if the one branch of this great united art-institute bore the name of a German National-theatre, the other that of a "Royal Kapelle"?

Both branches will be opened in the manner aforesaid to the full free partnership of all the nation, and consequently declared its intellectual property. On principle, moreover, their subvention is not to be exceeded, and thus there will remain no recourse to the bounty of the King to cover any deficits. It therefore would be at once more expedient and more correct, if the second department of this institute were likewise given that more befitting predicate, especially as even the name "Kapelle" will no longer be appropriate: the Chapel was the place in which the musical body fulfilled its exclusive function in olden times, and thence it took its title; but now this place is called the "Orchestra," a name which therefore serves better to denote the fellowship of instrumental musicians. This institute, however, will also include the vocal choir, so that the most accurate title would be:

German National-institute for Music in Dresden; the musicians accordingly to be called its "Members," the Kapellmeister its "Director."

————————

To the question: Would His Majesty the King be hereby deprived of the Patronage of the united institute, and how should His position toward it be defined?—the answer is:

The first, the head of the nation is the King: nothing can be assigned to the nation, in which its Head will not participate; the success of the nation's free agency is the honour of the King, the flourishing of a national institute his glory. Wherefore the King does but lift this institute to a higher level, when he appoints the officer through whom He makes known to it his will, no longer from the placemen of the Court, but from the members of the Ministry of State. As to the nation, to Him this minister is equally responsible: through him will He therefore rule the institute to His especial honour; every part thereof will think

SUMMARY.

and the human "; on his Last Symph. and Schiller's verses (42). "People want me to write according to *their* ideas of beauty." Farewell, interrupted by remembrance of E's roll of music; where to put the crosses. The "damning shroud" transferred to R's galops; goodbye to E, who sets out for Rossini (45).

AN END IN PARIS.

R in Paris; his gentle nature and love of animals. Accidental meeting with him and his dog in the Palais Royal: his ambitious projects; operas and how to get them accepted in Paris (49). Instrumental music proposed, but it needs a reputation, even where Beethoven is deified; drawing-room ballads, but who will sing them? Press-notices and their fallaciousness; singers and their patronage. "In one year from now!"—he leaves me (53). Fruitless search for him; my self-reproaches and growing belief in his success; but nowhere does his name appear on posters. One autumn day, nearly a year later, I overhear him soliloquising before a Punch-and-Judy show: the white cat and chromatic scales, that way lies Fortune. An Englishman on horseback gallops by, with Newfoundland dog; R rushes after (58). Lose sight of him again for two months; at last receive a note, "come and see me die"; find him propped up in bed, gazing on panorama of all Paris from his garret window. He tells his tale: the swamps and quagmires round all temples of Art; ante-chambers of Hunger; his dreams and rude awakening; his starving dog restored to beauty by the pawning of his belongings (62). Goes out to find the Devil, and meets the Englishman outside the *Concerts Musard*: E's offer to buy the dog, R's flight in terror; as R slept the dog was stolen; nothing more to live for; a horrible horn-scale from the Englishman's mansion followed by an agonised yelp; R laughed and went away (64). After a pause R continues: "I felt my end was near, and came to die on the Mount of Martyrs." Last will: his *credo* and peaceful death. Who knows what died with him? His modest funeral; the Englishman; the dog remained (68).

A HAPPY EVENING.

Advantage of not seeing the orchestra. Moods when the idea of the music overpowers the senses and makes them uncritical; people who wince when they *see* a note has gone wrong. Mozart's Symph. in E flat, Beethoven's in A: there graceful Feeling, here virile Strength; idiocy of inventing tales to interpret such music (73). Popularity the curse of every grand and noble thing; "they shall have no *merit*, these symphonies!" Sensation of the Infinite on hearing a Beeth. Symph.: the instrl. composer's realm is supra-mundane; tone-painting rejected, save in the province of Jest (76). Mozart's instantaneous creation; Beethoven's advance to higher altitudes (78). The *Eroica* no "musical bulletin of the Italian campaign"; the hero Beethoven, inspired by the idea of the young conquering demigod, intent on achieving a deed as great in Art. Music expresses, not the individual's passion, but Passion, Love, Desire, itself. Invocation to the God of Music (81).

ON GERMAN MUSIC.

Paris amateurs enthusiastic for highest products of German music, but do they really understand it? In Germany music is cultivated in the humblest cot, for its own sake; transfer these naïve artists to a salon, and they are covered with shame. Through division into many principalities there is no art-centre, no great public, and only from abroad can a German opera-composer succeed in attracting the whole of Germany; whilst Nature has denied the German the Italian throat (88). Yet in smallish German towns you find most capable orchestras, and the German bandsman is generally good on at least three instruments, besides his often being a composer himself. Music in Germany has issued from the home, and is regarded as a religion; instl. music, needing no outer trappings, is therefore the peculiar province of the German (92). The glory of German vocal music appeared in Protestant Church; the Chorale, the Motet, especially S. Bach's; Passion-music; congregational singing. Down to end of last century, Opera in Germany was Italian; yet the universal tendency in German genius was to lift that too to Universalism (95). Mozart this Universal genius; delicate of sense, quick of penetration, solidly schooled, he raised both Italian Opera to its highest and German Singspiel to a quite new genre (97). His imitators, honest but feeble. Weber's *Freischütz* another great event, but he failed with Grand Opera. Spohr and Marschner, not distinctive. Rossini's influence commenced a livelier era in French Opera; Auber's *Muette* brought it to its climax. Union of French and German spirit may found a new artistic epoch (101).

PERGOLESI'S STABAT MATER.

Importance of reviving old masterpieces for performance: limits to be observed by the adaptor; Mozart's revision of Handel's *Messiah* a model (104). Detailed criticism of M. Lvoff's adaptation; difficulties he has overcome (107).

THE VIRTUOSO AND THE ARTIST.

Fable of the magic jewel and the two poor miners—Mozart and Beethoven—succeeded by the gold-diggers (110). The composer's intention and its interpreters; after *himself* would come an executant endowed with some creative power and much affection; then the man who, no producer, will sink himself in the performance. But the public wants trick; Thalberg contrasted with Liszt, though even Liszt makes concessions (113). Conductor as virtuoso, with false tempi, added instruments, and cuts (114). Singers: surely here are the true artists, for the composer's music comes from *inside* them; but the human voice is an expensive instrument, and needs humouring; you'll have to write to please them. The Italians, see how they're glorified! Can they really catch fire at the wonder-stone? (117). "Don Giovanni" at the *Italiens*: Grisi and Lablache, true artists, make no effect; the whole audience strangely impassive; why this abstinence? Don Ottavio (Rubini) duller than ever; till at last the fans begin to stir, the audience wakes up, for—Rubini is about to do his trick: an inaudible tenor suddenly explodes, and lands on his high B flat. Take care how you play with the Devil (122).

DU MÉTIER DE VIRTUOSE.

(French version, 1840, of the preceding article. The last half differs much in tone, however, and ends with a tribute to French composers' tact in keeping their concessions to the singing virtuoso outside the framework of the drama itself; an appeal to Gluck as model : 133).

THE ARTIST AND PUBLICITY.

Solitude and the inner chords vibrating into melody. What drives the genius to bring to the ears of the crowd what it can never understand ? It cannot be Duty; for all men would run away from Genius, did it shew itself naked. The saint, the wounded soldier, the taunted woman, bear less humiliation than the genius: happy the world, that knows so little of his pains ! (137). Duty of supporting one's family can never prompt a work of genius. Freedom he wants, not honour or money. Laughter his only salvation (139). Happy the genius whom Fortune ne'er has smiled on ! His awkwardness in dealing with the world ; concessions asked of him. Wait and dream ; 'tis the best ! (141).

ROSSINI'S "STABAT MATER."

Religious fervour in Parisian salons ; duchesses and countesses singing their little *Ave* etc. ; re-interment of Bonaparte's remains to accompaniment of Mozart's *Requiem*—they melt away, then try its music, "it tastes like physic"; so they get their quadrille-composers to write Latin pieces (145). Rossini's retirement at Bologna; his tour in Spain with Aguado; a *Stabat Mater* of contrition. Disputes about its copyright (147). The maestro learning counterpoint ; at last the duchesses will be able to sing fugues. A "friendly ray" impounded (149).

ON THE OVERTURE.

Origin from the spoken prologue to plays ; at first a mere conventional, not characteristic, introduction ; then distinction between grave and gay, but still a contrapuntal structure—Handel. The so-called "symphony" came next, two quicker sections connected by a slower ; Gluck and Mozart perfect this form and give it character and independence (156). Development by Cherubini and Beethoven. Weber pursued their dramatic path, whilst Spontini started the "potpourri" form adopted thereafter by Herold and Rossini (158). Two unexampled masterpieces : *Don Giovanni* overture with its conflict of two motives undecided, *Leonora* overture with its dramatic progress—a musical drama complete in itself (160). Gluck's *Iphigenia in Aulis* a perfect model of an overture, preparing us for the ensuing work ; the character of its two chief themes determined by the drama, but their working-out purely musical (163). Subsidiary themes in moderation admissible, but only such as are important in the ensuing opera. The termination should accord with the drama's *idea*, and this should triumph though the hero falls. Gluck, Mozart and Beethoven the triad, as model, not one of them alone (165).

"DER FREISCHÜTZ."

I. To the Paris public.—The old legend of the Wolf's-gulch and its horrors ; a sweetheart as the guardian angel instilling pity for wild animals ; the young gamekeeper and his failing hand, his comrade and incantations to evil spirits, the magic bullets and destiny of the seventh (173). Characteristics of the German saga : gentle sadness, mystic converse with Nature and her sounding silences. Weber's music to *Freischütz* understood at once from end to end of Germany ; everyone humming it (176). Pieces from it already heard in Paris, but will the French understand the whole ? Surely not, if dressed à la Grand Opéra, even by a genius like Berlioz (178). Interpolation of ballets and recitatives will swamp the brief original numbers and damp the humour of the dialogue ; impossible to square it by canons applicable to the *Huguenots* and *Juive* ; a new work will be added to Berlioz' creations, but you will not get the freshness of our woodland air (182).

II. Report to Germany.—Needs must I love the German Folk that loves the *Freischütz* ; tears of joy. French curiosity to see what this twenty-years' success is really like ; high-flown phrases and a publisher's speculation ; a "discovery-council" appointed (185). The Statutes of Grand Opéra object ; logic to be added ; "Let there be dance," so ballet-tunes concocted from Weber's other works ; "Ye shall not speak," and Berlioz commissioned to add recitatives. My own preparatory article ; my fears all realised (189). Second-class singers employed : Samiel, and his sprightliness and shivering scene ; Max dreams himself into his boots ; a good-natured Kaspar from the Chorus, and his laudable efforts to shorten himself ; his terrible end (192). The Prince and his motley Court (192). Contrary to expectations, Berlioz' recitatives wearisome ; their singing execrable. Agatha and her knowing confidante in a ball-dress (195). Scene of the bullet-moulding, its dearth of incident, and Samiel's laziness (197). Paris verdict : "a mass of rubbish ; no logic in it ; why *seven* bullets ?" Way to manage a bad shot. We poor deluded Germans ! (199). Conflicting criticisms in journals, but all agree in condemning the work. *Charivari* says we have banished it from Germany ; here my laughter gives out, for *no* French journal will print my rejoinder, owing to their party-system (201). French and Germans radically opposed in taste ; they laugh at our welcoming their cast-off goods ; let us revenge ourselves by sending back their *Fra Diavolo* in exchange for our own *Freischütz* (204).

HALÉVY'S "REINE DE CHYPRE."

A first night at the Grand Opéra ; the Director, the publisher and his hack, etc. ; the Fifty-two German Directors on the lookout for French novelties ; imaginary conversation with one of these spectres : "German texts are impossible" (209). German composers' dearth of opera-texts ; but where is the difficulty ? A little Poesy and heart, with a subject that takes your fancy, will do the thing ; your drama glows, inspires the composer, and you then have the finest opera in the world (210). But if you have no poesy, at least you must have Knack ; then read up novels, history etc. ; distribute your interest, and you get a good working text. If you have *no* knack, give it up. But don't make characters all clouds and flowers, eternally spouting lyrics ; how to treat an operatic Major. The text of *La Reine de Chypre* a specimen of what knack can do (212). M. de St. Georges found a subject in Venetian history : what he made of it. Summary of the plot (218). Though no one could call this text an artwork, it holds the spectator from end to end ; an artful touch of patriotism introduced, adaptable to any nationality. Example the Germans might follow, especially as their Censorship is not so strict. And this text offers the composer every facility (220). Halévy's music shews unexpected grace and simplicity ; the orchestration unequal, a tendency to abjure modern use of brass in striving for historical effect ; not so grand as *Juive*, but due to lack of a grand poetic idea in book. Perhaps we yet may find a German dramatist to give us such a book (222).

AUTHOR'S INTRODUCTION TO GES. SCHR., VOL. II.

Reference to *Communication* for history of this period. The artist also can be practical in his proposals (226).

WEBER'S RE-INTERMENT.

Report.—Earlier attempts, by others, to obtain the transference ; alleged Royal objections ; Lüttichau on invidious distinctions (230). Benefit-perform-ances to collect the requisite funds ; arrangement of two themes from *Euryanthe* for processional music ; an unusual rehearsal (232). Sudden death of Alex. von Weber revives superstitions ; this subject used for my funeral speech ; a curious hypnotic experience. Sad outlook, from Weber's grave, upon his living followers (234).

Speech.—Most German of musicians, we bring thee back from foreign admiration to homely love (237).

Chant, sung after the entombment (238).

THE CHORAL SYMPHONY AT DRESDEN.

Report.—Palm Sunday concerts for benefit of widows and orphans of Royal Band ; opposition to my choice of this work, as it had been a failure in other hands ; intrigues by the orchestral committee. But I persisted, and bor-rowed the parts from Leipzig ; reflections on memories awakened by sight of these dumb notes at a time when I felt my career so futile (242). Steps I took to kindle public interest ; pains to secure a proper rendering, especially with the double-basses' recitative and the difficult choruses. Acoustic advantages of an entire reconstruction of the platform. Success in the teeth of my enemies (246).

Programme. An aid for those who wish to grasp the master's poetic aim : moods to which the various movements correspond ; illustrations from Goethe's *Faust* (252). At entry of the Word, light breaks on chaos, a sure and definite mode of utterance is won ; victory, brotherhood, awe, shouts and laughter ; the joy of Man to whom God gave the earth as home of happiness (255).

THE WIBELUNGEN.

Ur-Kinghood.—Origin of European races in Asia ; the Deluge ; the Patri-archate ; Despotism remaining in the East, free Communes rising in the West ;

the King's original Priestly power devolving on the heads of families, whilst he retains the final verdict in matters of worldly dispute ; reverence still cleaving to the royal family of the Franks till the "Ghibelines" go under (262).

The Nibelungen.—Saga tells us more, than History, of a race's essence. The Hoard as symbol of earthly power ; who wins it, becomes thereby a Nibelung. This saga the peculiar heritage of the Franks, whose royal race presents us with the name itself. Conquests of the Franks, culminating in Karl the Great ; with the death of the last male Karling the dissolution of the German Reich commences. Dukes of various subject tribes, allied by marriage to the Karlingen, now assume dominion ; but not till the beheading of Konradin at Naples does the ur-old royal race die out, and with it the ideal Kaiserdom (266).

Wibelungen.—Saga versus History, the Folk *v.* its learned Schoolmaster. Bishop Otto of Freisingen derives the title from a trumpery hamlet, Waiblingen ; but it really is a perversion of Nibelungen to make a stabreim with Welf. The Welfish element becomes a Churchly one in time, in Chivalric literature ; the Wibelingian paganism preserved in the Nibelungen-Lieder (269).

Welfen.—"Welf" originally meant a "whelp," a pure-bred scion ; the name became a symbol of German tribal independence. Historic conflict of the Welfen, the popular principle, with the Nibelungian rulers (270).

Nibelungen-hoard and Frankish Kings.—First historic appearance of Franks, on lower Rhine ; tribal division, but only from the oldest race were Kings and Commanders chosen. Chlodwig, his victory over Roman legions and assumption of supremacy ; his orphan children deprived of their patrimony by Siegfried von Morungen ; one of the sons, called "Pipingen" by the sympathetic Folk, was saved ; Karl the Great, his descendant, assumes title of Cæsar, or Kaiser (273).

Origin and development of Nibelungen-myth.—Man and first ideas of Nature ; opposition of Light and Darkness, Warmth and Cold etc., the common basis of all religions of every people. Distinction of the Frankish saga its combination with historic deeds and personages through the Hoard, the symbol of worldly might : the Night-elves (Niflûngar), their work at golden toys and keen-edged weapons, and the Ring of World-Rule ; their conqueror's death bequeathing vengeance to his heirs and incessant strife to regain possession of supreme power. Karl the Great knew this, when he had the Nibelungenlieder collected and transcribed (277).

Kaiser = Cæsar ; the Roman legend.—Outside Germany no power save Rome retained historic claim to rule, in time of Karl. Awe at the rank of Cæsar a memory of the Gallic wars. Divine descent attributed to Julius Cæsar ; Numa and the "sacra" ; the Pontificate had passed to Cæsar, sprung, so they said, from Troy (280).

The Franks claim Trojan descent.—They identify Pharamund with Priamus, write poems on Trojan War, and give Greek names to towns, in emulation of the Roman Cæsars. The ancient Mother-city of every race ; wars of independence waged by succeeding generations. The Franks claim to be the oldest race of all, and find all younger races *kingless.* But Rome had reared a worldwide Church ; Karl the Great allies himself with her (284).

The Hoard material and spiritual.—The actual worldly dominion crumbling down, the Kaisership attains a more and more Ideal significance, whilst the Roman Church claims more and more Material power. The Franks identify their Wuotan with the Christian's God, their Siegfried with Christ ; the Church sees in this Pagan legend her deadliest foe (287).

"Ghibeline" Kaiserdom and Friedrich I.—Struggles of the Kaiser with the Church, culminating in Friedrich Rothbart (Barbarossa) ; he claimed, not worldly possession, but spiritual rulership, the Pope to be his highest officer. He makes the various princes his feudatories, and reverses a papal election ; but finds a third foe in the spirit of Freedom in the .Lombard communes. How this latter, purely human principle, not racial, commences a new era in world-history under Friedrich's auspices (292).

Hoard transformed into the Grail.—Friedrich's last Conclave ; then he fares to Palestine ; beyond the Holy Land he presses farther east to find the Grail —none saw him in this life again. The Keeper of the Grail is priest alike and king ; thus ends the Nibelungen-saga in the pure Idea (294).

Its Material residue in " Property."—Post-Wibelingian Kings typified in Charles d'Anjou. In the Nibelungen-myth Man and his valour were accounted the highest ; since then, Man but a slave to Property. Feudal system degenerated into hereditary ownership, and even rights conferred by purchase. But the Folk still nurse the memory of Friedrich, who once shall come again to free them (298).

THE NIBELUNGEN-MYTH.

(Preliminary draft of *Siegfried's Tod*, which later on, with certain radical changes, became *Götterdämmerung.*—311).

TERCENTENARY TOAST. ·

The Dresden Kapelle founded 300 years ago, at commencement of third great period in History ; its evolution in step with progress of human spirit ; to be thoroughly useful, it must train and educate ; to be thoroughly sound, it needs a wife, the Orchestra a proper Choir attached thereto (318).

A GERMAN NATIONAL THEATRE.

How the idea originated at a time when Reform was in the air, 1848 ; its submittal to the Government and derision by the Court ; Dresden catastrophe of 1849 prevented its introduction into Parliament by one of the Deputies (322). Preamble.—Essence of Theatre is association with full retention of rights of individual. Its powerful effect on taste and manners demands its transference from the Courtier to a Minister who represents the nation ; under his supervision, it should be governed by the embodiment of the nation's best intellectual and moral forces (324).

Proposed new title : "German National Theatre." Its organisation :— Union of Dramatic poets and composers in Saxony appoints a Committee to watch over æsthetic, ethical, and national interests of dramatic art and see that authors are duly recompensed ; in association with Committee of active Stage-personnel they form a Jury to decide acceptance of pieces and to elect the General Director. He is appointed for life ; his salary arranged with Minister ; with other stage-officers he forms a Council of Internal Management. Voting arrangements, and right of appeal to Minister. Treasury and its principles (327). Branch-theatre for Leipzig to have a portion of the subsidy, and be managed on identical lines. No other town in Saxony large enough to maintain a standing theatre ; strolling companies must be done away with, and their places taken by troupes sent out from the central theatre, as below (330). Establishment of a Stage school, with free education of the young in every branch of dramatic art, also lectures to the older actors. Examination and classification of the pupils ; a trial-stage ; then drafted into the national travelling companies, retaining right of entry on principal stage when vacancies occur. Engagement by and from outlying theatres, as need arises. Director to see that minor theatres do not undertake works unsuitable to their stages (333). Number of performances : in a city of size of Dresden, where pieces cannot be frequently repeated, seven nights a-week are too much ; should be reduced to five, thus enabling proper preparation and giving employés opportunity of social intercourse (336).

The Musical Institute.—The Kapelle originally a body of musicians for Divine Worship ; gradually put to secular uses, and now the instrumentalists' chief duty accrues to the Court-theatre, though the *number* of church-services remains undiminished.—Present condition of the Catholic church-choir and the stage-choir ; *one* proper Choral-institute should be established (341). Debased condition of Catholic church-music ; needs restoration to its earlier purity of style. For this, it is necessary to do away with orchestra in church and return to unmixed vocal music with organ accompaniment, whilst a few women's voices might be introduced to strengthen the choir ; the Kapellmeister should. be commissioned to hunt up earlier compositions, and prizes be offered for purely vocal works (344). The Choral institute : its finances and scheme of education ; every pupil of the stage-school is to share in the instruction, as chorus-practice is most important for developing musical gifts. Provision for employment, remuneration, and pensioning of choristers ; concerts in aid of pension-fund ; Chorus-director and Committee (347). Duties of Orchestra to be reduced in number by abolition of ordinary entr'acte music ; its futility and demoralising effect on bandsmen and audience ; then real music written for particular plays, as Beethoven's to *Egmont*, will be duly welcomed (349). The Summer-theatre to be handed to one of the subsidiary companies, relieving the Kapelle of that addition to its labours, and enabling orchestra to be simplified. Necessary number of bandsmen ; their salaries and plan of regular promotion ; *one* head, not two or three. Balance left over for prize-compositions ; benefit-performances in concert-room for needy members of choir and band. Orchestra-school, to be united with Stage and Chorus schools, with removal of Leipzig Conservatorium to Dresden (354). Music and morals : those inspired by Beethoven's music have been worthier citizens than those bewitched by Rossini ; Auber and cancan. Therefore the State must concern itself with public taste here also, and through machinery like that for Theatre. Union of Composers and its committee ; furtherance of unknown talents—a proper hearing of their own creations supremely important for further progress ; public concerts. Inner

INDEX TO VOL. VII.

As in previous volumes, the figures denoting tens and hundreds are not *repeated* for one and the same reference unless the numerals run into a fresh line of type. Figures enclosed within brackets refer to my own footnotes etc.—W. A. E.